P9-CLU-293

Novels by Luanne Rice

LUANNE RICE

BANTAM BOOKS TRADE PAPERBACKS

NEW YORK

Sandcastles

A Novel

2010 Bantam Books Trade Paperback Edition

Copyright © 2006 by Luanne Rice

Published in the United States by Bantam Books, an imprint of
The Random House Publishing Group, a division of
Random House, Inc., New York.

BANTAM BOOKS and the rooster colophon are
registered trademarks of Random House, Inc.

Originally published in hardcover in the United States by Bantam Books,
an imprint of The Random House Publishing Group,
a division of Random House, Inc., in 2006.

LIBRARY OF CONGRESS CATALOGING-IN-PUBLICATION DATA
Rice, Luanne.
Sandcastles / Luanne Rice.
p. cm.
Novel.
ISBN: 978-0-553-38683-7
I. Title.

PS3568.I289S35 2006
813'.54—dc22   2006042764

Printed in the United States of America
Published simultaneously in Canada

www.bantamdell.com

2 4 6 8 9 7 5 3 1

Book design and title page photograph by Virginia Norey.

For Maureen (Max) Onorato
May we be walking beaches together
for the rest of our lives…

The house felt almost as much like a ship as a house. Placed there to ride out storms, it was built into the island as though it were a part of it; but you saw the sea from all the windows and there was good cross ventilation so that you slept cool on the hottest nights.

from *Islands in the Stream*—ERNEST HEMINGWAY

HELLO HELLO HELLO HELLO HELLO HELLO HELLO HELLO HELLO HELLO
LOVE AND KISSES CHALES

It was a long time before X could set the note aside, let alone lift Esmé's father's wristwatch out of the box. When he did finally lift it out, he saw that its crystal had been broken in transit. He wondered if the watch was otherwise undamaged, but he hadn't the courage to wind it and find out. He just sat with it in his hand for another long period. Then, suddenly, almost ecstatically, he felt sleepy.

You take a really sleepy man, Esmé, and he always stands a chance of again becoming a man with all his fac—with all his f-a-c-u-l-t-i-e-s intact.

from *For Esmé–with Love and Squalor*—J. D. SALINGER

Frightening, isn't it?—CHARLES SCHULTZ

Acknowledgments

Many thanks to my agent, Andrea Cirillo, and everyone at the Jane Rotrosen Agency: Jane Berkey, Don Cleary, Meg Ruley, Peggy Gordijn, Annelise Robey, Kelly Harms, Kathy Lee Hart, Christina Hogrebe, Chris Ruen, and Gillian Roth.

I'm deeply grateful to Ron Bernstein.

Thank you so much to everyone at Bantam: Irwyn Applebaum, Nita Taublib, Tracy Devine, Betsy Hulsebosch, Carolyn Schwartz, Cynthia Lasky, Barb Burg, Susan Corcoran, Theresa Zoro, Sharon Propson, Gina Wachtel, Melissa Lord, Kerri Buckley, Kenneth Wohlrob, Jennifer Campaniolo, and Igor Aronov.

Also to Paolo Pepe, Virginia Norey, Kathleen Baldonado, Ruth Toda, and Deb Dwyer.

Love to Rosemary, Roger, Kate, Molly, and Emily Goettsche.

Thank you to Amelia Onorato and the BDG, as well as Monique Colarossi, Ashley Elliott, and Marianna Scandole of Regis College.

Love and thanks to Emily Rose Walsh for meeting me in Ireland.

Thank you to Dan Walsh and the Fordham contingent: Matt Murphy, Matt Bockhorst, Eric Schwendimann, John Raymundo, and Will Healey.

Thank you to Suzanne Strempek Shea for her wonderful writing and for her suggestions on where to find what I was looking for in Ireland.

I'm grateful to Annie, of the Skibbereen Book Shop.

Much gratitude to James Lee for showing me Cork and Kerry.

Sandcastles

Prologue

It was the land of their ancestors, and Honor swore she could hear their voices crying in the wind. The storm had been building since morning, silver mist giving way to driving rain, gusts off the sea now blowing the hedges and trees almost horizontal. The stone walls that had seemed so magical when she'd first arrived now seemed dark and menacing.

From the plane yesterday morning, Honor had been awed by the green, by the emerald grass and hedgerows and trees. Her three daughters had gazed down, excited and hoping they could see their father's sculpture from the sky. He had written them letters about Ireland, and about the West Cork farmhouse he had found for them to stay in, and how he'd built his latest work on the very edge of a cliff overlooking the sea. They had fought to open the letters when they came, and be the one to read them out loud, and sleep with them under their pillows.

"There it is!" Regis, fourteen, had cried out, pointing at a crumbling castle.

"No, it's there," twelve-year-old Agnes had said, crowding her sister to point out the window. Square green fields ran along the coast, each dotted with tiny white farm buildings. Stone towers and ruined castles seemed to crown every high hill.

"They all look like the pictures he sent," Cecilia, just seven, had said. "It doesn't matter which house it is, as long as he's in it. Right, Mom?"

"Right, sweetheart," Honor had said, sounding so much calmer than she'd felt.

"It'll be just like home, Mom," Agnes had said, forehead pressed to the plane's window. "A beach, and stone walls . . . only now we'll be on the other side of the Atlantic, instead of home in Black Hall. It's like going across a mirror. . . ."

"Look at all that green," Cecilia had said.

"Just like our green fields of home," Agnes had said, unconsciously echoing the lyrics of a song her aunt used to sing to her.

"What's the first thing you're going to do when you see Daddy?" Regis had asked, turning to peer at Honor. There was such a challenge in her daughter's face—almost as if she knew how troubled her mother felt.

"She's going to hug and kiss him," Agnes said. "Right, Mom?"

"That's what I'm going to do, too!" Cece said.

"The first thing I'm going to do," Regis said, "is ask him to show me his sculpture. It's his biggest one yet, and it's right at the edge of the highest cliff, and I want to climb up on top and see if I can see America!"

"You can't see America across the Atlantic Ocean, can you, Mom?" Cece asked.

"I'll be able to see it, I swear I will," Regis said. "Dad said he could see it, so why wouldn't I be able to?"

"Your father was speaking figuratively," Honor said. "He meant he could see it in his mind, or his heart . . . the dream of America that our ancestors had when they left Ireland."

"And Daddy's still dreaming," Cece said.

Cece had counted the days till this trip. Agnes prayed for his safety. And Regis followed in his footsteps. Although she didn't want to be an artist, she did want to live life on the edge. Over the past year, she had been delivered back to the Academy by the police twice—once for diving off the train bridge into Devil's Hole, and once for climbing to the top of the lighthouse to hang the Irish flag.

Instead of being upset, John had gone straight to the lighthouse with his camera to take pictures before the Coast Guard could climb up to take the flag down. He had been touched by his daughter's Irish pride, and by her way of making a statement—regardless of risk.

Almost like his sculptures; he called them "sandcastles," which called to mind gentle beaches, families building fragile towers in the sand at the water's edge. But John's installations were sharp, kinetic, made of rock and fallen trees, dangerous to build.

Now, on this craggy headland in West Cork, the spiky top of his latest—the bare, unadorned branches of a tree that had fallen somewhere, hauled here by John—was visible over the next rise, at the edge of a cliff, ninety-foot granite walls that dropped straight into the churning sea.

Honor stood at the bedroom window of the farmhouse he'd rented, looking out. John came out of the shower to stand behind her, putting his arms around her and leaning into her. Their clothes lay in a heap beside the bed. Her sketchpad, abandoned yet again, sat on the desk. She had made a few drawings, but her heart wasn't in it.

"What were you drawing before?" he asked, his lips against her ear. He sounded tentative, as if he wasn't sure how she'd respond.

"Nothing," she said. "You're the artist in the family."

Honor pressed against his body, wishing she could turn off her thoughts and give in again to the desire that overtook her every time she saw her husband. She wished he hadn't asked about her drawing.

She gazed down at the small pile of moonstones—luminous, worn smooth by the waves at the foot of the cliff, a gift from John the minute she'd stepped off the plane—on the desk beside her sketchpad. She knew he'd meant them as a peace offering, but her heart was reluctant to accept it. She felt turned inside out, frayed from the stress of trying to keep up with him. He turned her toward him, pulled her body against his, and kissed her.

"The girls," Honor said.

"They're sleeping," he whispered, gesturing toward their daughters' room as he tried to pull her back to bed.

"I know," Honor said. "They're jet-lagged and exhausted from the excitement of being here, seeing you."

"But what about you?" he asked, stroking her hair and kissing the side of her neck. He sounded so hopeful, as if he thought maybe this trip could stop what they both felt happening between them, stop what they had always had from slipping away forever. "You're not tired?"

"Yes, me too," she said, kissing him. She was beyond tired; of wanting him to come home, of worrying that he'd get hurt or killed working on his installations alone, of wishing he'd understand how worn out she was by the demands of his art. At the same time, she was tired of being blocked. It was as if his intense inspiration had started killing the fire of her own. Even her drawings, such as they were, were of his soaring sculpture just over the next rise. She peered out the window, but the structure was now obscured by the day's wild storm.

He had taken them all to the cliff edge yesterday, when they'd first arrived. He'd shown them the ruins of an old castle, a lookout tower built a thousand years ago. Sheep grazed on the hillsides, impossibly steep, slanting down to the sea. The sheep roamed free, their curly white wool splashed with red or blue paint, identifying them for their owners. They grazed right at the base of John's sculpture.

It affected Honor deeply to see her husband's work here in Ireland. They had dreamed of coming for so long—ever since that day twenty-five years ago when she, John, Bernie, and Tom had found the box in the stone wall. Honor knew that John had always felt a primal pull to be here, to try to connect with the timeless spirits of his family, as Bernie and Tom had done years earlier. In this green and ancient land, his own family history meshed powerfully with his artistic instincts, an epiphany in earth and stone.

His sculpture awed her, as his work often did—she found it inspiring, disturbing, stunning, rather than beautiful. She knew the physical effort it took him to drag the tree trunks and branches here to the cliff's edge, to raise them up and balance them against the wind, to haul rocks into the pile—cutting his hands and forearms, bruising his knuckles. John had hands like a prizefighter's: scarred and swollen. Only, it had so often seemed to Honor, the person he was fighting most was himself.

The sculpture rose up from the land like a castle, echoing the ruins just across the gap. It seemed to grow from the ground, as if it had been there forever, a witness to his family who had worked this land, farmed these fields, starved during the famine. He was descended from famine orphans, and as he and Honor and their daughters walked the property, she had to hold back tears to think of what their ancestors had gone through.

And what John experienced now. He was an artist, through and through. He channeled powers from far beyond his own experience—became one with the ghosts, and the bones, and the spirits that had suffered and died. That's why he'd come to Ireland alone—to haunt the Cobh docks from which his family had emigrated, to drink in the pubs, and to build this monument to his Irish dead.

His sister Bernie—Sister Bernadette Ignatius—was probably the only person who really understood him. Honor loved him, but she didn't get what drove him, and she was also a little scared of him. Not that he'd ever hurt her or the girls, but that he'd die in pursuit of his art. It wore her down, it did.

She'd felt exhausted yesterday, standing at the base of his huge, ambitious, soaring, reckless installation. How had the wind and the weight of his materials not carried him over the edge of the cliff? How had the storm-scoured branches, the bark stripped right off them, not fallen on him and crushed him? Alone on this headland, he would have never gotten help.

"You did this alone," she'd said to him while the girls explored the headland. The sculpture rose above them—in silhouette it had what she had failed to notice before, a cross set at the top, to mirror not the castle ruins, but Bernie's chapel across the sea.

"No," he said. "I had some help."

"Who? Did Tom fly over?"

"No, Tom's too busy at the Academy," John said. "This was a local guy, an Irishman I met..."

Something about the way he trailed off made Honor stop asking. Strange people were sometimes drawn to John because of his work. He unlocked the souls of all kinds of people—there was something about the soaring, spiritual, seeking nature of what he did that spoke to the hurt and troubled. She shivered at the way John looked now, his lips tight, as if there was a backstory to his assistant that she was better off not knowing.

"Have you taken the pictures yet?" Honor asked.

He shook his head—was that sorrow or regret? He glanced around the headland, as if on guard against a threat.

"What's wrong?" she asked, her skin crawling.

He hesitated. She saw him peer at the sky, then at the sea, at low black clouds gathering along the horizon. And he decided to lie; regarding the weather, it was true in its own way, but it obscured his real concern, so Honor wouldn't have to worry, too.

"I haven't gotten any decent shots yet," he said. "The days have been too sunny, which is great, and makes me so glad that you and the girls got to see Ireland in the sun. But I need some shadows and rain, to get the atmosphere the piece needs."

His work was a two-part process; he built sculptures from materials gathered entirely from nature. Then he photographed them and let nature take the work apart again. The wind, or the sea, or a river, or gravity would destroy what he had done, but the photographs would last forever. Very few people actually saw his installations— Honor and the girls, Bernie and Tom were among the people who did. But the world—art lovers, environmentalists, and dreamers—knew the photographs of John Sullivan.

"Looks like you're getting your wish," she said, pointing at the dark clouds scudding along the horizon.

"Maybe," he said, hugging her. "Then we can go home."

It had struck her, almost bitterly, how tender he sounded. John was never in a hurry to get home; he made a life of his work, and his family had to fit in around his trips and installations. But she also felt some hope—he *wanted* to come home this time. She wasn't begging him. She believed he knew how close they were to losing their marriage.

He had called the girls over yesterday, let them pet some of the sheep, showed them the stone walls, famine walls built during the 1840s by his ancestors, starving to death and worked to the bone. He pointed at the maps he'd brought from Connecticut, shown them how the walls corresponded with the ones built by his great-grandfather across the water, on the grounds of Star of the Sea. He told them that the cross on the top of his sculpture lined up perfectly with the one on the top of the Academy's chapel.

Agnes had wanted to walk on the walls, and Regis had wanted to climb the sculpture, all the way to the cross. Cece had clung to her mother, afraid the wind might blow her off the cliff—even though the sun had been shining, brightening the green, making the blue sea gleam down below, as the wind, barely a whisper that morning, began to pick up.

Honor had pulled Cece into a quiet hollow, sheltered from the stiff wind, and pulled her sketchpad from her jacket pocket. Sitting there, hearing John and the older girls talking and laughing, she had sketched John's sculpture. An artist herself, she had once been passionately inspired by John's work—and he by hers. But lately she had just felt daunted. Sketching his sculpture on what felt like the edge of the world, holding her youngest, she remembered some of the joy art used to bring her. As John's work had gained power, she had lost track of herself. Maybe she could turn that around....

Today Ireland's gentle green was gone, washed away by sheets of cold rain. The fog was gray and constant. Instead of reinforcing her bleak mood, it made her feel happy to be safe and cozy with her family—all together again. An east wind had whipped into a full gale, howling off the sea, blowing whitecaps into spume, churning up the dark bay. Honor felt as if they were on a peninsula at the end of forever.

She felt John's warm body against hers, wanted to follow him into bed; something about the coziness of their cottage juxtaposed to the dangerous cliff edge made her want him more than ever. But as she started to turn away from the window, she saw the flash of someone passing by.

"Did you see that?" she asked. "Someone on the path—right there."

John glanced out the window. He frowned and pressed his head against the glass and tried to see through the rain—there were big, muddy footprints through the side yard, leading toward his sculpture, and he caught a glimpse of a tall man hurrying along.

"Who is it?" she asked, watching John pulling on his jeans.

"I don't know," he said.

"Then why are you getting dressed so fast?" she asked. "I thought—"

"Where are the girls?" he asked.

"In bed," she said. "We just said...they're tired from traveling..."

"Honor," he said. "That guy I told you about. I met him down at the docks in Cobh. I went to do research there, to find out about the ships my family emigrated to America on. And I stopped into a bar, and got to talking to someone—he's from Connemara, but came down here looking for work. I needed some help with the heavy lifting, and I hired him. Gregory White."

"He helped you?"

"Yes, I paid him. But now he won't leave me alone. He keeps coming back for more work, more money, and when I told him there wasn't any more, he vandalized my sculpture. Tore off some of the branches and threw them off the cliff. Knocked the cross off, so I had to climb up and put it back."

"Why did he do that?"

John shook his head. "I don't know. Greg's messed up. Drinks a lot. I made the mistake of telling him about the gold ring, and now he's convinced there's pirate gold buried on the land. He's nuts. We got into a fight, Honor. He was screwing with my work, and I told him I'd kill him if he did it again."

"What makes you think that was him just now? Couldn't it be someone else, just taking the coast path?" Honor asked, even as she started to shiver. Grabbing her robe, she suddenly felt cold, as if the wind were rattling through the windowpanes and into her bones. She felt her heart plummet. She and John had been doing so well since she and the girls arrived, and now this....

"On a day like this?" John asked. She saw the rage building in his muscles; his shoulders seemed to double in size when he got this mad. It was never at her, but she felt it all the same. "Goddamn it. Goddamn it. If he does something else to the installation, I swear to God...The whole bar heard me tell him what I'd do to him. I warned him!"

"John, stop it!"

"Call the gardai, Honor. The police. The number's by the phone. I've had it with this. Tell them to come to the Old Head. Ballincastle, right?"

"John, don't go out in this," she said, staring into the bleak, ferocious weather. Even as she spoke, he opened the door. The wind howled, blowing papers in a cyclone around the room. John's eyes met Honor's, but he didn't even speak. He just left the house, slamming the door.

This was her life, she thought. One minute in John's arms, and the next—if the spirit moved him, impelled him into a fifty-knot gale—left standing alone to wonder what had just happened. She heard her own words of the last moments echoing in her ears: *"John, stop it—please, John—don't!"* She felt as if she had somehow become the mother of a stubborn, willful boy. What had happened to the Honor who'd climbed hills with him, stretched the limits with her own art?

"Where's Dad going?" Regis asked, sleepy, coming through the door in her nightgown.

"He's checking on his sculpture," Honor said, picking up the phone, wishing Regis hadn't chosen this moment to wake up.

"Who are you calling?" Regis asked.

"Go in with your sisters," Honor said, covering the receiver. "Right now, Regis!"

Looking alarmed, Regis backed into the bedroom as her mother dialed the telephone. Honor reached over, pulled the door tightly shut, just as the Irish voice answered: "Gardai."

"This is Honor Sullivan," she said. "My husband asked me to call you—he's built a sculpture on Ballincastle, at the Old Head, and he said someone, Gregory White, has been damaging it. We saw some-one pass by on the coast path outside our house—John thinks it was him, that he's here now, and he asked that you send help."

"What's that name again?"

"My husband's name is John Sullivan, and the man is Gregory White. We're at Ballincastle," Honor said, edging toward the window, her heart starting to pound. She could barely see ten feet in front of the house, through curtains of rain. The footprints seemed deeper, closer. Peering over the rise, she couldn't even glimpse John's sculp-ture, couldn't see the cross.

"Would Gregory White be the same man whose life your husband threatened? We've been called to pull your husband off him before."

"Just get here!" she cried.

Then, just before the connection was broken, she heard the voice chuckle and say "the monstrosity..." As if the person had spoken to someone standing there, speaking of John's sculpture.

"The *what*?" Honor asked.

But the phone line was dead. She pulled her robe around her tighter. John got lots of reactions to his work; people loved it or hated it. Not like Honor's paintings and drawings—her landscapes of the countryside and seashore around Black Hall were quiet, pretty, popular... safe. She had lost the way to her deepest forces and inspi-ration, but her students at Star of the Sea, where she was the art teacher, wouldn't know that.

Right now, hearing the police belittle John's work, she felt her blood boiling. Should she go after him now, try to help? She wavered, leaning against the windowpane. What if he needed her? Who was Greg White, and why was he trying to destroy John's work? Her skin crawled at the thought that her husband could be in danger. She felt the pit in her stomach, deep and terrible. The police said John had threatened his life. What kind of fight had they had in that bar?

Oh God, she was so on edge. And she always was; this trip to Ireland had felt like a walk across razor wire. Her chest hurt; it felt so heavy, as if her heart was turning to stone. When it came to John, she hardly knew what to do anymore. She had three young daughters, and she was always worried and afraid that they would lose their father. Almost worse, she felt that she and John had lost their connection. There were moments when she didn't think she could take it another day.

Regis had seen her crying just before they'd come over to Ireland. She'd found Honor in her studio, bending over a handful of John's photographs—silvery pictures of the ice caverns he'd sculpted when they were young, after a blizzard had blanketed the Connecticut shoreline. She remembered that John had worked until he had frostbite. He had wound up in the ER. Honor had wept for the young couple they had been, for her young husband who had thought he had to push himself that far, for the way he hadn't let up on himself at all. Regis had seen her weeping and asked in a strangled whisper, "Are you and Daddy going to get divorced?"

"Mommy?" Agnes called now, from inside the farmhouse bedroom.

"What, honey?" Honor asked, not wanting to move away from the window.

Outside, a siren sounded—thread-thin, it was swept away by the wind, making Honor wonder if she had heard it at all.

"Mommy..." Agnes said again, slowly and quietly.

"Don't tell her," Cece said in a stage whisper. "Regis said not to!"

Honor turned quickly at that. She walked into the bedroom shared by all three girls—just like at home—and saw her two youngest daughters sitting on Agnes's bed.

"Where's Regis?" she asked.

"That's what I wanted to tell you," Agnes whispered.

"But we're not supposed to," Cece said. "Regis said not to."

"Said not to tell me what?"

"Don't," Cece warned, looking at Agnes.

"She went out to help Daddy!" Agnes blurted out.

"No," Honor said. "Please, no."

Honor was frozen. She heard the siren again, or thought she did.

Doubting her hearing, she couldn't ignore the feeling in her blood. It was cold, as if her heart had started pumping ice, and she knew before she knew.

She ran to the window, then to the door. Pulling it open, she felt the storm's force flatten her against the wall. She was barefoot, dressed in her robe, but she ran outside. Her feet sank in the cold mud. The younger girls were right behind her, beside her.

"Get back inside!" she ordered them.

"We're scared!" Agnes shrieked. "Don't leave us alone!"

She grabbed their hands. Breathless, they ran toward John's sculpture. It had looked like an ancient castle against the sky, but now she couldn't see it at all. Driving rain and fog obliterated everything, blurred the rocky cliffs, the green hills. Even the sheep looked like clouds blowing off the sea. Honor heard another siren, and had to jump back with the girls, allowing the police car to pass on the narrow road, blue lights flashing.

"Mommy, what's wrong?" Agnes cried.

"What's happening?" Cece wailed.

Honor was scared, too. Trembling, she held the girls' hands. Small rocks on the road cut her feet. The blue lights sparked up ahead, showing the way. She scanned the hillside for John's sculpture, but couldn't see it—until they rounded the corner, and she saw the trunks and branches toppled over, lying on the ground at the very edge of the cliff. The gardai had clustered at the precipice, looking down.

"Regis!" Honor cried. "John!" Then, "Girls, stay here—right here!"

Dropping her younger daughters' hands, she tore across the field. Breathless, she stopped at the brink. Daggers stabbed her eyes— silver knives of wild rain. She couldn't bear to look. The cliff was ninety feet high; the wind blew her back, and she had to inch her way forward. Weighted with dread, she made a superhuman effort to look down the jagged cliffs falling to the sea.

Expecting to see everything she loved crashed on the rocks ninety feet below, she gasped to see the narrow ledge just twenty feet down. A man's body lay crumpled on the rock, blood spreading from his head. Regis, her lips blue-white with shock, stood beside his body, a woman officer's arms around her. John looked up at Honor, his blue eyes sharp with rage, meeting hers just as the gardai snapped hand-cuffs on his wrists.

"John," she called down the ledge.

"He tried to kill Regis," John said.

"But what—"

"He tried to kill my baby," John said. "So I killed him."

"Don't say anything else," Honor said.

"It's too late," an officer said, shoving him. "He's already proved he has a history of violence, and fifteen people heard him threaten this man. The fall didn't do that to his head. You heard him. That's a con-fession."

They led John and Regis up the narrow path from the ledge to the hillside, past the destroyed sculpture, and Honor grabbed Regis, her sobs a muffled keening as the wind shrieked in their ears and the rain pelted their faces, and John was taken away.

One

Six years had passed, and sometimes it seemed he was gone from their lives forever. It hadn't happened all at once: first they had seen him as often as they could, but as time went on, the visits had dwindled. He always wrote letters to the girls, and they to him. But for Honor, it was another story. She had stopped writing to him over a year ago. There was so little she felt she could say to him now.

So when Honor woke from this particular dream before dawn that late summer day, she felt stunned and couldn't get back to sleep. She felt the fresh salt air blowing through the window, climbed out of bed, looked in on her sleeping girls, fed Sisela, the cat, put the coffee on, and walked through the vineyard to the beach. Summer vacation was winding down, with school looming again in September.

The stars were still bright in the sky, bits of white fire in a field of dark blue. Honor stared up at them, shivering in the early chill. Wide awake, she tried to call back the details. What had startled her out of sleep? The real-life wedding plans of her daughter Regis filled her waking hours with lists and worries—but last night's dream had taken her away from all that.

It had been a John dream. She felt it in her skin, before remembering the details. The press of his hand on her back, his lips against her ear, telling her a secret. In the dream, her mouth had been about to smile. Until the end, the sound of his voice had prompted everything in her body and spirit toward happiness. The dream might have been of Ireland; it might have been in that farmhouse bedroom, the moment before everything ended. She wanted that feeling of closeness back more than anything.

Barefoot, she walked across the cool, hard sand to the water's edge. Her white eyelet nightgown brushed her ankles as she splashed into the shallows. She startled an egret standing among the rocks at the end of the beach, and it took off with slow white wings, reminding her of something graceful and prehistoric.

The tide was outrageously low. Honor looked up at the sky, remembering that there had been no moon last night.

"New moons and full moons do crazy things to the sea," John had said one night long ago, when they'd walked along the edge of the waves. Last night it had seemed so real—every word and touch coming back to her now. They'd been twenty-three years old, and so in love it hurt.

In her dream—and during the real walk, twenty-two years ago, when she had first started teaching at Star of the Sea—it was twilight, dawn's opposite, when the sky was taking back all the light, pulling it up from the waves, the sand's hard silver. John had his camera out, as always, ready to capture it all. And walking on the beach, he was safe for once. There weren't too many risks he could take on a warm summer night, with Honor holding his hand.

"They make the high tides higher and the low tides lower," Honor said. "Flood tides, neap tides..."

"With the right wind," he'd said, stopping to stare out at the water. Crouching, holding his camera to his eye, adjusting the lens. "A flood tide will fill the marshes, overflow the banks, come all the way up to the door. And a neap tide, like this one, will uncover stretches of sand that have been underwater all year."

She heard the shutter clicking as he took his pictures. When they were children, and her family stayed at Hubbard's Point and his stayed on the grounds of Star of the Sea, the two homes had been connected by this same wild, long barrier beach—of her dream, and the one she walked right now.

After a winter storm, an especially low neap tide had revealed timbers from a Revolutionary War ship. Honor, John, his sister Bernadette, and their friend Tom had found it, reporting it to the nuns. A local archeologist had scrambled to collect data, but after three days, when the tides returned to normal, the ship had disappeared.

"Do you think anyone ever came back to find that ship?" she asked.

"Probably, but those treasures don't count. I only want the ones I come across by accident."

"Right, like those ice fields you climbed Mount Robertson to photograph last winter. And the bear den you practically crawled into—"

He gave her a look, shook his head. This was their dance—John courted danger to be closer to nature, get the shots he wanted, and Honor teased him about it. She'd never tell him that it was one of the most exciting things about him, and that sometimes she felt that as long as he came home safe, she wouldn't really want him to stop.

He handed her his camera. It felt so heavy, and she held it carefully so she wouldn't drop it. She watched John, barefoot, his khakis rolled up, his hair windblown, bent from the waist, picking up what looked like wild stars.

Moonstones.

Far out on the tidal flats, long submerged, uncovered only by the grace of the new moon, the pebbles were smooth, iridescent white, no bigger than her fingernail. They lay on dark sand, catching the last light, shimmering like fallen stars. She wanted to paint the scene as Van Gogh would, the year he was in the asylum—with streaks of midnight blue and gold, and magic swirling through the night. Inspiration was a type of madness, and she loved how crazy and inspired she and John could be together.

When John finished scouring the tide line, he came back to her. Took the camera from her, slung it over his shoulder by the strap, put his arms around her. He looked into her eyes, his blue eyes, shining, his mouth breaking into a smile. He had always had a face full of secrets, but that night he was wide open, all hers.

"Honor," he said.

"John," she answered.

Holding her, he rocked her, back and forth gently, as if they were moving with the tide itself. She felt as if they were part of each other; they'd always been that way, ever since they were kids. He kissed her, turning her into salt water, liquid and surging. And then he fumbled for her hand.

"Honor," he said again.

Then, "Love, honor, and cherish."

"What?" she asked.

"That's what I'm going to do," he said. "Love and cherish you, I swear...."

She knew but she didn't know. She had loved him so much, for so long. Was this the moment she had always dreamed of? On the beach they loved, barefoot and sandy, with their pants rolled up and wet?

"Will you marry me?" he asked, taking her hand, filling it with the moonstones he had just gathered.

"Oh, John—"

"I can't afford a ring yet," he said. "But I love you, Honor. I'll love you forever. Will you marry me?"

"Yes, John!" She clutched the moonstones, flinging her arms around his neck to kiss him, overjoyed that he'd asked her here, on their beach, between their houses, knowing what stones symbolized to him, to his family. They lay on the sand, tucking the moonstones into a pocket of his camera bag, talking about the life they would have, the places they would go. He'd be careful and always come home to her—better yet, she'd go everywhere with him. They would have lots of kids, and they'd all grow up on the beach, right here.

"We'll teach them about the tides and the stars," he said.

"And art. They'll be photographers and sculptors like their father."

"Painters like their mother." He paused. "Will we get married at the chapel? At Star of the Sea?"

She nodded excitedly. "We can walk to our wedding!" As the new art teacher, she had a house on the campus.

Now, at dawn, on the same beach, Honor finally felt the dream drifting away. So many of the promises they had made that night had come true. They had gotten married at Star of the Sea. Bernie had been maid of honor, Tom had been best man. There had been lots of travels, lots of art, lots of students, and best of all, three children. Three beautiful daughters. Regis, the oldest, had been the light of her father's life. When John had asked Bernie and Tom to be her godparents, he had told them he was holding them to the fire on it—if anything ever happened to him or Honor, she was in their hands.

Honor had been expecting that Tom would give Regis away—her daughter was rushing to have the wedding in October, over Columbus Day weekend, desperate for the security she thought marriage would provide. Honor had asked herself, would Tom walk his goddaughter down the aisle, because John wouldn't be home yet? Would he dance with her at the reception? Would he be the one to tell Agnes and Cecilia, Regis's sisters, that they were as beautiful as the bride?

Questions Honor had never wanted to ask. Because among all those promises made that moonless night so many years ago, all the promises so faithfully and lovingly kept, there had also been one broken.

Honor didn't think about it very often anymore. Her life was fine, busy, very full. The girls still needed her, even Regis. Over the years, Honor had gone through the motions of painting, saving most of her energy for her daughters and students. And the shoreline was still her home. It had soothed her heart during the time John had been gone, with salt breezes and sea glass and beach roses. But the one thing she never did—not since Ireland—was walk the tide line to gather handfuls of moonstones.

Until now. Because she knew that something was about to happen. She hadn't told the kids yet, but Tom had told her the rumor. And some rumors were too real not to be believed, especially when they came from Tom Kelly.

Honor shivered in the dawn chill, looking down at the hard sand.

The new moon had pulled the tide out so far, the flats were completely exposed. The sun had not yet risen, but its light was spreading up from the horizon, across the dark water, onto the tarnished silver sand, rippled with tiny salt streams, glittering with tiny white stones. Seeing them took Honor's breath away. Leaning over, she picked them up, cupping them in one hand. Each pebble shimmered like a jewel.

"I can't afford a ring yet...but I love you, Honor...I'll love you forever...."

She wheeled around. If the moonstones were back, it seemed impossible that John wasn't here, too. A cool breeze blew off the water, whispering through the marsh grass growing along the top of the beach. It sounded almost like a voice, and she started toward it. She saw Sisela whisk across the stone wall leading up to the Academy, one of the walls built by John's ancestors.

Emerging from the shadows, she saw a person running toward her. Tall and lean, with his long legs and strong shoulders. If she closed her eyes, she could see his face, his blue eyes, forever in her memory. But she didn't have to remember, because she saw those eyes every day. In their twenty-year-old daughter Regis.

"Mom," Regis called from down the beach, waving something in the air.

Was this it? Honor wondered, her own heart starting to race. Regis ran faster, although Honor could truly say she'd never seen her daughter move at a normal pace. Everything with Regis was full speed ahead.

"What is it?" Honor asked. "What do you have there?"

"Oh, Mom," Regis said, holding up the blue envelope. "Read it! It's addressed to you!"

Honor's hand shook. She held the moonstones so tight, they pressed into her palm and left marks. The sun was coming up, throwing light onto the beach. Regis stared at the envelope, Honor's name in John's handwriting.

"Where did you get it?"

"It was stuck in the screen door."

Sometime between when Honor left the house for her walk and now—had he been watching them?

"I think Aunt Bernie put it there. I saw her standing outside the convent just now, when I came down. What does it matter how the letter came? Read it! What does it say?"

As always seemed to happen, the wind picked up as the sun rose. It blew gently off the land, bringing with it scents of beach plums, sassafras, grapes, and pines. It carried the sounds of Star of the Sea— the nuns' voices, singing lauds, and the bell, tolling half past the hour. The breeze ruffled Honor's hair, and even though it was summery and warm, it sent an arctic chill into her bones as she read John's letter.

There were several paragraphs, and each one answered a question. Honor held it so her daughter couldn't see.

The moonstones, Honor thought, feeling electricity. There are no coincidences....

"What does he say, Mom? You have to tell me!"

Honor looked up at her, stared straight into those gray-blue eyes. She saw all the pain of John's absence, and the joy of having just found his letter. The tide had turned, was starting to come in, licking their bare feet with the first splashes of foam. Honor's whole body trembled. She knew she could try to smile, but Regis knew her too well, would know that it was forced.

"Mom?"

Honor held the letter, the sheet of pale blue paper. She thought of what she had just read, but she knew that Regis cared about only one line.

"He's coming home," Honor said.

Regis had to go straight from seeing her mother to meeting her fiancé. She had never felt more torn in her life. She wanted to run back home to her sisters, tell them the news about their father. Or to Aunt Bernie, who would know the whole, real story—she had stayed in touch with him more than anyone. The six years had passed with horrible, excruciating slowness. Like six years in fairy-tale time, or legend time—six years when people grow old, and other people go a little crazy, and still others forget entirely.

But Regis had made plans to go out on the water with Peter and his family. That was the thing about being in love—you had to train yourself to love, or at least care for, or at least spend time with, his family, when you'd really so much rather be with your own.

Regis left her mother standing on the beach near Star of the Sea, and ran along the sand toward Hubbard's Point. Because it was so early she was practically alone, except for egrets and herons standing in the shallows, and rafts of seagulls and terns gathered just off the rocks.

She ran along the empty, deserted nature sanctuary, then emerged into the stretch of beach cottages—each almost identical to each other, almost like Monopoly houses, in a tidy row along the strand—and then the honky-tonk section of Black Hall, with one guy sleeping on the sand in front of the beer hall.

As her feet pounded, her heart soared. Just seeing her father's handwriting could do that to her. Her sisters were younger, and didn't quite get it. Not the way Regis did. What did they remember about him? She was never sure, and they hardly ever talked about it. During the six years, the family had visited him seven times. Three times the first year, twice the second year, then once a year after that until the summer before last. They hadn't gone back after that. During the long stretches between visits, Regis noticed strange things happening. She would forget what her father's voice sounded like, or how his eyes looked. How his laugh would start out slow, with a chuckle, and then grow. How his hands were so strong. How her parents looked together.

Her mother had made various excuses for why the visits stopped. The airfare was too expensive; studies and school activities demanded too much time; and Regis's favorite: seeing their father in prison was traumatic for the girls. Regis had tried to tell her mother that *not* seeing him was traumatic. But her mother seemed to have secret reasons all her own, and she stopped listening.

Running along the beach, Regis felt exalted. She'd played varsity tennis at Star of the Sea, but only because her aunt had made her. Team sports weren't her thing. Like her father, she was more of a solitary athlete—running, swimming, biking, climbing, preferably with an element of severe danger and a major adrenaline rush involved. Even now—approaching the big houses of Tomahawk Point, she chose to run along the craggy, jagged rocks close to the water's edge, instead of cutting across the coast path higher up, through the yards. One slip of the foot and she'd break an ankle or fall into the sea. But Regis didn't think about it—she just trusted herself to make it across.

Running along, she saw some driftwood washed up on the rocks and felt cold. The sight reminded her of Ireland: her father's sculpture vandalized, driftwood branches torn off, lying on the ground. Regis shuddered as she ran, a memory shimmering, not quite there.

Tearing over the rocks now, then forsaking the last stretch along a pristine beach to run through the woods, along narrow paths, over streams, into the swamp, across a makeshift bridge—a splintered plank someone had laid across the inlet, thick with blue crabs and slithery marsh creatures—to Hubbard's Point. Even before Ireland, her father had taught her to take the path less traveled. The instincts were in her blood, and even when she tried to choose the safest route, she seemed compelled to go the more dangerous way.

Dashing the last quarter mile, along sleepy beach roads to the Drakes' house, she was sweaty and out of breath when she came face-to-face with Peter and his mother. Peter lit up to see her. His mother looked displeased.

"Hi!" Regis exclaimed, going straight to Peter and kissing him. He held on, but she pulled back because his mother was right there. "Hi, Mrs. Drake."

"Hello, Regis."

"Am I late? You said seven o'clock, right? For our trip out to Block Island?"

"The boat's in the mud," Peter said. "We had a really low tide this morning."

"It was a moonstone tide," Regis said. She tried to smile, but couldn't. She thought of how her parents had gotten engaged, not with a diamond, but with moonstones. What if her mother couldn't forgive her father? What if that day in Ballincastle had destroyed them?

"Maybe so, but look," Peter said, pointing.

Regis peered between the cottages, and yes—the family vessel, a big white fiberglass powerboat on a mooring out in front of the house, was listing seriously to starboard, clearly aground.

"There could be a lot of damage," Peter's mother said. "Stuck in the mud like that. Structural damage."

"I don't think there will be, Mrs. Drake," Regis said. "Really, I don't. When we were in Ireland, there was this tiny fishing village. Just past Kinsale, Timoleague . . . Some boats were tied to a long stone jetty, others were on moorings, and when the tide went out, they would all rest right there on the bottom of the harbor. Then the water would flood in again, and the boats would float and head out to sea."

Mrs. Drake gave Regis a long look, as if she was trying to figure out whether she was for real or not. Her expression made Regis squirm and take Peter's hand. "That's not an Irish fishing boat," Mrs. Drake said, gesturing. "It's a brand-new, top-of-the-line Jetcruiser. You don't want to know what it cost. It has an intake system I don't under-stand, but let me tell you, getting filled with sand or mud or eelgrass or whatever is out there on the bottom won't do it any good. Peter, go out and help your father."

"Mom—"

"What's he doing?" Regis asked.

"He's trying to dig it out."

"But the tide's coming in soon," Regis said. "If we just wait, nature will take care of everything."

Again Peter's mother gave her a long, scary look. Her nostrils trem-bled and her lips thinned. "You and Peter have decided to interrupt your college educations and get married," she said. "How you're going to support yourselves is the question. It makes me think you're very naive in the ways of the world, to think that nature takes care of things. As often as not, it ruins them. Business 101 would teach you that once an engine gets clogged with sand, you can kiss it goodbye!"

Mrs. Drake wheeled and walked toward the house. She was dressed for the boat ride: white slacks, a red T-shirt, and a blue and white sweater tied around her neck. Regis felt herself blush, and looked down at the ground, picturing the colorful Irish fishing boats and how much more beautiful they were than the fiberglass gas-guzzler of which Mrs. Drake was so proud.

"She's right," Peter said. "This isn't Ireland."

"My father's coming…" Regis began. But her throat caught, and she felt herself shaking. She stepped forward, reached up to put her arms around him. They leaned gently against an oak tree, and he started kissing her long and slow. The morning heat touched her face and arms, and Peter's kiss made her feel like liquid sunshine, warm from the inside out.

When they pulled apart, he looked into her eyes. "Okay, tell me what you meant," he said. "About your father coming."

"We got a letter from my father. He's coming home."

"Your father?"

Regis nodded. She couldn't even speak the words.

Peter's expression darkened. "But that can't make you happy, him coming back here," he said.

"How can you say that?" Regis asked, feeling slapped.

"Because of what, well, what happened. Because of what he did."

"He saved my life," Regis said. "That man was attacking me, and my father fought him off."

Peter glowered. Regis recoiled, remembering how he had once told her his parents felt sorry for her mother, because of what had happened. It had almost been enough to make her break up with him.

"He killed that man," he said.

"Stop, Peter," Regis said, feeling the blood flow out of her head, her face, just as it had from Gregory White's skull on the rocky coast. "I know."

"Goddamn it, Millie!" came Peter's father's voice calling from across the tidal flats. "Will you and Peter get out here? There's seaweed in the intake."

"Seaweed in the intake," Regis murmured.

"Should we go and help him out?"

Regis felt stunned. She looked around at the window boxes and garden. Peter's mother had an eye for bright flowers, and had planted multitudes of geraniums, petunias, zinnias, and cosmos. The yellow cottage had fake blue shutters bolted to the wood. The windows were hung with white curtains tied back with colorful ribbons. The overall effect looked just like the house pictures Regis had drawn when she was a little girl.

"Regis?" he said, taking her hands. "You're not like your father. I know that, okay? I love you."

"I love you," she murmured, feeling prickles race around her lips, across her cheeks. Didn't Peter know she was *just* like him? She felt almost faint, but then she looked around at the pretty gardens, and up at the man she was going to marry. She and Peter would love each other and be safe forever. Their biggest worry would be seaweed in the intake.

"Okay?" he asked.

She nodded, resolute. Peered out at the water, saw the tide starting to trickle back into the rock pools and across the sand flats. The Drakes' shiny white boat looked so ungainly out there, nothing like the bright wooden hulls in Kinsale harbor. It looked plastic and aggressive, with silver pipes and ducts, like something that might harm the sea. But because Regis loved the man whose family owned it, she knew she'd do anything to help.

"Come on, then," she said, tugging his hand. "Let's go rescue your boat."

And together she and her fiancé hurried across the yard to the steps down to the rocks, instead of where she really felt like going—home, to see what was going on, to hear what everyone was saying about the letter.

Two

The wedding plans were moving along, and Agnes hadn't seen Regis so sparkly since their father had gone away. Nothing had been the same since then. Their family had once been so happy. They lived at Star of the Sea Academy, the most beautiful place in Connecticut. They were Irish Catholics who practiced their faith, who believed in being good.

But then life had changed. Her father had gone to Portlaoise Prison for six years, for killing a man. How could that be—Agnes's good, gentle father? She couldn't stand thinking of what he'd done; she couldn't believe that he'd raised his hand so violently to someone, even in defense of Regis.

No one really talked about it. Regis couldn't remember anything, from the minute of running out into the rain, into the murky salt mist that had obscured the whole thing. Only three people had been on that cliff—their father, Regis, and Gregory White. The news stories in Ireland had said that Greg White was a drifter, originally from Connemara, with a history of theft and violence. He'd seen their father as a mark, a successful artist, someone to get money out of.

Agnes had sneaked into the Academy library, where her aunt kept copies of Irish newspapers. The country seemed just about evenly divided on whether her father should have been punished or not.

Some said that his manslaughter conviction was an outrage—that John Sullivan had only been defending his daughter. Some articles portrayed Greg White as a parasite, reporting that he had previously been associated with gypsies, "travelers," in Connemara, breaking into farmhouses and beating up the owners. They said that White had bragged about the riches he was about to get.

Other papers said that Agnes's father had acted with undue force. Police had been called on him before. White had attacked the sculpture, and Agnes's father had confronted him in a bar. Fighting had ensued, and Agnes's father had had to be restrained. Worst of all, people had heard him threaten to kill White if he touched the sculpture again. Some news accounts seemed to say that he hadn't just defended Regis—he had gone over the line between manslaughter and murder, that his real anger at the victim had been caused by White's vandalism of the sculpture, and that six years in prison wasn't enough.

Agnes couldn't bear thinking that, and she refused to believe it. The worst part was, the prison was far away, and over time they had stopped visiting him. He wrote letters home, and Agnes and her sisters wrote back. But not her mother.

Agnes sat on her bed, writing in her notebook. It was Tuesday, a day of silence. Looking around the room she shared with her sisters, at Regis's bride magazines, at the pictures on the bureau of their father, of his photographs on the wall, and at a photo of Regis and Peter, Agnes held in a shiver.

Regis was making a mistake. She wanted love and romance, a fairytale dream. It killed Agnes to see her sister working so hard to invent something that could never be real. Because Agnes knew—she was sure—that Regis was trying to make everything right. If she and Peter could be in love, then she could pretend her family hadn't fallen apart.

Peter wasn't right for her sister. He was nice, fine, but he was so ordinary. And Regis was awesome beyond words. She could climb trees so tall, Agnes had once believed her sister was going up there to inspect the moon at close range. She once swam all the way across

Long Island Sound, with Agnes and Cecilia rowing the boat along-side to make sure she got to Orient Point safely. She was an honors student at Boston College, she worked two jobs, and she was the best sister in the world.

Regis had taken care of Agnes after their family had broken up. Cecilia too, but she was almost too young to know what was happening. Regis had pulled herself back after Ireland—put the trauma away and locked it shut forever. Agnes admired Regis's ability to block out and forget. The sisters had that in common. It had always been Regis and Agnes, sticking together through thick and thin.

No one had ever had a better sister. When she'd gone off to college, Agnes had missed her so much; now, with her getting married, Agnes couldn't even imagine.

All Agnes could do was pray. That's what got her through life. She climbed out of bed, walked over to the window. Knelt down, gazed out at the Academy grounds, with the long and beautiful stone walls. They held such secrets and mysteries. In a way, they were responsible for their family tragedy, and they held the promise of their salvation. They had been built by their beloved ancestors.

Kneeling, she gazed out at the land and the walls, and started praying the Memorare. Beside her, on the windowsill, was Sisela, their cat. She was ancient, in feline terms—eighteen, just slightly older than Agnes—pure white, nearly toothless. Agnes wondered whether Sisela remembered her father. While Agnes prayed, Sisela purred. She touched her nose to Agnes's cheek. She was a saintly, supernatural cat, Agnes was convinced—always bringing comfort to the family, always alert to passing angels. A sea breeze blew in, and girl and cat turned their faces toward the window. There in the glade, leaning on the oldest wall, Agnes saw her mother. She started to wave out the window, but her mother wasn't looking.

Her mother's head was bent. She seemed to be staring at the sheet of blue paper she held in her hands. Even from here, Agnes could see her mother's shoulders shaking, could see that her mother was crying.

❧

After the boat debacle, Regis borrowed Peter's Jeep to drive home. She couldn't stay away any longer, no matter what the Drakes thought. With the top down, she kept her eyes peeled for cops hiding out in their favorite spots. Her aunt had pointed them out—not just here in town, but also on I-95—teaching her that state troopers liked to hide under the bridge, behind the bank of mountain laurel in Niantic.

Driving along, Regis felt the sun on her face. Like her mother, aunt, and two sisters, she had fair skin and freckles. When she was young, her father had always reminded her to use sunscreen. They would play on the beach, building driftwood and sand sculptures and setting up his shots, and he would always call her over, quickly smooth sunscreen on her shoulders and nose, risking losing the play of light on water and marsh grass in order to protect her skin.

Her eyes welled up, thinking of how he had always tried to protect her. Her mother seemed to have forgotten that—the gentleness he had for the family, how he would remind them to put on sunscreen, take their jackets when it was cold, how he would tell them bedtime stories and sit with them if they had bad dreams. Was he really coming home? Her stomach flipped as she wondered what was in his letter and what her mother would have to say about it.

Regis's ring glinted in the bright light. It sparkled like a star, as if Peter had climbed a ladder into the night, pulled Arcturus straight out of the velvet sky so she could wear it on her finger. But seeing her mother gather those moonstones this morning had really hit her; her parents had been so much in love, they hadn't needed anything like a diamond.

By the time she saw the big stone walls and wrought-iron gates, her heart was pounding. A stretch of marshland eased up to the Academy property, serene with silver-green grass waving in the late summer breeze. Pulling over, she stared through the iron fence at the cluster of stone buildings, at the cross atop the chapel spire silhouetted by bright blue sky. For the second time that day, she shivered to think of her father's last sculpture.

"Pssst," she heard.

She scanned the area, saw nothing but a muskrat across the marsh and a pair of osprey circling above the glowing water, not far from where she and Cece had found the herons' nest. She watched Sisela, the family's white cat, stalking mice in the reeds. Suddenly Cece poked her head out of the drainage ditch, grinning insanely, pollen-glittery brown curls springing from her head and tangled with twigs and bits of grass.

"What are you doing in there?" Regis demanded.

"I came through the tunnel, of course," Cecilia said.

"The tunnels are only for seniors," Regis said.

"Dream on, if you think I'm following that stupid rule. I've known about the tunnels since I was five. And guess who showed me?"

"Me, I know," Regis said. "I've been ruing the day ever since. Where's Mom?"

"Waiting for you to get home."

"Where's Agnes?"

"Well, that's why I'm in the tunnels," Cecilia said, flashing the smile of a slightly demented spy. "I've been following her."

"And...?" Regis asked, trying not to look or sound too worried.

"First she went to the Blue Grotto," Cecilia said. "She walked around the statue of Mary five times. Also, Mom thought she finished her bagel at breakfast, but she didn't. She brought it as an offering, and she left it at the Blessed Mother's feet."

"I'm sure the birds enjoyed it," Regis said. "Or the chipmunks. Then what?"

"Then," Cecilia said, her spy bravado faltering slightly, "the walls..."

"The walls," Regis said, closing her eyes. "Are you sure?"

"I saw her."

"How far did she get?"

"All the way to the edge."

"Did she go in?"

Cecilia nodded gravely.

"And you saw her come out of the water?" Regis asked, her heart starting to kickbox.

Cecilia nodded again. "Why does she do it?" she asked.

Her nutty-young-adventurer expression was gone, replaced by something completely vulnerable and quite painful to see, and suddenly Regis knew that Cecilia had been hiding in the ditch waiting for her—that this wasn't an accidental meeting at all. Cecilia blinked, her eyes huge, waiting for Regis to say something big-sisterly and wise.

"I'll tell you some other time," Regis said, shaking off the weird emotions pouring through her, the ones she'd really do anything, anything to get rid of. Checking the time again, she shook her head.

"We should get to the convent now," Cece said. "Mom and Aunt Bernie are over there, and I think they want to talk to us."

"Where is Agnes?"

"Drying off."

"Okay. Come on—hop in. Let's go see Mom."

"No, I'm going to get Agnes first. We'll meet you there."

Cecilia took off in a blur. Regis watched in admiration as Cece disappeared through the chink in the stones, taking a shortcut through the tunnel. Regis knew how protective Cece felt of Agnes, how protecting someone else could make you feel much braver in your own life, brave enough to go into the dark, damp tunnels. Sitting very still, Regis remembered the first time she had ever been in there. Like Cece, she'd been five. It was so black and slippery, with hardly any light coming through the stones, and with moss growing on the path underfoot; it should have felt scary, but it wasn't. She'd been with her father. Her hand had been in his.

"When we're together, we can do anything!" she'd said to him. She had believed it, too. If only it had been true; if only the last time they'd been together hadn't ruined their family. She felt a headache starting behind her eyes, the way it always did when she started to remember that day.

Putting the Jeep in gear, she drove slowly through the stone gates, up the hill to the convent. She parked next to the nuns' station wagon, took a deep breath, and went inside.

⚜

Honor sat in a green chair, holding a cup of tea. She watched Sister Bernadette Ignatius—her sister-in-law, the girls' aunt Bernie—pouring tea for Agnes, plunking in a sugar cube, handing it to her. Agnes shook her head.

"She doesn't want any," Cecilia said.

"Agnes. You were in the water so long, your lips are still blue," Sister Bernadette said. "Drink the tea."

Agnes shook her head again, but as if she hadn't noticed, Bernie placed the delicate white teacup on the mahogany table at her elbow. Agnes stared at it, as if she could read messages in the tea leaves.

"She won't touch it," Regis said.

"She won't," Cece chimed in.

"Well, it's there if she changes her mind," Bernie said. She stood tall, straightened her habit, and sat down at the Windsor chair beside her desk. Honor gazed over at her. Sometimes, even after all these years, it still gave her a shock to see her old best friend, John's sister, in a nun's habit. Bernie looked so much like her brother, with all the bright wildness Honor remembered from their childhood. Honor knew that there had been parts of herself Bernie had traded away, to fit into her life as a nun.

"Mom, will you tell us what's going on?" Regis asked. "A tea party is really nice, but honestly—"

"Is this your shower?" Cece asked, confused. "I know we're having a tea party for your shower…"

"Cecilia!" Honor said.

"Great, Cece," Regis said, trying to smile, as if she wanted to make everything normal. "You just let the cat out of the bag. A tea party for my shower? Mom, Aunt Bernie, I thought you didn't approve of my getting married, so I never thought you'd throw me a shower."

"We'll talk about that later," Honor said.

"I screwed up the surprise!" Cece wailed. "I'm sorry! It's just that with everything happening…"

"It's okay, honey, I hate surprises anyway," Regis said, hugging her from one side as Agnes, not speaking, hugged her from the other side.

Honor stared at her daughters, comforting each other. The love among them was extraordinary, and always had been. She glanced over at Bernie, met her eyes. Was she thinking of her own beloved sibling?

"Okay, everyone," Honor said. "I want to talk to you about something. A letter from your father."

"Daddy?" Agnes asked, the first word she had spoken all day.

"I saw it," Regis said. "I held it in my hand. It really was from him, and he said he's—"

"Girls, he's coming home," Honor said.

"He's getting out of jail?" Cecilia asked.

"He didn't even deserve to be there," Agnes whispered. "All he did was save Regis. How could they punish him for that?"

Honor's stomach tightened, as it always did when she talked about John with the girls. She had to reassure them, and she had to try to explain why John had been so adamant about not fighting the charges. Honor had begged him to claim self-defense, to call one of Tom Kelly's powerful Irish barrister cousins. But he wouldn't even discuss it. And once his mind was made up, she knew that was the end of it.

"He'll be so upset," Cece said. "That we stopped visiting him."

"It's true, Mom," Regis said. "Won't he?"

"I didn't even know he was coming home this soon," Agnes said. "I thought he wasn't supposed to get out till the end of the year."

"Did they pardon him, Mom?" Regis asked. "Is that what happened? Did his lawyer, or his barrister, whatever it's called, finally get the court to realize that he's not a killer?"

"He did kill that man, though," Cece said in a low, terrible voice.

"Manslaughter," Agnes said bleakly.

"He's being released for good behavior," Honor said. "Sweethearts, it's complicated. You love your father, and he loves you. That will never change. When I read this letter to you, you're going to have some questions. You might feel upset at me for not telling you more sooner."

"Read it, Mom!" Regis demanded.

"Let your mother finish," Bernie said, frowning slightly.

"I'm going to read it, Regis. I just want to prepare you all. It's not exactly what I expected to hear, and I'm sure that's true of you, too." Honor looked over at Bernie. Did she know what was coming? Was she in on it somehow? Honor was close to her, as a sister-in-law, but she knew that Bernie's first loyalty was to her brother. If Bernie did know, she was giving nothing away: she sat there, both impassive and on the edge of her seat.

Honor pulled the blue stationery from the blue envelope, lowered her eyes, and began to read.

Dear Honor,

How are you? How are the girls? I think of you all, every day, all day. That is a fact, and the same as it has always been. Thank you for letting me know about Regis. It seems impossible to believe that she is old enough to have a boyfriend, much less get married. She hasn't said one word about it in her letters. Thank you for forwarding them to me, by the way. I wonder what it means, that she didn't see fit to tell me about her marriage. I have a lot of thoughts about that.

You could probably tell me her exact reasons, you know her so well. One thing that comes to mind is, maybe she doesn't want me to feel bad. Doesn't want me to think of her walking down the aisle without me holding her arm. Is that crazy? After all this time, is that the last thing she would want?

I'm assuming the wedding is at Star of the Sea. You didn't mention it, and I've wondered about that, too. Don't worry or feel bad, Honor. I might not tell you either, if the tables were turned. How could I do that to you, evoke a place so important to us, to our family, the chapel where you and I looked into each other's eyes, promised to love, honor, and cherish, where we said our "I do's," where our life together began? I hope that's the reason you didn't tell me, and not a fear that I would show up.

At that, Regis gasped, and Honor looked up from the letter.

"He really thinks that?" she asked. "It's not true! I just didn't think he'd be home in time...."

"Just listen, sweetheart," Honor said.

"Let your mother finish," Bernie said.

Here is what I want, Honor: to be at our daughter's wedding. And I believe you want me to as well—or you wouldn't have told me about her getting married.

I've respected your wishes, Honor. I agree with your reasons, most of the time. They made more sense to me when I was in prison.

Back then—

"Back *then*?" Regis asked. "When did he get out? Why didn't anyone tell us?"

"Sshh," Bernie said. "Listen."

Back then, it was so clear. I had screwed up so badly. I'd messed up things with you so ridiculously—what right did I have to even question your wishes? Life in prison, everything is black and white. Good and bad. There were no doubts. I hated myself so much for what I'd done to land inside there, I judged myself unworthy to question you. But these last six months, everything has shifted.

Nature will do that. Staring out at the sky through bars keeps you from wondering too much. Honor, I used to think I'd go crazy if I wondered too much. But being on the mountaintop, or the tundra, or the seaside, or the sea itself breaks all the questions wide open.

Honor stopped, scanned the next part of the letter, which she would not read to the girls. She felt their tension, wanting her to go on. Clear, blue light slanted through the arched windows, falling on the letter she held on her lap.

*The questions all have to do with the same thing, you see.
And there is only one answer. Think about that, Honor. You're
the one who first told me, so long ago. My wise…*

Again, she stopped, unwilling to read his words out loud. She should have edited the letter before bringing it before the children.

*I will see you soon, all of you. And I will be at Regis's
wedding unless you, or she, wishes otherwise.*

"That's the end of the letter," Honor said.

When she looked up, she saw the shock in her daughters' faces. She wanted to rush into the explanation, tell them everything she wanted them to know and understand. Instead, she sat quietly, waiting.

"He's out?" Regis asked.

"Yes."

"Since when?"

"Six months. Just as he said in the letter—"

"Weren't you going to tell us?" Regis shrieked.

"Regis," Cecilia said. "She probably was. And besides, who cares, as long as he's coming home!"

"But why didn't you, Mom?"

"Because I didn't know myself until just a few days ago."

"Why didn't he come home right away?" Regis asked. "How could he have stayed away from us?"

"Your father carries his own burdens," Bernie said, and Honor felt grateful to her for jumping in. "He feels guilty for what he did. He took a man's life. And he's sorry about that. There's also the fact that he went to jail. He feels terrible for what you've all gone through."

"So he wanted to stay out of our lives?" Regis asked. "Agnes, did you hear that?"

Honor looked at Agnes, who sat there silently, eyes closed tight, hands balled into fists.

"He must be lonely," Cece said.

"Where is he now? Where did he write the letter from?" Regis asked.

"I don't know. It didn't have a stamp or postmark, it was delivered by hand. Bernie, thank you for dropping it off at the cottage...."

"I didn't," Bernie said.

"Isn't it obvious?" Cece asked. "Dad must have put it there himself!"

"Thank you, God," Agnes whispered.

"He's already here!" Regis said, and Honor felt a shiver go down her spine, because she was thinking the same thing.

Three

The weather turned rainy that evening, and it poured straight through till dawn. Sister Bernadette had been up since vigils, and now, as she stood in the passage between the chapel and house, she gazed through leaded glass as gray light from the east washed over the Academy's grass and trees, its stone walls and buildings. Two sisters walked by, and she exchanged silent nods with them.

Life behind the enclosure had a rhythm all to itself. Her order was unusual, in that it had both contemplatives and teaching sisters. As a young novice, she had been a contemplative. She had lived in the cloister at the back of the house. Her days had been spent in meditation and prayer, not speaking, communing only with God. That had been a very intense time; Bernadette had had much guilt and sorrow to expiate.

After two years behind the enclosure, Bernadette felt forgiven. She also felt the calling to teach.

It shouldn't have surprised her. She was a classic older sister; her younger brother John had been her first student. Back when they were young, growing up in New Britain, and then coming down here to Black Hall, she had taught him everything she learned. Not so much school things as life things. Their joke was, Bernie would learn how to drive, and she'd drive home and give John the wheel.

She had taught him how to climb trees, ice-skate, ski down the tall hills at the WASP country club up the street from their house in New Britain. Their father had had a motto: "Buy the smallest house in the best neighborhood, even if it's all you can afford." Bernie and John had watched their father shop at fancy stores, spend his life smiling and selling insurance to the rich people at the country club that wouldn't have him as a member. Bernie had taught her brother to listen to his own deep, inner voice, the one that told him not to become an insurance salesman.

"There's more," Bernie told him as they rode the bus downtown one cold December day to go Christmas shopping.

"More what?" he asked.

"You'll know," she said, gazing out the window at the three-family houses on the west end of Center Street.

"Dad says I'd be good," John said. "He said I could sell someone their own car."

"That's not a compliment," Bernie said, turning to her brother. "And it's not true, either. He's talking about himself. You couldn't sell someone blankets if they were freezing."

John gave her a sharp look. He was thirteen, and Bernie fifteen. She had the Sullivans' "Red Irish" coloring, with fair skin, strawberry blonde hair, and gray-blue eyes. He was Dargan all the way—"Black Irish" with striking dark hair and clear blue eyes. She smiled at her handsome brother.

Bernie wanted to touch his cheek, but he was just at that age where it would bother him. If only he knew what she saw. Bernie had always adored her brother; she felt that she could see straight into his heart. She wanted to tell him that he had a beautiful soul, but she held back, for all the best older-sisterly reasons.

Instead, she pointed out the bus window. This end of Center Street was mostly tenements—small apartment blocks and three-family houses. In a city of Polish factory workers, the Irish had dominated this neighborhood at one time. Now it was other nationalities. The buildings needed painting. Some of the porches were sagging. Bernie knew that one of their neighbors owned several of these buildings. His family had been landlords to shifting waves of immigrants.

"Dad would sell them insurance if he could," Bernie said.

"So would I," John said.

"He would sell them insurance," Bernie said. "But he wouldn't see them. Look at them, John."

"There's no one outside to see," he said, peering out the bus window. The streets were lined with high, dirty snowbanks, and everyone was inside.

Then look inside, she had wanted to tell him, but she held back. He would have to discover the ability to see for himself. She gave him his first camera for Christmas that year: the Swinger, a Polaroid camera. It was the only one she could afford, a white plastic camera with a black wrist strap. John had torn open the package, looked up grinning as Bernie began singing the TV ad:

"Meet the Swinger, Polaroid Swinger..."

"Wow, Bern," he said, beaming. "Thanks."

"You're welcome."

"It's the film that they get you on," their father said. "The camera's plastic, made cheap in China. How else would they sell it for under twenty bucks? But it's the film that costs an arm and a leg. That's where the company makes their money. That and the film developing."

"No developing, Dad," John said, reading the instructions, starting to load the camera. "It does it itself, right here. Hey, Bernie, smile!"

He'd snapped the picture. Bernie could remember it still; the family gathered around, waiting for the murky image to clarify. The harsh, acrid chemicals mingled with the smells of their white spruce tree, bacon and coffee from Christmas breakfast, their parents' cigarette smoke, and the last-night stale whiskey smell coming off their father.

And then, when the picture came to life, it was as if John did, too. He put on his boots and parka, went out into the snow with his new camera. He took shots of white powder sifted on glossy green rhododendron leaves, stones and tar bound up in clumps of snow thrown back by passing snowplows, branches broken under the snow's heavy weight.

Standing at the convent window now, Bernie knew that her brother had had the gift inside him the entire time: the ability to see and photograph nature. He had it for people, too. She remembered that first Polaroid picture he'd taken of her—her coppery red hair sleep-tousled, flannel nightgown buttoned to the throat, crooked grin and happy Christmas-morning eyes.

Staring across the grounds, Bernie wondered where he was now. Before the trouble, his life had been about traveling, making do, going to ground, in order to get the best shots—taking Honor and the girls with him when school wasn't in session, going alone when it was. He would follow the light in Manitoba as he completed some project having to do with snowy owls, the boreal forest, and the transit of Venus. He had chased the spirit to Ireland, looking for his version of the Holy Grail—and it had landed him in the deepest trouble there was.

Nuns passed by, coming and going. Sister Bernadette nodded, and they nodded back. Simple greetings, a friendly spirit, were part of monastic life, dating back to the rule of Saint Benedict. If only it were so easy in the outside world. After vespers last night, just before the rain began to fall, Bernie had gone for her evening walk to the Blue Grotto. She had spotted Honor hurrying along, on the path between her cottage and the art building, and when she'd raised her hand in greeting, hoping for the chance to talk things over out of earshot of the children, Honor hadn't seen—lost in her own thoughts.

A buzzer sounded, indicating that someone was at the front door. Bernadette turned her head, listening for voices. Moments later, Sister Ursula poked her head into the passage and said, "Tom Kelly."

"Ah," Bernadette said.

Sister stood there. Their eyes met, but Bernadette didn't react or look away. She held her place.

"He needs to see you about something on the grounds."

"Thank you. Tell him I'll be right there."

Sister Ursula stood there another instant, looking almost curious, but then nodded and walked away. She had been a nun nearly as long as Bernadette had. She had grown up here in Black Hall, part of a well-known Episcopal family. Back then, her name had been Charlotte

Rose Whitney. She had gone to Miss Porter's with Tom's sister Anne. Her brother, Henry Tobias, had gone to Hotchkiss, dated girls here at the Academy. After their parents died, Charlotte converted to Catholicism and became a nun, named for the martyr Ursula, patron saint of girls' education.

How life changed, Bernadette thought. She sometimes wondered how much Sister Ursula knew, what her brother Henry had told her about those old days at the Academy. They never talked about it, but occasionally when Tom was around, she caught Sister Ursula giving her a certain look—more compassionate than judgmental, or so Bernadette told herself.

The hallway was long. It was really a passageway, built after the fact, to connect the building where the nuns slept with the chapel and the rest of the school. Rain-washed light slanted through the diamond-paned leaded glass windows, spilling on the terracotta floor. Bernadette's heels clicked as she walked.

When she got to the administration building, she spied Tom's green pickup outside. A load of squared-off stones glistened in the truck bed. She entered her office and saw him standing by the window with his back to her. She stared at the back of his head. It was soaking wet, his wavy dark hair dripping onto the shoulders of his faded green oilcloth.

"Good morning, Tom," she said.

"Sister Bernadette Ignatius," he said, half turning around, blue eyes glinting, a half smile tugging his sulky mouth. He bore a striking resemblance to John.

"It's raining out," she said. "You don't have to work today."

"Any wall builder who'd let the rain stop him had better find another job," Tom said. He had turned his back on his family wealth and power so completely, she sometimes forgot he had it at all.

"I suppose you're right," she said. "It's only a drizzle, really."

"And besides—I got your message."

"I left it in haste."

"I could tell. You were babbling."

"I don't babble."

"Let's just say you weren't your usual rapier-sharp self on my voice mail."

"Well, I've had a lot on my mind. Things are tumbling down around here. Literally. There are chinks in the mortar."

He gave her a really wicked smile. It was basically three-cornered, wider on the right side of his face. His eyes narrowed and sparkled, and he said, "Good."

"Good? What do you mean?" she asked.

"Get your umbrella, Sister Bernadette. Let's take a walk, so you can show me where you want the repairs done."

She glanced at her desk. It was piled high with last spring's report cards. She had planned to go through them all, get an idea of where the senior girls should be heading for college next year. Regis was at Boston College; if only the Jesuits could take hold of her before October, get her more excited about her own intellectual capacities and help her connect with Ignatian spirituality, maybe she would think twice and not get married.

"C'mon now, Bernie," he said. "Spend the morning away from your desk. Come take a walk with me now."

"Oh, Tom," she said, smiling and starting to shake her head.

She gazed across the room at her old friend. They were both forty-seven. His skin was ruddy and lined, from a life spent all day, every day outdoors—except for that year in Ireland. She and Tom had been the first to go—long before John and Honor's disastrous journey. He had wanted to search out his and Bernie's family roots—because even though the Kellys had employed the Sullivans here in the States, back in Ireland they had all been equal: fighters and farmers.

They had flown over to Shannon, made their way to Dublin. Just north of the city, no more than four miles, the Kellys had played their part in Irish history—in A.D. 1014, at the Battle of Clontarf, Tadhg Mor O'Kelly had died defending Ireland in a bloody battle against the Danes. A great sea monster rose from the waves during the fight, protecting Tadhg's fallen body and those of his O'Kelly kinsmen; the sea monster could be seen on the Kelly crest today, proudly featured on Francis X.'s signet ring—the one that Tom now wore, his only trapping of family power.

Bernie thought back. At the time of the trip, she already knew she was going to enter the convent. She had very persuasive reasons for doing so. But she and Tom had known each other so long, and their fascination with Ireland was tender, deep, ineffable. She had needed to make the trip before making her vows.

On the plane, holding her hand, he had promised her everything. "I'll introduce you to the Kellys' Dublin, and then we'll go to Cork for the Sullivans and Dargans, trace your brother's pirate blood...." John's Black Irish coloring was long assumed to have come from some ancestor's romance with the Spanish or Algerian pirates that had buried gold on Dargan family land. "We'll figure out why stone walls mean so much to us and our families."

"Who can resist that?" Bernie had joked. But deep down, she was serious. Entering the order, Sisters of Notre Dame des Victoires, would mean trips like this would cease. It was her last hurrah, and who better to take it with than Tom Kelly?

The memories flooded in; she slipped her hands inside her sleeves for warmth now, and shivered. His eyes were sparkling, teasing her, just like when they were children, and just like during that life-changing trip to Ireland.

"Take a walk with me," he said, holding the door open.

She nodded, taking a long black umbrella from the brass holder. He took it from her without a word, opened it and held it over her head as they left the building and walked across the campus.

The rain tapped the silk overhead. Their arms touched as they walked. Bernadette's shoulder came to the middle of Tom's biceps; he was tall, and she remembered the year he had shot up over six feet. He had been just thirteen years old.

As children, they had played together right here, on these grounds. His great-grandfather was Francis X. Kelly—the land's original owner. And her great-grandfather, Cormac Sullivan, just off the boat from

County Cork, had been hired to form a crew and build all the walls. Tom's great-grandfather eventually donated these rolling hills and grand buildings to the Sisters of Notre Dame des Victoires, to open an academy for young girls. The family property, called Stella Maris, became Star of the Sea Academy.

It had twenty acres of rolling hills and stone walls on the seaside; big stone buildings that were warm in the winter and ocean-breeze cool in the spring and fall; a convent vineyard that produced a fine chardonnay; a faculty of first-rate teachers; a fine library, containing all of Francis X.'s rare books on Ireland and the church and medieval France and Rome, including an illuminated manuscript collection that rivaled Yale's; and a warren of secret tunnels that seniors revealed to juniors on the first day of fall term.

And beautiful walls, all of which told of longing for Ireland and families left behind; of starvation and suffering; of Bernie and John's family history; and all of which were useful in keeping the nuns, and later the students, inside.

Once a year, on the Fourth of July, the nuns would let the Kellys hold a big celebration here. In gratitude to America, for all it had done for the Irish, the family would invite all the descendants of all the workers who had made Stella Maris such a showplace back for a day.

Thus, Bernadette and John Sullivan, great-grandchildren of a poor stonemason, had become friends with Tom Kelly, great-grandson of the lord of the manor. John would dare Tom to climb the tallest trees, balance on the sharpest rock pinnacle. Honor, from a family down the coast at Hubbard's Point, had become a scholarship student here.

Tom had rebelled against his family's life of privilege, and here he was building walls. Bernie was running the place, and John and Honor were separated—whether they called it that or not. How things had changed, she thought for the second time that morning. Yet, looking up at Tom Kelly, how very much they had stayed the same....

"Tell me what you're thinking," he said.

"About the repairs you're about to tell me we need and how much they're going to cost," she said.

"That's bull, and we both know it. Come on, tell me. What are you thinking?"

"Just remembering the Fourth of July parties," she said as they walked along.

"Ah, yes," he said. "Where we were all supposed to kiss the soil of the country that made us so prosperous."

"It was generous of your family," she said. "John and I used to love coming down to the sea for the day. All the kids did. We felt so special, coming to such a grand place."

He chuckled. "We were nothing if not 'grand.' My family out-WASPed the WASPs," he said. "They wouldn't let us into the country club, so we built a better one. Star of the Sea was prettier than Miss Porter's, and my father never stopped saying so—even though Miss Porter's is where he sent Anne. The famine drove us out of Ireland in 1847, and we never looked back."

Bernie heard the bitterness in his voice. "You did," she said. "You and John looked at what was hidden in the stone wall, and then you both looked back."

"Yeah, Bernie. We did, didn't we?"

She remembered how excited they had all been by the discovery of the small stone box—Honor had called it a time capsule. It had set everything into motion, sent the four of them to Ireland in two different waves.

"I saw Charlotte Rose Whitney giving me a look today," he said.

"Sister Ursula," Bernie corrected.

"She used to hang around with Annie, come to our house for weekends. I'd go to Farmington, to pick them up on Friday nights. Never thought she'd turn out to be a nun...."

Bernie's stomach tightened. She knew what was coming next.

"Never thought you would, either."

"Enough of that, okay?" Bernie said as they walked across the wide green lawn, under a canopy of tall maples lining the path. The rain dripped down, and her black shoes felt soggy.

"Anne probably told Charlotte Rose a few things about us."

"Nothing important," Bernie said, her heart beating fast. "Because she didn't know. Did she?" She watched as Tom shook his head slowly. "Then why do you say such things?"

"Because I think about them," he said, walking in furious silence for a minute. Then, "Do you believe in destiny, Sister Bernadette Ignatius? Fate?"

"Should we have a theological discussion now?" she asked.

"I tell you what," he said, eyes glaring. "I believe in love. I believe that what is meant to be will be. As long as it takes."

"Six years," she said quietly to hide the anger she felt growing, pretending they were talking about John and Honor. "That's how long John has been gone. That's how long Honor has waited, and it hasn't been easy."

"Who ever said love is easy?"

"John never understood his own limits," Bernie said, shoving her hands into the sleeves of her habit, to hide the fact that they had started to shake. "That was one thing—learning how to fly his own plane so he could land in the Alaskan bush, going out on thin ice to get the best shot, traveling to Ireland to seek out our family history—and building spectacular sculptures in the process. But putting Regis in danger...that's the part that made Honor crazy."

"He's afraid she'll divorce him."

"You've been in touch with him since he got out?"

"Bernie," he said, his voice patient, but his eyes still dark and quite dangerous.

"Have you?"

"What do you think?"

"Why didn't you tell me?"

"Honor among rogues," he said. Tried out a smile on her, then dropped it. "He asked me not to."

"He had six months more on his sentence."

"Good behavior. He's had a barrister working for him, to make sure it was noticed."

"Paid for by whom, I wonder?"

Tom didn't reply, just kept walking. The rain pattered overhead.

"Bernie, I'm walking a fine line here. John's my friend, and there are confidences..."

"You think I don't understand confidences?"

"Oh, fighting words."

"If you think those are fighting words, Tom Kelly, think again. And you should know better, with Tadhg Mor O'Kelly in your family tree. What do they say about him? 'He died fighting like a wolf dog' against the Vikings?"

"Go on, Sister Bernadette—take your best shot." He thrust his shoulder at her, and she landed a punch.

"Ow, Bernie," he said, and she could tell he was surprised that she'd connected so hard. She was a little shocked herself. Knowing her brother was free, and that Tom probably knew just where he was—and the surfacing of all the other memories—filled her with emotion. Tom had said John feared that Honor would divorce him. Would she?

Her brother had been gone for so long, some of the young nuns didn't even know he existed. Just last month, when Tom had come to work on the seawall and the stone cottage on the beach, Sister Gabrielle had laughed, said, "Sister, I think we should find a way to fix up your sister-in-law and the hot Irishman." Bernie had wondered what Tom and Honor would both think of that. The fact was, many of the young nuns knew next to nothing of Honor's and Bernie's past. And they didn't know Tom's history with someone else in the family.

"You blame me," Tom said.

"I don't blame you for anything," she said. "How could I? John has free will. He made his own choices."

"I know," Tom said. "It stirred us all up—me, John, even Honor, even you. You can't deny that."

"I wouldn't dream of it," she said, uncomfortable with this rising level of tension between them.

"Will Honor see him?"

"I don't know."

"What did she say about the letter?"

Bernie wheeled to look at him. "What do you know about that? Is he staying with you? Did he tell you he wrote it? Tom, I don't care about confidences—tell me where my brother is!"

"Bernie, I don't know."

"Then the letter—"

"He sent it to me to give to Honor. The postmark was Quebec. But he said he's on his way here. That's all I know, I swear."

"Honor's really on the edge with all this," Bernie said to Tom. "Regis is giving her the devil of a time...."

"A lot like her aunt at her age, if I'm remembering right," Tom said.

"None of that," Bernie warned.

"I don't know, Bernie," he said. "I remember you giving your mother a few sleepless nights when you were her age. You gave me a few, as well. What's Regis done?"

"She's in love and she's getting married and she's only twenty... nothing much more needs to be said," Bernie said. "You already know that."

"She's as passionate as her parents were."

"Yep," Bernie said, willing him to say not one word more.

"But as much as they loved each other, as strong as their passion might have been—Bernie, ours..."

"Stop it, Thomas."

They just walked along, the only sound their feet hitting the wet ground and the rain falling on the umbrella. His anger poured off him, waves of heat that she felt through the black fabric of her habit. Nearing the Blue Grotto, they were startled by a white streak—Sisela, running away.

"Now, is this the problem?" Tom asked as they approached the Blue Grotto.

"It is," she said, stepping closer to the arch, holding out her hand to touch the crumbling stone. Most of the Star of the Sea walls had been built without mortar, the friction and weight of one large, square stone upon another keeping them in place, but the grotto was different. Here the stones had been cut smaller, rounder, and were held together by cement mortar. The walls formed something like a cave, with a beautiful archway at the entrance and a delicate statue of the Virgin Mary inside.

She watched Tom exa * .ng the place where three stones had fallen from the arch. They lay on the ground, the size of softballs. He picked one up, held it in his hand, tried to fit it back in place. Then he tried it with the other two.

"Can you fix it?" she asked.

He nodded. "Something's missing, though," he said.

"What's missing?"

"A fourth stone. See here?" he pointed, beckoning her closer. She stood beside him, seeing the empty space. His breath was warm on her cheek. It made her shiver, and she wanted to step back. But he was pointing at scratch marks made on one of the existing stones.

"What are they?" she asked.

"Someone pried the stones out with a knife," he said.

Her heart pounded, and her mouth was dry. "Vandals?" she made herself ask. This missing stone was one thing she had no idea about.

"Looks that way," he said. He reached into his pocket, pulled out his reading glasses, and leaned closer to the crumbling mortar. Bernadette walked straight over to the statue. She examined it for damage, saw none. Carved from alabaster, the statue was three feet tall. The virgin's face was exquisite, her delicate features filled with love and compassion. Her gown was draped in graceful folds, and her arms hung at her sides, hands upturned. A serpent writhed beneath one bare foot.

Since the Academy grounds and chapel were open to the public on Sundays for mass, worshippers often left gifts here. The statue was set on granite, a natural outcropping. The rock was covered with mass cards; notes asking for prayers; the names of people living and dead in need of intercession; miraculous medals; scapulars; Alcoholics Anonymous anniversary coins; devotion candles in tall red glass holders; coins; even pieces of fruit. Although many years had passed since the apparition, and even though no official announcement had ever been made, and, in fact, the bishop had ordered it suppressed, word had trickled out, and the devoted continued to come.

"Bernie," Tom said. "You'd better look at this." The tone of his voice made her feel cold inside as she turned to walk over.

"What is it?" she asked, peering up at the faint scratches, made where the arch began its overhead curve. Tom pointed; his gold Kelly crest ring glinted dully in the grotto's dim light.

Without a word, Tom handed her his silver-rimmed reading glasses, and she slid them on. She had to stand on tiptoe to really see the knife marks, where the vandals had chiseled the rocks right out of the wall.

"I have no idea what these words mean," Tom said. "Do you?"

She stared, not replying.

Tom pointed, putting his arm around her slightly to give her a little boost up. Leaning closer, she held her breath as she felt Tom's heart beating against her back, as she read the words etched in stone:

I WAS SLEEPING, BUT MY HEART KEPT VIGIL.

Four

"When do you think Dad will come home?" Agnes asked as the first rays of Wednesday's morning light came through the filmy white curtains.

"She speaks!" Regis said, grinning from her twin bed across the room.

Agnes just smiled back, holding the covers up to her chin. A small stuffed bear came flying down from the bunk bed above, and Cecilia's head appeared, upside down, in Agnes's face.

"She spoke Tuesday, too," Cecilia said, whipping her head around to look at Regis, curly brown hair whirling over Agnes's face. "Didn't you hear her yesterday, when Mom was reading the letter?"

"That hardly counted," Regis said. "We were all in shock."

"Mom left some of it out when she was reading it to us. Did you notice?" Agnes asked.

"I noticed," Cecilia said. "Now that he's coming back, why do there have to be secrets?"

There was a long pause; then Agnes broke the silence among them. "Will he be home for your wedding?"

"That's what he says."

"If Mom lets him," Agnes said.

"Of course she'll let him."

"Don't you ever think about what he did?" Cecilia asked.

"You sound like Peter," Regis said.

"Then you don't?"

"We think about it," Agnes said. "We all do...."

She glanced at Regis. She knew that it was different for her—they had all been in Ireland, but Regis had actually been with their father. She had seen the fight, probably felt Greg White's hot breath on her own cheek.

"I don't think about it," Regis said stubbornly. "I barely remember it. Everything happened so fast."

"But you dream about it," Agnes said. "Because you wake us up saying—"

Regis shook her head fast and put up her hand so Agnes would stop. She had never been able to bear talking about it. During the investigation, Regis had been so traumatized—in St. Finan's Hospital, being treated for shock. By the time she was well enough to testify, her father had entered a plea of guilty, and the court didn't call her.

"You yell, 'Help, help, help,' over and over," Cece chimed in. "Sometimes you say something else, something I can't understand."

Regis was silent.

Agnes knew that Regis was dreaming of their father in prison, of the bars at his window, blocking his view of the sky. Things Regis couldn't think about while awake haunted her sleep. Sometimes Agnes felt so close to her sister, she believed their dreams merged; that they traveled the same roads, trying to be with their father in their dreams because they couldn't in real life.

"What will he be like when he gets home?" Cece asked.

"I don't know," Regis said. "I wonder whether he'll speak to me."

"Speak to you?" Agnes said. "Why would you even ask that?"

"Because if I hadn't followed him, it might not have happened," Regis said.

"Oh God," Agnes said. She had her own guilt. She could have stopped Regis from going to the headland. Watching Regis pull on her raincoat that day, gesturing not to tell their mother, Agnes had felt chills. She'd had a premonition—not specifically of death, but just of some terrible thing. Agnes had glimmers sometimes...sparks of perception, hints of a vision. That day she had grabbed Regis's hand. "Don't go," Agnes had said. "Daddy will be back in a minute."

"I have to," Regis had replied, pulling away. And the way she had said "have to" was every bit as compelling and electric as Agnes's own feelings about holding her back. So Agnes had let her sister go that day, and their family had fallen apart, and Regis still had it all locked inside.

"Agnes," Regis said now. "We have to straighten this out before Dad gets here. You can't blame yourself because of what I did."

"But I *knew*," Agnes said.

"She knew what would happen," Cece said. "She has the power."

Agnes wished it weren't true, but Cece was right. Agnes—not always, but sometimes—saw and felt things, and she couldn't deny it. She had once dreamed their mother was going to take them blueberry picking the next day, and she had. A dream had once shown Regis tripping on the way to the bathroom in the middle of the night, knocking a framed picture off the shelf—and it happened. The glass had shattered, and she'd fallen on it; Agnes glanced over now, saw the white half-moon scar, smooth, shiny, just below Regis's left kneecap. There was something spooky and prescient about Agnes.

"Let's be practical, not magical," Regis said. "We have to get over this so we don't upset Dad."

"I agree with that," Agnes said.

"What will he be like?" Cece asked wistfully. "Sometimes it's hard to remember him. Will he be happy to see us? Will he and Mom be happy again? Can you tell us, Agnes?"

"No," Agnes said, holding herself tight, wishing she didn't always picture her father staring out through those bars for just a sliver of blue sky, his muscles in knots from being locked up, pent up like a lion in a zoo, and his heart in tatters because his family had forgotten him.

"You can, but you don't want to," Cece said.

Agnes bowed her head. When the family was in Ireland, everyone else had loved the beaches, stone walls, and pubs. Agnes had loved the fairy forts, stone circles, and standing stones. She loved any Irish town whose name began with "Lis," because it meant that fairies lived there.

"Stop pushing, Cece," Regis said. "Agnes doesn't know any more than we do. We'll have to wait and see."

But Agnes did know. Whether it was second sight or just common sense, she wasn't sure. But she knew that nothing was right. How could it be? Her father had killed a man.

"Do you ever think about him?" she asked softly now.

"Dad? Of course," Regis said.

"Not just Dad," Agnes said, with a funny fishhook feeling in her throat. "I mean Greg."

"She means Greg *White*," Cece said, as if she thought her sister's use of only the first name to be unseemly.

"Not if I can help it," Regis said through teeth clenched so hard her words came out in a whistle. "And you shouldn't either. He tried to kill me and Dad, and he's the reason why Dad went to prison."

"I just wonder," Agnes said. "Who he was, and why he did it...."

"Mom told us he was a *drifter*," Cece said, as if that was the worst thing in the world, as if she could just as easily have said "devil" instead. "And he was angry at the world, and he hated Dad's sculpture because it had a *cross* on the top of it."

Agnes knew that, and it made her sad. Why did people do things like that?

"I just want—" she started to say.

"You just want world peace, universal happiness, and goodness," Regis said, climbing out of her bed to grab Agnes by the wrists. The sisters locked eyes, and Regis gave Agnes a good, gentle shake and kissed her hard on the forehead. "You'll drive yourself crazy wishing for things you have no control over."

"But," Agnes began.

"That's why you have to grab for happiness yourself," Regis said, still holding her wrists, fire in her eyes as she stared into Agnes's. "You have to stop running on walls, Agnes. Diving into the water... do you think you're going to walk on it someday? You're not. Stop thinking about Gregory White. Stop thinking about Dad in prison, because he's *out*. Do you realize that?"

"I heard Mom read part of the letter," Agnes said.

"Well, there you go. What don't you believe?"

"She said 'part of the letter,'" Cece said. "Maybe she's wondering what was in the rest."

"Stop worrying about it," Regis said. "It's summer. We have to make our own happiness, don't you know that?"

"Is that why you fell in love?" Agnes asked.

"I fell in love because I met Peter," Regis said. "I'm going for it. Let other people be 'safe,' and wait till they graduate, and not tick off their parents. I love him, and that's that."

"You love him because he makes you forget—"

Regis shook her head hard. "Don't say that. Our love is real and true. You're making it sound like getting drunk, or getting high, doing stuff to block out stuff. Agnes, I swear, the only boy good enough for you would have to be a saint or an angel. But for me, it's Peter."

The two sisters stared at each other. They had been together for so long, through so much. Agnes had never known a day of life without Regis; she had always been there. Agnes had been born five days after Regis's second birthday. The two girls gazed at each other without words.

"It's time for work," Regis said. "I have to get going now."

"Which job? Ice cream or books?" Agnes asked.

"Books, this morning," Regis said. "Dusting tomes in the library for Aunt Bernie."

"At least you get to be with the books," Agnes said. All the school archives, the missals, the Latin books, the old catechisms...Her own job was cleaning the art and photography studios.

Regis nodded. Agnes saw her glance up at the tall bureau, at the picture of their father smiling down. Regis had placed it there a long time ago, shortly after they'd returned from Ireland. Someone had moved the frame, shifted it back on the bureau top, and Regis gently moved it forward now.

Agnes knew why.

When they were little, their father would always come into the room to tuck them in. He would stand right there, at the end of their beds, smiling down at them—and then he'd sit at the end of one of the beds, to read to them. He had been such a good, loving father. Regis liked to pretend that his picture was really him. Not just an old photo, a moment frozen in time, but their real, live dad.

"He's really coming home," Agnes said.

But Regis didn't reply. She just lingered, her hand on their father's picture as if it were more real than her sister's words, then smiled at her sisters and left the room.

Five

Honor felt a shiver in her body and a charge in the air, almost as if the seasons were changing and fall was crackling down from the north. But it was late summer, with heat rising from the grass and rocks; the water was calm and the sky a cloudless blue. Doing the breakfast dishes at the kitchen window, she saw Regis stepping out the side door.

"Regis," she called. "I want to talk to you."

"Peter's coming by for ten minutes before I have to do my library job—can't we talk later?"

"Come on, Regis. It won't take long."

Honor watched her stiffen, give a dark glance, and reluctantly come toward the kitchen door.

"What is it?" Regis asked.

"I wanted to talk to you alone," Honor said. "About your father's letter. Just you and me, without the other girls."

"Why?"

Honor took a breath. This was their own private Sahara—conversations about John. It was arid and treeless and unutterably vast, and they'd never once managed to cross it safely.

"Because I want to know how you are."

"I'm fine, Mom," Regis said.

"Regis, talk to me."

"What do you want me to say? He's finally coming home, and I can't wait. Can you?"

"Never mind me. You're the one..."

"What? I'm the one who's responsible for him going to jail? I know, Mom."

"That's not what I was going to say!" Honor exhaled. How could Regis always get under her skin so fast? "I mean that you're the one I'm concerned about. I know you've been waiting for this day for a long time. I just want you to..."

Regis looked over at her, listening intently, and at that moment Honor lost the courage to say what she'd wanted to say: that she just wanted Regis not to get her hopes up.

"What, Mom?"

"Do you think we should make an appointment with Dr. Corry?" Honor asked.

"I don't need any more therapy," Regis said. "I'm totally well adjusted now. I haven't dived into Devil's Hole in three years, I haven't scaled the chapel steeple in at least four, I kept my promise about not swimming to North Brother again, and I'm getting married."

"Regis, I'm not sure that belongs in the plus column."

"What are you talking about?" Regis asked, outraged.

"Darling, you're so young. That's all I'm saying. Why don't you let me make an appointment with Dr. Corry, and you can—"

"Just because you don't want to be married anymore doesn't mean everyone feels that way, and it doesn't mean I need to go back to a shrink!"

"Regis, honey—"

"One thing about Dad going to jail—it made things easier in a way. You didn't have to kick him out."

Honor took a deep breath. Regis was gazing at her, begging to be contradicted. She veered back and forth between seeing her parents' love as idyllic and seeing it as doomed.

"On the other hand," Regis continued, although her mother hadn't said a word, "you've seemed more charged up about painting again."

Honor's heart kicked over. She hadn't thought anyone knew. Art had become a job. Something to teach. Her own work had felt so stale.... "Yes," she said. "I've started something new. It feels good."

Regis grinned. "He inspires you," she said. "And the other way round. You're both artists. You could never live without each other."

Honor looked away. Regis had hit a nerve. Her daughter couldn't know that Honor's love for John made almost any other love look shallow and small. She had loved him with everything she had. For good and bad, he was the most passionate man on earth, and the idea of him coming home had unleashed a flood of ideas she wanted to explore on canvas.

"Just don't hold it against him anymore," Regis said.

"What are you talking about?"

"You know. My being on the cliff. That was my fault, not his."

"You were fourteen," Honor said.

"I know! I was old enough to take care of myself. So don't blame Dad for anything. It was my responsibility...."

"Tell me that after you have kids," Honor said.

"I will," Regis said. "I hope it's soon."

Honor wanted not to take the bait. She really did, so badly she dug her fingernails into the palms of her hands. But she couldn't help herself—Regis was so single-minded, and once she got an idea in her head, it was all over.

"That would be a very big mistake," Honor said. "As a matter of fact, I think you should postpone your plans to get married. October is coming up so soon...."

"That's the point! You know that Peter and I are in love, and you know that we've been together forever, and you know that I believe in love more than anything in the world—so why are you giving me such a hard time?"

"Because you haven't thought it through. Because..." Honor trailed off, not knowing how to put into words the fact she worried that Regis was operating from fear, from a compulsion she didn't understand.

"Mom, if you're trying to talk me out of marrying Peter, or into waiting till we graduate or something like that—forget it. We want

to get married and be each other's family. Have kids and be happy together. And now that Dad will be here, he can give me away!"

"This is such a big event in your life, Regis, and you're so young.
How can you be talking about kids when you haven't even finished
growing up yourself?"

"I am grown up!" Regis said, her voice rising dangerously.

"I know," Honor said quickly, going for a different tack. "I know
you are. Twenty just seems so young to me. Honey, you're the oldest
daughter; your sisters look up to you so much. I wish you would just
take a little time, to be sure of yourself and what you want. Wouldn't
you want that for Agnes and Cece?"

"I'd want them to fall madly in love and feel what I feel for Peter."

"I'm not trying to say you don't love Peter," Honor said.

"Then why shouldn't I marry him?"

"Because you don't always know what you want at twenty. You
think you do—"

"*You* knew. You loved Dad."

"But I didn't marry him until we were older—"

"But you *knew*. And you were together—you only waited because
things were more conventional back then."

Honor winced at the word "conventional." "We waited until after
graduation, and until your father saw that he could make a living.
He'd chosen to be an artist, and even with my teaching job he thought
it would be irresponsible to just get married and start a family without knowing he could afford it."

"Peter is responsible!"

"He's a college student." Honor spoke slowly, knowing that she had
to be careful. "I know he works part-time at the golf course, but his
parents are supporting him now. You have two jobs, and he works
part-time. What will happen after you're married?"

"He'll get a better job! Of course he will. We both will!" Regis exhaled, paced around the kitchen. "You and Dad struggled when you
were first married. I remember all the stories about you cleaning
houses before you started teaching, and him trying to sell his photo-

graphs, having to take school photos and pictures of kids with Santa at the mall."

"It wasn't easy," Honor said. Had she and John romanticized their starving-artist years to the kids? Even as she wondered, she felt a sharp longing for those days, when they had lived on bread and cheese and wild grapes and apples, when they had been living for their dreams and shooting for the stars.

"No, but you loved each other and believed in each other," Regis said. "Like Peter and I do."

Honor reached for Regis's hand. To her surprise, she let her hold it, and their eyes met and locked. "Your father and I wanted to live as artists. We knew that, and it drove us. That's what made it possible to know what we wanted, and what we had to do." She held herself back from saying that she had almost given up on making real art while John's had flourished. "Do you and Peter know what you want?"

Regis stared into her mother's eyes for a long moment, and Honor had one of those startling senses of disbelief, seeing the baby Regis had been, suddenly watching her grow up here and now.

"Each other," Regis said. "That's what we want." She eased her hand away, kissed Honor's cheek, and walked out the door. Peter was waiting in the driveway; Honor watched Regis run toward his car and climb in. She saw him lean over to kiss her, watched Regis throw herself across the gearshift for closer contact. They held each other in the driveway for a long time. Then Peter shifted, and they drove away.

Honor leaned out the window to see them go. Her body hurt, watching her daughter's passion for her boyfriend. It wasn't so much because she disapproved, but because she remembered being twenty. She remembered having that kind of love for John.

Abandoning the sink filled with dishes, she walked into her studio. Her fingertips tingled, wanting to paint. Sisela was curled up on the window seat, one paw over her eyes. Sunlight slanted in, turning the old cat bright white. Honor paused, her heart in her throat. For a second, she'd thought Sisela looked like the kitten she'd been when she and John had found her in the stone wall.

Regis had been a tiny girl, just learning how to walk. They'd been on a painting excursion and picnic in the vineyard. Both John and Honor had brought their easels and paints, with paper and crayons for Regis. Suddenly they'd heard a sound, and there was the little kitten—all alone, just sitting on a flat stone as if she was waiting for them. John had gone to her, and the kitten had practically jumped into his arms, meowing with hunger.

"She's starving," John had said.

Honor had rummaged through the picnic basket, broken off a tiny piece of smoked salmon, held it out; the cat ate, mewing for more.

"Kitty cat," John had said, holding her out for Regis to touch.

"Kee-cah," Regis had tried to imitate.

"That's right, sweetheart," John had said, delighted, as always, with everything Regis did. "Kee-cah."

"Sisela," Regis said then, trying to hold the kitten.

"Where does that come from?" Honor asked, like John taken with the wonder in Regis's eyes, her joy at seeing the kitten.

"I have no idea," John said.

And it wasn't until later, when they were walking home along the path that led past the nuns' enclosure, that Regis laughed, pointing at Bernie in her black habit standing among a group of novices, looking like apprentice angels in their all-white habits and veils, saying of them "Sisela!"

"Sisters," John translated, gazing from their bright child to the tiny white cat, her head poking out from the crook of Regis's elbow.

"She named the kitten after Bernie," Honor said, reaching for Regis's hand. Her father was carrying her, and Regis was holding Sisela.

"And the young nuns," Honor said, looking over at them.

Now, nearly nineteen years later, Sisela lay curled up in the sunlight. She was a constant reminder to Honor of those old, precious days—for a long time after John's arrest, Honor was barely able to look at the cat. She still ached to say her name—it reminded her too much of that day when the three of them had been together, so purely happy.

"Oh, Sisela," Honor said now, petting the cat. She purred, stretching her neck so Honor could tickle the spot under her neck.

After a minute, Honor walked over to the sideboard and opened a cabinet door. Pushed deep inside was an old paint case. It had belonged to John—she had given it to him when they were Regis's age, and he had been using it that day when they'd found Sisela.

John had left it behind—not just physically, but spiritually—when he'd given up painting entirely for photographs. Honor sometimes opened it, smelled the oil paints and linseed oil, remembered the days when they'd gone to the beach to paint and swim, where they could be all alone.

He had kept some of her notes inside. She pulled one out now, read it:

> Oh cute boy,
> Really intriguing new images. I am as ever impressed with your fluidity, use of color, and integration of emotion. What made you decide to do a stone wall series? There are stories to be told in your pictures, that's for sure. Mysteries of the Connecticut River, mysteries of Long Island Sound. Mysteries of Ireland.
> I was interested in the exchange with your mother. I'm glad she's inquiring about "the artwork." I put the words in quotations, because that makes it sound like a hobby—which I know it isn't. It's only your lifeblood. Asking you how the artwork is going is a little like asking someone else if they still have red and white blood cells and platelets. It's a little like asking whether you've exsanguinated lately.

Her eyes filled with tears, and the words blurred. She wanted to read it over again, but she couldn't. John's mother hadn't approved of his becoming an artist; his father had been ashamed of the fact that he hadn't wanted to go into sales, join the family business. Honor remembered laughing with John, knowing that his parents could never understand anything as impractical as art. If work didn't make money right away, what was the point of doing it?

His work had never been about money, even though he had become very successful. John's art never originated outside himself; he didn't rely on his eye, like other artists. He had such darkness inside; it informed his work, and he'd been edging toward it for such a long time.

Of all the things John had found in the box hidden in the stone wall, the one that had fired his imagination most had been the ticket stub from the passenger ship leaving Cobh for New York. He had pictured his ancestors starving to death in West Cork, the terrible conditions that had driven them to emigrate. Fired by Tom's revolutionary leanings, haunted by his family's suffering, he needed to explore the same things they had—the emotional loss, the leaving home, the quest, the exile.

In that, he had succeeded.

John and Tom had found the box on a hot summer morning, clearing the field so the nuns could plant their vineyard. It was years before Sisela. The children weren't born yet. John and Honor weren't married. Bernie wasn't yet a nun, hadn't told anyone but Honor about thoughts she'd been having about entering the convent.

She and Honor had spread out a blanket in the shade, and Honor was helping her paint a watercolor. Clearing the top two feet of soil in a meadow atop glacial moraine was grueling, backbreaking work—John was hot and sweaty. He had thrown his T-shirt over a tree branch as he used a pickax and dug with his hands, pulling rocks from the earth, throwing them into a pile.

Bernie had gazed proudly as her brother stopped digging and started to pile the rocks into a pyramid. Then he'd pulled fallen pine boughs from the edge of the woods, made a triangle around the rocks. To Honor, it had looked primal, symbolic, filled with the power of the earth and forest. After a while he came over to get his camera, and Honor and Bernie followed him back to watch him take pictures.

"Jesus Christ, the nuns are never going to get their grapes planted if you don't knock that off," Tom said, wiping the sweat off the back of his neck.

"Nuns making wine," Bernie said. "Do you think they drink it?"

"Your ancestors would roll in their graves to see him making art out of goddamn rocks," Tom said.

"I think they'd understand he has it in his blood," Bernie said.

"These rocks were the bane of their field-clearing, wall-building existences, and here he is making extra work. Know how I see it?"

"How?" John asked, setting up another shot.

"You're making it twice as hard. We dig the stones out of the earth, you do your Picasso thing, and now we have to cart the rocks all the way over to the walls, and somehow manage to make them look as if they've been there forever."

"You're the new generation of stonemasons," John said, laughing. "You gave up the family bank account to do this shit, so why don't you show us how it's done?"

"Yeah, that's what I'd like to do—"

"Tear down my masterpiece?" John asked.

"Damn right," Tom said.

They started jostling, as if about to start a fight, but John pushed him away. "There's only one place to bury the hatchet," John said, laughing.

"And that's right between the eyes," Tom said, laughing harder, the two friends teasing as they had since they'd first met. "Come on, let's knock down that eyesore and get to work."

"Fine, you're on," John said.

"Really?" Tom asked, sounding surprised. "But you just built it—I was just kidding."

"He sculpts from nature," Honor said.

"And nothing in nature is permanent," John said, reaching out to tear the stones down, throw them into the wheelbarrow. They clanged against the metal and each other. Something in his willingness to destroy what he had just created seemed to shock Tom, but Honor was beginning to know John's work style, how he took his inspiration from what was ephemeral and wild.

"Okay, so you can handle the abstract," Tom said. "Now let's see you pile these rocks onto those walls, and make them look right."

"You're the rich boy. *I'm* descended from the best wall builders in Ireland," John said. "I think I can handle it."

"Put your money where your mouth is, Sullivan."

Bernie smiled, watching them. Strands of her copper-colored hair slipped out from under her sunhat, glinting in the sunlight. Honor glanced over, noticing how Bernie couldn't take her eyes off Tom. Because the attraction between them had always been so obvious, John said he bet Bernie and Tom would be engaged by Christmas. But Bernie had confided in Honor the terrible conflict she felt—she loved Tom, but she'd been feeling a deep calling, something she couldn't ignore, to become a Sister of Notre Dame des Victoires. Honor had held back, keeping the secret Bernie had made her promise not to tell.

Honor and Bernie laughed and cheered as John and Tom finished filling their wheelbarrows, then raced at top speed over the hill to the longest wall, stretching down from the chapel to the water—the same wall where, several years later, Honor, John, and Regis would find Sisela.

The women walked over to meet them, Bernie's hair blowing in the sea wind as she tucked it back under her hat.

"Some things never change," Bernie said. "They've been trying to one-up each other since they were twelve."

"I remember," Honor said. "Look at them now—John's trying to prove he's got the stonemason genes..."

"And Tom's got his working-class-hero bravado going," Bernie said. "Trying to make everyone forget his great-grandfather owned all this land. But look—he does seem to be doing a pretty great job."

The existing wall was five feet high, a foot and a half wide, a dry wall built without mortar. Its ancient stones were covered with lichens. They watched Tom choose a section where the land sloped and the wall was lower, placing the new stones flat on top, as they would have lain on the ground. He had a knack for arranging them, working them in so no continuous lines appeared, making the top of the wall even with the stretch that rose up the hill.

"Not bad, Kelly," John said. "You might be the better sculptor after all."

"What the hell are you talking about, Sullivan? That's just your hobby—this is man's work!"

"Oh, yeah? I'll show you man's work," John said, flashing a grin straight at Honor as he lifted the biggest stone from his wheelbarrow.

His knees bent under the weight, and Honor watched him stagger over to the wall, jump up, hold the rock over his head. His hands must have been slick with sweat, because he bobbled it like a basketball, nearly dropped it, recovered, and then sent it crashing into the old stones, falling in after it, headfirst into the wall.

Honor cried out, and Bernie ran to him, but Tom was already there—giving him a hand and pulling him out.

"Good one," Tom said. "You okay?"

"Yeah," John said. He had smashed his elbow into a jagged rock, was raising it up to look at the damage. Honor's stomach clenched as she saw blood.

Bernie handed him a handkerchief. "I don't think you have to show off for Honor anymore," she said. "I'm pretty sure she already likes you."

"Are you all right?" Honor asked, holding his hand, helping him hold Bernie's handkerchief to the cut.

"I'm an idiot," he said, bending to kiss her, stumbling as he came close, steadying himself against her, one hand on the wall as he laughed at himself. His hand found unfamiliar purchase, and he let out a low whistle.

"Look at this," he said.

"What is it?" Tom asked, moving closer.

All four of them huddled close to the wall, trying to see what was there. John reached in, pulled out a dirty, ragged piece of dark blue cloth. The fabric was dry and ancient and torn, edges frayed, wrapped around an object vaguely square, a cube. As the others stood watching, John unwound the cloth. It was stuck with spiderwebs and a thick white cocoon, and it fell apart at his touch. Bits of acorns spilled out.

"It's old, that's for sure," John said.

"It's gone," Bernie said. And it was true—the fabric had just disintegrated, fallen to the ground like dust. What was left inside appeared to be a stone box. There were markings on the lid, the shape of a Celtic cross, and words in what might have been Latin.

"Oh, open it," Honor said, holding John's arm, feeling the excitement of discovery, finding something so old and incredible together—there with the man she loved and their best friends.

And he did. He opened the box that would change all four of their lives forever.

She took a breath now, remembering all those years ago. She burrowed deeper into the paint case—looking for something much more recent. It was the letter from John, delivered straight to her door, and she pulled it from its envelope and reread the last part, the section she hadn't read out loud to Bernie and the girls.

> *Here is what I want, Honor. One question keeps coming up, and I have to ask you:*
>
> *Will you let me see you?*
>
> *If you do, I know that the other questions will be answered. Do you remember the box we found, how we felt that day? How all those mysteries spread out before us, and we couldn't imagine solving them if not together? There had been love before us—deep, impossible love. We went to Ireland to understand it, because we knew no love was deeper than our own, and we wanted to trace those predecessors.*
>
> *We have to find a way for us all to go forward from this.*
>
> *Let me come home, Honor. If not to return for good, then at least to hear you say goodbye, so I'll really believe it. Let me be at Regis's wedding. Please, as her father and as the man who until now has loved her more than anyone.*
>
> *As I still love you.*
>
> > *John*

She didn't know the answer. She wasn't sure what she would say or do when the moment came and she saw him again. Replacing the letter in the case, she sat beside Sisela on the window seat.

Stroking the old cat, she gazed out the window, at the stone wall that ran along the crest of the distant hill. A figure appeared—Tom, pushing a wheelbarrow.

Her fingers brushed lightly over Sisela's fur. The cat purred softly.

Honor's easel beckoned. Staring at it now, she thought back to that day long ago, when she and John were painting in the summer air. Their hopes and dreams had been so exciting and sustaining, their need to make art. Honor felt that need flood through her again.

"Where is he?" she whispered to the cat.

Sisela meowed, sounding exactly like the tiny kitten who'd been starving until the Sullivans had found her on the old wall. Honor kept petting her now, staring at her easel, feeling the stone in her chest, where her heart used to be. Then she picked up her palette and began to mix colors.

Six

The Academy grounds were deep and green, even in the heat of summer. Thursday morning, Tom Kelly wheeled a barrow full of stones toward the grotto, his T-shirt soaked in sweat. He had been down to the beach cottage, getting it ready. Damp and musty, it needed about a month of airing out. Well, there was time....

Two young novices walked past him, said hello. He acted polite, even though he wanted to tell them to leave while they still had a chance. Who would willingly lock herself inside this place?

As he pushed the wheelbarrow, he thought of how often he had walked these paths. As a young boy, he and his whole family would arrive here for the annual Fourth of July picnic in a cortege of black Cadillacs. His mother and father, his brothers and sisters, his aunts and uncles, all his cousins.

They would drive down from Hartford, all in a row, black cars following close, almost bumper to bumper. No cop would dare stop or ticket them. They were the Kellys, Connecticut's unofficial first family. They had gone from poverty to power, and—just like in Ireland—their ranks included lots of cops, politicians, lawyers, and judges. No one messed with the Kellys.

Tom knew that his father and most of their ancestors would roll in their graves to see him carting stones on what had once been the crown jewel of the Kelly real estate empire: Stella Maris, Star of the

Sea. That Irish immigrants could buy and own the most beautiful piece of property in New England, where the great Connecticut River flowed into Long Island Sound—and could then turn around and donate it to the nuns, establishing one of the finest girls' schools in America—well, that had filled Tom's family with great pride and a big "in your face" to the Connecticut Yankee establishment.

But to Tom, it had seemed that his family was just like the WASPs. All they cared about was climbing up in the world. The richest of them had owned property on Merrion Square in Dublin, and over the decades their goals included owning the newest Cadillac, living in the best houses, buying more property, building the tallest skyscraper in Hartford. The family had sent Tom's father's generation to Jesuit schools; they had sent Tom and his siblings and cousins to Hotchkiss and Taft and Miss Porter's, as if trying to forget where they'd once come from.

Tom had found a book of poetry at school, and it woke him up: Brendan Kennelly's *My Dark Fathers*. It was about the Irish famine, and how it had killed the spirit of a people:

> *When winds of hunger howled at every door*
> *She heard the music dwindle and forgot the dance.*

Tom began wondering about his own family. None of his relatives ever mentioned the famine; they never talked about the old country. They only talked about winning, getting ahead, beating their opponents. But Kennelly's poetry had unlocked a curiosity in Tom, and a need to find out about that dance they'd all forgotten.

As he approached the Blue Grotto, Tom's heart pounded. While he had learned about Irish pain from John Sullivan, he'd learned about the dance from John's sister, Bernie. She had come here for the Fourth of July parties with her family, stonecutters in the Kellys' employ. She was so tall and beautiful, with a willowy body and soft gold-red hair, but some kind of superstrength behind her blue eyes.

The first time he'd met her, they'd been twelve years old. She and her brother had climbed the steep stones to get on top of the grotto, where no kids were supposed to go, to look out over the mouth of the river. Tom had spotted them and walked over.

"Hey, get down from there," he'd called up to the red-haired girl in a yellow dress.

"We're just looking at the water," she'd said.

"Yeah, well, you're not allowed. That's off-limits."

"Our great-grandfather built this grotto," she'd said, gazing down with her arm around her younger brother, and the most withering expression Tom had ever seen. "I don't think he'd mind."

"Well, *my* great-grandfather paid him to do it," Tom had retorted. "And I'm telling you you'd better get down."

"Ah. So you're a Kelly."

"That's right. Now get down. You might fall off and sue someone, Red."

She had given him a long, hard stare. It wasn't exactly defiant—at least, not by Kelly standards. But it was thorough, and it definitely took his measure. Tom had shivered, turned inside out by the way she'd looked at him with those dark blue eyes. He'd thought she was the coolest thing he'd ever encountered, but the funny part was, her gaze was so warm.

"Come on, John," she'd said, holding her brother's hand.

"Let me help you," Tom had offered.

"That's okay, Kelly," she'd said. "We can take care of ourselves."

And she'd jumped down, catching her younger brother. They had run off to join the picnic; Tom could see her still, yellow skirt flowing behind her like sunshine over the green grass.

From then on, he'd always looked for her at the family parties. Her red hair and blazing eyes made her hard to miss. But it wasn't until they were seventeen that she'd taught him about the dance. It was right here, he thought, entering the grotto with his wheelbarrow. The hair on the back of his neck stood on end, as if the ghosts of the teenagers he and Bernie had once been were right here beside him, dancing in the moonlight to the music of the wind.

"Tom," she said now.

He jumped, startled.

There, in the semidarkness of the grotto, she knelt before the Virgin's statue. She must have heard him coming; she was half turned around, her black veil shielding her face. He saw her pale skin and delicate cheekbones, her blue eyes catching the dim light.

"Sister Bernadette Ignatius," he said. "I didn't expect to find you here."

"I knew you were coming today," she said, blessing herself and standing up. There were grass clippings and smudges of dirt on her long skirt, from kneeling on the ground. It killed him every time, seeing her in her nun's habit.

"I have a lot of work here on the grounds to finish before school is back in session. I was just down at the beach cottage. How'd you know I'd come to the grotto this morning?"

"Intuition." She smiled.

"So you came here to meet me?" he asked, something in his chest catching and tugging like a fish on a line.

"Yes," she said. "To give you instructions."

"Instructions?" he asked, laughing. "You think I need help fixing the stonework?"

"No, of course not," she said. "I just want you to make sure to leave the words uncovered."

"The words?" he asked, looking up at the spot where someone had gouged the stone. "That's vandalism," he said.

"That's the Song of Songs," she said, standing beside him to read what had been scratched into the granite. The grotto was damp, the north wall covered with moss. The place smelled of earth. But Bernie gave off warmth that got right into Tom's skin, made him remember other times they'd come here, when he'd held her in his arms. She looked up at him; was she recalling those days, or had she buried them forever?

"Is that a song you can dance to?" he asked, his voice hoarse.

She didn't reply, and she looked away.

"Sing it to me, Bernie," he said.

"Don't, Tom," she said.

He closed his eyes. Even with Bernie standing beside him, the chill was back. Being in the grotto reminded him of a tomb, or a prison cell. He thought of the Bible she had given him to take over to John at Portlaoise. It had belonged to her great-grandfather, who had carried it over on the boat from Cork. Tom wondered whether John had taken comfort from it, whether he had read it much during those long six years.

"Sister Bernadette," he said now. "You didn't have to come all the way here to tell me that."

"Maybe I just wanted to make sure," she said.

"That I didn't cover it over?"

"Yes."

"Well, why *are* you saving it?" he asked.

"Being Irish, you ought to know the power of words, of expression, when a person is trapped."

"I don't see any guards, or locked doors or barred windows," he said.

"There are many ways of being trapped," she said.

"Who carved it?" he asked. "It's someone you know, I can tell."

But she just ignored him; if she did know the author, she was choosing to remain silent.

"Isn't the grotto like a chapel?" he pressed. "Are you saying it's okay for crazy people to carve their messages into the altar? Prayers that will never come true anyway?"

She'd been staring up at the words, but now she turned to look at him. Maybe it was the fact that she'd spent most of her life out of the sun, but her skin looked as smooth as it had those summers so long ago, her eyes as blue and still as the deepest rock pool at the sea's edge.

"Prayers aren't wishes," she said. "They don't 'come true.'"

"Spoken like a true nun," he said.

She opened her mouth to reply, seemed to think better of it. Her unspoken words hung between them, shimmering like ghosts. Water from yesterday and Tuesday's rain trickled onto the rock floor in a steady drip, drip, drip.

"For all your idealism and poetry, all your Irishness, Thomas Kelly," she said quietly, "I'd say that you've stayed very bitter."

"How can I not be, after—"

"Don't, Tom."

"Do you ever think of him, Bernie? That's what I want to know. Tell me that, at least... do you ever?" Tom stared into her eyes, wanting to take her by the shoulders and shake her. They had worked together without trouble all this time, but suddenly he wasn't sure he could stand it another week. John's release had tipped the balance.

"What I'm thinking about right now is my brother coming home. He's paid his debt, and now he's free."

"Free," Tom said, thinking about the word. He traced the words in the stone. Funny, how Bernie was on the same wavelength regarding John's release.

"You think he wrote this?" Tom asked, gesturing at the words. "Sneaked back in the dead of night and left a message for Honor?"

"I don't think so," she said abruptly.

"I don't know. I wouldn't put it past him," Tom said. "And we both know he has stonecutting in his Sullivan blood."

She just stared at the wall.

"It's what took us to Ireland, remember?" he asked. "We went there wanting to find out where we came from, and we ended up leaving our hearts behind."

He had gone too far. She whirled around and walked out of the grotto, leaving Tom alone with the broken wall and the mysterious words. He read them again:

I WAS SLEEPING, BUT MY HEART KEPT VIGIL.

He wouldn't have given Bernie the satisfaction of knowing that he had looked up the passage again last night:

> I was sleeping, but my heart kept vigil.
> I heard my lover knocking;
> "Open to me, my beloved, my dove, my perfect one."

He took out his trowel, began mixing the mortar. His shoulder ached. It always did when he worked in the rain or places that were very damp. The pain didn't stop him, didn't even slow him down. He had a job to do, and he did it. That had been his way, ever since he'd become an adult—single-minded focus, eye on the ball, finishing what he started.

. The quality had gotten him more trouble than he'd ever bargained for: him and Bernie, both of them.

Fireflies twinkled in the tall grass, a big yellow moon was rising out of the sea, and Paradise Ice Cream was hopping. Twenty-eight flavors and a short-order grill were housed in a small white cottage on the edge of a marsh, with beach traffic meandering past on Shore Road. Bright, colorful lanterns swung from a wire above the packed parking lot. People sat at picnic tables under a willow tree, gazing across the mouth of the river toward the lighthouse on the other side.

Regis wore her embarrassing uniform—chinos and a blue shirt with the Paradise logo over the breast. She'd felt nervous and on edge—a cross between Christmas morning and final exams—ever since her father's letter had come, and especially after the talk with her mother that morning. Twice tonight she had dropped scoops of ice cream—splat on the counter, instead of into the cone or cup.

Partly it was the look in her mother's eyes that had her so upset. That morning, when her mother had tried talking to Regis about her father and marriage and going back to see Dr. Corry, her gaze had been so distant and tormented, Regis had almost wanted to turn the tables and ask her mother if she wanted to talk about it. Her mother said she was too young to get married and have children? Hah! Maybe her *mother* should go to therapy, just for a reality check.

One of the curses of what had happened to their family was that Regis had had to grow up so fast. With her father gone so long, she had stepped in to comfort her mother, pull her weight by working two jobs, and look after her younger sisters.

Getting married almost made her feel like a kid in comparison.

"You okay, Reeg?" Jennifer, her coworker, asked, glancing over as if to see why Regis's line was moving so slowly.

"Just a little clumsy tonight," Regis said, wiping a streak of butter pecan off the counter. "Sorry."

"Don't worry," Jenn said. "Only three and a half hours till closing, and then this will all be just a bad memory."

Regis laughed and took the next order. As always, there was a big crowd—people who had spent the day at the beach or on boats, wanting a treat to finish off their day. She stood behind the counter, working fast, occasionally glancing up to see who was there. Every time a man approached with his kids, she felt herself tilt, her stomach flip. Every father reminded her of hers; every tall man made her think that tonight was the night, that her father had finally come home. But those were childish thoughts. She was a grown-up now. Her father had missed the last years of her childhood.

Serving ice cream to all the hot beach girls—some still in wet bikinis, from swimming after dark, others in capri pants or sundresses—and to all the cute beach boys in shorts or jeans, some with their shirts off, Regis felt like the unsexiest, dorkiest kid in Black Hall. Dusting the books in Aunt Bernie's library, which she had done that morning, seemed glamorous in comparison.

Scooping ice cream all evening, the only thing that kept her going was the knowledge that her father was on the way. No one knew what it was like for her, realizing that he'd gone to jail for six years because of her. Even though she couldn't remember the details of that stormy day, certain sounds had recently started becoming more vivid: thunder crashing out at sea, Gregory White screaming he was going to kill them, the sound of her father's fist smashing his face.

She pushed those flashes away with happier memories: Irish accents and green fields, gorgeous old ruins of towers and castles on so many hilltops. Their first day there, after spending time on the headland with her father's amazing sculpture, their family had visited the graveyard in Timoleague, where her great-grandmother lay buried—at the mouth of the Argideen River, with wide marshes so reminiscent of the ones here in Black Hall.

In Skibbereen, the family had gone to the Paragon, a pub with dark walls and stained-glass windows. All the tables had been taken, and the proprietor had grabbed Regis's father by the arms, said in a friendly, wonderful Irish voice, "Whatever you do, don't leave!" He found chairs, pushed tables together, and the next thing Regis knew, the whole family had been seated, and someone took the stage and started playing a fiddle, and Regis had been so happy, she could almost ignore the tension between her parents.

"Hey," she heard now as she cleaned up the spilled ice cream.

"Peter!" she said, glancing up to see him standing in line with Jimmy, Josh, Hayley, Kris, and some other kids from Hubbard's Point. "I didn't expect to see you!"

"We decided that Peter needed some ice cream and cheering up," Kris said. "We were hanging around on the boardwalk, but all he kept saying was, 'Regis's working tonight.' "

"It's true," Josh said, his arm around Hayley. "It was getting boring to hear him."

"What can I say?" Peter asked, his eyes burning into Regis's. "I have a one-track mind."

"You're ridiculous," said one of the girls Regis didn't recognize. Her laugh was a seductive, electric trill. She was small and blonde, with a dark tan everywhere. Regis knew, because she was wearing so few clothes: a tiny bikini top, short denim shorts with the top button gone, and legs up to her chin. "Boys and girls in love—it's so our parents!"

"You got a better plan?" Kris asked.

"Love the one you're with," the girl said. "It's the only way to go."

"Not for Peter," Hayley said, smiling at Regis.

"Life's too short," the girl said, giving Peter a sizzling look.

Peter seemed to be ignoring her, still gazing at Regis, keeping their intense connection. So why did Regis feel like vaulting over the counter and smashing a cone of mint chocolate chip into the girl's face?

"Down, Alicia," Josh said.

"Well, that's how we do things in New York," Alicia said, elbowing him. "You are all so provincial out here! Last year Peter seemed like fun, and this year he's totally boring. *Next* year I'm making my parents take a house in the Hamptons instead of Connecticut."

"That's a great idea," Regis said.

"Oooh, bitch-bite," Alicia said, fixing Regis with a moderately amused stare. It actually sent a shiver down Regis's spine as she realized that she was suddenly on the girl's radar screen.

"Hey," someone called from the back of the line. "Could we get some service here?"

"You know," Alicia said, leaning her elbows on the counter, "he's right. Looks like you'd better get to work...."

"What will you have?" Regis asked.

Peter and his friends stepped in, ordering ice cream cones. But Alicia just stayed there, never taking her eyes off Regis. She looked as voracious as a wild dog, and not half as nice. "I'll have a butterscotch sundae," she said. "Hot butterscotch always makes me think of sex." As she said the words, she wiggled her hips, brushing them against Peter.

Josh and Kris rolled their eyes, and Hayley shook her head. Peter just stepped back, gazing at Regis in a reassuring, protective way, letting everyone knew they were together. "Knock it off, Alicia," he said.

"Oh, poopie," she said. "You're all such a bunch of New England puritans. Get me back to the city!"

As she went to get their order, Regis's hands were shaking. By the time she brought back their ice cream, Peter was standing off to the side, talking to some other kids. Regis had seen them at Hubbard's Point, but she didn't really know them. It was a whole different, self-contained world there—Peter's old childhood friends, and the new ones from this summer, all gathered together in the idyllic land between the railroad trestle and Long Island Sound. Some of them had full-time summer jobs, but some, like Peter, took it somewhat easy Regis thought of what her mother had said, and tried to push the words away.

Regis's love for Peter was tender and private. She knew that some people, including her family, questioned it. He could seem a little spoiled, even arrogant. But Regis loved him. She loved how he looked at her, with amusement and longing in his eyes, as if he knew she was about to make him smile, as if he'd never wanted anyone more.

When they were new, he had once come to their house to pick her up. It was raining. For most of the day there had been occasional soft showers, just misting the trees, but now it was really coming down. They had planned to go to the movies with his Hubbard's Point friends, but Regis had wanted to run down to the beach in the rain. She'd kicked off her shoes, tugged him by the hand.

She remembered the expression on his face—hesitant, reluctant, as if there was nothing in the world he wanted to do less than go running in the rain. But she'd stood on tiptoe, looking him in the eye. His gaze had been so direct; she remembered the feeling that he was taking her in, that she was really registering with him, that he was trying to figure out what made her tick.

He'd held her, one hand on the small of her back, the other stroking her cheek.

"Would it make you happy?" he asked.

"More than anything," she said.

He'd slipped off his loafers, fancy and Italian, left them in a corner of the kitchen. He hadn't asked for a rain jacket, hadn't grabbed an umbrella from the stand beside the door. Grabbing Regis's hand, he'd held the screen door, and they'd gone tearing across the field. Rain pelted their faces and shoulders, their backs, soaking them through.

They'd gone puddle-jumping, through pools of water collecting in the hollows at the base of the hills, up and down the rows of trellised grapevines in the vineyard, and into the wildflower meadow. Their feet squished through the mud, stomped on the wet grass, all the way down to the beach.

Holding his hand, Regis had run across the sand. Their bare feet were covered with mud and sand, and they couldn't stop, they ran together, fully dressed, straight into the water. They were already so drenched, right down to their underwear, that they could barely tell the difference. The rain water had felt cool, but the sea felt like a warm bath.

Regis had clung to Peter, her arms around his neck and her legs around his waist, the salt water holding them both, making them buoyant. Peter had kissed her, their mouths open and hot, and his expression so full of excitement and joy, and Regis had known that he had never, ever done anything like that with any other girl. It might have seemed like a small thing to other people. But to Regis, it was huge, and she knew it was for Peter, too. They had crossed a line. And she loved him for following her where she wanted them to go.

"Mmm," Alicia said now, taking her sundae, then licking the whipped cream and eating the cherry without even using her hands. "Yummy."

"Enjoy your ice cream," Regis said to everyone.

"Regis," Peter said, bounding over, taking his coffee cone. "Thanks. What time do you get off?"

"Eleven," she said. "At closing."

"I'll come pick you up. I can't wait, Regis. I never can…"

"Oh, Peter," she said, overwhelmed with love, leaning forward for a quick kiss. The people in line were crowding up, impatient to get her attention.

"I love coffee ice cream—give me some," Alicia said, leaning toward Peter's cone and licking it. "Yummy," she said again, looking over his shoulder, straight at Regis.

Why was Peter letting her do that? The sight felt like a punch in the stomach to Regis. She closed her eyes for a moment, to block it out, and something weird happened: she flashed back to Ireland, when they were all there, Gregory White dead on the cliff. Regis had been in shock, her memories frozen in amber. Driftwood, fallen from the sculpture. No—pulled loose by Gregory White. Lying on the ground. Then covered with blood, flung into the sea.

Just last night, that image had poked through—as if it were alive, a memory she wished she could push back into the sticky ancient mess, never to emerge, jumbled together with her mother crying, yelling that she should never have brought the girls to Ireland, that she had always known something terrible like this would happen.

"There are no rules with you," her mother had wept. "It's so dangerous..."

"Honor," her father had said as the police led him away. "I didn't know this would happen—I had no idea. I didn't want Regis to be here."

"But of course she would be," her mother had said. "She would follow you anywhere—to the edge of the world. That's what she did, don't you get it, John?"

"Don't hurt him," Regis had whispered, just like a little zombie. "Don't hurt him, don't hurt him, don't hurt my father."

No one could understand her. They thought her teeth were chattering, couldn't make out the words. *Don't hurt him, don't hurt him.*

Don't hurt him, Regis thought now, watching Peter leave. What a thing to remember. Had she really said that, and why? Or was it just her crazy mind conjuring things out of nowhere, nothing better to do while she waited on pins and needles for her father to come home?

The Hubbard's Point kids climbed into their cars. Regis's hands were still trembling as she filled the orders of everyone in line. Once Peter had driven away, Regis's thoughts went back to what they'd been at the beginning of the night: drawn to fathers and their kids, coming to Paradise for some ice cream. Once she glanced up, thought she saw her father standing under the trees at the edge of the parking lot.

"Dad!" she said under her breath, dropping a scoop of chocolate chip right on the toe of her sneaker.

When she looked up again, the man was gone. She busied herself, cleaning up the floor, starting from scratch with the person's order.

Hurry home, she thought, making a chocolate chip ice cream cone. *I need you, Daddy....*

After midnight, when everyone but Sisela was asleep, Agnes made her rounds. The Academy was a different world then. Everyone slept so peacefully; her mother and sisters never even heard her leave. Regis was exhausted from working late at the ice cream stand, and she'd fallen asleep in her uniform. Agnes kissed her sisters' foreheads before she left, and they barely stirred. Only Sisela saw her go, watching her with wide green eyes, giving her blessing and encouragement.

Once last year, Agnes had sneaked into the convent, tiptoeing into the enclosure where the nuns lived. Laypeople weren't allowed in there. Agnes had been afraid she might be committing a sin by trespassing there, but then she remembered how Aunt Bernie had once taken her and her sisters behind the wall. They had been very young, curious about nuns. Aunt Bernie had said, "We're just like everyone else, except we live in a convent. It's not so mysterious." And it hadn't been, not really. There were normal bedrooms, bathrooms, a kitchen, a living room, a dining room with one long table.

But to Agnes, it was wonderful. And she thought nuns *were* different. They saw the world uniquely; that was why they had to leave it. Because no matter what Aunt Bernie had said, Agnes knew that nuns weren't like everyone else. She thought their hearts were more tender. They felt things so deeply. They cared about everyone and everything so much, it sometimes hurt to breathe. Whenever she heard them chanting the hours—vigils, lauds, terce, sext, none, vespers, and compline, beautiful psalms full of emotion and longing and praise— she thought the nuns sounded like angels who had somehow come to earth.

At vespers, in the early evening, with lights just beginning to go on in the convent and the refectory, Agnes would stand still and listen, and very faintly, just above the sounds of the waves gently rolling in and the wind rustling the leaves, she would hear the nuns chanting. The sound was ineffable, so beautiful, tugging at her heart.

The soft, piercingly lovely voices would chant the psalms, one hundred and fifty of them. The nuns chanted them all through the hours of the day, starting at vigils, three-thirty in the morning. The sisters faced each other in two rows on either side of the aisle, with one side singing the first two lines, and the other singing the second two, sounding like dueling angels climbing ladders to the sky.

The time she had snuck into the convent, she had walked past the part where Aunt Bernie and the school nuns lived, all the way to the back of the house, to the cloister. This was where the contemplatives lived, behind the filigree cast-iron door, in the enclosure. Aunt Bernie had lived here at the beginning, when she had first become a nun. Agnes didn't know why, but she knew that Aunt Bernie had suffered greatly. She could tell by the shadows in her blue eyes.

Agnes had gripped the iron curlicues with both hands, wishing she were on the other side. Her heart had ached, tears welling up, her whole body shaking; that was how badly she'd wanted to be in there. She was so positive that she belonged in the cloister. To be shut off from the world, away from all the pain. Not because people out here were so terrible—no, not that at all. Because they were so dear. Because Agnes loved them so much. She couldn't bear it sometimes. She thought that she would die of love—for her family, the way they had been before everything broke in Ireland; even more in the six years since.

No one had caught her that night. And no one had caught her any other night, either. Sometimes she thought someone was watching her. Once she glimpsed a flash of red—like a fox, or a redheaded spirit—peeking out over the stone wall. Other times, there were streaks of white, like angel wings.

Agnes believed that she was having visions of an angel with red hair.

Visions were not new here. No one knew the details, but all the girls whispered that Sister Bernadette Ignatius had once had a visitation from the Virgin Mary. Agnes's Aunt Bernie! Right here at the Academy. So why shouldn't Agnes have visions as well?

Right now, slipping out of her family's cottage, she looked left and right. She had her camera, the better to record what she had been seeing, slung over her shoulder. The salt breeze was so warm, she ran across the grass wearing nothing but her nightgown. She probably should have changed, but she was in a hurry.

When she got to the first wall, she jumped up and ran along the top. The stones felt rough under her bare feet, but she didn't care. She felt breathless with excitement and anticipation of what she was about to see. The moon seemed caught in the treetops, its light broken into shadows on the lawn and stones. Agnes prayed as she ran, jumping from one wall to the next.

At the top of the hill, she took a deep breath. Here there were no trees; the moon was alone in the sky. Its light flooded down the land, sloping gently into Long Island Sound. Agnes's heart began to race; she hoped she was right about what was going to happen next. Wishing for visions was one thing; planning for them was another.

She had prayed for guidance. Knowing that these moments were a gift, she had doubted whether she should ask for more than what was freely given. But she was only human, her mind was full of doubts. Was this a real vision?

Why did the visions never occur at home, when there were others around? Some days she wondered whether she was imagining the whole thing. So, to be sure, she'd made a plan.

Holding her camera, she arranged it on the edge of the wall. She pointed it down toward the water's edge, directly in line with the angle of the wall running down to the sea, and set up the shot. A ribbon of silver streamed from the moon onto the waves. Adjusting the timer, Agnes knew she was ready.

She jumped onto the wall and began walking down to the water. Where was he? Would he be here tonight? Her heart was beating so hard, she thought she might fall off the wall. The tide was high; it came almost to the base of the seawall. She heard the waves, felt them in her body.

So much in her family had been lost. They had loved each other so much...to have parents like hers, so devoted and in love. And then, when Regis had chased her father into the rain at Ballincastle, and when he fought to protect her and the man died—why couldn't their mother forgive him for that? He'd only been trying to save Regis.

Agnes felt ripped apart because her family was in tatters. She had knelt and prayed for God to make them whole again. And when that didn't happen—when her father had gone to jail and her mother had stopped speaking of him, or planning visits to him—Agnes had nearly given up. She had told God the only way she would keep believing was if he'd send her a sign.

And he did—sent it over and over again, in this vision of angel wings. Only Agnes and Sisela had ever seen it. In fact, hearing a meow, she knew that Sisela must have followed her, was with her now, just out of sight.

She shivered, her heart opening wide. The camera forgotten, she was in only the present moment. Her spirit yearned for something she couldn't name. Running along the wall's narrow, curving top, she scanned the beach where she'd seen the shadows moving on other nights.

On those nights she'd had visions, a man had been standing in the shadows, a saint she'd called or conjured, a red-haired angel, someone to look over her because her father was gone. She thought if she ran fast enough, jumped high enough, trusted completely, he would come out of his hiding place, radiant with love, spread his wings, carry her to safety—tonight. And if it could happen here, on the beach, maybe they could rewind time and it could happen in Ireland, undo what had happened, bring her family back together.

Agnes heard the waves splashing against the rocks. She sped up, running as fast as she could. Then she leapt.

One long jump off the end of the wall, soaring over the waves splashing the beach, her toes skimming the surface. The water felt cold on her feet, and she plunged in, headfirst. She saw stars, blackness. Blinked the salt water from her eyes, touched her forehead. She must have struck a rock. Hot, wet—blood pouring down.

"Please," she cried now. "Please!" Unwilling to give up her dream, or her vision, she brushed her wet hair back, pressed her fist into the cut above her eye, felt the waves lapping at her body.

The tide was high, and the waves felt strong. They weren't just splashing, but tugging her, pulling her into the sea. Her blood mixed with the water, and all she tasted was salt, and all she wanted to do was go with the sea. She was too weak to fight it, or swim against it, or do anything but let it take her away.

She heard splashing. He was there—he came forward and caught her, lifting her up. His arms grabbed her, made sure she didn't fall back. Agnes heard a voice, felt him take her hand. She was so cold and tired now, too sleepy to understand what he was saying. The voice sounded so familiar, saying her name:

"Agnes, my child...hold on, don't give up, I have you now."

She looked skyward. A gust of wind blew off the Sound, caught her between the shoulder blades, and lifted her up. She gasped, feeling wings brush her cheeks. There were arms around her, pulling her up, higher and higher. The wind made her nightgown flutter against her legs.

From down below, if her sisters happened to look out the window, what would they see? Agnes thought of them glimpsing the sparkles and imagined that they might think they were witnessing mist blowing in from the sea. Or they might believe they were spying angels visiting the convent. Or maybe they'd think they were seeing shooting stars. But it would be none of those things. No, the glimmer visible from earth was nothing more than shiny bits of mica on the soles of Agnes's feet, from running along the tops of the walls.

That's all it was....She tried to brush the blood from her eyes, but it was a flood now. So she just closed her eyes tight and felt herself fly through the night.

Seven

Cecilia hadn't been able to sleep. She never could, on nights when Agnes went out. Everyone always thought the youngest sisters were so clueless, when actually they were the most aware. They had to be vigilant, to make sure their older sisters got home safely, that their mother didn't catch them, that everything was okay.

Regis never caused Cecilia to worry like this. With Regis, you knew exactly what you were getting: trouble. Everyone knew and expected it. She just had that way about her—daring and wild. The good part, for Cecilia and Agnes, was that Regis didn't keep all the fun for herself.

The minute Regis got her license, she had taught Agnes and Cecilia to drive. That was one thing for Agnes, who was fifteen at the time. But Cecilia was just ten. She had started off sitting on Regis's lap—because she was too short to reach the brake with her foot. Zooming around the Academy roads, Cecilia had felt like Toad in *The Wind in the Willows*, driving his red motorcar with mad abandon.

Whenever something crazy happened at Star of the Sea, Regis was the first person everyone thought of. Last fall, when the pumpkins had started appearing on the tops of every chimney, there wasn't much doubt about who had climbed up to put them there. And three

years ago, when some nuns visiting from the mother house in Canada
went to the Blue Grotto and found that someone had placed a statue
of Saint Ignatius in one of their beds, Aunt Bernie had known right
away who had done it.

Now Regis was asleep in her bed right here in the room they all
shared, breathing nice and peacefully as if she hadn't a care in the
world. Cecilia sighed loudly, rolling over and jostling the bed frame—
maybe if she made some noise, Regis would wake up and then Cecilia
wouldn't have to handle this alone.

Cecilia really didn't know what to do. She would never betray
Agnes, not even to Regis. But several nights this summer, more regularly this past week, Cecilia had watched Agnes sneak out. It always
began right after midnight. Cecilia knew, because she'd hear the bell
toll. She'd open her eyes, and there at the window—once standing,
twice kneeling—would be Agnes, with Sisela on the sill beside her.

Cecilia had stayed as still as a statue, peering out through narrowed
eyes. She had watched her sister staring up at the sky, scanning the
stars, hands clasped as if in prayer. Cecilia could almost feel Agnes's
heartbeat across the room—moving the air, it was so strong. The first
time it happened, with a half-moon shining through the trees, the
white cat jumped out the window, and Agnes slipped out to follow
her through the silver moonlight.

"Where were you?" Cece had whispered when Agnes returned,
sopping wet.

"Do you believe angels can have red hair?" Agnes asked, sounding
so crazy, Cece almost wondered if she was dreaming the whole thing.

"What are you *talking* about?" Cece had asked.

"Nothing," Agnes had replied, smiling in her beatific way. "Go back
to sleep."

The second time, the night had been so dark, every tree and bush
coated with thick fog, it was as if the whole world was under a spell
of sleep. Cecilia had watched Sisela flying out to disappear into the
shadows, Agnes climbing out after her again, and her heart had fallen.
Because she'd caught just a glimpse of her sister leaping up onto the

wall that ran behind their house, through the vineyard, and this time Cecilia had known: Agnes was doing that thing with the walls.

Usually she did it during the day—she'd jump up and run along the tops of all the walls that crisscrossed the Academy property. Cecilia had thought it looked so fun, she'd tried it once. Agnes had caught her and stopped her, hands on her shoulders. The cold look in her eyes had shocked Cecilia.

"You can run on the beach, or through the vineyard, or into the marsh, Cece," she had said. "But the walls are different. You could twist your ankle and fall off...."

What was Agnes doing at night? Why did she have to run after dark? Animals lived on the land, and big fish swam in the sea, and they all hunted at night—you only had to watch Sisela to know that. Cecilia shivered to think of her sister out among the wild things. She wanted Regis or their mother to wake up and see that Agnes was gone.

But everyone was sound asleep, so Cecilia bit her lip and decided to follow her sister. Tracking her through the main campus was no problem—the lawns were groomed, the paths well lit. Once she got to the vineyard, though, it turned scary. No lights at all, and lots of ruts in the ground. Cecilia heard animals scurrying into the vines, and she saw the silhouette of an owl hunting, flying low over the land.

Agnes was far ahead; she had had a head start, and she had the advantage of knowing every step of the walls. Cecilia smelled the spicy grapes, felt twisted vines and leaves brush her face as she crashed through the rows. She shivered when she ran head-on into a huge spiderweb; she never even saw it, but just felt the silken strands all across her nose and lips.

At the far side, where the vineyard ended and the land sloped down to the beach, Cecilia slowed down. She had lost sight of Agnes. There was no one around, and the realization that she was alone made her heart pound in her throat.

"Agnes?" she whispered.

There was no answer. The only sounds were the wind in the leaves and the waves upon the shore. Cecilia held her breath, feeling over-taken by terror. Not for her own safety, but for her sister's.

She stumbled down the hillside, starting to run. She had last seen Agnes dashing down the wall to the beach, straight toward the water. Cecilia had seen her sister do this during the day, and it always ended with Agnes plunging in.

"Oh God!" Cecilia cried out. What if Agnes had dived in, hit her head? It was so dark, Cecilia would never find her. As she ran, she spotted Agnes's camera on the edge of the wall. It was directed at the beach, and a little red light was blinking as if it were on a timer. Even as Cecilia approached, the shutter clicked, and the camera flash lit up the sky.

"Agnes?" Cecilia called. "Where are you?"

"What are you *doing*?" came the voice, but it wasn't Agnes's—it was Regis, chasing Sisela, hurrying down the hill after Cecilia.

"What are *you* doing?" Cecilia asked.

"I heard you leave, woke up just in time to see you running out-side. Cece, it's the middle of the night—come on home and get back in bed before Mom—"

"I'm following Agnes," Cecilia blurted out.

"What are you talking about?" Regis asked, obviously only half awake. "Isn't she asleep?"

Cecilia shook her head.

"Jesus, Mary, and Joseph. Where is she?"

Regis stood there peering into the darkness. Sisela was dashing down the hill toward the beach, as if on the trail of something.

"I don't know," Cecilia said, starting to tremble. "I saw her running along the wall...here's her camera..."

Regis went over to the camera, picked it up, examined it. Cecilia wasn't very good at taking pictures, but she knew enough to recog-nize that this was Agnes's digital camera, not the one that used film.

"If we push the right button, we'll be able to see the last picture she took, and the one before that, and maybe we'll be able to figure out where she went," Regis said. Pressing a button, she got the small screen to light up. It filled with an image of what looked like Agnes's white nightgown, glowing in the silver moonlight, just before she hit the water.

"Not now, Regis," Cecilia said, tugging her hand. "We have to check the cove. That's where she was headed. She does this all the time, during the day...runs along the top of the wall and dives in...."

Regis didn't need another word. Holding hands, the two sisters ran the rest of the way down to the narrow strip of beach. It was littered with driftwood, gnarled and twisted, looking like monsters and beasts in the dark. The stone beach cottage was shuttered and empty, casting shadows on the sand. Trembling, Cecilia ran up and down the tide line, scanning the waves for Agnes.

"Agnes! Agnes, answer me!" Regis cried.

"Agnes!" Cecilia yelled.

Suddenly, they heard noises on the beach. Narrowing her eyes, Cecilia watched as a real-life monster rose up, kneeling over Agnes lying on the beach. Grabbing Regis, Cecilia shrank back, too frightened to speak.

Not Regis, though. Cecilia heard her sister's intake of breath, and she would have sworn it sounded more like relief than anything close to shock. Cecilia wanted to run, call for her mother and Aunt Bernie, get the police, but Regis went running toward the man.

"Dad," Regis cried, throwing herself onto the sand beside him.

His oldest and youngest daughters flew at him. Oh God, he wanted so badly to hold them, but he couldn't—Agnes was lying still, blue, and he had to try to save her. She lay on the sand—he had pulled her from the waves—on her back, head tilted back, airway cleared, not breathing. He bent over her, giving her mouth-to-mouth resuscitation, his hands covered with her blood.

"What happened to Agnes?" Cecilia—she was so much bigger now—started to cry.

"Oh, no," his darling Regis gasped, taking Agnes's hands, shaking them, trying to wake her up.

"Can you call for help?" he asked between breaths. "Get your mother—call an ambulance."

"Go, Cece," Regis commanded. "Go *now*!"

Cecilia took off, flying down the beach, sobs flung back into the wind, climbing up the bank to where the wall slanted down, the wall Agnes had taken off from.

"Dad, tell me what to do," Regis said.

"Hold her hand," John said between breaths. "Keep her with us."

"Talk to her, right? Agnes, it's me, it's Dad, he's come home..."

John breathing, counting one, two, breathing again, holding his unconscious middle child in his arms, lowering her, pressing her sternum, one, two, breathing again. Stars tilting in the sky, every time he turned his head. His daughters here—he had seen all three of his daughters tonight. God, thank you for that, for letting me see them. God, keep Agnes alive. God, God... Prayer came hard, bitter man that he was, but still, God, God...

"Agnes, can you hear me?" Regis asked.

John breathed into his daughter's mouth, trying to grab life from the air, give it to Agnes, make her heart beat, make her breathe.

"Be here, be okay, be fine," Regis said. "Dad is home, he's here, we're together again. Can you hear me? We're all together!"

John's own heart pounding so hard, drumbeats in his chest, his head. His skin could barely hold his heart inside, and he felt nearly stone mad with seeing his daughters again, Agnes lying on the cold ground, and he couldn't lose her.

"I need you," Regis pleaded.

A night bird screeched in the brush at the top of the beach; small animals rustled through the briars. The waves broke on the sandbar. The night was so still, except for Regis's quiet weeping. John kept breathing into Agnes's mouth.

A cough—and then retching. Agnes turning her head, sea water pouring from her mouth. Sobs—not Agnes's, but Regis's. And John's, too. In the distance—footsteps, pounding down the beach. Small cries, out of breath, full of panic. John would know that voice anywhere.

Still holding Agnes—*can't let her go*—looking up into the stars, into the face of his wife.

"Honor."

"Oh my God!" Honor cried out. "What happened? What have you done?" Honor crashing into his body, pounding him, pushing him aside, trying to take hold of Agnes.

"Mom, she just started breathing!" Regis cried. Honor burying her head into Agnes's face, hand over her mouth, feeling the slight breath, pushing her eyelids open—she was unconscious.

"Honor," John said, trying to hold her, wanting more than anything to just hold her.

But she couldn't hear him. Or wouldn't. She was ministering to their daughter—the same as the last time. Pushing John aside, hating him for something he didn't even understand. Six years in a cell, he'd remembered that feeling, his wife's fury, loving her more than air, but tasting such bitterness for what he couldn't even let himself imagine.

"I didn't know she was coming," John said. "I didn't see her until she'd jumped into the water—"

"We didn't know you were here," Regis said. "Why didn't you tell us?"

Ask your mother, he wanted to say. But he couldn't—he was mesmerized, staring at Honor, wanting to hold her but unable to touch her. She had a shield around her as she sat there holding Agnes, an invisible, impenetrable force field keeping him away. He stared at her, though. She couldn't stop that.

He stared at her soft skin, her blue eyes weeping salt tears, the lines around her mouth and eyes deeper than six years ago, but her face even more beautiful. He stared at her long hair, thought of all the times he had dreamed of it. He saw the way she held their daughter, remembered how she had flown to Regis on that cliff edge while the gardai had dragged him away.

Their last free moment together—by the sea. And now this. What a homecoming, what a way to see his wife and daughters again. The salt air brought the past right back to them, and the look in Honor's eyes showed how much she despised him. Suddenly Agnes began to convulse.

"Oh God," Honor said. "Where's the ambulance? I sent Cece to call!"

"Mom, what's happening to her?" Regis cried. Crouching down, shouldering in between her parents, trying to hold her sister.

"She's having a seizure," Honor said. Then, to Agnes, "Hold on, sweetheart. We're right here with you."

"Mom and I," Regis said. "And Dad, Agnes. Dad is here...."

John's heart capsized as he heard Regis call him "Dad" and tell Agnes he was there, as if it would help her. He watched Honor and Regis, trying to hold Agnes, panic in their eyes. Her body was rigid, face contorted, and then she went slack.

"It's stopping," Regis said as Agnes relaxed.

"Is she breathing?" Honor asked, holding her now.

"Oh God," John whispered. "Keep her from going away..."

He bent down, felt his daughter's warm breath on his ear. It was faint and unsteady. He took her hand, and it felt sea temperature. "She's breathing," John said.

"Where's Cece? Where's the ambulance? Regis, will you check? Tell Bernie—" Honor said.

John reached under Agnes, arms raking the sand, scooped her up against his chest. Honor gasped, let out a cry.

"Come on," John said. "We'll take her in your car."

"Hurry, John," Honor said, running ahead.

His feet felt so heavy in the loose sand. He ran down, closer to the water, to get better purchase. It was more like a road here, hard and packed by the waves. To his left, the Sound was bright with starlight, and ridges of white waves crashed on the rocks. Eyes full of salt spray, he resisted his fears. He just held his daughter close, as if his heart could warm her, keep her alive.

Regis led them up a beach trail John and Honor had walked so often as kids and later, in their marriage, leaving the girls with Bernie or Tom, sneaking down to be alone.

The night was black, but John's feet knew the way. As a boy he had explored all the walls and trees and caves and tunnels, loving the landscape with everything he had.

Honor, slightly ahead, turned back to him, her voice breaking. "How is she?"

"She's with us," John said, and he thought of all those nights when he'd thought the world was empty of love, but here he was walking beside his wife, and he was carrying Agnes, and Regis was with them.

"Agnes, be okay," Regis said, alongside again, holding her sister's hand. "You have to be." Then, looking up at John, her eyes wide, "She's so cold. Was she in the water long?"

"I don't know," John said. "I heard a noise, and she was there, in the water, and I pulled her onto the sand...."

"What were you doing there?" Regis asked. "Why didn't you come to our house?"

John glanced at Honor. She was the reason. He wouldn't go anywhere too close unless she said it was okay. Tom had cleaned the stone beach house, driven him here. John thought maybe Tom would have told Bernie, who would have told Honor. But if that was the case, she wasn't letting on. She just stared ahead, her lips so thin.

"Lights," Honor said, before John could say anything. "They're here."

The flashing blue lights looked almost like sea fire coming across the field. Faint, distant, blinking through the trees and marsh grass. The Academy chapel was silhouetted, the cross eerily lit in the sky. Regis began to run, and to call and wave her arms.

"Over here!"

Once the ambulance cleared the Academy buildings, the blue light turned stark and garish, and John realized that it was coming from an accompanying police car. His stomach clutched, and he held Agnes tighter.

Ten seconds later, and everything changed. It felt like sped-up slow motion: things happening in rapid succession, yet John taking every detail in, not knowing which one might change his life, the lives of the people he loved. He had been here before.

The vehicles stopped. EMTs jumped out, had him lower Agnes onto a stretcher. They instantly went to work—taking vital signs, repeating her name, "Agnes, can you hear me?" A man and a woman, white shirts, dark pants, strangers with stethoscopes. The police car, lights still flashing, illuminating the scene.

Two officers slowly getting out. One with very short dark hair, a military-type haircut, the other a woman with blonde hair in a ponytail.

"Hello, Honor," the woman officer said, and Honor was gone in tears, sobbing something incomprehensible to John as she clutched the officer's hands and dragged her closer to Agnes.

Where was Regis?

"Good evening, sir," the male officer said.

The policeman was young—he couldn't be thirty. He was six feet tall, a couple of inches shorter than John. Broad, as if he lifted weights, with that laser-beam expression the police and guards always seemed to have. They could see past who you were, straight into the worst of what you could be.

"Good evening," John said.

"What's your name?"

"John Sullivan," he said, reading the officer's name tag: SGT.KOSSOY.

"How did you come to be involved in this?"

"Involved—"

"Can you tell me what happened?"

"I was on the beach," John said. "When I heard a splash, and a cry. Or maybe it was the other way around—"

"A cry?"

"Like a small scream."

"Was someone being attacked?"

"I don't know, I didn't think so—I thought she just lost her footing and fell."

"But you just said she screamed."

"She must have been afraid—once she realized..." John's attention went to Agnes. She had begun to convulse again. He saw Honor lunge, the female officer pull her back. Honor sobbed, and the EMTs prepared a shot of Valium. They injected Agnes, and she stopped. The radio crackled.

"May I go to her?" John asked.

"Go to her, to the patient?" the officer asked, confused.

"I need to be with my wife and child."

"I have more questions," Sergeant Kossoy said.

Out of the darkness, car lights emerged. And from the car, a person climbed out—it was Regis, running toward him. She was out of breath, holding her side. She took John's hand, looked straight into the officer's eyes.

"We need my father now," she said. "You can ask him more questions later."

And as the EMTs loaded Agnes into the ambulance, John followed Honor and Regis, and got into the car to follow it to the hospital, holding himself together as he thought of the last time he and Regis had faced the police.

Eight

Honor couldn't breathe. Once they got to the hospital, she had to sit down, lean over, let the blood rush to her head to keep from passing out. Regis and Cece paced, running back to ask her and John if they wanted anything. She gave them five dollars and asked for tea with milk and sugar, just so they could feel they were doing something.

John sat beside her. Her skin might as well have been peeled off, her nerves were so raw. Her heart was beating hard, right in the soft hollow below her throat. She had gotten tough over the years, and stopped herself from crying; now she felt all those unshed tears hardened in a knot. But as tough as she was, she couldn't look straight at John.

The lights were so bright in the waiting room. Too harsh for a place of such worry and heartbreak. Even the shadows seemed cruel. She looked around, saw other families huddled together. Why were they here? It was easier to imagine other people's suffering than face how scared she was about Agnes.

"Honor," John said.

She couldn't bear to look at him—just a glimpse of his face filled her with panic. The deeply scored lines, down from his mouth. The short hair, shot with gray, so short, chopped off; she remembered when it had been so dark and wavy and handsome, so Black Irish—

sexy and dangerous. He said her name again, and now she had to look: his eyes were the same pale blue. Ice blue they were called, but what a joke, when his expression had always been so warm, and was now. His gaze made her shiver.

"I'm scared, John," she said.

"I know. She took a bad fall."

"Was it a fall, or did she jump?"

"I didn't see." He paused. "You don't mean jump, do you? You mean, did she dive in, right?"

Honor didn't want to face what she meant, so she just squeezed her eyes tight. Why did the only real harm that had ever come to their daughters happen when John was there?

"Is she depressed? Has she done anything before?"

"She's not depressed! And she's never done anything like it before. Did you say something to her? Did you—"

"I didn't even know she was there!"

"Was she going to meet you? Did she sneak out to see you?"

"Honor, no. None of the girls knew. I just got here."

"I hope that's true—because I swear, after what happened with Regis, I'd kill you if you ever did anything like that with the girls again."

"Honor—"

"If you want to risk your life—I'm past worrying about you, okay? Go ahead and do whatever you want. Stand on as many cliff edges as there are. But leave my daughters out of it! I want them safe. Agnes is in there now..." Honor choked, unable to think about what might be happening.

"I know, Honor. I know, I agree. That's why I asked you... what made her go into the water like that?"

"John," she said, feeling the scream in her chest. "What does it matter right now? She's unconscious, and she's in there, and that's all I can think about!"

His eyes were full of high-velocity worry now, and that killed her. Made her shudder, thinking of all the small worries he had missed, all the minor ways the girls had gotten hurt, the emergency rooms she had sat in without him—for inconsequential things, not like Regis, and not like this. Fevers, a sprained ankle, an earache. It felt surreal to be with him now, just as for so long it had felt surreal to be without him.

Just then the doctor came out, and they both stood up. She was tall and lean in green scrubs, with long brown hair held back in a pony-tail and circles of Tibetan prayer beads around her wrist, and she in-troduced herself at Dr. Shea. Honor wanted to jump at her, pull what she knew about Agnes out of her.

"What is it?" Honor asked. "How is she?"

"She has a concussion," Dr. Shea said. "And a hairline skull fracture. How long was she in the water?"

"Just a few seconds," John said. "I ran to her the minute I heard her go in."

"Do you know how long she wasn't breathing?"

Honor's knees nearly gave out. This was the territory she'd been dreading. She thought of all the near drownings she'd ever read about, people who'd swallowed water, stopped breathing, stopped the flow of oxygen to the brain. She thought of her quicksilver Agnes, and couldn't bear to think another thought. She heard herself crying, felt John's arm slide around her shoulders, strong and solid.

"Not long," John said. "I started mouth-to-mouth right away. Did that for a few minutes. And then she coughed, and started breathing on her own."

Dr. Shea nodded. The look in her eyes was reassuring, but Honor didn't feel it yet. She was still too shaken and nervous about that question—*how long had Agnes not been breathing*?

"She's regaining consciousness," Dr. Shea said, "and that's a good sign."

"Is she alert?" John asked.

"I wouldn't say alert, not yet, but she knows her name. She told me she has two sisters..."

"She does," Honor said.

"We'll give her a more complete mental status test in a little while, but I wanted to just get out here and let you know the main things. Her EKG showed seizure activity. It could be temporary, or it could last for a while."

"Head injuries can cause seizures," John said, and Honor looked at him.

"Yes, they can," Dr. Shea said. "She must have hit her head on a rock. She has a bad cut just above her left temple—we've stitched it up here in Emergency, but we'll have a plastic surgeon look in on her tomorrow. Neuro's in with her now."

"Neuro?" Honor asked.

"Neurosurgery. To evaluate the hematoma, keep track of the swelling. Swelling's not good for the brain."

"Is there swelling?" Honor asked, and she felt so frantic she thought she might vaporize. John's arm was still there, holding her steady.

"Listen, I shouldn't have said it like that," Dr. Shea said, without quite answering the question. "It's just something we look out for with head injuries. But honestly, from what I can see, this is a good head injury. There's no appreciable swelling. She's stable. She wasn't without oxygen for very long. And she's here now, you got her here quickly, and we're watching her."

"Did I..." John began. He was holding on so tightly to Honor, but when she looked up at him, she saw that he was lost. His face so thin and drawn, and so tense, and his blue eyes filling. "Did I make a mistake by moving her?"

"Moving her?" Dr. Shea asked.

"Yes. I picked her up and carried her, instead of waiting for the ambulance. Did I do more harm? Should I have kept her lying flat?"

"That's what we tell people," Dr. Shea said. "It's probably optimal to wait for the EMTs. But she's your daughter, right? You did what you had to do."

"But did I hurt her more?"

"If she had a spinal cord injury, I'd say yes. Plenty of dives into shallow water in the dark can end up in broken necks—but that didn't happen here," Dr. Shea said. "The way I look at it, your carrying her got her here just that much faster, and that's good. That's very good. She was in shock."

John stared at her, waiting.

"We want to keep her overnight, run some more tests, keep an eye on her. Okay?" the doctor asked.

Honor just stood there. The doctor looked from Honor to John, waiting for one of them to speak.

"That's fine," John said finally, once he realized Honor was frozen. "Thank you."

Honor wanted to say thank you too, but she couldn't. Her throat was blocked. When she looked up at John, she saw the bruise on his cheek from where she'd hit him.

"I haven't done that in a long time," John said harshly.

Honor looked up at him. "Done what?"

"Made a decision about one of my daughters."

As the doctor walked away, the waiting-room door swung open and Regis and Cecilia ran in, Regis holding the tea and looking up at her parents as if she were five, with big round eyes waiting for them to make the world keep turning.

"What is it?" she asked.

"She's doing well," Honor said.

"Are you sure?" Regis asked.

"When can she come home?" Cece asked.

"Probably tomorrow," Honor said. "They want to keep her here for observation."

"Can I see her?" Regis asked.

"The doctors are still with her. They'll tell us when we can. Come here," Honor said, holding her arms open. In one quick move Regis put the tea down and threw herself into her mother's arms. Honor felt her shaking. She herself felt unsteady. She looked across Regis's shoulder at John, saw him watching them. Cece approached him, and he looked surprised and happy.

Cece handed him the tea she'd brought up from the cafeteria.

"Thank you," he said.

"It's hot," Cece said. "Don't burn your mouth."

"I won't," he said, staring at her, trying to smile.

Honor closed her eyes and swayed. They had been so happy. John had loved them all so much. She raised her eyes to look at him now, but what she saw made her heart clutch. His face looked so hard, his jaw set, his cheekbones so gaunt. He looked like a man who had spent time in prison. But his eyes streamed with tears. He coughed, turned away.

Not before Regis saw. Her mouth open slightly, she put her hand on Cece's shoulder. Now both girls looked shocked. John and Honor stood with only a few feet of space between them, but it was a hopeless gulf. She couldn't comfort him, because her tenderness had instantly melted, and she felt herself locked up again. So much hurt and pain because of his recklessness.

"Dad, it's okay," Regis said.

He shook his head. "It isn't," he said.

"All that matters is that we're together again," she said. "Now." Regis looked to Honor for support, but she couldn't nod, or in any way give it.

They weren't together, not in the way Regis meant. Tonight fate had brought them to the same place, but that was all it was. Honor's eyes fell on Regis's left hand, on the engagement ring Peter had given her. Honor had taken her ring off long ago, and that said everything. Her heart was pounding as both girls were looking up at her, waiting for her to make everything right.

She knew she couldn't. Her silence was like a ticking bomb, and it went off with Regis exploding out of the circle, running through the ER door, into the enclosure where Agnes was.

"Regis!" John called, but she didn't stop. She wouldn't, Honor wanted to tell him. Regis always went places she wasn't supposed to, where she wasn't allowed.

It was a lesson she had learned from her father, long ago.

The lights were so bright. The cubicles were separated by curtains, some of them not drawn. As Regis hurried past the nurses' station and down the row, she looked in on an old man, a young woman, a child, none of them Agnes. It was very late; all of the doctors and nurses seemed to be busy with patients. No one stopped her, even though she was wearing a T-shirt and her drawstring pajama bottoms—soaked and sandy from kneeling over Agnes on the beach.

When she got to the last cubicle, she saw feet moving behind a closed curtain. Hesitating, she peeked through the crack. There were two doctors standing there, one of them shining a light into Agnes's eyes. Her sister was lying there, head bandaged. She must have been unconscious, because the doctor had to hold her eyelids open.

Regis ducked behind a linen cart, her heart smashing around her chest. She wanted to run right in, but she knew she had to wait for the right moment. A few minutes later, she heard the doctors leave, and she ducked behind the curtain.

Agnes's eyes were closed. She had a turban of gauze on her head. Lying on the floor was a pile of shaved hair and squares of bloody gauze. The sides of the bed were up, so Regis reached over, took Agnes's hand. It felt so cold, even though Agnes was covered with heated blankets.

"Hey, Agnes," Regis whispered. "Wake up."

When her sister didn't stir, Regis leaned over, put her mouth next to her ear. "Did you see him? Dad's home. He's really here."

Agnes's lips twitched. Regis saw—she was sure it was her sister trying to smile. Her eyelids flickered. There—a flash of recognition.

"Regis," Agnes said, her voice croaking.

"You're awake!"

"How'd you . . . find me?"

"Cece followed you."

"Excuse me, what are you doing in here?"

At the sound of the irate voice, Regis looked over her shoulder, still holding Agnes's hand. She saw a male nurse standing there, with shockingly bright red hair and blue eyes, and dressed in baggy blue scrubs. "I'm her sister, it's okay."

He stared at her for a few seconds, as if maybe he knew her from somewhere. "She's supposed to be resting," he said eventually. "She really hit her head. Maybe just a few more minutes, okay? I wouldn't do it, but someone might call security."

"She needs me," Regis said.

"I understand," he said. "But just a few more minutes. What she needs most right now is sleep."

"Thank you..." Regis broke off to read his name badge. "Brendan. She and I have shared a room together our whole lives. Except when I went to college last year."

"You'll be apart after you get married," he said.

"What?" she asked, shocked.

He gestured at her engagement ring. "After your wedding," he said and stepped closer, pulled the covers up higher on Agnes, right around her chin. The gesture seemed so protective and tender. Regis thought of Peter, wondered whether he'd do that for her if she were ever hurt and cold.

"Look," Brendan said, "why don't you let her get some rest? She's getting good care, I promise. She'll be a lot more ready for visitors tomorrow."

"I'm not a visitor," Regis said.

"I know. You're her sister. You make me think of me and my brother. But still. Let her rest, okay?"

"You promise to watch over her?"

"I promise."

"Her name is Agnes."

"I know," he said, breaking into a big smile, pointing at her chart. "And yours is Regis. I heard her call you that."

"Yes."

Just then the curtains parted, and a female nurse stood there. She looked surprised—not to see Regis standing there, but to see Brendan.

"What are you doing here?" she asked. "I thought you were off tonight."

"I switched my shifts," he said.

"Must have been pretty recently," she said. "You're not on the schedule. Better tell the office, so one of us can go home."

"I'll take this patient," he said, gazing down at Agnes.

"She's on my list," the other nurse said, frowning.

"That's a mistake," he said. "Because she's on mine, too."

"Like I said, you'd better clear it with the office."

"I will," Brendan said. He gave Agnes and Regis a quick glance, as if to make sure he should really leave, then followed the other nurse.

"I swear," Regis said, holding Agnes's hand. "I don't want to leave you."

"You can," she said weakly. "Just come back tomorrow, okay?"

"I'll leave you in the care of Brendan," Regis said. She looked into Agnes's eyes and chuckled lightly. "He has red hair."

"So?"

"Cece told me about you chasing an angel with red hair when we went to get Mom tea. Jesus, Ag!"

"She shouldn't have told," Agnes said, not laughing at all, closing her eyes.

Brendan returned. Something about the way he smiled, standing close to Agnes, the way he had tucked the covers around her, made Regis realize that it would be okay to leave.

"Brendan," Regis said, "I'll be back tomorrow."

"That's good," he said. "Like you said, she needs you."

"Look after her, okay?" Regis asked.

He nodded, not saying a word.

With that, he let Regis kiss Agnes's forehead, and then gently eased her out of the cubicle. Regis glanced back, just happening to see the hem of his jeans poking out from under his green scrubs. She saw some burrs stuck to the denim—the kind that grew in the Academy field, along the stone wall.

Regis stood there in the glow of fluorescent hospital lights, feeling as if she had encountered something strange and wonderful. She knew about her sister's penchant for visions—something Regis thought was basically hooey. She didn't even believe in what she'd heard her aunt had seen, so she wasn't about to believe it about her sister.

Brendan was *real*; he wasn't any mere vision, but he had certainly appeared tonight just when Regis needed him most, for peace of mind. He was a true-life angel, that was for sure. Since he was taking care of Agnes, he deserved elevated status. Regis dubbed him Brendan, the redheaded archangel of the ER.

She would leave her sister with no one less.

Nine

The tide had risen high during the night, and now it had ebbed all the way out to the end of the jetty. Rockweed and Irish moss glistened in the morning sun, and periwinkles studded the glossy rocks. Crabs scuttled for cover as John walked through the tide pools.

He kept his eyes peeled, scanning for the rock that had done it. Orienting himself by way of the wall and the spot where he'd pulled Agnes onto the beach, he narrowed in. The water would have been a good two feet over the top of the rock last night. Even in the blackness, the stars had illuminated the surface, the ridges of breaking waves. She never could have seen what was underneath. But she'd lived on this beach her whole life. Wouldn't she have known better than to dive here?

He looked up at the hillside—to the stone wall that snaked down the hill, all the way to the edge of the bank—where it became a breakwater, jutting out into the cove, meant to prevent erosion of the Academy land. What had she been doing, running on top of the wall? And what had possessed her to go crashing into the water?

John walked over to the spot where she'd gone in, pebbles crunching underfoot. The tide was still going out, rivulets through the mud. Green weed stuck to his feet. He didn't care. His baby had hit her head on a rock, one of these right here, and he had to find the one.

It wasn't hard to figure out. He scanned the immediate area; most of the rocks were too small, and last night they'd have been too far underwater to do much harm. But this one, taller than he was, massive and broad...he ran his hand over its rough surface. Was that a slash of blood on the granite, or just a streak of rose quartz? John felt it in his soul: this was the rock that had injured Agnes.

Throwing his shirt up on the beach, he went to work. Took the shovel and crowbar and pickax and sledgehammer he'd borrowed from Tom's toolshed—behind the convent, out where he kept the mowers and landscaping equipment, and John's great-grandfather's stonecutting tools.

Using the shovel, he dug around the rock now, throwing sand off to the side. It wasn't part of the moraine, wasn't attached to the ridge of granite left behind by the last ice age. No, it was just a boulder from the field. John knew that one of his ancestors had rolled it down the hill, into the water—at the same time he'd cleared the Kelly land, built the walls.

Digging was a waste of time. Grabbing the pickax, he started swinging. Every blow jolted his whole body. He found a crack and felt something give. Chips flew. He shut his eyes, swung again and again.

After a few minutes, he was covered with sweat and stopped to rest. As he did, he heard a loud meow. It startled him, and he looked around. He was used to cats; many strays lived in Portlaoise Prison, and over the years, he had welcomed several into his cell. Each of them had comforted him, but there was one that had become his favorite: a small white cat that had reminded him of Sisela.

He heard rustling in the brush at the top of the beach. Pausing, he walked closer to investigate. A cat meowed again and again, as if in distress. He crouched down, leaning on the shovel's handle, peering into the tangled vines and beach roses.

She sat so still, he almost missed her. There, nearly hidden, he saw glowing green eyes, those of a white cat. God, she looked so much like Sisela, she took his breath away. He felt a quick sting, just behind his eyelids. His old cat, his old beloved life...But it couldn't be her—she would be almost nineteen by now. He knew that she must have died

while he was in Portlaoise; he had grieved for her along with everything else. But maybe this cat was one of her kittens.... His eyes
blurred with tears.

"It *is* you! You're really home!"

John heard the voice, and when he looked up, there she was—
running down the hill through the grapevines and wildflowers, her
black veil and habit flying out behind her. John let the shovel fall to
the sand, caught his sister as she jumped down from the bank.

"Johnny," she said, breaking into sobs.

"Bernie," he said.

Holding his sister, he let himself cry. He'd held the emotion in for
so long. It cracked his chest now, making him shudder, flowing out.
Bernie felt so real, here on the beach they'd loved as children. She'd
been there for him from the minute he was born.

"You're really here," she wept.

"I sometimes thought I'd never see this day," he said.

"You have no idea how much I missed you."

"And I missed you," he said. "Your letters really got me through."

"Johnny, they were nothing. You don't know how much I wanted
to be with you. Those few visits felt like nothing..."

"You had to keep this place running," he said. "I understood."

She reached up, held his face between her hands. Her cheeks were
streaked with tears. He felt her staring into his eyes, trying to gauge
how he was doing. With anyone else he would have pulled away, but
not Bernie.

"You're still my little brother," she said. "I'd do anything for you."

"You did, Bernie. I know how hard it was to get permission from
the order to fly over. And all your letters and prayers—I had you with
me every day. Believe me, you were with me in my cell."

"It wasn't enough," she murmured. "I felt so helpless."

"You looked after Honor and the girls, just like you promised."

"I love them," she said. "Honor is my sister—that's how I feel about
her. And the girls are..." she trailed off, tearing up again. "They're the
closest I have to children of my own. Bless them all."

"Bernie..."

They hugged again. Then stepped apart and, as if by agreement, dried their tears.

"You don't look any older," he said, smiling. "Not one bit." And she didn't. Her face was unlined, her eyes clear and bright, and the wisps of hair he saw sticking out from under her wimple looked as red as ever.

"John, you still look exactly like my little brother." She reached up to touch his face again.

"But old now," he said. "I got old in prison, Bernie."

"Johnny," she said. Her eyes were filled with pain, and he could see that she had counted the days right along with him.

"I'm sorry for what you must have gone through, worrying about me," he said.

"No," she said, taking his hand. "Not me...you, Johnny. I prayed for you every day. The entire community did."

"Nuns praying for a murderer," he said.

"Stop it. You are not a murderer. It was a terrible thing, but not intentional. You had to fight that poor man to keep him from hurting Regis."

"That's how you see it?" he asked.

"I know your heart, Johnny."

"Maybe you don't," he said.

His heart was thudding so hard, his ribs hurt. He flashed on the rage he'd felt that day, one memory that hadn't dulled: the sight of Greg White descending on Regis. John remembered what his fists had done. As terrible as that was, he wished the story had ended there.

"I know my brother," she said stubbornly.

"Thanks for saying that, Bernie," he said.

"Has Honor been down to see you today?" Bernie asked.

"Not yet," John said.

"Agnes is improving. She's awake and alert. They're going to do an MRI at ten, but Honor said the doctors sound very positive. They'll probably release her soon."

John felt scalded; Honor hadn't even bothered to come tell him.

He felt color rising in his neck and face and saw it register in Bernie's expression.

"It will get better, Johnny," Bernie said, reading his mind. "Honor is a little bit in shock. Because of Agnes, but also because she wasn't expecting you to be here this soon—none of us were. It's a gift, beyond belief.... But for her, with the girls and all, it will probably take some getting used to."

"Tom helped me," he said. "He got one of the Kellys involved, and they got me out early, for good behavior."

"Tom loves you like a brother," Bernie said, keeping her voice even.

"Well, I'm your brother, and we both know he'd do anything for you," John said.

She didn't nod, didn't acknowledge what he'd just said. She just gazed at John, as if she was afraid he might disappear again. "Six years was too long," she said. "Remember the outcry in Ireland...a lot of people thought you never should have gone to jail."

"Yeah, well..." John wanted her to stop.

"John, I still don't...I'll never understand," Bernie said, taking his hand. "Why you pled guilty the way you did."

"They had witnesses who'd heard me threaten him, Bernie. I told him I'd kill him, and I did."

"Regis would have told the court that *he* attacked *you*," she pressed.

"I didn't want to put Regis through it," he said. "Or Honor."

"They would have welcomed the chance to tell what happened," Bernie said. "They wanted to stand up and fight for you...."

"Well, I didn't want them to," he said, his voice rising. Then, seeing the hurt in her face, he shook his head. "I'm sorry, Bernie."

"It's okay, John," she said. "You've been under such a strain."

He nodded, wanting her to let it go at that. He gazed up the hillside—he couldn't help watching for Honor. There was something he wanted to do before she came—if she came—and he was itching to get it done. He glanced over at the pickax and sledgehammer, and Bernie saw.

"I want to ask you what you're doing," Bernie said. "But I have the feeling it's between you and that rock."

He didn't reply. Bernie stood right beside him, sandals on her feet. Overhead, one seagull hovered and dropped a mussel on the rock, cracking the blue-black shell. Then it dropped down and ate the meat.

"Do you still feel the need to do hard labor? Didn't you get enough of that at Portlaoise?"

"It's not like that," he said.

"It's just that you're doing a really good imitation of Sisyphus. 'The gods had condemned Sisyphus to ceaselessly rolling a rock to the top of a mountain, whence the stone would fall back of its own weight. They had thought with some reason that there is no more dreadful punishment than futile and hopeless labor.' That's Camus. You don't have to do penance, Johnny."

"That's not what this is," he said.

"What, then?"

"She's so beautiful," he said.

"Honor?"

He nodded. Who else?

"She looks the same, yet I can see the years that have gone by. They're in her eyes, in her skin…the color of her hair. But it's not a shock to see, it's just what's right. I feel I've been with her all along. It's what I always imagined: going through life with her."

"It's what we all imagined."

"She's moved on, though. I can tell by the way she looks at me."

"Don't be so sure of that."

He shrugged, staring at the boulder. He touched the red line— Agnes's blood, the vein of rose quartz. "I want to know it all. How long did it take for her to forget me? Or was it already over, even before I went to prison?"

"She hasn't forgotten you," Bernie said softly.

"Is she going to keep the girls from me?" he asked, his chest tightening. "She didn't even let me know about Agnes. Doesn't she know it's killing me? Seeing them all last night, for such a short while. And to know they're all there, just over the rise. And I'm here. I feel a million miles away."

"But you're not," Bernie said in her steady, realistic way. "Give her a little time. She has a lot on her mind with Agnes. I'll keep you informed about everything. She asked me to. If you want to go to the hospital, you can use the convent car. Or I'm sure Tom would drive you."

"Thanks, Bernie."

"Are you okay here?" she asked, gesturing toward the stone cottage.

"I'm fine."

"I don't even have to ask you who got it ready for you."

"Nope."

"Thomas X. Kelly strikes again." She swallowed hard, her eyes welling up again. "I'm just so glad you're back home. You have no idea, John."

He nodded, and just then he knew he couldn't handle this anymore, the tension of being with someone he loved. The feelings were too huge. She must have read his mind, because she suddenly kissed him.

"I'd better get back to work," she said. "I'll find out about the MRI and let you know. Depending on what they find, Agnes could even be released later today."

"If she's not, maybe I'll take you up on your offer about the car," he said.

"Okay," Bernie said.

John gave her one more hug, and then he watched her scramble up the path to the top of the bank. She followed the wall straight up the long hill, looking back to wave at him.

John waved back. He felt ready to explode. The tide had turned. It had just started to flow back from the sea, filling the tidal pools and swirling in the sand. Six hours between tides, six years since he'd been here, with his family. He pictured Honor as she'd looked back then, and as she'd looked last night, so terrified about Agnes.

He couldn't hold it all inside. He grabbed the pickax and started swinging. Six years of pent-up longing came tearing out of him, and bits of rock began to fly. He couldn't stand anything that hurt his daughters, and he attacked the boulder as the gentle tide swirled in around his feet.

Ten

"You have to tell me," Regis said, scrunched up next to Agnes on the bed. "What's in the picture?" Cece had run down to retrieve Agnes's camera last night after they got home (or that morning?) and brought it with her when she visited earlier.

"I don't remember," Agnes said, lying back against the pillows. Her head was pounding so hard, she couldn't think. Sunlight was flooding through the windows, and even though it was so bright and beautiful, she knew it was making her headache worse. "Tell me again—how was he, what did he look like?"

"He's like he always was. Our wonderful dad. I'm not sure I remembered that he was that tall. It's weird." Regis shook her head. "You should have seen him give you mouth-to-mouth resuscitation, lug you up the beach. He totally saved your life."

"Nothing like that ever happened before..."

"You mean, having to have your life saved from bleeding to death and drowning? Jesus, Agnes...you really could have died."

"No. I mean hitting a rock. I've dived off that wall a hundred times. I know exactly where that rock was supposed to be; I swear, it moved. Or maybe I'd just lost my bearings..."

"Looking for your lost vision," Regis said wryly.

"Don't make fun of me," Agnes said.

"It's just, people don't look for visions," Regis said. "They either have them, or they don't. Aunt Bernie, supposedly..."

"Exactly! That's my point. She had one on the Academy grounds, and I swear I did, too. And besides, don't you think that Dad being there, right at that exact minute, was pretty much a miracle? The way he saved my life?"

"That part's pretty cool," Regis agreed. "But look, Agnes. Cece told me about the angel with red hair. You know? It sounds nutty. And the vision thing..."

"Regis, it's on my camera."

"Let's see that," Regis said, and Agnes handed it over.

She watched Regis's expression. Her sister was skeptical about religious matters, believed that nature held enough wonders to cover the mysteries of life. She was completely practical, relying on her own strength and willpower to make things happen. So, watching her expression change as she gazed at the digital camera's screen, Agnes felt triumphant.

"See?" Agnes asked.

Climbing up on the wall, the stones had felt warm beneath her bare feet, holding on to the last of the day's heat. And then she had started running. She had felt as if she could fly, take off like an angel into the sky. For all the light of the stars, the night was still so dark and mysterious, but then the white light had seemed to wrap her up, lift her into itself.

"It's your nightgown," Regis said.

"What?" Agnes asked.

"A filmy white blur," Regis said, staring. "That's what it has to be."

"You're ruining it," Agnes said, trembling.

"Agnes," Regis said, taking her hand. "Maybe it's seagulls taking off. You scared them when you dove in. It's just a white flash, not a vision."

Tears popped into Agnes's eyes.

"What's wrong?" Regis asked, looking scared.

"Don't you know how badly I need to believe in something good?" Agnes asked, breaking down. "That there's someone looking out for us, after everything? With Dad gone, in jail for something he didn't mean to do...and Mom just lost...and you marrying Peter..." The words were out before she could stop them.

"Peter?"

"Yes!" Agnes said, tears streaming as her head started to pound. "He's just your version of a vision, or an angel. Someone you need to keep the darkness away..."

"Agnes," Regis said, blanching as her sister buried her face in her hands and sobbed.

"I want to know someone is protecting us," Agnes wept. She couldn't bear the idea of Regis taking it away from her, the knowledge that she had seen something holy, mystical last night, that there was a good force keeping watch over their family.

Regis took her hand. When Agnes looked up, her sister's face was nearly in hers, eye to eye. "We do that for each other," she said. "And yes, Peter does that for me. If you say those are angel wings in the picture, then so be it. What do I know?"

Just then the door opened, and Agnes's heart thumped. She sank into her pillows, depleted from everything, and tried to smile through her tears. Last night he'd promised to come back today, and here he was.

"Speak of the devil," Regis said. "Brendan, the redheaded archangel."

"Excuse me?" he asked.

"Never mind," Regis said with a quick squeeze of Agnes's hand. "Private joke."

"Feeling better?" he asked, looking straight at Agnes.

She nodded. "Yes. Thank you."

"That's really good to hear," he said. "It's a good sign."

"Are you her nurse today?" Regis asked.

Brendan didn't reply. He gazed at Agnes, eyes sparkling. He looked a few years older than Regis—maybe twenty-two or twenty-three. He was about five-nine, very thin, with bright red hair. Agnes had never seen such clear blue eyes, and she tingled, knowing they were trained on her.

"Brendan McCarthy?" Regis asked, leaning forward to read his name off his badge. "Hello? Are you her nurse today?"

"Uh, no. I'm in the ER...they told me Agnes had been moved to the sixth floor. I just wanted to check and see how she was doing. And..." he said, trailing off, looking at Agnes again, "and bring you this..." He placed a shell on her tray. She reached for it—a perfect channeled whelk.

"Thank you," she said. "How did you know I like shells?"

"I didn't," he said. "But I found it and thought of you."

"Hey, were you on the beach last night?" Regis asked, starting to hold up the camera for him to see. "Before you came to work? I think my sister got a shot of your wings."

"Regis, stop," Agnes said, red with embarrassment.

"Plus," Regis said, "I noticed you had a burr on your jeans last night. Like the kind that grows on the top of the beach..."

"That's some other angel," he said, glancing at the screen.

Agnes felt absurdly pleased as he looked back at her, ignoring Regis's odd question about the burr.

"I'll make sure the nurses on this floor take good care of you," he said.

"Did you straighten out your work schedule?" Regis asked.

"Yeah," he said. "No problem."

"It's funny," she said. "Most people *miss* work when they screw up their schedules—not show up for extra shifts. But then, angels probably work a lot of overtime, right?"

Brendan shook his head, bemused. "Whatever you say. Look, I'll check back later, okay, Agnes?"

Agnes just nodded. She held the shell in her hand.

"Okay," Regis said for her. "Check back."

Brendan left the room, and Regis smiled down at Agnes. "He likes you," she said.

"That's because I was his patient last night."

"You should have seen him standing guard over you. His supervisor came in and was all confused, because he wasn't even scheduled to work. It's as if he knew you were going to be here and came rushing in. Do you know him?"

"No," Agnes said. "Not before last night."

"He was wearing jeans under his ER clothes, and he had a burr stuck to the hem. I swear, it came from the thicket between the beach and the vineyard."

"What would he be doing there?" Agnes asked, frowning. Her head hurt, listening to Regis's theories. They were so practical and earthbound.

"Maybe he was looking for his one true love...and maybe that's you."

Agnes gasped, and the intake of breath hurt her bruised ribs. "Don't say that," she said. "Don't you remember?"

For once, Regis was silent. Agnes looked up, saw that Regis remembered very well. "It's what Dad used to say about Mom. That she was his one true love."

"I know." Regis held Agnes's hand softly, as if she were a bird with a broken wing. She stroked it gently.

"Well, he's home now," Agnes went on. "He saw his one true love last night..."

Regis didn't say anything.

Agnes hurt all over; the doctor said it was from being revived, having her rib cage nearly cracked by CPR. Her father had given her mouth-to-mouth resuscitation. Agnes was alive because of him. It was all so miraculous; why did it have to feel so tragic? The confusion made her shimmer and start to cry again.

"Did I upset you?" Regis asked, surprised.

"It's not that," Agnes sobbed. "I just hurt all over."

"You'll get better fast," Regis said. "Mom's out there talking to the doctors, but they already told her—you're going home tomorrow. You're going to be fine."

"That's not why I hurt," Agnes said.

"Then what?"

"Why isn't Dad here?"

Regis didn't answer. Agnes knew her sister didn't think she was strong enough to take it. Drifting in and out of consciousness last night, before being loaded into the ambulance, she had heard her mother yelling at her father—screaming, really, as if her insides were pouring out like black fire.

"She won't let him see me, right?"

"It's more like he doesn't want to rock the boat. All he cares about is you getting well now. He's just waiting to see if you come home today. You're all he's thinking about right now."

It made Agnes so sad, to think of him so near, yet so far. How must her father feel, knowing everyone was gathered together but him? Agnes wept. Why couldn't her parents realize that they all needed to be together?

"You know what I like thinking?" Regis asked. "How happy Dad will be when he sees Sisela. He loved her so much, didn't he?"

But Agnes couldn't reply. All she could do was hold the shell Brendan had given her, and think of her father, and try not to break apart.

That night John borrowed the nuns' station wagon to drive to the hospital. Bernie had told him they wanted to keep Agnes in the hospital one more night, to be safe. It felt strange, driving these familiar roads again. He remembered coming this way the night Agnes was born—for the births of all three of his daughters, in fact.

Parking in the visitor's lot, he felt a steady breeze blowing off the harbor. He entered through the main doors, and his whole body tensed. The plaster walls and linoleum floors reminded him of being in an institution; it was a visceral reaction, and he tried to shake it off by running up the stairs.

When he reached Agnes's room, his only reaction was to the sight of his daughter. She lay back against her white pillow, her head bandaged, her eyes closed. Her mother and sisters had left for the evening; she was all alone.

"Sweetheart," he whispered.

Her eyes fluttered open. "Daddy!" she said.

"How are you feeling?"

"My head hurts," she said.

"I'm sorry, honey. It probably will for a while, but not too much longer. You really gave us a scare."

"I didn't know that rock was there," she murmured, tears squeezing from the corners of her eyes.

"The tide must have been covering it."

"I'm sorry for making you worry," she said. "And for hitting the rock…"

"Please don't be sorry for anything, Agnes. As long as you're okay, that's all we care about."

She nodded, but her shoulders began to shake with helpless sobs. It had all been too much for her. John sat beside her, holding her softly. She cried against his chest, her tears soaking his shirt. He thought of that treacherous boulder protruding in the bay, of how close they had come to losing her to it.

"You need some rest," he whispered now.

"Don't go, Dad," she wept quietly, fists balled like a small child's. "Don't leave before I go to sleep."

"I won't, Agnes. I promise I won't," he said.

And he didn't; he stayed until she had fallen back to sleep, and just to make sure, for quite a long time afterward.

The next day, after Agnes was home safe, in her bed, Honor stood in her studio, covered in oil paint. The craziness of it—preparing a canvas, setting out her paints, getting to work, after Agnes had had such a near miss—sort of stunned her. But she'd gone to bed last night, wrung out with worry and relief and about a million other emotions, and found herself completely unable to sleep—or even shut her eyes.

All she could see was John. Soaking wet, covered in sand, lifting Agnes into his arms…It all felt so unreal. It had haunted her all through the hours she couldn't sleep last night, the sense of John there, holding their daughter. First Agnes, then Regis—the image shifted.

She had practically run into her studio to paint it. The color and lines had flowed, keeping her focused on the canvas instead of her child in the hospital.

She stroked paint onto the canvas, a rough image of John with their daughter in his arms. Was it Regis or Agnes? She didn't even know, and she wasn't sure it mattered. Her emotions came gushing out in the work. He looked so tender, yet his intensity came through as well. His darkness had caused so much turmoil, and she didn't want to leave any of it out.

Now, in the background, the vanishing point: the top of the hill, crowned by the old stone wall. She lowered her brush. Why was she painting that *now*? Yet she couldn't leave it out.

There, her brush rounding the stones, dotting on specks of white, lichens softening the contours. She left a dark spot, the hole in the wall where the box had been hidden.

Oh, what a scavenger hunt the box had provided. There was the ticket stub, and a gold ring, a death certificate and a hand-drawn map of Ireland had shown the places most precious to Cormac Sullivan: Counties Cork and Kerry, their jagged peninsulas reaching into the Atlantic Ocean like long, rocky fingers; at the tip of one, Ballincastle, was the word "home."

Tom and Bernie had gone to Ireland first. They fell in love with Dublin—land of the Kellys—and every week they sent John and Honor postcards of castles, the River Liffey, and flower-bedecked pubs. Slowly painting now, Honor remembered reading those cards, dreaming of Irish romance and magic.

Not John, though. He had his own dark obsessions about the box and what it meant, took it to the deep, hidden part of himself that nurtured his work. His family's struggle and suffering, and the choices they'd made to create a better life for their children grew in him with a kind of rage and fury that Honor had never seen in him before.

The famine; not enough to thrive, not enough to live. The British versus the Irish—hoarding food, and work, and life. The famine shrinking John's ancestors' bodies, leeching the strength from their bones. They had lived on the westernmost land in Ireland: what must it have been like, knowing that salvation lay across the waves, in America? How could they leave their beloved land and families— and how could they not? Oh, and the famine ships—families piled in, crammed together, the stench of illness and death. Losing what they loved, every inch of the way.

John had always known his installation had to be on a cliff, at the very edge of Ireland—to symbolize how young Cormac, his great-great-grandfather, had yearned toward the opposite shore of America.

Cormac Sullivan had been born August 1, 1831, in West Cork, and had died on November 14, 1917, in Hartford, Connecticut. He had become a stonemason in Ireland, working for his father, Seamus, who had learned the trade during the famine—a token job created by the British, indifferent to their suffering. Every bit of strength had gone into survival, but the Sullivans had become artists at the stone trade. Clearing land, building stone walls, starting their own stonecutting firm, becoming well respected in the county and beyond.

It was on a job, clearing some seacoast property on West Cork's Beara Peninsula, that Seamus Sullivan's shovel struck gold—literally. Working for the Dargans, a family that owned a farm on Ballincastle Head, he uncovered two objects: a gold chalice and the gold ring with the red stone.

He'd gone straight to the family, given them the treasure. They had been so grateful to receive them, Mr. Dargan had given Seamus the ring—and told him the story.

Algerian and Spanish pirates had sailed north—with the Armada and in fleets of their own—during the late 1500s. Ireland, jutting out into the Atlantic, had been irresistible, and the pirates had laid siege all along the west coast. One group had kidnapped an entire Irish town, taken them back to Algeria as slaves.

"Dargan" was derived from "D'Aragon"—and the family's Black Irish looks, with dark hair and blue eyes, had come from the invasion. Some of the pirates had stayed in the area, hiding their treasure in the many sea caves scored into the rocky coastline, burying it on land marked by distinctive outcroppings. The family's dark coloring came from pirate blood.

During the time he worked on the Dargan land, Seamus Sullivan fell in love with their daughter, Emily. She was a feisty beauty, and in a letter, he wrote, "She has black curls and blue eyes the color of Bantry Bay." Because he had been so honest with the family, Seamus won her hand in marriage. But when he tried to give her the pirate's ring, she gave it right back. Hating the greed and violence the pirates had visited on her family, she told Seamus to throw it into the ocean.

Seamus knew he should have. He wanted so badly to please Emily. But his family had also been scarred, by the first famine's poverty and starvation. Two of his brothers had died, and so had his mother, pregnant with his sister. His aunt and cousin, a neighbor, and a family friend had starved to death as well. So although Seamus had pretended to cast the ring into the ocean off Ballincastle—told Emily so—he had kept it.

So he and his beloved Emily were married, and for such a long time, she didn't know that he'd told her a lie. They inherited the farm when her father died; they lived there with their eight children—the oldest being John's great-grandfather, Cormac. Perhaps Seamus considered the ring to be an insurance policy. Or maybe he just felt it had brought him so much luck—the love and trust of the Dargan family, and the hand of Emily in marriage.

Then, in 1847, a second famine struck.

Back then, so many Irish were emigrating to America, it sometimes seemed there'd be no one left. People boarded steamers in Cobh, bound for Boston, Providence, and New York. The news that flowed back was always good—never bad. People in the States weren't doing well, they were doing very well. They weren't making a good living, they were prosperous.

Seamus knew he had to save his only son, Cormac. He had learned of work in the United States. The Kellys of Merrion Square in Dublin needed stonemasons to build walls on their properties in Hartford and Black Hall, Connecticut. Seamus and Emily were heartbroken to send Cormac off, but they had seen what the last famine had done, and they couldn't bear to risk his life.

With his parents at his side, Cormac walked over the hills to the old stagecoach road. He carried a suitcase in his hand; in his heart he carried his family's love and all the skills his father had taught him as a stonemason. Just as the stagecoach came, his father reached into his pocket and pulled out the pirate's ring.

"This is your inheritance," Seamus said. "I found it on your grandfather's land, years ago, and he gave it to me. It's precious, because in some ways it brought me and your mother together. In case times get hard, you can sell it."

Emily never said a word about Seamus's keeping the ring. She cared only about her son, that he have enough to help him get started in a new life. She held her tears until the stagecoach came, and Cormac climbed in. Her beautiful, young, skinny, hopeful boy... When the coach pulled away, the moaning of the wild wind blowing hard across the western hills was all mixed in with her keening for her oldest son.

He was only sixteen, and she never saw him again.

Honor knew all this from Emily's diary, which John had eventually found in the West Cork Heritage Center, along with many other family documents. It had sent him to Cobh, to literally climb into the holds of the famine ships, touch the wood that had soaked up so many tears. And there on the docks, he had met up with Gregory White.

Thinking of all that, standing at her easel, Honor heard a strange sound. It was hollow, clanging, like the tolling of a bell. It was dull, not clear like the chapel bell, and it seemed to be coming from the beach. Putting down her brush, cleaning her hands with a linseed oil–soaked rag, she opened the screen door.

The sound drew her outside; she walked barefoot across the yard, feeling each hammer strike in her heart. She knew where she was going, of course. John couldn't have summoned her more effectively if he'd called her name. The sound drew her across the lawn, down the hill, through the tangled gorse that grew upon the bank.

The cottage was built at the very top of the beach, as far above the tide line as possible. It had been used by the Kellys, long ago, for beach parties, a place to dress for summer dances. Normal high tides reached the sand twenty-five yards down. Run-of-the-mill summer storms sent their strongest waves fifteen yards from the front steps.

But hurricanes and winter gales were another story, and they had done damage to the small stone cottage, chipped away at its foundation, sent cracks up the walls.

Just beyond it, she saw John standing on the sand, his legs braced, attacking a rock with a sledgehammer. She started to run, sand giving under her feet; when she got to the spot where John had revived Agnes last night, her heart jolted—she flashed back to the indentation where she had lain, dark bloodstains on the sand.

"What are you doing?" she shouted.

He didn't even hear, just kept smashing the boulder.

"*John!*"

He stopped, looked over at her. Stunned, he dropped the sledgehammer, brushed his hands on his jeans. His body was slick with sweat, and his face had tiny cuts from flying stone.

"Jesus Christ," she said under her breath. "It never ends."

Then she took a deep breath. "She's home," she said. "I wanted to let you know. Agnes is home."

"I know," he said, catching his breath. "I walked over before, but she was sleeping on the sunporch."

"Why didn't you come in? She would have liked to see you."

"And I'd like to see her," he said. "All of them. All of *you*. I've missed you so much." He stared at her, but she couldn't hold his gaze. She thought of her painting, how she'd been trying to capture his intensity. Well, here it was.

"I didn't go in," John continued, "because I didn't want to disturb her. I would have knocked, but I saw you in your studio."

She nodded, but didn't speak. She didn't want to let him into her work. It was private, *hers*. "Why are you staying here?" she asked instead.

"You want me to go back to Ireland?" he asked.

"I mean here, on the beach. I'm sure Bernie would find a place for you at the Academy. Or Tom..."

"This just seems right," he said.

"A ramshackle, moldy stone house, on its last legs? If we have a nor'easter, you could get washed away in your sleep."

"Would that bother you, Honor?" he asked, blue eyes glinting with dark fire. "Never mind. I won't put you on the spot."

"I *am* on the spot," she said, her heart pounding. "I don't know how to be around you. What to say, how to feel. God, when I saw Agnes on the beach, just lying there, all I could think of was Regis, in shock and broken; I was sure she'd never be the same again..."

"I know," John said.

"Seeing Agnes's blood on the sand." Honor glanced over at the spot. It was pristine now, scoured by wind and waves, but she swore she could still see it. "I thought of that day, seeing *his* blood."

"I think of it every day," John said.

"You left us then," she said.

"Left you? It wasn't my wish—they arrested me."

"You could have fought the charges!" Honor yelled, exploding. "If we meant so much to you, why didn't you try harder to come home to us? You were defending Regis! Your daughter! What could they have expected you to do?"

"Nothing," he said, his eyes blazing.

"Then why didn't you speak out?" she rapped out. "Why didn't you fight?"

"You don't understand," he said.

"I know, John. And I didn't understand in Ireland, either. Not the first time I visited you in prison, or the time after that. Or even the last time. I've never been able, not once, to get it through my head. Why you just went to jail... you're so stubborn. You always were."

"I killed Gregory White," he said. His voice was even, but his eyes were wild.

"I know that," she said. "And I know he attacked you. Explain it to me someday, will you? Tell me what you had in mind, going to prison without one word in your own defense?"

"Honor..."

"And I'll tell you how it's been for the girls. Okay?" She was crazy now, and she knew it. Her fury had started simmering in her studio, at her easel, but now it was boiling. "They're desperate. They've missed you so terribly, I don't know if they'll ever be okay. Regis getting married? She didn't have a father to hold on to, so she latched onto the first boy she found. Cecilia's okay. She's young, though. And Agnes? Jesus, where do I start?"

"Agnes?"

"She has visions. That's right, you heard me. She knows that Bernie had one once, and she's frantic to have one of her own. She's silent on Tuesdays, because that's the day you killed Greg White."

"Oh God," John said.

She turned away, started walking as fast as she could. He ran to her, grabbing her arm. The look in his eyes scared her—the skin was stretched over his skull, and his eyes were blue fire.

Their eyes met and held for a few seconds; she saw old hope in his, something she recognized from long ago. A spark, as if for that instant he believed that everything just might be okay, that it *had* to be okay. She felt spent, almost sorry for throwing the blame for everything at him. She looked in his eyes, saw tears brimming there and how terrible it had all been for him. She waited for him to speak, but instead he exhaled with excruciating frustration and turned away.

He walked over to the big rock and hefted the sledgehammer. He started swinging, attacking the rock as if it were his enemy. There was that sound again—the metal against stone she'd mistaken for a bell.

"John," she cried. "What are you doing?"

"This rock is going to be gone," he said over his shoulder, swinging again and again. "It hurt Agnes, Honor, and I'm getting rid of it."

"It's a rock," she yelled. "You can't just pulverize it!"

He didn't even reply—just kept pounding with his sledgehammer. His muscles tensed and bunched, and he swung at the rock as if he hated it. Sparks flew. Honor stood back, in shock and speechless, both moved and appalled.

As she backed away, she could see that he was lost in what he was doing. She saw his passion and rage, and was gripped with the realization that this was the man she had always loved, the man she sometimes feared. It was the same thing all over; nothing had changed. The entire way back to the house, she heard his violent hammer strikes. They didn't stop or even let up.

The sound went on all night.

Honor didn't sleep at all.

She gave up and went to her studio. The desire to paint came over her, and the work began to flow. As charged up as she felt about John, she couldn't deny the effect it was having on her work. This new painting was primal, coming from deep within, nothing like the delicate seascapes and portraits she did for her art classes. From her window, she watched the stars wheel across the sky, rising and setting to the rhythm of John breaking apart the rock.

By the time the sun began to rise, turning the sky deep blue with a ribbon of rose along the horizon in the east, Honor put down her brushes. She felt exhausted but exhilarated. Morning haze lay gently on the ground. She walked out the back door, through the vineyard. Birds were starting to sing in the trees, and gulls called from the tidal flats.

Honor followed the stone wall, her heart beating faster with every step. She startled a red fox; it leapt onto the wall, running a few steps before jumping down the other side. As she approached the crest of the hill, looking down at the beach, she already knew what she would find.

The rock was gone.

One night—that was all it took for John to destroy something created by fire and ice a million years ago—the boulder that had hurt their daughter. The sound of the sledgehammer was finally silenced. John sat on the beach, staring at the sun rising over the peaceful bay. Honor stood on the hill, watching him for a few minutes.

John was lost in his private thoughts. She couldn't imagine what they were, and in that moment she wanted to know more than anything in the world. When he didn't turn around, didn't even move, Honor just backed away.

And she walked silently back through the lush green vineyard, home to their sleeping daughters.

Eleven

Time moved differently for John. In jail it had been scheduled down to fifteen-minute increments. Wake up, meals, head counts, work, exercise, bed. Here, it was measured by tides, sunrises, shifting weather patterns, and the moon moving across the sky. Through it all, he watched for Honor. He wanted her to come back, see what he'd done to the rock. At the same time, he was worried that she'd be afraid. He had scared even himself.

He had attacked the rock with white fury. His muscles ached and cramped in his back and shoulders, burning hard. Ever since seeing Agnes in the hospital, he had known he had to do this. Honor always said his passions got the best of him, and right now he knew she was right. Her grief had been palpable; her rage, over being left in confusion and doubt, his going to jail without a fight, had spurred his own. Not at her, at all, but at just about everything else.

His hatred of the thing that had hurt Agnes—all the ways his being locked up had damaged his daughters—had taken hold of him, and he'd poured all his frustration into the rock. Now, looking at the rubble in the shallow water, he felt almost embarrassed to think of what Honor would think.

Meow…

He looked around, saw the white cat sitting on the wall. She was so still and thin, the age showing in her eyes and the texture of her fur, and the sight of her sent a jolt through his entire body.

"Sisela," he said.

It couldn't be...

No, John thought, his heart racing as he slowly approached the cat on the wall. It couldn't be her; it had to be another cat. One of her progeny, perhaps. Or maybe this was her ghost, coming back to haunt him.

She meowed again, and when she opened her mouth to make the sound, he saw that she had barely any teeth left. This was an old, old cat. He reached out his hand. The cat didn't just inch forward, but leapt into his arms—just as she had when she was a kitten.

"Sisela," he said. Regis used to say she was the fourth Sullivan sister, and that's how John felt now. He cradled the old cat as she purred against his chest, the sound like a low sobbing. She craned her neck, nuzzling his chin. John's eyes stung as he stroked her, thinking of all the years they'd been apart. He thought of how often he'd held his daughters like this, and how often Sisela had wedged her way into the embrace.

"Well, that's a pretty sight."

Hearing the words, John looked up and saw Tom there, grinning.

"It's really her, isn't it?" John asked.

"That old cat of yours, yes, it is," Tom said. "She's on that damn wall every time I pass by. Must've been waiting for you to get home. It's good to see you, John."

"You made it happen," John said. Sisela remained snuggled against his chest. He held on for comfort—but for his or the cat's, he wasn't sure. "You got me out, and you brought me home, and you got this place ready for me."

"How're you doing?" Tom asked.

John nodded. His throat was closed so tight, he couldn't talk. He petted the cat some more, and then set her down in the tall grass at the top of the beach. She circled once, then stalked away.

"You're really back," Tom said. "And the first thing you do is attack a boulder." Tom gestured at the crowbar and sledgehammer leaning against the cottage. Then he looked out at the empty bay. "Where did it go?"

"Let's not go into it," John said. "It's just gone."

"Honor gave me a call."

"Really?"

"She was worried about you. Let's see, what did she say? 'John's acting extreme.' I think she said '*very* extreme.'"

"Yeah, well..."

Tom just shook his head, smiling as he jumped down the bank. The old friends hugged, and John laughed, feeling a sudden exuberance. The sun was in his eyes; he squinted to see Tom better, and he saw Tom doing the same: John felt Tom assessing him, just as Honor and Bernie had done, seeing how he'd weathered prison.

"You look good," Tom said finally.

"Liar."

"I'm serious. You sure look a hell of a lot better than the last time I saw you."

"In the waiting room, surrounded by other inmates?" John said.

"Yeah."

"Well, freedom makes everyone look better," John said. "At least you and Sisela didn't cringe when you saw me."

"Did Honor?"

John nodded. "Once she saw me in the light of day. Our first meeting was right here—after Agnes's accident. And then yesterday she came to blast me."

"Well deserved," Tom said.

"You want to take your shots, too?" John asked, anger rising.

"Whoa, calm down," Tom said,

"Yeah, fine," John said, shaking it off.

"Bernie tells me Agnes is making a really great recovery," Tom said. "The question is, how about you? What kind of recovery are you making?"

"Recovery?"

"From prison."

"You mean, am I rehabilitated?" John asked, laughing bitterly.

"I mean, do you lie awake wanting to rip someone's head off for sending you to jail in the first place? Do you have nightmares of being locked up for being a good guy who just encountered the wrong person? Nice stuff like that. That's what I mean."

"Look, I'm fine. Putting it all behind me."

Tom stared through narrowed eyes. "Right. That's why you annihilated that big goddamn rock that's been sitting here since the last ice age."

"It wasn't so hard to do; the thing had a big crack right down the middle. I just worked on the weak spots."

"Whatever you say. It took you all night. Come on, let's take a walk. I'll show you my latest work assignment from Sister Bernadette Ignatius. I'd like to get your expert opinion."

John grabbed his T-shirt from the beach, shook off the sand, and pulled it on, trying to hide the fact that he was shaking. Tom had some idea of what John had been through, but no one could really know.

John's body ached—from pounding on the rock hour after hour, but even more, from all the years he'd spent apart from everything he loved. There had been times he thought he would die from longing. Missing Honor had never seemed greater than in the middle of the night, an ocean away, locked behind bars. But he thought maybe it was even worse right now, with her and their girls just over the hill.

The two men climbed the bank. They followed the wall, heading down the opposite side of the hill from Honor's house, through the western edge of the vineyard, to the Blue Grotto. John remembered coming here with Honor, kissing her in the dark. She'd always shiver in here, and he'd hold her close.

And the summer before his arrest, he'd helped Bernie out, wheeling in a barrow full of rocks and a tray full of mortar, wielding his great-grandfather's trowel and smoothing out the cement's rough edges.

"What does Bernie want done here?" John asked, walking into the moss-cool cave made by his great-grandfather, looking around.

"She wants some repointing, new mortar, a few stones put back. It started out with one stone pried away—vandals, we figured..."

"Students?"

"Who knows. Spiritually inclined, from the graffiti," Tom said, gesturing.

John read the message:

I WAS SLEEPING, BUT MY HEART KEPT VIGIL.

"Who wrote it?" John asked. When he glanced over, he saw Tom scrutinizing his face. "What, you think I did?"

"Hell, yes."

"How? I flew home from Ireland during recreation period?"

Tom shook his head. "It was written sometime within the last month. You've been out all that time. Besides, who else would have made such a meaningless poetic gesture?"

The two men chuckled, their teasing intact after all this time. Tom always said he built walls and John built art, and only one of them was worth his pay.

"I was in Canada, getting myself ready to come home. It would have been too intense to just fly straight from Dublin here—I told you that. I flew into Halifax and made my way south slowly. And you know it, because you shipped my camera up for me, and paid my way. I took my time getting down here, that's all."

Tom narrowed his eyes, as if he could tell by John's expression whether he was being truthful or not.

"You don't believe me?" John exhaled. "Listen, you want to know if a person's lying, it's just not that hard. In prison, Dermot McCann told me that people always look down, to the left, when they're lying. With the population in Portlaoise, that was just about everyone all the time."

"Who's Dermot McCann?"

"He was an old guy in for forging documents for the IRA. He claimed he'd been set up by his son-in-law. But then, everyone claimed they were set up by someone."

"All except you."

"Shut up, okay?" John said, trying to stay even-tempered. Being in the enclosed space, the Blue Grotto, made John's chest tighten. He felt the sweat pouring down between his aching shoulder blades.

"Okay," Tom said. "You're out, what did or didn't happen up there doesn't really matter now, anyway. There were only three people on that ledge, and..."

John felt the rage building in his skin. The statue of the Virgin Mary, surrounded by trinkets and handwritten prayers, gazed at him with outstretched arms. He stared at her without turning around.

"This is where it happened, isn't it?" he asked. "Where Bernie made her choice."

"Hey, knock it off," Tom said. "That's not fair."

"You have your hallowed ground," John said. "And I have mine."

"Fine," Tom said. "Truce, okay?"

"Can we get out of here?" John said, feeling the walls close in on him. "I need some air."

When they walked outside, he leaned over, taking huge gulps of fresh air. The dampness and chill, the lack of light, the feeling in his chest had all reminded him of Portlaoise.

"It was a violent place to live," John said, after a minute. "I lived with those feelings for six years, and they're still with me. That's why I needed to take my time getting home. I'm trying to shake it. The way everyone dealt with everything was by attack."

"Did you want to attack me just now?"

John shook his head, even though he wasn't sure. It was the mention of three people on the ledge. "I haven't talked about what happened in all the time since that day..."

"No kidding. That's why the judge gave you six years. You didn't leave him any choice."

John stared out across the fields. It was so beautiful from here, the soft green landscape ending in blue sea and endless sky. He had dreamed about it so often in his cell. The smell of grapes filled the air. One October he and Honor had picked bunches of grapes. They'd lain on a blanket, and they'd made love, and afterward he'd fed her grapes, one by one.

"Just tell me the judge had it right," Tom said.

"The judge had it right."

"Man, you're looking down and to the left," Tom said.

"We going to rehash this all day and all night?" John asked.

"Whatever you say, John," Tom said, after a brief silence. "Let's go to dinner."

"Should I change?" John asked.

"No need," Tom said. "Not for where we're going."

John followed him to his truck, out behind the classroom buildings. He noticed how Tom threw a glance toward the offices, the administration wing, where Bernie held court. John shook his head and smiled, and Tom noticed.

"Still carrying a torch," John said. "For a nun."

"What do you know? You haven't been around in..."

"Six years. I know."

Tom gestured at a green pickup truck, and they climbed in.

The landscape was so familiar, yet so foreign. Years away made John raw to the changes—a tract of houses where the ghost woods used to be, all those trees he and Tom used to climb, saying they were haunted. And there, the little boatyard on the inlet—the narrow waterway had been dredged, turned from a creek to almost a river, the weathered wood docks now concrete, and big enough to accommodate huge powerboats.

"Look at that," John said. "Charlie's boatyard—"

"They call it a 'yacht basin' now," Tom said.

"I don't see any rowboats," John said.

"Nope. Everyone wants bigger boats now. Kids don't like to row around the marshes—they have Jet Skis. Their parents have big ugly stinkpots."

"Does Charlie still run the place?"

Tom shook his head. "Some developer paid him enough to retire to

Florida, and he's in a condo down there, going crazy because he lost the only thing he ever cared about—boats, docks, the water. You can't sell out and keep your heart intact. I hear he had a heart attack last spring."

"It's not the same," John said, looking at the boatyard, but meaning everything.

"Some things are," Tom said, getting it, getting him, shooting him a look. "Wait'll you see where I'm taking you."

And he was right. A couple of miles later, he pulled into Paradise Ice Cream. It was still a little shack on the edge of the marsh, picnic tables overlooking the creek leading to the mouth of the Connecticut River, into Long Island Sound. John, Honor, and the kids had always come here for lobster rolls and fried scallops. They served the best ice cream around. People stood at the window, and John and Tom got in line.

"Smells good," John said.

"I could have taken you somewhere fancy for your welcome-home dinner, but—"

"You know me well," John said. "There's nowhere better than Paradise."

Tom smiled, as if he knew something John didn't. John wanted to ask what the secret was, but he was too happy just standing there. People drove in and out, radios playing. A family walked past with their trays. Numbers were called over the loudspeaker. A young couple leaned against the big tree by the street, eating ice cream cones.

"May I help you?" the young girl asked.

"You sure can," Tom said, grinning, and suddenly John looked up and realized the secret: it was his daughter.

"Regis!" he said.

"Hi, Dad," she said, sounding equally happy and surprised. "Hi, Tom."

"You work here?" John asked. He saw her eyes shining, the same little girl he'd always known. She looked so excited, just the way she'd always looked when she wasn't expecting to see him.

"When I'm not working at the library," she said. "Got to earn money for the wedding."

"The wedding, yes," John said. "I want to hear all about it...."

"You gonna order?" someone called from the back of the line. John turned to glare—saw a muscle-bound bleached-blond beach bum standing there, arm around his girlfriend, showing off his toughness.

"I'm talking to my daughter," John said.

"John," Tom warned.

One punch and the guy's teeth would be down his throat. Tom jabbed John, gave him a sharp look, brought him straight back to the present, out of Portlaoise Prison and lessons learned there.

"He's just rude, Dad," Regis said. "He comes here every day, and he's always like that. Give me your order, and I'll take my break—okay?"

"Sure, we can do that," Tom said, stepping in. "Two lobster rolls—we're celebrating your father's homecoming. Fries, coleslaw, the works. And how about two root beers?"

"Except, make mine a scallop roll," John said.

"You've got it," Regis said, faltering slightly. She took Tom's money and made change, giving John a quick glance. "Number twenty-five. I'll meet you back at the picnic tables."

"Easy, now," Tom said as they walked past the beach guy. John wanted to tell him not to worry—the moment had passed. He barely even glanced at the jerk, staring at him as he walked by.

"There she is," John said, relieved, as they rounded the building and saw Regis heading for a picnic table.

"Yep," Tom said as they approached Regis.

There were ten tables set in the yard behind Paradise, and John figured he'd sat at every single one with Honor and the kids. They'd all loved coming here—it was a summer tradition, repeated many times throughout July and August. Everyone had their favorites—Honor and Agnes would always order lobster rolls, John and Regis liked fried scallops. And for dessert, they'd always get their favorite ice cream cones....

"Hi!" Regis said.

"Hi, beautiful," Tom said. "So, how about this, Regis? Having your dad back home?"

"It's incredible," Regis said, her eyes sparkling, staring at John.

"I second that," John said.

"I'd almost given up believing it would ever happen."

"Did you really?" John asked, her words piercing him.

"It's just been so horribly long," Regis said. "We've missed you so much."

"You have no idea how much I missed you...."

"Cece was so little when you left," Regis said.

"I know," John said. "Agnes, too. All three of you, really."

"Did you see Sisela?" Regis asked.

"I just did, today," John said. He looked down, rocked by a wave of emotion.

"She loves you, Dad. We all do."

John looked out across the marsh, to the lighthouse at Saybrook Point. It was twilight, and its beam flashed in the rose-colored sky. He had done some of his favorite work around lighthouses—driftwood piled up on their beaches, assembled on the sand, photographed and mounted. Wreckage and lifesaving.

"Tell your father about your job," Tom said, jumping in.

John gave him a quick, grateful glance, then smiled at Regis. She looked so pretty, ridiculously young, in her blue uniform.

"Well, it's hard work. Really busy, and sometimes there are idiots, like that guy in line. But mostly it's fun. Families and their kids are always so nice, and my friends stop by to torture me."

"Your aunt worked here for a summer," John said. "We did the same to her."

"Aunt Bernie! No way! Before she became a nun..."

"Yes, before that dark day," Tom said, and John raised his eyebrow and threw him a look.

"She never told me," Regis laughed. "I'll have to tease her."

"She'll love that," Tom said wryly. "Sister Bernadette Ignatius, flipping burgers..."

"Remember coming here when we were little?" Regis asked, eyes glued on John.

"I was just thinking that," John said. "You and I always got scallops."

Regis's eyes filled with tears. "I don't get them anymore," she said.

"Why?" he asked. "You don't like them?"

"They reminded me too much of you. I couldn't eat them while you were gone."

John nodded. He knew exactly what she meant. Every night for six years, locked up, he would have to stay busy just past the dinner hour. Funny, it wasn't eating dinner that got to him—it was the time just afterward, when he would be helping his daughters with homework, or telling them stories, or going outside to look at the stars with them and their mother. He reached over to take Regis's hand.

"I'm home now," he said.

She shook her head, and he saw tears freely running down her cheeks. "You're not, though," she said. "You're not in the house."

"Regis...it'll take some time," he said.

"She won't let you in, will she?"

"It's not your mother's fault."

"Why won't she forgive you? It's not as if you meant to hurt anyone...."

John felt Tom's eyes on him, and he didn't dare look over. His stomach tightened, and he felt sweat running between his shoulder blades. "I shouldn't have gone out...I should have known you'd follow me...." he said carefully. "I think that's what bothers her most."

"But you couldn't have stopped me if you tried," Regis said.

John almost smiled. She was right about that. From the time she was a little girl, Regis had been his shadow. He had taught her to rock climb—cautiously at first, but amazed when she'd scramble faster than him to the top. He had always loved the adventure in life, and Regis had embraced it right along with him.

"We could talk about this all day long," John said. "It won't change what happened, sweetheart."

"I know," she said, and he chilled hearing the desolation in her voice.

"Number twenty-five!" the voice crackled from the speaker.

"That's us," Tom said.

"Let me," John said, jumping up. This was his job—as dad, he always went to pick up the food. Sometimes Regis would scamper alongside him, wanting to help, offering to get the napkins and plastic forks. But today she stayed where she was, sitting with Tom. The fact gave John a tiny pang of grief—another way the world had changed while he was gone.

But he had something else on his mind. Hurrying over, he told the boy at the window his number. When he handed him the tray, John patted his money, to make sure he had enough.

"That's okay," the boy said. "It's already paid for."

"Actually," John said, pushing money across the counter, "can you add on one more thing?"

"Sure," the kid said, taking the order.

It seemed to take forever, even though John knew he had rushed it ahead of the others—maybe because John was waiting with his food, maybe because the boy knew he was with Regis. In either case, five minutes later, John was on his way back to the picnic tables with the tray.

"Hey, you got me a root beer, too!" Regis said, seeing the three tall paper cups.

"I did," John said, handing one to her.

"And what's that?" she asked, staring down at the paper plate, at the crusty roll filled with golden-brown scallops, fries and coleslaw on the side.

"It's a scallop roll," he said, sliding it off the tray, onto the table in front of her. It wasn't much, but he had to give her something.

She looked up at him, and he saw tears glittering there. He bent over to kiss her forehead, kiss the tears away.

"I'm home now, Regis," he said.

Twelve

Agnes knew there was something wrong with her, but she
didn't want to tell anyone. Visions were one thing, but
this was too much, even for her. Ever since hitting her head, she'd
been seeing white wings everywhere. At the kitchen window, when
she was making herself toast; in the bathroom mirror, while she was
washing her face; in the sky at night, reflecting moonlight.

Agnes spent a lot of time looking at the image on her camera. What
was it she had captured? Sometimes she'd stare at the small screen,
expecting a saintly apparition to fly out. Her father knew everything
there was to know about cameras and photography, and she knew
she had to ask him.

"Mom," she said, walking into her mother's studio. Her heart leapt,
because her mother had her sleeves rolled up, painting with total
abandon. The studio was a mess, and even though it was Agnes's job
to clean it, she didn't care.

"What is it, honey? Are you okay?" her mother asked, hardly able
to look away from the canvas she was painting

"I'm fine," Agnes said, hiding a smile.

"Are you sure? How's your headache?"

"It's okay." Agnes made her way through the room. She had always
loved it in here—the smell of paint, the clarity of light streaming
through the north window, Sisela sleeping on the windowsill, and

her mother's happiness everywhere. Back when she was a little girl, she had somehow known that her mother found peace and contentment in her work as she did nowhere else. Maybe that's why she had lobbied to make this her campus job. Grabbing the push broom, she began going over the floor.

"Is Cece still in her room?" her mother asked. "I asked her if she wanted to go for an after-dinner walk on the beach with me, but she said no."

Why do you think she said no? Agnes wanted to ask. Cece was dying to see their father—and so was Agnes. But her mother was being so odd and secretive about him, being so vague about when they were all going to get together. Even going to the beach—instead of going to their usual spot, on the stretch near the wall where Agnes had wiped out, her mother had been steering them to the other end of the beach, the bight where the oysters grew.

"Mom," Agnes began, sweeping around her easel.

"One second, honey. Let me finish this…"

Her mother was squinting at the canvas, squeezing cadmium red onto her palette, using her palette knife to apply a dot of paint. Agnes pushed the broom closer to look. What she saw took her breath away.

It was a painting of Agnes and her father. So clearly—his eyes and hands, her hair and the shape of her shoulders. It showed the night of Agnes's fall, with a canopy of stars overhead and the waves leaving white ripples of lace behind, the sand wide and dark, and Agnes's father holding her like a baby, carrying her up the beach. A ghostly white cat crouched on the mica-sparkled wall. The cadmium red was for Agnes's blood, smeared on her father's shirt.

"Mom," Agnes said again. But instead of waiting for her mother to be ready, she stuck the broom in a corner and walked out of the studio. Her heart was beating so hard, she felt it might break out of her chest. She walked down the hall, into their bedroom. Cece wasn't there, so she put her camera on the shelf and went onto the porch, found her sister curled up on the glider.

"What are you doing?" Cece asked. "I thought you were supposed to be lying down."

"I'm tired of lying down, and I'm bored," Agnes said.

"Bored because you can't go wall-running at night anymore?" Cece asked.

Agnes tried to smile. Something about her mother's painting had shaken her right down to her bones. She kept seeing her father's eyes; the way her mother had painted them, filled with terror and sorrow and tragedy. Those eyes said everything there was to say about their family.

"Mom would probably ground you for life," Cece said, "if you ever went back to that wall again."

"Because I got hurt..."

"No! Because she doesn't want us to see our father! Haven't you noticed? Why is she acting like this?"

Just then Peter's Jeep came squealing up the driveway. Agnes and Cece watched as Regis leaned across the seat to kiss him, then jumped out. He drove away fast, leaving a little cloud of dust under his tires.

"Hey," Regis said, climbing the steps. "How are my girls?"

"Where's Peter going?" Cece asked glumly, instead of answering.

"He's going fishing with the Hubbard's Point kids."

"What about you?"

"I don't feel like going...."

"Why do you look so happy?" Agnes asked, suspicious because Regis was never happy to be left behind by Peter, and picking up on a new radiance in her sister that hadn't been there this morning.

"I'll tell you in a minute, but you first. Why do you look so *unhappy*, both of you?" Regis asked.

"Why won't Mom let us see Dad?" Cece asked. "It's crazy. He's my father, and I love him, and I want to see him."

"She's in there," Agnes said, gesturing at the studio, "painting up a storm."

"Really?" Regis asked. "She hasn't painted at night in such a long time."

"I know! And you should see the painting she's doing," Agnes said. "It might be the best thing she's ever done, and it's of *him*. Carrying me up the beach. But the part you *really* notice is Dad."

"Really?" Regis asked, gazing toward the studio, all lit up, yellow light splashing onto the bushes and grass. "Dad?"

"Yes," Agnes said.

"Well, speaking of Dad, I saw him tonight," Regis said, her eyes shining.

"What happened?" Cece asked, bouncing on her knees.

"It was wonderful," Regis said. "He came to Paradise with Tom…"

"To see you!" Agnes said.

Regis nodded. "He wants to see both of you, too. He's burning to come home, you can just tell. He's trying to do what's right for Mom, but…it's all wrong! Obviously, especially if she's painting him. We have to convince her…"

Just then the headlights rounded the corner, down by the curved stone wall and privet hedge, and a car came into view. Cece gasped, and Regis laughed out loud. It was an old car—a Volvo or a Volkswagen, something round all over—every inch of its surface painted with tiny figures in a million bright colors.

"Who is it?" Cece asked.

"It's the archangel," Regis said, smiling.

"Brendan," Agnes said as he got out of the car.

His bright red hair glinted in the porch light. He had a smile big enough for everyone, but eyes only for Agnes. She felt herself blush as he came closer, not looking away.

"Hi," Agnes said.

"Hi, Agnes," he said.

"Hey, Brendan," Regis said. "What brings you out here?"

"I had to come see about Agnes," he said.

"Perfect timing," Regis said. "Cece and I were just going inside."

"No, we weren't! We were just talking about Dad, and—"

"C'mon, Cece," Regis said, hand on her shoulder. "I'll play you in chess."

"You always beat me. It's no fun."

"I'm the oldest sister, which means you have to listen to me. Besides, if you want to be in my wedding, you have to toe the line."

"You're being cruel and unusual!" Cece wailed, but she followed Regis into the house.

Alone on the porch with Brendan, Agnes straightened her head bandage. She hoped she looked okay. She sort of wanted to throttle Regis for leaving her alone with the boy from the hospital, and she also sort of wanted to thank her. Her head was spinning. The dizziness made her wobble, even though she was sitting down, and she touched her forehead to steady herself.

"You okay?" Brendan asked, leaning over to touch her shoulder.

"I'm fine. I get dizzy."

"That's not uncommon, after a closed head injury."

"A what? I thought I had a fractured skull."

"You do," Brendan said, sitting beside her. "Luckily it was just a linear fracture; the more serious injury was the concussion. You sustained a blunt-force trauma by striking that rock. That's what caused your seizure, and what's making you feel dizzy now. It will pass, as you heal."

"You sound like a doctor," she said.

"That's what I want to be," he said. "I just took my MCATs."

"Your what?"

"Medical school admissions tests. I went to nursing school first, because that's what I could afford. I knew I wanted to go into medicine. I don't like to see people suffer; I want to make them better."

Agnes looked into his eyes, saw the fire there. She thought of how Regis called him an archangel, wondered if there was some truth there. Agnes had been waiting for a vision for so long, she had just about given up hope. But gazing at Brendan, she felt ripples under her skin.

"Who do you know who suffered?" she asked.

"My brother," he said. "He had leukemia."

"I'm so sorry," she said. Without even having to think, she reached for his hand.

"It was when we were young. I was seven, and he was two. He had just started running—not walking, *running*. And he could throw…

man, he could whip a ball at you like he was Roger Clemens. His name was Patrick, but we called him Paddy."

Agnes held her feelings inside. She knew the power of nicknames. They were tribal, like drumbeats, calling you straight to your family campfire. Glancing at the window, she saw Regis and Cece peeking out, to see what was going on. When they were small, her father had called Regis "Owl," because she never slept. The memory came flying back.

"What happened to Paddy?"

"He got sick. We didn't know what it was at first; it seemed like a really bad cold that wouldn't go away. But it just kept getting worse, so my mom took him to the ER. They tested his blood, and that's when we knew."

"And you tried to help him..."

"As much as I could. I'd play catch with him, even when he was in his bed. But he bruised so easily. They made me stop—the ball hurt him if he missed." Brendan paused. "There were some periods when they wouldn't let me in his room at all. He was so susceptible to infection."

Agnes blinked, imagining the brothers being kept apart, how hard it must have been.

"I wanted to give him my bone marrow; brothers can sometimes donate for each other, you know? But we weren't compatible. That's how I found out I was adopted—my parents couldn't conceive for a long time, so they adopted me."

"You didn't know before?"

Brendan shook his head. "We're Irish. That means we don't talk about anything."

Agnes nodded. That sounded very familiar.

"Paddy lost his hair from the chemo," Brendan said. "I gave him a Red Sox cap. He was just learning to talk, and he'd say 'me hat,' and smile, pointing at his baseball cap. He was so proud of it. When he died, we buried him with it."

"I'm so sorry he died," Agnes said.

"I know. Me too. He was the greatest kid."

"He's the reason you're going to be a doctor," Agnes said. "And help lots of other kids."

"I hope so," Brendan said.

"Your parents must be so proud of you."

He shook his head. "They can't see it."

"What do you mean?"

Brendan was looking down at her hand, still holding his. His gaze felt like a laser beam on her skin. She felt trills across her nerve endings, all up and down her arm. When he raised his eyes to meet hers, she felt the same tingling sensation in her face, in her eyes. "There are two ways of dealing with grief," he said. "One is to open up to it— to love people and the world more than ever, because you know how short life is, and how precious. The other way..."

Agnes waited, on the edge of her seat. She thought of her own family, knowing that they had faced grief all their own, that her father's going to jail had been the death of how they had once been. She had felt so abandoned, as if all the world's goodness had drained away, and as if bad things were closing in, waiting to harm them even more.

"The other way is bad," she said. "You feel so shut out, and alone. Closed off from help. It's so dark."

"Yes," he said. "It's like prison."

Agnes felt a sharp pain in her heart, thinking of her father behind the Portlaoise walls, locked in, away from everyone he loved. What did Brendan know about that?

"Do you mean like actual prison?" she asked. "With bars and locks?"

He shook his head. "No," he said. "I mean the kind you put yourself in. Anyone can go to prison. Anyone. You can take drugs, like some people. Or you can drink booze, like my parents. You build walls, lock yourself into your misery, until it becomes the only thing you know. You're alone in there with your demons, and the people you love can't get in, and you and the demons can't get out."

"Your parents have been in there since Paddy died?"

"Pretty much. They try to get sober now and then, but they always go back to the bottle. It's so much easier for them. See, once you get used to living that way, all numb and locked in, real life can start to feel really raw. If they ever really decided to stop drinking, they'd have to face the truth about Paddy. That he's gone. Their real son is gone, and I'm left."

"You're their real son, too," Agnes said. "If they adopted you, you are...."

"I wish they saw it that way."

"You're as Irish as they come. That red hair."

"Yeah," he said. "They made sure of it. Irishness was a requirement of the people at Catholic Charities and Adoption Services, they told me that much when they told me the truth, after Paddy got sick. Before they hit the bottle, and locked themselves in. Time passes people by in prison..."

"I know," Agnes said, lowering her head, thinking of her father. All the time they'd missed together, and all the time they were still missing...

"Anyway, I came to see how you are," Brendan said abruptly. "And because of what you said that night, when I was with you in the ER."

Agnes smiled, but inside she felt unsettled. What had she said? She tried to concentrate and remember. She could feel the bright lights shining in her eyes, the doctors suturing her head, the pressure of her headache, bursting at her temples. She remembered weeping, wanting her parents. Then darkness, and a tunnel, a feeling she was falling. She was dying.

Her heart stopping. Black all around. A voice, a clear voice. What had it said? And what did she say in response?

"You," she began. "You want to be a doctor...one who helps children, who treats leukemia?"

"No," he said. "I want to be a psychiatrist. I want to treat families."

"But Paddy..."

"Paddy died," Brendan said. "But we're still alive. My parents and I. You and your family. I want to keep the living alive, keep them from dying in prison, here on earth."

"What did I say?" Agnes whispered. "When I was in the ER?"

His arm encircled her, so protectively, with such gentleness.

"You said you've been praying for a vision," Brendan said. "To help you know what to do. You said you'd been wishing for one ever since you were twelve, ever since your father went to jail. And you asked me to help you."

"Help me what?"

"Bring your family back together."

Thirteen

"M om, can we invite Dad for dinner?" Regis asked, and watched.

Her mother didn't look up from the sink, where she was washing tomatoes from the convent garden. Running each one under the water, holding it there under the cool stream, placing it on a folded-up paper towel to drain. Her gaze flickered, looking out the window. One little question, and her mother was lost.

"Mom?"

"Not tonight, Regis," her mother said.

"Why not? He's back, right there on the beach, so why can't he come for dinner?"

"It's complicated," her mother said.

Regis stared. Now, lifting another tomato, her mother's hands were trembling. Regis could see it from all the way across the counter. She had a hard time holding on—there, now she had a grip, and she held the tomato under the water and there, onto the towel.

"I'm twenty, Mom. I'm getting married. I think I can handle hearing."

Now her mother started on the basil. A big, shaggy bunch of it, bright green, with its sharp licorice smell. One of the novices had brought it over that morning, along with the tomatoes and some zucchini. Regis had answered the door. The young nun hadn't been much older than Regis, if at all. Her hair was hidden by a white veil.

"Mom?" Regis prodded.

"I don't like to bother you girls with my problems," her mother said. "But this is hard."

"Dad coming home is *hard*?" Regis asked.

"Don't be sarcastic, Regis Maria."

"I'm sorry." Regis exhaled. She wanted everything to happen faster: her parents to get along and be happy, Agnes to heal completely, her own wedding day to arrive. She wanted life to flow in harmony, the way it was supposed to. The nightmare of the last six years was over, wasn't it? A sense of injustice brought sharp tears to her eyes.

"No, honey," her mother said, seeing. "I'm sorry. I know it's hard for you. It's just that your father and I have a few things to work out."

"But you're not even trying," Regis said.

"What makes you think that?" her mother asked. "I'm trying, and so is he. We've talked."

"*Yelled*, you mean. Everyone heard you two fighting on the beach. Your voices carried on the wind."

Her mother looked a little shocked at that. "Really?"

Regis nodded. She dabbed angrily at her eyes. "You don't even know what's going on," she said.

"What do you mean?"

"Mom, you haven't been this happy in over six years. You're in your studio all the time now, working away. The music's on. We can hear it coming from your studio at night, and it makes us feel so good. And then we go in to see your work, and it's *amazing*."

"It is?" her mother asked, frowning.

"Yes! And it started after Dad got back."

Her mother stared down at the tomatoes and basil. Then, to Regis's surprise, her mother began to talk. Really talk.

"Regis, your father and I fell in love when we were very young. He was so creative, full of passion for life. I didn't know artists like him existed." She paused, trying to come up with the right words. "He launched himself into life, and took me with him. He incorporated his art into our marriage, and everything, even a walk over the hill, became a big adventure."

"That's Dad," Regis murmured, thinking of how cold and dull the world had looked without him.

"But honey," her mother said, "it just wore me down. I spent so much time worrying about him. It was like living on thin ice. I never knew when he'd fall through—and once you got big enough to go with him, and you always did, I felt you'd fall through with him."

"He wouldn't have let me," Regis said.

"Think about what happened in Ireland," her mother said. "You were so traumatized, you didn't stop shaking for two days. You still have nightmares. Do you know how often you cry in your sleep?"

"That was because I missed Dad," Regis said. "Because he was in Ireland, and we couldn't visit him enough."

"It's because you nearly fell off a cliff into the sea," her mother said. "And because you saw him kill a man."

"*That's* why Dad can't come for dinner?" Regis asked.

Her mother looked at her as if she were just a child—exasperated and frustrated.

"You're forgetting!" Regis said. "You're painting again. Deep inside, you know that's because your heart is finally whole again. Dad fills the world with color. He makes everything so vivid and beautiful, and exciting. You love that as much as we do."

Her mother's eyes darkened, as if Regis had just struck a nerve.

"When Sister Julie came over earlier, bringing the tomatoes and basil," Regis went on, "I was trying to figure out how old she was. Twenty, twenty-one at the oldest, so pure and holy in her white habit. I looked at her face and thought of Agnes. My sweet holy sister...who nearly killed herself looking for a miracle."

"What are you talking about?"

"Are you kidding, Mom? Don't you know? Agnes is desperate to have a vision, like Aunt Bernie. She thinks that divine intervention is the only way to bring the family together. We want Dad to come home."

"Oh, Regis," her mother said.

"All I know is, Peter and I will *never* be like this," Regis said. "We'll stay together forever."

"I hope you do," her mother said steadily in a way that made Regis feel furious—because deep down, she thought her mother felt the opposite.

Regis grabbed the car keys and walked out of the kitchen. As she drove down the long drive, she thought of how Gothic the Academy looked. Even on this bright summer day, it was all stone, all gray and dark and imposing. The main building's slate roof glinted like cold steel in the hot sun. The chapel's steeple looked like a black needle piercing the sky. A group of nuns, walking from the convent toward the vineyard, looked like shadows in their black habits. Although Regis loved the nuns, had always felt as if they were extra aunts, she shivered now.

She had said her father filled the world with color. Well, not *this* world. Regis had always loved living here, but right now it just seemed lonely and full of mystery and disappointment. She floored it, pulling out of the dusty drive, and drove the two and a half miles from the Academy to Hubbard's Point. She stopped under the railroad trestle to speak to the guard. He waved her through, and she took the first two lefts.

This section of Hubbard's Point was built directly on rock ledge slanting into Long Island Sound. The cottages were exquisitely proportioned, wood-shingled with candy-colored shutters, shaded by white pines and scrub oaks, surrounded by small, brilliant gardens. They were built close together, as if somehow the original builders had decided that all the inhabitants should be best friends.

The families here all seemed so happy. They barbequed together. They had clambakes and birthday parties. Their kids rode bikes in wild packs, just *shrieking* with fun. The parents all went to the beach together. The dads all mowed the lawns and painted the cottages, shared ladders, hedge clippers, things like that. The parents here stayed together; everyone was so normal.

Regis's mouth felt dry. She felt like an outsider everywhere she went. At home, with her mother, and here, at Hubbard's Point. Her mother had grown up at this beach. Things here felt so safe. Maybe her mother never should have left, if that was what she wanted so badly.

The kids here had their first kisses with each other. Regis knew that Peter had had girlfriends before. One from two summers ago, with whom he had exchanged love letters. She lived in New York; Regis had recently learned that Alicia was a friend of hers. To Regis, she sounded like the most sophisticated girl ever: she went to the same school as young movie stars, and she had once ridden on a motorcycle with Josh Hartnett. Her father, a surgeon, operated on celebrities. He had once golfed with Derek Jeter.

In her worst moments, Regis wondered why Peter would want her, after being with the girl from New York. When she'd asked him, he'd just looked at her as if she was a sweet idiot. "Because I love you," he'd said. "You're different from anyone I know."

Her stomach flipped. Was that why her mother had married her father? Because he was different? Regis knew that she and her father were alike in so many ways—her mother had been right, about liking to walk on thin ice. Well, what if Peter got sick of it, the way her mother had? What if Regis wore him out?

But then she would remember how much he had loved running in the rain, jumping into the bay. She'd seen the emotion in his eyes, known that she had unlocked more love and wildness than he had ever known.

Regis had been good for so long. Holding herself back—no cliff diving, no steeple climbing, no across-the-Sound swims. Right now she felt she might explode from being so good.

Parking at the curb, she climbed out. She heard music blaring from his upstairs window, knew he was home, so she picked up a pebble and flung it upward. Just then she noticed his neighbor, Mrs. Healey, standing on the other side of her hedge, watering her garden. They waved, and Regis smiled.

"Hi," Regis said.

"He's in there," Mrs. Healey said, nodding up at his window.

"I just, I just…" Regis began, embarrassed.

"You think it's more romantic that way," Mrs. Healey said, dimpling as her smile grew. "I understand."

Regis nodded, quivering and confused. She wondered whether she could ever be like Mrs. Healey: wearing her husband's shirt over her turquoise bathing suit, flip-flops on her feet, watering a square of bright pink petunias, not tormented. Was angst a Sullivan family specialty?

"Regis," Peter said, coming out the back door.

She was flooded with relief at the sight of him, and nearly burst into tears. He was six foot two, tan, with dark hair and just the right kind of muscles. He put his arms around her. His lips brushed hers, and her body turned to jelly in his arms.

"What's wrong?" he asked. "You're shaking."

"I'm just so glad to see you," she said, fighting back tears. "You have no idea how crazy it is at home."

"I think I have an idea," he said. "Considering you're dealing with a convict for a father."

She cringed, as if he'd slapped her. He didn't mean it, she told herself. He just didn't know her father yet—no one did, because he was in exile on the beach.

"How was your fishing last night?" Regis asked, to make things normal again.

"Stripers are running. We drank a lot of beer, caught a lot of fish, a good time was had by all."

She grabbed his hand, wanting to pull something out of him, the love and understanding she needed so badly right now. She started to run, and he followed along, down shady Coveview Road, to the place where the train tracks ran along the narrow private beach. The sun was shining, but she knew if only she could get him alone, to where they could be on their own, they could recapture the feeling of that magical rainy day.

Scrambling up the bank, they watched a flock of sandpipers scatter along the tide line. They walked along the railroad tracks, past a tidal marsh, golden with silt and tall grass. Regis looked down and saw blue crabs glinting in the shallow water, scuttling into hiding holes. As she and Peter approached the high, rusty train bridge, her heart skittered. The bridge spanned Devil's Hole, the swift, rocky creek spinning down below in wild swirls and eddies as the tide rushed in.

"When's the next train?" he asked nervously.

"Because you want us to get on board?" she asked, squeezing his hand.

"The tracks are dangerous," he said.

"If something happens, we'll die together," she said, and he gave her a dark look.

This was the scariest place; if a train had come before, they could have just run down the bank to the beach on one side, or the marsh on the other. But if a roaring locomotive came now, when they were on the bridge—they'd have no choice but to jump into Devil's Hole. Regis's heart was pounding. She had jumped in before, and felt the powerful, primal urge to do it now.

Looking both ways and listening for approaching trains, Peter ran as fast as he could across the high, narrow bridge. Regis watched him go and felt disappointment; she had wanted him to feel the thrill with her.

The railroad ties seemed splintery and ancient. Looking down between them, Regis saw straight into the violent current below. Even the bravest Hubbard's Point boys, the ones who would sneak onto the catwalk under the Connecticut River bridge at midnight, hang from cables as long as their arms could stand it, then drop into the deep middle of the river, wouldn't dare jump into Devil's Hole. She felt like impressing Peter and doing a cannonball.

But she didn't. She just leapt onto the smooth granite boulder, leading him up the sloping gray rocks to a pine-covered crest. Even now, the cliff was littered with fallen limbs, stripped of their bark by the harsh sea wind. At the very top, overgrown with vines and small oak trees, was Sachem Cave. Most people didn't even know it existed, but Regis's father had shown it to the world in his art.

They crawled under the ledge. Once inside, they held each other, her heart beating hard and fast. Peter felt like stone.

"Isn't this great?" she asked.

"Why does it always have to be..." he started, trailing off.

"Have to be...what?" she asked, afraid to hear.

"Nothing," he said, pulling her close, kissing her.

They lay down on the cool rock floor, gazing into each other's eyes and starting to feel something like calm again. Regis pressed her lips to the sun-warm skin above his collarbone, and she tasted the salt of his sweat. She wanted to drown in his arms, right here and now, and never leave the cave.

"Who went fishing with you?" she asked.

"A bunch of guys," he said.

"Just guys?" she asked.

"Regis, cut it out."

"Just tell me," Regis said. "Did the New York girl go?" Insecurity, lodged deep inside, had started bubbling up.

"Regis, she's not the girl I want to marry. You are."

"Did your parents like her more than me?"

"Stop."

"Is that why they're upset we're getting married?" she asked. She couldn't help herself.

"You know the reason. It's because we're young. They think we should wait."

"Your parents are so happy," she said. "And they were each other's first boyfriend and girlfriend."

"Yeah, but they keep telling me they didn't get married till after law school," he said, holding her, seeming angry as he stroked her back.

"But wasn't that a waste?" Regis asked. "When you think of all the time they could have had together but didn't?"

"Well, I guess they were going to class and everything."

"We're going to go to class," she said, kissing him, then pulling her head back so she could look into his eyes. "But we'll be together at night. We'll have dinners, and breakfasts, and the whole night in between."

"We could just wait," he said. "Three more years, till we graduate."

"Three years!" Regis said, stung.

"I'm not saying we should," he said quickly. "I'm just telling you what they said. You know they'll help us out with money and all, but they keep asking all these practical questions. Insurance, and a car, stuff like that."

She shook her head, and the movement dislodged hot tears. She closed her eyes, to keep the tears inside. Who cared about those things? Didn't Peter know that it was impossible to make up for lost time? Three years was half of six years; every day, every minute in life was all its own, and could never be replaced with another.

"When you love someone," she said, with her eyes shut tight, barely recognizing her own voice, "you want to be together whenever you can. If you want it badly enough, you just make the practical things work out."

"Regis…"

"Insurance, cars," she said. "Who cares about them? Love fills the world with color, and if you lose someone you love, one day you'll wake up and the world will be black and white."

Peter touched her cheek, kissed her mouth. Everything was so smooth and hot, and she and Peter were flowing into each other.

"We could be doing this at Little Beach," he said when they broke apart. "A whole lot easier. And it would be just as colorful."

"But it wouldn't be as magical," she said. "It wouldn't be so private—and we wouldn't have this view." She pointed over the treetops at the Sound, an explosion of light and every shade of blue—azure, slate, turquoise, navy, cobalt. Sunlight sparkled on the surface, and white birds, seagulls and terns, wheeled in slow circles through the bright sky.

"It's just…" he said. "Just this… why does everything with you have to be such a big ordeal?"

"Ordeal?"

"Walking on the railroad tracks. Crossing Devil's Hole. There are plenty of places to go on Hubbard's Point. Little Beach, the marsh, even the cemetery. But you always want to do the most dangerous thing."

Regis squeezed her eyes tight. *Thin ice*, her mother had said. But why couldn't Peter feel the sweetness and magic, just like that day in the rain?

"Is it because of your father?" Peter asked. "Because he brought you here that time? Why do you want to be like him so much?"

"It's not that I *want* to," Regis whispered. "It's that I *am*."

Regis closed her eyes. Peter was right: without her father, she wouldn't even know this place existed. He had once climbed this cliff to build one of his wood and stone sculptures.

"I want to go with you, Daddy," she'd begged. Her mother and Agnes sat on the curved beach; he had his camera bag slung over his shoulder, getting ready to carry his supplies across the tracks and bridge. "You need me to help you build the castle."

"I know, sweetheart," he'd said. "And I want you to. You help me build the best things in the world. But remember what I told you about children walking on railroad tracks?"

Regis had shivered, because she did remember. When she was five, her father had held her in his arms, pointing at the rail bed and telling her that when he and his sister were young, a friend of theirs had been killed walking the tracks.

"Then don't you go either!"

"I'm an adult," he'd said. "And this is my work. Look at all that fallen timber up there, caught in the rocks. I want to make something fast, today, and take the picture just before sunset. Won't it be pretty, with the whole Point stretching out into the bay?"

"Then you should take me!"

"Regis," he'd said. "There are some places fathers can't bring their daughters. I don't like it, but it's the way life is. I told you about that boy I knew, who got hit by the train. I want you to promise me that no matter what happens, you'll never walk on the tracks."

"I won't promise unless you do," Regis had said.

"John," her mother had said, and even then Regis had heard the edge in her voice. "Maybe your daughter has a point."

Oh, Regis remembered the look in her father's eyes as he'd smiled back. Those glinting blue eyes had been so happy. Regis had watched him waver; take in his wife and daughters, then sweep his gaze across the train bridge, up the granite cliff. He had wanted to promise, but he couldn't; he chose his work, and the risks that came with it, instead. Or maybe it was his love of those risks that had made him choose that work in the first place.

Regis had had to make her own choice: stay safe on the beach with her mother, or climb to the sky with her father. She loved them both equally, but she knew that adventure was in her nature, part of her spirit.

She remembered that day every time she crossed the high trestle. She thought of it every time she looked at the photo he had taken that day. Sepia-toned, it appeared as if it had been taken a century ago. The shot showed the fallen, wind-silvered pine boughs he had gathered and made into a castle, the flat rocks he'd stacked like crenellations at the mouth of the cave.

He must have set up his camera just inside. The photo had a feeling of shelter. Yet it also had a sense of outlook; as her father had planned, the Point jutted out into the cove's golden water, giving the right side of the picture a solid edge. His sculpture reminded some people of an earthly sandcastle, others of something more spiritual. One review had used the phrase "yearning toward heaven." Aunt Bernie said the tower was Celtic, like a standing stone or dolmen. To Regis, it had always been a ruined castle, just like the one he eventually found at Ballincastle.

"Didn't you learn your lesson, over in Ireland?" Peter asked now. "You could have died there—on a cliff that was probably just like this one. Your father didn't protect you then, and he ended up in jail."

"That's *why* he ended up in jail," Regis retorted. "Protecting me!"

"He killed someone. My father called a friend of his in Dublin. He looked the case up, and he said your father pled guilty. He didn't even try to claim self-defense. He beat that guy, then pushed him off the edge."

"Your father checked *up* on him?"

"What do you expect, Regis? My dad's a lawyer—of course he was going to find out the details. That's what court documents are for."

"Your father wasn't there," Regis said, shaking. "And neither were you. You don't know what happened!"

"How am I supposed to know what happened," Peter said, "when you won't tell me? You've never talked about it. Never told me about that day, about Gregory White..."

"Stop it!" Regis said. "And don't ever call him a convict again, like you did before."

"But he is one. And he should have done a better job of keeping you safe."

He did, Regis thought. More than anyone knows... She shook her head. Where did that thought come from? It was like a half-remembered dream, shimmering in her mind, just beyond consciousness.

"Never mind Ireland," Peter went on. "Even this place—instead of letting you follow him up the cliff, he should have been happy with you staying on the beach with your mother."

"He didn't let me," she said. "That's the whole point."

Regis wished she'd never told Peter. When she had begged her father to let her help him build his wood and rock castle, he had told her to stay with her mother and Agnes and play on the beach instead.

And then he had set off. Regis had stood there, watching him get smaller and smaller, walking down the railroad tracks, his folded-up tripod over his shoulder. She had built him a sandcastle, waiting for him to return. Her mother and Agnes had drizzled wet sand for the turrets. Twenty minutes later, the waves had washed it away.

Just now, her gaze fell upon a piece of wood, scoured of its bark and needles, weathered silver and white as a bone. Regis wondered how long it had been there, whether maybe her father had gathered it as part of his castle tower thirteen years ago.

"I love you, Regis," Peter said. "I want to take care of you. Instead of scaling cliffs, I want to stay on the beach and build sandcastles in the sun with you," he said. "What do you say to that?"

"I'd say sandcastles don't last," she whispered, looking deep into his clear blue eyes as a train whistle sounded in the distance, droning high and long and mournful, seeming to announce that something terrible was about to happen.

Fourteen

One thing about running a convent, school, and vineyard, Sister Bernadette was used to making lots of decisions and, to a large degree, running a lot of lives. She set the curriculum, holiday schedules, prayer times, fasting policy, dates of release for the new varietals.

Certainly, she couldn't affect the weather—a dry spell made for sweet grapes, and that could wreak havoc with the chardonnay. Just as too much rain could cause root mold, and once an entire hillside of vines had been compromised. Still, she had gotten Tom to help her dig drainage trenches that year, and the crop was saved. As she always told the incoming freshmen, "God steers, but you row. And rowing is what will get you into the colleges of your choice." And the grape harvest of your dreams...

Right now, with dust covering her habit and dirt under her fingernails, she stood on the highest hill in the vineyard, gazing down at her brother working on the beach below, and knew that he was rowing in the wrong direction. Just then she heard creaking, and turned to see Tom wheeling his wheelbarrow up the path. She tried to duck behind a leafed-out stretch of vines, but he'd already seen her.

"Morning, Sister," Tom called.

"Hi, Tom," she said.

"What are you up to?" he asked, letting his wheelbarrow clatter as he left the path to climb the rise.

"Just cutting back the vines," she said. "I think we're going to have a good yield this year."

"Yep," he said. "Looks that way. Is the irrigation system working better?"

"Seems to be. I wish we'd get some rain, though. I'm worried about the well running dry."

"I've got my eye on it," Tom said.

"When your great-grandfather had it dug, I don't think he envisioned supplying water for a whole community of nuns running a school and a vineyard."

"He would have thought it was far-out. Two of his favorite things: nuns and booze."

"It's not 'booze,' you philistine," she said, smiling sharply. "It's 'fine wine.'"

"Who are you calling a philistine?" Tom asked, stepping closer.

Bernie stepped back, turned away. The sea wind swept up the hill, blew her veil into her face. She felt Tom standing beside her, following her gaze down the hill. She brushed the veil out of her eyes.

"Look at my brother," she said. He stood on the beach by the broken rock. He had wrapped the biggest pieces in chains, hauled them above the tide line. Bernie had watched him go at it all day. Now he lifted one onto his shoulder, stumbling slightly as he heaved it onto the pile.

"He claims he's building a new sculpture, but come on," Tom said. "Isn't there something you could tell him, get him to 'lay his burden down'?"

"I wish I could. I wish I could talk sense into both him and Honor."

"Really? What would you tell them?"

"I'd tell them to stop fighting what they know to be true. They love each other. They have three children..."

"You saying children should hold people together?" Tom asked.

She glared at him. "I'm not saying that," she said.

"Sounds like you just did," Tom said.

"Why are you suddenly making things so difficult?" she asked. "We've been working together for all these years. Day in and day out. I see you all over the grounds—you keep the place running for me. Never a problem. Until now. What's going on?"

He shook his head, staring down at John. "It's seeing them throw it all away," he said. "John and Honor."

"What does that have to do with us?" Bernie asked. Tom gave her a dark sidelong glance that made the blood rise into her face. She refused to back down though, and stared right back. "Answer me, Thomas Kelly."

"Look," he said, grabbing her shoulders. "You might get a lot of mileage out of being mother superior here. But that gets nowhere with me. You might be Sister Bernadette Ignatius to everyone else, but to me you're Bernie. My Bernie..."

She was frozen, unable to speak.

"Isn't love supposed to be holy?" he asked. "Even as religious as you are, is there anything more sacred?"

"No," she said softly.

"Then what more do I need to say?"

"Love is different for everyone," she said. "I love God. That's the choice I made, and it's the life I've chosen."

"I know that," he said, still holding her shoulders, staring into her eyes. She felt him trying to shake her loose from something.... Suddenly he let her go. "I'm sorry."

"That's okay," she said.

"It's just, having John back home. It makes me want us all to be the way we used to be...remember that, Bernie? When we were all young, and we'd play on these hills? Remember we sneaked wine out of my grandfather's wine cellar and drank it behind the wall?"

"I remember," she said.

"Back then, you broke the rules as much as anyone."

"You're right," Bernie said, and looked away.

"I thought we'd all raise our children together."

"You should have gotten married," Bernie whispered. "You still should...you can still have a family."

"Really?" he asked. "You wouldn't mind seeing me with my wife, pushing our kid in a stroller?"

"I wouldn't mind," she said. "I want that for you."

He looked down at her, and she tried to ease the stress from her face. She felt it in her whole body, but all that mattered was that Tom didn't see it.

"Ah, Bernie. This is my family," Tom said, looking around, taking in the Academy grounds, the vineyard, the beach, and Bernie standing beside him. She felt tears slip from her eyes.

Tom reached over. He used his thumb to wipe the tears from her cheeks.

"You have dirt all over your face," he said. "Doesn't the mother superior have better things to do than clipping back grapevines?"

"What's more important than tending the earth?" she asked.

"We've got to do something about those two," he said, gesturing down at John.

"They're in God's hands," Bernie said.

Tom squinted, shaking his head. "That's not good enough," he said. "Look at the mess he made with us. We've got to help them, Bern."

Together, they looked down at John, standing on one of the pieces of rock, smashing it over and over again with the sledgehammer. Every strike seemed to hit Bernie in the abdomen. She folded her hands, as if in prayer. The truth was, she was folding them in self-protection. Protection from the feelings she had had so long, that she felt just might kill her.

"John's work has always saved him," she said. "He loves doing it so much, it keeps him going."

"He's going to wreck his body," Tom said.

Bernie stared down at her brother. He had revolutionized the art world with his freewheeling spirit, the way he built temporary sculptures, incorporated elements of nature and light, photographing them with his handheld camera, then letting the wind and sea take them away. It all sounded so peaceful, but watching her brother now, she felt the violence.

"He hates himself," she whispered. "For what he let happen in Ireland."

"Are you talking about your brother?" Tom asked. "Or yourself?"

"We Sullivans have made a mess of things," she said.

"Well, you didn't do it alone," Tom said.

She knew Tom was right, and she knew what she had to do. Touching his cheek, she felt her hand trembling. He grabbed her wrist and held it. He had always tried to hold on, when she had always prayed to let go. She closed her eyes, backed away. When she turned to run down the hill toward the convent, she thought she heard someone call her.

It wasn't Tom, and it wasn't God. It was the voice Bernie heard in her sleep, and she wondered again—as she had so often over the years—whether the time had come for her to answer the call.

It was Tuesday, and Agnes was being silent, sitting with the cat on her lap. Honor found it frustrating on even the most ordinary Tuesdays, but how was she supposed to monitor how Agnes was feeling if she wouldn't say anything? Regis's words, about Agnes seeking a vision to save their family, still stung.

She took her daughter's temperature, peeked under the dressing to make sure the wound looked okay, made sure she ate lunch and drank plenty of water. They had a doctor's appointment in two days, and Honor was glad to know they had an MRI scheduled.

"Does it hurt?" Honor asked.

Agnes shook her head.

"Have you been feeling dizzy today?"

Again, Agnes shook her head, petting Sisela.

"What about that vibrating feeling you had yesterday—when you thought you were about to have another seizure? Has that come back?"

Agnes shrugged.

Honor exhaled. "Agnes, I know you feel that silence is a sort of prayer, and I try to respect it. The problem is, because you've had a head injury, I really need to know what's going on. If you won't do it for yourself, do it for me—alleviate my stress. Tell me how you're feeling."

"I'm fine," Agnes mouthed, but not a sound came from her lips.

Honor placed her hand on her daughter's shoulder. She was seated at the window, holding Sisela and gazing out across the field that led to the wall where the whole thing had started. Just then the phone rang, and Honor answered.

"Hello?" she said.

"Hi, Mrs. Sullivan. It's Brendan—may I please speak with Agnes?"

Honor threw her a look. "Funny you should ask, Brendan..." At the sound of his name, Agnes looked up eagerly. "She's sitting right here."

Honor hoped that Brendan's calling would make Agnes decide to talk, but instead, she just motioned at the telephone and shook her head.

"I'm sorry, Brendan," Honor said. "She is here, it's true, but she doesn't talk on Tuesdays. And it's a Tuesday."

He laughed. "Okay," he said. "Well, if she doesn't talk, does she listen?"

"Yes," Honor said, watching Agnes, her daughter's shining eyes.

"Would you mind handing her the phone?" Brendan asked.

"Not at all," Honor said. She gave the receiver to Agnes and grabbed her painting smock. When she left the room to go into her studio, Agnes was just sitting there, phone to her ear, saying nothing, petting Sisela with her free hand.

Heading into her studio, Honor went straight to her easel. She uncovered her palette, stared at the painting. She had to work on John's eyes. They were too calm, when her memory of that night had them wild, fiery. As she started working she felt her heart pounding.

The tap-tap-tap that came from beyond the hill's crest was John, working down on the beach. The sound of metal striking rock rang in her bones. He had already destroyed the boulder, but now he was turning it into art. She could only wonder what soaring composition would come of it, what topsy-turvy masterpiece would result.

She worked on her own painting, touching the brush to John's eyes. There. A sweep of blue, sharpening his gaze. But it wasn't enough. Maybe the blue was too soft—she added a dot of black, mixed it with her palette knife. Now the clarity was gone—she's pushed it too far. No painting could ever do justice to her husband's spirit. She had tried, over and over.

If only she could capture his passion on canvas. The secret had always seemed to be in his eyes. The clear color, the direct gaze, the way they reflected the sky. He saw so much in the world, but it was never enough. He always wanted to see more—and he wanted to go everywhere, and touch everything, and bring it home for Honor.

What had Regis said? That he filled the world with color... It was so true. That was John. He made her feel so alive. Listening to him work on the rock, she felt a sort of companionship. He was right out there, bringing his artistic dynamism to their own beach, to that rock he'd reduced to a pile of rubble.

Now, staring at her painting, at the eyes, she shivered. That's where it got so tricky. Her husband was a brilliant sculptor and photographer; he had discovered his own way to experience and represent the world. But it included smashing a rock to smithereens during the course of one night. That was John as well....

Hearing footsteps on the flagstone walk, Honor looked up from her painting and saw Bernie standing in the doorway, staring at her. Her black habit was streaked with dust; she was obviously just down from the fields. But she held an envelope in her hand, so she must have been to her office....

"Bernie, are you all right?" Honor asked, alarmed.

"I'm fine," she said, advancing into the big, bright room, blinking. Honor found herself blocking her view of the easel, steering her over toward the chairs by the window.

"What brings you here?" Honor asked. "Would you like some iced tea?"

"Sure," Bernie said. "I've just been up in the vineyard, and I'm pretty thirsty."

Honor went over to the little refrigerator, pulled out the plastic container she had filled that morning. She filled two tall glasses, handed one to her sister-in-law. "Red Rose tea, half a lemon, a splash of orange juice, fresh mint from the herb garden, and one small bottle of ginger ale," she said.

"My mother's iced tea recipe," Bernie said, sipping. "Nothing tastes better on a summer day."

"Or takes us back to when we were kids."

Bernie held up her hand. "Please," she said. "I've had enough trips down memory lane for one day."

"Were you talking to John?"

"Tom," Bernie said.

"Oh," Honor said, watching Bernie bow her head. She might have been praying, but when she raised her eyes, Honor could see she was blushing instead.

"Our old friend Tom sometimes forgets himself," Bernie said. "He forgets that times, and people, change. He forgets that I took vows, and that he's my employee."

"I guess he counts on friends staying the same," Honor said.

"But they don't necessarily," Bernie said. "Do they?"

"What are you talking about?"

"If friends stayed the same, you and John would be together now. You were the best friends ever."

"We all were," Honor said. "You and I were best friends before I fell in love with your brother. And John and Tom were, before Tom fell in love with you."

"You and I are still right there in the best friend department. At least I hope we are," Bernie said. She gave Honor a gentle smile, and Honor felt grateful for it.

"I'm so glad, Bernie. Thank you."

"So, friend to friend, what's the deal with you and John?"

"I don't know what you mean."

Bernie, in that instant, became Sister Bernadette Ignatius, the nun that all the students feared: the one who knew all, saw all, and expected everyone to meet the highest standards. She tilted her head and narrowed her eyes, and she wouldn't look away until Honor gave in.

"Listen to him out there," Bernie said.

"I know."

"It wasn't enough that he destroyed the rock. He's making his presence known. He doesn't want you to forget he's home."

"How could I forget that?" Honor asked. "What do you want me to say? It's hard."

"Yes," Bernie said. "I'll grant you that. How can it not be, considering what you've all gone through?"

Honor's chest felt tight. "You know what Regis said to me the other day?"

"Tell me."

"That Agnes is searching for a vision. Where do you think she got that idea?"

"Good question," Bernie said. She drained her glass. She stood up from her seat, smoothing her sleeves and long black skirt. She straightened her veil. Then she walked around the easel so she could look at Honor's painting.

Honor saw the work with Bernie's eyes: a man wearing jeans and a rough jacket, his hands strong, his eyes tormented, bending over with the weight of a child. Honor had deliberately blurred her features—it might be Agnes, and it might be Regis. The landscape was of ocean, rocks, and hills. There were stone walls in the distance, and the green suggested Ireland—or the Connecticut shoreline. And there was Sisela, the white cat, crouched on the wall, her green eyes seeing all.

"It's John," Bernie said.

"Yes."

Bernie stared a few minutes longer. "And Sisela, and one of the girls…"

Honor nodded. Bernie met her eyes; Honor saw deep hurt and pain, and somehow she knew it didn't have to do with her and John. Bernie handed Honor the envelope. On the front was a spidery drawing of a sandcastle at the water's edge…and, rising from the waves, in the distance, a sea monster.

"Don't throw everything away," Bernie said.

"Bernie…"

"Choices matter," Bernie said. "I know that better than anyone. Read what's in the envelope, what you wrote to me, and see if you know what I mean. I have the feeling you'll remember. At least, I can't imagine you forgetting."

"Do you ever think you got the vision wrong, Bernie? That she was trying to tell you something else?" Honor's skin felt electric, remembering the day Bernie had told her. Honor's hair had stood on end, especially when she realized what it was going to mean for Tom, for all of them.

"I'm nothing if not fallible," Bernie said. "We all are. Read the letter. You were pretty wise back then."

Honor held the envelope in one hand and put her arms around her sister-in-law. Of course she remembered; she knew without reading a word. Holding Bernie, she thought of the choices they each had made. There was no greater risk than love, she thought, hearing John strike the rock.

No greater risk in the world.

Fifteen

Dark silver, the tidal flats shimmered under starlight. Long past sunset, John took advantage of the ebb tide, gathering the last fragments of the boulder, hauling them out of the shallow water, onto the beach. He left the largest rocks just below the high-tide line, carried the smaller pieces up toward the tall grass at the top of the beach. Working from pure emotion, not intellect, creating a physical manifestation of what he felt inside, a circle took shape.

His muscles burned from exertion, and he knew that his reward would be a long swim and a good sleep. Dreams and work were his sanctuary. Even in his deepest dreams, he worked on the sculpture. Fitting the pieces together, arranging every broken piece into a new and completely different whole.

In some of the dreams, Honor was right there with him. She had such a sense of form and composition; he had always wished she would come with him to his work sites. Over the years, he had seen such spectacular places, mainly in the northern hemisphere: Greenland, Labrador, Hudson Bay, Denali, the Magdalen Islands. He had always wanted her to be with him, but there was always a reason why she couldn't be.

The girls, mainly. Even when Bernie had offered to have them stay at the convent so Honor could be with John, it never seemed to work out. Honor would decline, saying she didn't want to disrupt their daughters, or the trip was too expensive, or that she didn't want to distract John from his work—so he could return home sooner.

Until Ireland, John had never really pushed her to change her mind. He understood that people were who they were: the drive-to-the-edge recklessness he had inside himself was the exact opposite of Honor's nurturing, stay-by-the-fireside grace. And even though his large-scale work got the attention, she was ten times braver than he: her canvases of people captured such depth of heart, nuance of emotion, it was almost as if his wife could see beneath people's skin.

He rolled another large chunk of rock into place, stood back to survey the emerging stone circle. It felt so good to be working again. Reaching for his camera, he recorded the latest placement. He'd lost the chance to photograph his last work-in-progress in Ireland, and he never wanted that to happen again. Waves broke on the sandbar a hundred yards out, and for a moment, he thought he was hearing things.

"John?"

He looked up, scanning the beach. A shadow caught his attention, up on top of the bank. His heart skipped to see Honor standing there— silhouetted by light coming from somewhere at the Academy.

"Is everything okay? Is it Agnes?" he asked.

"Everything's fine," she said.

He walked up the beach, over the far edge of the stone circle, past the stacks of driftwood that he'd gathered over the course of the last week. She made her way down the narrow path, through the beach roses to the edge of the seawall. He jumped up on the granite out-cropping, to give her his hand.

"Thank you," she said, and laughed softly.

"What's so funny?" he asked, shocked and thrilled to hear her laugh.

"Just that I know this beach as well as you do, but you've always tried to help me find my way in the dark."

"We've been here many nights."

"Yes, we have."

All the times he and Honor had come down to this beach—he pictured their entire history contained in the stone circle, and he felt electricity sizzling through his skin. Her hand felt small and cool. He held it and wished they could just stand there all night.

When she pulled away, he saw the trouble in her eyes. What had she come here to tell him? His heart clutched, but he knew he had to let her say what she had to say. Her eyes grazed the tidal flats, dark silver in the starlight, coming to rest on the circle of stones.

"What are you doing?" she asked.

"Did you come down here to see my work?" he asked.

She didn't answer, but walked over to the largest rock fragment. A long cube at the water's edge, nearly the size of a refrigerator, with jagged edges—she ran her hand over the top, feeling the broken rock. John stood right behind her.

"What is all this?" she asked without turning around.

"It's a stone circle," he said.

"Like the one near Clonakilty?"

"Drombeg?" he asked. "Yes, but on a much smaller scale," he said.

He watched her walk around the circumference. The smaller pieces were at twelve o'clock, at the top of the beach, and the largest ones were just below the high-tide line of seaweed and driftwood. She seemed to be absorbing the placement, wondering about the meaning.

"The effect I'm trying to achieve—" he began.

"I'm not an art magazine," she interrupted quietly. "I'm not asking you about your sculpting practice. I want to know what made you attack the boulder and then pull the pieces out of the water. This is glacial rock. You broke it apart in one night. What does that mean, John? Do you know how extreme that seems?"

"Honor, Agnes came running down that wall, free as can be, wanting only to swim in the Sound—and she dove in, and this rock nearly killed her."

"I'm not sure that's what Agnes had in mind," Honor murmured. "A swim…"

"What do you mean?"

Honor shook her head as if he wouldn't understand, and he felt frustration rising, just below boiling.

"God, Honor. I feel so out of sync with our family, or at least with you. I love you all so much, but it seems all I do is screw up."

Honor turned to stare at him. Her eyes blazed in the starlight. "It's been awful for the girls," she said. "Having you away."

"I know."

"It's been awful for all of us," she said. "We couldn't bear to think of you there—"

"Honor, what can I do?" he asked, despair welling up. "What can I do to make it better?"

"I don't know—"

"If I can't make things work between us, what's the point? I thought if I showed you...I wrecked it, this rock, because of what happened, but now I'm going to put it back together, in a circle. I know it's just a sculpture, a symbol..."

He stepped forward, took her in his arms. He had no choice, and because she didn't pull back or say no, he didn't even hesitate. They swayed together, moving to the rhythm of the waves rolling in, one after another, regular as heartbeats. The water rushed around their ankles, and the blood pounded in his ears.

"Forgive me, Honor," he said.

"I have forgiven you," she said. "I just don't know if I can go on with you."

"What do you mean? Did you meet someone else?"

"John," she said. "Of course not."

He held her tighter; as impossible as it would be to imagine Honor with another man, it had also been one of John's worst fears. She was so beautiful, and she had so much love inside—how had she gone six years without letting it out?

"I had the girls to think of," she said. "They needed me twice as much. We all missed you terribly."

"Then why aren't you sure if we can be together? I love you more than ever. I'm the same person," he said.

"That's what I'm afraid of," she whispered.

"Afraid of?"

She pushed away, and even in the darkness, he saw the exhaustion in her expression. "John, it got to be too much. I thought I could handle it, and I tried to—but what happened in Ireland, with Regis, was the last straw."

"You've made up your mind?"

"I thought I had," she said. "Counting down to your release, I'd pretty much decided."

"To divorce me?"

She nodded. He felt as if she'd just punched him in the stomach. He wanted to turn away, but he couldn't. She was two feet away and he was frozen like a stone statue. He felt despair, the failure of their marriage swirling around him. The idea of Honor had kept him going in prison—the hope of returning home and being a family again. He burned now, wanting to tell her everything—maybe she'd understand then, and change her mind. But he'd sworn he'd go to his grave with it all, and he swallowed his words.

"You're leaving me," he said, numb.

She shook her head. "Then I saw you," she said, the words barely intelligible.

"What?" he asked.

"I called a lawyer," she said. "I'd planned to have papers drawn up, have you served when you got home."

"I get it, Honor," he said. "You want a divorce."

"No," she said harshly. "I *did*. But then I saw you. It's one thing to imagine how much easier life would be without this. Without the constant drama, the worry—being married to a man whose idea of a solution is to smash a boulder to bits. And then put it back together!"

"It's just a symbol," he said.

"I need more than symbols, John," she said, her voice cracking. She raised her eyes to meet his. He wanted to feel some hope, but reading her eyes he saw only anger and despair.

"I do it for you, Honor. So you'll be proud of me. It's like when we were kids. The only way I could be sure you'd notice me was if I took bigger risks than anyone else. Sure, the other boys might cross the railroad tracks, but who else would dive into Devil's Hole?"

"Don't remind me," she said, softly punching him in the chest. John caught her fist, holding it as they rocked back and forth. His heart was pounding; he had to let her know how much he loved her, how he'd do anything to keep her.

"I climbed the water tower, just so I could hang a flag with your name on it."

"And I watched you from the ground, terrified the rusty ladder would give way, that you'd fall to your death."

"But I didn't," he said.

"Not then," she said. "But I've never stopped worrying about you. All these last years—every time the phone rang, I thought it was going to be your lawyer..." She stopped, swallowing as her eyes filled with tears. "Calling to tell me someone had *stabbed* you in jail."

"I kept myself safe," he said. "So I could come home."

"This is what I did every day," she said, facing the water. "Stood on the beach, looking east. I'd imagine the water flowing out of Long Island Sound, into the Atlantic Ocean, all the way to Ireland. It was the closest I could get to you."

"What would you have said to me?" he asked, holding himself back from telling her his version of the same thing.

"I don't know," she whispered, but he didn't believe her. He saw the thoughts racing behind her eyes. Her face was alive with emotion— he tried to read it all, but didn't trust himself. He could swear he saw love in there, but he couldn't be sure.

"Try," he said.

"There was a whole ocean between us."

"There isn't now," he said.

"I left you there," she said. "In Ireland. In prison. I stopped visiting you...I stopped taking the girls. I just couldn't stand it anymore. I couldn't stand it. I couldn't bear thinking of you there."

Her eyes blazed, and his heart began to race, wondering what she'd think if she'd actually seen the horrors of that dark day.

"John," she said, "you were my heart. And the heart of our family. You were everything." She shook her head, looked down for a long minute. Then she seemed to make up her mind about something. As he watched, she reached into the back pocket of her jeans, held a paper in her hands. His blood froze as she held it toward him.

"What is it?"

"Just read it."

"Do the girls know?" he asked, holding the paper, unable to look.

"It was their idea..."

"Honor," he said, staring at the paper's edge lifting in the soft wind. This was it, the end of their marriage; it felt like the end of the world. "Don't do this."

She handed it to him, backed away. He watched her walking down the dark beach toward home, and his hands were shaking as he raised the paper to his eyes, peered at it in the dim light.

He looked at the piece of paper, expecting to see legal letterhead. Instead he saw pale gray stationery with Honor's monogram at the top. There, in her handwriting:

> *Come for dinner, tomorrow night, six o'clock.*
> *We will be waiting.*
>
> > Honor

John read the words over and over, and he felt the ice in his veins at last beginning to thaw.

Sixteen

It felt like the way holidays used to be, with everyone pitch-
ing in to help, and a growing excitement—not just about the
meal itself, but about what it all stood for: a time to celebrate, give
thanks, and be together. It was going to be a real feast, too—with
everything their yard, beach, and region had to offer.

Regis had dug clams and gathered mussels from the waters near
Tomahawk Point; she had asked Peter to take her fishing at dawn,
and in the morning mist she'd caught three big flounder. Peter had
seemed quiet, out of sorts, his thoughts a million miles away—as he'd
been ever since they'd crossed Devil's Hole. Cleaning the fish, Regis
had felt her stomach clench, and wanted to ask him what was wrong.
But she held back, afraid of what he might say. And she was so happy
about her father's coming for dinner that night, she couldn't bear to
rock the boat.

Cecilia had ridden her bike through the vineyard, to the nuns' veg-
etable garden. She met Sister Angelica and Sister Gabrielle there—
dressed in their black habits, with the sun beating down, they had to
be boiling hot... but the nuns just smiled so kindly and happily, as if
they knew that Cecilia's father was coming for dinner that night.
They helped her fill her big wicker basket with fresh corn, tomatoes,
zucchini, basil, and lots of raspberries.

Agnes went with her mother to the doctor, to check the results of the MRI, make sure she was healing well, and have her dressing changed. They took off the huge gauze turban and put on a smaller bandage instead. The shaved part of her head, right around the stitches, itched like mad, and she thought it made her look ugly and a little crazy. Dr. Grady's office was attached to the hospital, so Agnes wore a cap, just in case she saw Brendan, but he was nowhere to be seen.

On the way home, they stopped at the A&P. Agnes's mother asked if she wanted to wait in the car while she ran in for a few things, but Agnes felt like moving around. Although she got a little dizzy at times, she felt stronger than ever today; knowing that her father would be with them for dinner that night was like the best medicine any doctor could ever prescribe.

She pushed the cart while her mother got the items she needed: stuff for piecrust, cheese and crackers, heavy cream, butter, fresh bread. When they got to the greeting-card aisle, Agnes stocked up on a bunch of paper products for the night's decorations. As she threw crepe paper streamers into the cart, she thought of how she had planned to give Regis a shower this summer. As reluctant as she was about her sister's engagement, she knew she had to get back on track there.

The air-conditioning felt too cold. She shivered, wobbling slightly. Just then someone took her arm, to steady her.

"Thanks," she said, thinking it was her mother. But when she looked up, it was Brendan.

"Oh!" she said. "It's you! We were just at the hospital, and I looked for you."

"I'm off today," he said. "How was your checkup?"

"The doctor looked at my stitches," she said. "And took some X-rays. I'm fine." She reached up, touched her head to make sure her hat was covering the razor track through her long dark hair.

"Honey," her mother said, coming down the aisle with a bag of flour. She stopped short, peering at Agnes. "You're pale."

"I thought so, too," Brendan said. "Hi, Mrs. Sullivan."

"Hi, Brendan."

"I guess it's just my first time out since I hit my head," Agnes said, leaning on the cart.

"That's it," her mother said. "Let's just leave the cart here, and I'll take you home."

"Mrs. Sullivan, I'll drive her," Brendan said. "You can finish your shopping..."

Agnes's blood jumped, and her eyes locked with his. He looked so bright and sweet, making her heart kick. She felt excited, if not exactly energetic. Sensing her mother's hesitation, she smiled. "I'm really okay, Mom. Just tired."

"I'll take good care of her," Brendan promised.

Her mother nodded; perhaps she was remembering him at the hospital, taking such good care of Agnes those first twenty-four hours after her fall. Agnes remembered them almost as if they were a dream: images of him taking her temperature, bringing her extra blankets, sitting with her till she fell asleep.

"Okay," her mother said. "Thank you, Brendan. Take her straight home."

"I will."

"And go lie down," her mother said, gazing at Agnes. "As soon as you get there."

Agnes kissed her. Her mother sounded worried, but she looked excited. Her eyes were shining in a way Agnes hadn't seen in a long, long time.

Brendan put his arm around Agnes, and they walked through the parking lot to his car—the wild, surrealistic, painted car she'd seen the other day. The temperature had to be about ninety, and it made Agnes feel weak. But she couldn't bear to get into the front seat until she'd looked at some of the images: white whales flying, bears riding bicycles, a little girl turning cartwheels across a lake, swans kissing, a boy walking a tightrope between stars.

"Better get in," Brendan said gently. "I promised your mom I'd get you right home."

"I want to see more," she said, gazing at foxes in a green rowboat, dolphins sliding down a snow-covered hill, a boy riding a sea monster, and one white cat on a dark stone wall. But the heat was searing, and she felt really weak, and Brendan was standing there with the door open, so she nodded and climbed into his car.

The vehicle was old, the leather seats cracked at the seams. A baseball cap sat on the dashboard. A Christmas ornament hung from the long gearshift. Brendan turned the key, and the car sputtered and started.

"Who painted your car?" she asked.

"I did," he said.

"You're good," she said.

"Thank you. Coming from you, with such talented parents, that means a lot."

"You know about my parents' work?"

He nodded. "One of the doctors at the hospital was telling us your father is really famous. I looked him up. His photographs are amazing. But your mother's work is even more beautiful. The way she captures people..." He trailed off.

Agnes laughed. "You should tell her. She'll love you forever. He's the one who gets all the acclaim. I love her paintings, though."

"She's a storyteller," Brendan said. "Her paintings, the ones I found on the Black Hall Art Colony website, could be really amazing illustrations of a great story."

"Well, so are yours. You really want to be a doctor? You're obviously an artist."

"The kind of doctor I want to be listens to stories, tries to see the whole picture. I think psychiatrists have to be artists, in a way. I started painting before I got the idea to go to medical school. Art and stories are ways of finding power....I see it all going together...."

"Like my picture," Agnes murmured.

"Your picture?"

"On my camera," Agnes said. "I tried to take it the night I fell. I wanted to capture..." She stopped herself, embarrassed.

"Your vision?" he asked.

"You believe me?" she asked.

"I get it, Agnes. When life is really hard, it's okay to need help. I did it when Paddy was sick; I imagined his guardian angel taking care of him. It helped me a lot."

"Do you think they're not real?" she asked, worried that he'd try to talk her out of believing. "My vision, his guardian angel?"

"The opposite," he said, turning to give her a quick, bright smile. "I'm sure they are. They help us get to where we have to go."

"Where we have to go," she murmured, gazing at him. She relaxed, knowing that he understood her. Closing her eyes, she thought of the pictures she'd seen painted on his car: people, creatures, monsters, all going places, using unusual means to get there.

When they reached the Academy gates, Brendan read the sign out loud: "Star of the Sea," he said.

"It used to be called Stella Maris, when my parents were young," she said.

"Do you have your camera with you?" he asked.

"No," she said. "It's in my room. I'll show you."

He nodded. Obviously he remembered the way from the other night, because he followed the winding drive past the jumbled stone buildings, the convent and academic halls, around the chapel with its silvery slate roof and steep spire, through the thick and fragrant vineyards, along the tallest stone wall, straight to Agnes's house nestled in the hollow.

Her stomach jumped when she looked at the front door—soon her father would be walking through it, to be greeted by his family, to sit down to dinner. Agnes had been waiting for this night for so long. Climbing out of Brendan's car, she glanced around for her sisters— they were nowhere to be seen. Her eye fell on the picture he'd painted of the white cat—sitting on a stone wall, gazing at the full moon.

She opened the front door; a cool breeze blew through the house. The windows facing the Sound were open, white curtains fluttering. Sisela, the old cat, reclined on the top of the bookshelf.

"That's Sisela," Agnes said.

"Hello there," Brendan said, walking over, holding out his hand.

Sisela rolled on her side, letting him stroke her throat. Agnes stood still, watching. Sisela was usually very cautious about allowing strangers close to her. Was it possible that she and Brendan had met before?

"Oh dear," Agnes said, wobbling. She felt suddenly weak in the knees, and he helped her onto the sofa.

"Actually, Sisela's usually very timid," Agnes said. "I don't know what's gotten into her. Did you two make friends the last time you were here?"

Brendan didn't reply. He had slipped into medical mode and was very surreptitiously taking her pulse. What he didn't realize was that his touch was making her heart race. She gazed at him, concentrating as he counted her heartbeats. His blue eyes were so alert, almost electric, and Agnes felt the current.

"You painted her," she said.

"What do you mean?"

"Sisela. On your car," Agnes said.

He didn't reply, but just held her wrist. Slowly he changed his grip so he was holding her hand. It had been so hot outside, and at the store, but in here there was nothing but a cool breeze. Agnes felt it on her skin and shivered.

"Will you show me the image on your camera?" he asked, without answering her question.

She nodded. It felt almost as if she were dreaming as she led him through the house, down the hall to the room she shared with her sisters. No boys had ever been in here—not even Peter. But Agnes didn't even hesitate; she felt driven to show Brendan where she slept, and where she kept her camera.

"Here it is," she said, reaching up on the shelf. He stood beside her, steadying her, helping her bring down the camera.

They sat on the edge of her bed. Agnes glanced at him. She expected him to seem curious, welcomed into the Sullivan girls' inner sanctum. The room was filled with so many mysteries of sisterhood—books, paintings, posters, banners, scarves, jewelry boxes, clothes strewn everywhere—even, Agnes was embarrassed to see, Regis's lacy demi-cup peach-colored bra hanging off her desk, and her purple thong tossed aside and accidentally hooked onto her lamp. But Brendan had eyes only for the camera.

"Is the picture on there?" he asked.

"Yes," she said, checking to make sure it was charged, then turning it on. Brendan leaned over her shoulder, watching as she clicked through the images on her screen: Cece grinning, Regis and Peter waving, Sisela on the windowsill, Agnes's mother at her easel, and then...

"This is it," she said as the white flash came into focus. She passed the camera to Brendan.

He held it in both hands, and she could tell they were trembling. Reaching out, she steadied them with hers. His eyes were riveted, his mouth half open. He stared at the photo, a white blur. As he leaned closer Agnes caught sight of something she hadn't noticed before— a profile, just the hint of a face, in the field of filmy white.

"That looks like—" he began, sounding excited.

"An angel, right?" she asked.

"I was going to say something at sea," he said. "The Kelly sea monster, rearing out of the breaking white of a wave."

"The Kelly sea monster?" Agnes asked, thinking of Tom's ring. Brendan handed her the camera, and it slipped through Agnes's fingers, smashing on the floor. As Agnes lunged to get it, her hat fell off. She grabbed the camera, and saw that the fall had cracked the screen.

"Oh!" she cried, covering her head—the ugly shaved stripe, the bandage—with her arms.

"What is it?" Brendan asked.

"Don't look at me," she said, starting to cry. "I'm hideous."

"You're not," he said. "You're beautiful. Besides, I've seen it before. I was your nurse, remember?"

Agnes bowed her head and wept. She felt so embarrassed by how she looked, and the fact she somehow hadn't computed the fact that he would already have seen, and upset by the fact her camera was ruined. If Brendan was disappointed at not being able to see more of the picture, he wasn't showing it. In fact, he looked radiant—his eyes were bright, and his smile wide and so tender.

"It'll grow back," he said. "Hair does that."

"It's not just that," she cried. "The picture is destroyed. I thought I'd captured an angel, the only one ever, and now it's gone."

"At first I thought it was a monster," he murmured.

"It can't be," she wept. "It was too beautiful…"

"Sometimes monsters and angels are one and the same, I think," Brendan said, slipping his arm around her, brushing what hair she had left out of her eyes. "Besides, you don't have to worry. It's not gone."

"How do you know?" she asked, looking up at him.

"Because whatever you want to call it, monster or angel, it's here to protect you," he whispered, kissing her gently. "And because the important things are never really gone…"

Agnes's knees felt weak, and she was sitting down. His lips touched hers, so soft and warm. She was melting into him, into his arms and chest and skin. She saw stars, brighter than the angel's picture. Sisela meowed from the bed above, and Agnes barely heard. But Brendan did and, after another kiss, pulled slightly away to look up.

"Hi there," he said. Sisela was staring down with green eyes. "Are you our chaperone?"

"She likes you," Agnes said.

"I like her, too," Brendan said, reaching a slow hand up toward the cat. Sisela twitched her whiskers, purring as he petted her head.

"Do you like cats?" Agnes asked.

"I like this cat," Brendan said.

"You have met her before, haven't you?"

"Once or twice," Brendan said softly. "I've seen her on the walls a few times."

"When have you been here?" Agnes asked, feeling the hair on the back of her neck stand on end. She'd known there was something about Brendan, known he had met Sisela before—of course he had to have, to paint that picture of her sitting on the wall.

But just then the screen door slammed, and Regis came charging in. She slid into the bedroom on bare feet, grinning to see Agnes and Brendan there.

"A boy in our room! Zowee!"

"Hi, Regis," Brendan said.

"Kids, time is of the essence. Agnes, in case you've forgotten, our father is coming for dinner in just a little while! We have clams to shuck, pies to bake! C'mon, get a move on!"

"I'd better go," Brendan said, looking at Agnes, holding her face between his hands. He stared at her with such fire in his blue eyes, she felt it spreading through her bones.

"Okay," she said. "I want to hear more, though."

He gazed at her, and she wished he'd never leave. "I want to tell you more, too," he said.

When he left the room, Agnes could barely move. She touched the spot where he'd been sitting on the bed beside her; it was still warm. Up above, Sisela was now purring, as if whatever mysterious history had existed between her and Brendan made her happy to remember.

Agnes raised her gaze to Regis, who was staring down the hall after Brendan. She looked back, and the sisters locked eyes.

"Dad's really coming home," Agnes said. "I'm not sure I can let myself believe it."

"Do you think it will be the same?"

"The same as when?"

"As when we were little, when he and Mom loved each other so much? When we were all so happy? Do you think we can get it all back?"

"I don't think it was ever gone," Agnes said.

"Really?" Regis asked, frowning, wanting to believe so badly it brought tears to her eyes.

"Really," Agnes whispered, the feeling of Brendan still shimmering on her skin as she stood up to hug her sister. "The important things are never really gone."

Seventeen

Honor felt as nervous as she had at summer dances long ago. Even though this was all for the girls, she chose her dress carefully—a blue silk sheath, plain and sleeveless. The night was hot, and the dress would feel cool. She told herself her choice had nothing to do with the fact that blue was John's favorite color. She clipped a strand of jade beads around her neck, slid a silver cuff bracelet onto her arm, and stepped into a pair of blue sandals. Then she kicked them off. Summer dinners had always been barefoot.

By the time she got to the kitchen, the girls had all gathered and were at their appointed jobs. Regis was at the sink, a green apron over her pink sundress, expertly shucking littleneck clams, arranging them on a silver tray. Cece, in navy shorts and a pale yellow top, was mixing up cocktail sauce, wrinkling her nose as she tasted too much horseradish. And Agnes, wearing a white cotton dress, sat at the kitchen table arranging cheese and crackers. The aroma of raspberry pie, still in the oven, filled the room, and Honor felt almost overwhelmed with the moment.

"Oh no," Cece said, looking down at her shirt. "I spilled."

"C'mere, honey," Honor said, leading her to the sink. "We'll fix it."

"Should I change?" Cece asked as Honor let the cold water run, started to dab at the tomato sauce. "I don't want to have a big wet blotch on me the first time I see him!"

"It's not the first time you've seen him," Regis said. "You saw him when you were born, and you saw him till you were seven, and then on visits to Portlaoise, and you saw him again this week—"

"You know what I mean!" Cece said, sounding panicked. "I want him to think I look nice, and like me!"

"*Like* you, Cece?" Honor said, getting the last of the spot out. "He *loves* you."

"But what if he doesn't?" Cece asked. "He hardly knows me! What if he thinks I'm not as smart as Regis, or as pretty as Agnes? I've got to change."

She ran out of the kitchen, ignoring her sisters and Honor calling after her. Honor felt frazzled, but one look at the girls told her she had to run after Cecilia. She hurried into the bedroom, saw Cece tearing through open drawers—pulling out tops, throwing them on the bed. None of them were good enough. Cece dissolved in sobs, with complete abandon.

Honor hugged her. Cece shook, just falling apart. Honor held her tighter, soothed her with whispers.

"You're our little one," she said. "He loves you as much as I do."

"But he doesn't *knowwww* me," she wept.

"Yes, he does," Honor said.

"How can you say that? He's been *awaaayyy*!"

"But you're his daughter. He loves you for that reason alone."

"He loves Regis, because she's so smart and funny and scary wild, like him. And he loves Agnes, because she's so holy and blessed and sweet, like you." Cece's assessment of Honor took her completely by surprise, but she didn't react, just held on. "But what about me? Why would he love me?"

"Because you're Cecilia Bernadette Sullivan. You're our baby girl. His baby girl...I remember the day you were born. He was right there with me..." Honor smiled, but she had to stop and couldn't quite go on. She was seeing John's eyes, his smile, the way he had cradled their newest daughter in his arms. "And you know what he said?"

Cece shook her head. "No. What?"

"He looked you right in your blue eyes and said, 'I've been waiting for you.'"

"He did?"

"Yes. Those were his exact words."

"But how could he have been waiting for me, if he didn't even know who I was?"

"Because I think he did know who you were," Honor said. "We both did. That's why we love you so much, why we always have and always will. You have that certain 'Cece-ness' to you, that we couldn't live without."

"He's here!" Regis shouted. "He's just walking through the vineyard now! Hurry and get back here!"

"She's right," Honor said. "Now, honey...how about picking out a top?"

"This one?" Cece asked, holding up a blue-and-white-striped shirt.

"That's perfect," Honor said, catching the dismay in Cece's eyes.

"Oh no," Cece said. "I was all wet, and now you are, and it's my fault."

When Honor looked down, she saw that her dress was wet with Cece's tears. Her stomach jumped; looking after the girls kept her from making sense of her own emotions. She wasn't sure how she felt about anything. What if she let John back into their lives again, and something terrible happened? She felt so many conflicting things right now, she wanted to escape out the back door.

"Mom, your dress," Cece said.

"Don't worry," Honor said, patting her shoulder.

Walking into the kitchen, she reached for a paper towel. The girls rushed down the hall, in time for Regis and Agnes to unfurl the banner they'd made. The message had been painted, glued, and glittered by all three girls and flowed with crepe paper streamers.

Honor watched the kids get the sign in place—held up by two tall driftwood branches meant to pay homage to their father's favorite kind of beach sculpture. Then she went to the door.

He was coming up the path, head down. Honor could see that he thought himself unobserved. He wore khakis and a blue shirt, carried a bouquet of beach wildflowers—asters, black-eyed Susans, sweet peas. His once-dark hair glinted with silver—the sight of it gave her a pang. And when he raised his eyes, she got to see it all: the way they went from nervous and uncertain to surprised and overjoyed, to see all three girls and Honor and the sign crowding the entryway.

"Hi, John," she said, standing out in front.

"Hi, Honor," he said.

They just stood there, and for a minute Honor wasn't sure what to do. The sun was dipping down behind the Academy hills, glinting off the rock ledge and stone walls. The waves beat against the beach, their sound peaceful and constant. Her heart was pounding, and the front of her dress was soaked with Cece's tears. John's eyes met hers, as if giving her one last chance to back out.

"Welcome home, Dad," Regis said.

"You're here…" Agnes whispered.

"I've been waiting for you," Cece said, and at that, John's eyes flooded with tears. So did Honor's.

They stared at each other for a long time. This had been his home—she could see what it meant to him, to be back. She could barely breathe. There had been nights when she'd dreamed of this, and others when she'd made up her mind to never let him back again. He held on to the flowers, waiting for a sign from her.

"You're here," she said, staring into his eyes.

"I never thought—" he began.

The words filled her with panic. She didn't know what he was about to say, but she knew she couldn't handle it right now. She reached for the beach flowers, her hands shaking.

"Come in, John," she said, standing aside.

And he did.

John's skin was tingling as he walked through the door, right behind Honor. He took everything in—each sight, sound, and smell. The look in Honor's eyes was almost too much for him, and he fought the urge to bolt. At the same time, he wanted to freeze the moment, stay as happy as he was in this instant, surrounded by his wife and daughters in what had once been his home.

Cecilia hung back, looking up at him, a huge grin on her face.

"You're really here," she said.

"I really am," he said. Everyone stood there, waiting for him to say something more.

"What will you have to drink, John?" Honor asked suddenly.

"I'll have a beer," he said.

She went to put the flowers in water and get the drinks, and with that, John felt the new formality. Had he really expected to walk in and have it be easy? Have her know what he wanted, tease him and kiss him, the way she used to? Even the girls seemed stilted, gathering up cocktail things as if he were a guest. Only Cece stayed by his side, gazing up at him as if he were the most wonderful person she'd ever seen.

They walked onto the back porch, with its long view over the field and vineyard toward the beach. Off to the right, across the mouth of the Connecticut River, the lighthouse at Fenwick flashed. They gathered around a small table, sitting in wicker chairs. Regis placed a tray of clams right in the middle, and Agnes offered him a plate of cheese and crackers. Goat cheese from New York State, Camembert, and Vermont cheddar—his favorites. He took them from her, noticing how she sat there smiling, as ethereal as an injured angel, dressed in white, with her head bandaged.

"Thank you, Agnes," he said.

"I remember that you love cheese," she said.

Honor served drinks, and Cece pointed out the cocktail sauce.

"I made it," she said.

"Be careful, Dad," Regis said. "She likes it hot."

"I do, too," he said, and everyone watched him as he dabbed a little on the side of a clam, raised it to his mouth, and ate it. "Wow, that's good," he said.

"Thanks!" Cece said, and she beamed when he took a second.

The clam tasted so briny and fresh, straight from Long Island

Sound. He hadn't had shellfish in so long. Every bite was delicious and reminded him of how much he had missed—he had forgotten the relatively small things like snacks before dinner, because he had missed the big things—his life with Honor and the kids—so much.

"Tell me about everything," he said.

"There's a lot to tell," Cece said solemnly. "What should we start with?"

"How about you, Regis? When do I get to meet Peter?"

"Soon," Regis said, smiling. "In fact, I invited him to come for dessert. I thought the sooner the better, considering..." She glanced down at her engagement ring. John couldn't believe Regis could be wearing one, and when he looked up at Honor, she widened her eyes at him. Even after six years apart, John knew she had volumes to say on the subject.

"Regis isn't the only person with a boyfriend," Cece said.

"You have one, too?" John asked.

"Not me!" she giggled, bringing back memories of Regis when she was younger, when suggesting she liked a boy was the worst thing he could say.

"Who, then?" he asked, and for a moment his heart stopped, thinking she might say "Honor."

"Agnes," Cece said, giving her sister a look.

"He's not my boyfriend," Agnes said, blushing.

"Looked that way to me, too," Regis said.

"Could we please not talk about it?" Agnes said.

"At least tell me his name," John said.

Agnes gave him a sweet smile, and he had the feeling she was giving in only because it was him. "Brendan," she said.

"The archangel," Regis said.

"Don't tease your sister," Honor said, and John knew she was concerned, watching Agnes get paler.

"My camera broke," Agnes said, seemingly out of nowhere. "I got distracted and knocked it down."

"Oh, Agnes!" Honor said.

"That must have been upsetting," John said, his eyes on Agnes. She looked pale and worried. "What kind of camera?" he asked.

"Canon EOS 300D," she said.

John had kept up on what was new in photography equipment the best he could. The prison library had magazines, and Tom had donated a subscription to *Camera World*. Agnes had one of the good newer ones; was it possible she had the eye and feel for it, that she wanted to follow him into the field?

"Did you have images on it?" he asked. "Is that why you're upset?"

"It's expensive," Agnes said. "I feel bad about that."

But John could see something deeper in her eyes; she had regrets about breaking expensive equipment, but he understood the kick in the stomach of losing a shot you love—and that's what Agnes was feeling now.

"It's that picture she took on the wall," Cece confided. "The night she crashed into the rock."

"Cece, stop!" Agnes said.

"I wish I could see that picture," John said.

"I took it with a timer," she said. "And a flash set for backfilling, as well as illumination."

"Did you get something interesting?"

She paused, then nodded. "You might say so."

"I wish I could see it," he said again. "Maybe I could take a look at your camera, see what I could do."

"Maybe," she said.

"She's a good photographer," Honor said, sipping her beer. John noticed that she was drinking the same thing he was, instead of her usual summer rum and tonic; it made him happy, for no good reason. "Honey, why don't you get your camera, show it to your father while I get dinner on the table?"

"Okay," Agnes said. She went toward her room, and Honor and Cece went into the kitchen, leaving John alone on the porch with Regis. The late-afternoon breeze picked up, ruffling her hair, brushing it back from her face. He saw that she had her mother's exquisite bone structure, and his heart dropped. Regis had grown up while he was gone. He had missed it all.

"You okay, Dad?" she asked.

"I'm fine," he said.

"Then what are you thinking?"

"I was just wondering...where did all the time go?"

She nodded, as if she knew what he meant. But she couldn't. She couldn't imagine how it felt to have a little baby, and to hear her squawk in the nursery, and take her first steps, and learn how to talk, and name a white cat, and make her parents laugh, and go to school, make a Christmas wreath out of her tiny handprints, dipped in green finger paint and pressed in a circle on white cloth. How it felt to see her collect shells and pinecones, and climb the tallest trees, and beat boys in races, and beg to be allowed to follow him up the steepest cliffs—and then to miss six years of her life.

Sisela wandered out the back door. She stretched, looked up at John, leapt into his lap. Curled up, lay down. He stroked her back, and she started to purr.

"Remember when she was just a kitten?" Regis asked.

"Yes, I do."

"She was sitting on the wall just as if she knew we were coming, and she was just waiting for us..."

"As if she was waiting for the right family to come by, and we were it."

"Had you ever seen such a pure-white cat before?"

John shook his head. "No, never. And I missed her a lot while I was gone. There were cats at Portlaoise, a white cat in particular that reminded me of her."

"Dad, was it terrible?" Regis asked, reaching for his hand.

"Honey," he said, and stopped there. Her gaze crackled with intelligence and compassion; he stared into her eyes, wondering what she knew, what she remembered, how badly she had suffered from what he'd done.

"What was the worst part?"

He thought. There were plenty to choose from. The noise, the filth, the tension and anger, the bars and walls, the no-escape. But one thing loomed over all the others and made him shiver even now—that moment when he'd made his decision. What sort of harm had he done to her? He couldn't say it, though. "Missing your mother and you girls," he replied.

"That's how we felt, too. Dad, we missed you so much."

"I worried that you did. And that you'd give up thinking I'd ever come home again."

"I'd never give up on that," she said fiercely.

Just then Agnes returned with the camera. She placed it into John's hands, gazing at him with hopeful eyes. The camera was small and light, the perfect weight for a teenage girl. He turned it over, knowing the instant he saw the cracked display that it wouldn't be easy to fix.

He tried to open the lens cover, but it stuck. Something had bent, and he didn't want to force it. Looking up at Agnes, he saw the light go out of her eyes.

"Is it ruined?" she asked.

"I'm not sure," he said, not wanting to hurt her, but knowing he had to be truthful.

"Is the image gone forever?"

"Maybe, Agnes. It's possible," he said gently.

"You don't know how beautiful it was," she said. "Not just as a picture, but also what it meant."

"I know what that feels like," he said. "To capture something you've never seen before…"

"And want to show it to people," she said. "To everyone you love."

"It's a huge disappointment when you lose the shot," John said. "Or to take the picture, but lose the image, have it compromised by…"

"The camera crashing," Agnes said.

"You're a real photographer," John said, smiling and drawing her into his arms. "I can tell by the way you care about this one picture."

"She thinks it's of an angel," Regis said wryly.

"If that's true," John said, "and she lost the image, can you imagine how much worse that would be? To have taken the only known shot of an angel anywhere, and have it trapped inside her camera?"

Tears glimmered in Agnes's eyes, even as a smile filled her face. "Thank you, Dad," she whispered, hugging him harder.

"Agnes! Honey, I think your zucchini bread is ready!" Honor called from the kitchen, and Agnes hurried away.

"Isn't she doing well?" Regis asked, watching her sister go.

"She's making a really great recovery," John said.

"Seeing her on the beach like that, bleeding from her head," Regis said, and suddenly she went pale and a great tremor went through her. She buried her face in her hands.

"It reminded you..." John began, as the sickening realization hit him.

Regis blocked her ears. She shook her head violently, shocking him.

This was so hard, something that had haunted him the entire time he'd been in prison, and even before—from the moment the gardai took him away from Ballincastle, that last sight of Honor and Regis standing in the rain. "Regis," he said, taking her hand again. "How did you manage? After seeing what happened, being right there...They took me away before I could take care of you."

"Dad, I was fine," she said, resolute.

"But you..." He wanted to say, "But you couldn't have been fine." Not after seeing Gregory White charge at them out of the fog, seeing John beating him, picking up the rock...Blood pouring from his head, all over the rain-slicked ground, and all that happened afterward...

"I felt so guilty, Dad."

"Regis, no..."

She sobbed quietly for a few moments. He saw her shudder, and he wanted to reach for her, rewrite everything that had happened, erase the moment from her mind. Where was Honor? He wanted her now, to help him comfort Regis. Reaching for his daughter, he stroked her hair.

"It was my fault," she said.

He stared at her, stunned.

"If I hadn't followed you out to the bluff...you wouldn't have had to fight Greg White. You wouldn't have had to defend me."

John shivered, wondering what was going on in her mind. "He was crazy and violent," he said. "He was going to kill us. Do you remember?"

"Dad," she said, shaking her head. "That's the awful part. I barely even remember *anything*. I think I saw him fall..." Her eyes flickered, her voice faltered. "But then I looked away. I hardly saw anything else. I mean, I know what happened because Mom told me."

"What did she tell you?" he asked, his stomach turning.

"That you went crazy when you saw him attacking me. And you beat him..."

"I did," he said, his voice deep and low.

"But it's almost as if I wasn't even there. It's like a dream. The only thing I'm sure of is seeing you taken away by the gardai. Oh, Dad..." She dried her tears, looking at the doorway. "We shouldn't talk about it. Mom will get mad."

"What do you mean?"

"She can't stand what happened. Made me go to a shrink *forever*— do you know, she even blames my getting engaged on the fact that I was 'traumatized'?" Regis exhaled.

"Well..." he said.

"Don't you start, too," she said warningly.

"I'm looking forward to meeting Peter," he said, trying to be diplomatic. Regis held out her ring for him to see, and he held her hand. His heart jolted, and he looked out across the meadow, toward the edge of the vineyard.

Young people fell in love here, that was for sure. He looked up the hill, saw the stone wall. He thought of himself and Honor, his sister and Tom. So much passion on these hillsides—he still felt the fire, every bit as much as he had back then. The sound of Honor's voice in the kitchen filled him, made his pulse race. He could barely hold himself back from going inside, just to be near her.

"Tell me about the white cat," Regis said, as if she were trying to get back on solid ground.

"Well, she used to come into my cell, and I'd give her food."

"And she reminded you of Sisela?"

"Yes," he said. "Very much. Sometimes she'd sit on the table, silhouetted by lights in the cellblock, and I'd think she actually *was* Sisela, that she'd somehow come over to see me, with messages from you and your sisters and mother."

"I'm glad you had her there," Regis whispered.

"I'm glad, too. And I was even happier to get home and see the real Sisela. I wasn't sure she'd still be alive."

"We're all here, Dad. And now you are, too. We're a family again."

John smiled, as if he believed her. But his mind locked on the look he'd seen in Honor's eyes when she'd met him at the door, the way she had hesitated before taking the flowers he'd brought her, before inviting him into the house. He had broken something that day on Ballincastle—something more solid and eternal than the rock he'd destroyed right here on the beach.

No matter what Regis, in her youthful innocence, might wish and hope, John knew they had a long way to go before the family was really back together. But just then Cece came charging out, beckoning them toward the kitchen, and he and Regis went in to dinner.

Eighteen

It was the first time they had all been at a table together in over six years. Honor sat at one end, John at the other. Their eyes met; Honor tried to look away, but John wouldn't let her. Cece said grace, and then they started passing the food. Once everyone had filled their plates, Regis raised her glass.

"Here's to having Dad home," she said.

"Here's to that," everyone said, joining in.

"I wish Peter were here already," Regis said, bubbling over. "I want him to meet you, Dad, and see the greatest couple in the world—my parents!"

Honor flinched. Regis was pushing hard, but she knew that now wasn't the time to set her straight. She wanted this night to be wonderful for the girls. Her own mixed-up emotions left her feeling rocked and dizzy, and having John right here, in his place at the table, made them more extreme.

"I'm looking forward to meeting him, too," John said, still staring at Honor.

"I just want him to see you and Mom together. When I think of how I want us to be when we're married ... it's just like you two. The way it was when, well, before ..."

"Tell me something," John said, after a slightly uncomfortable silence. "What makes you know that Peter's the one? How did you two meet and fall in love?"

"He's from Hubbard's Point," Cece said.

"It's so romantic, isn't it?" Regis asked. "Just like you and Mom, only the opposite—a boy from Hubbard's Point, and a girl from Star of the Sea."

"But how did you fall in love?" John pressed. "How do you *know*?"

"We met at Paradise. Last year, when I was working. He used to come in with all his friends, on their way back from sailing lessons in Hawthorne, and they'd stop for ice cream. Once I was in a bad mood, from working two straight shifts, and he told me to smile..."

"He *said*," Agnes said quietly, "that you looked so cranky, you'd curdle the ice cream."

"I knew I should never have told you that. He was just teasing," Regis said.

"Sounds like he's a real kidder," John said, looking at Honor again. She wanted to roll her eyes, to show what she really thought, but she was afraid Regis would see. She didn't trust herself with anything regarding love—Regis's or her own—right now.

"It's very Peteresque, you have to admit," Agnes said. "Making jokes about your mood at work, while he's on his way back from sailing lessons. Or golf. Or seeing a Yankees game. Or—"

"So, Peter does lots of fun things," Regis said. "What's wrong with that?"

"I still haven't heard why you think he's the one for you," John said. "Out of all the other boys in Black Hall, or Connecticut, or Boston, or the rest of the world..."

"Well, how did you know *Mom* was the one?" Regis asked stubbornly, reaching right across the table for the bottle of wine. She drained her water glass and poured some wine in, giving Honor a daring look.

Honor's pulse was racing. Having John at the table felt both like the most normal thing in the world and the most odd. She watched him now, gazing back at her. His face was so gaunt, and the lively expression she'd always loved was layered over with darkness and grief.

The girls were on the edge of their seats, watching for signals passing between their parents.

"I knew from the minute I saw her," John said, gazing down the table. "Like Cece said—her family stayed at Hubbard's Point, and we were at Star of the Sea, and we all met on the beach, to stare at a ship that had been uncovered by a wild storm."

"A sunken ship," Honor said, and it calmed her to tell the story the girls had heard so many times, almost more legend than reality at this point.

"It was dusk, and the stars were out. Constellations rising straight out of the water. I remember there was a crescent moon, low in the western sky. Your mother's hair was so dark and shining, and her eyes were so bright—I wanted to stare at her all night."

"But she wanted to dig the ship timbers out of the sand," Cece giggled.

"Yes, she did," John said. "So we all tried to—your mother, Aunt Bernie, Tom, and I. We made it our project, and we met there the next day, and the day after that."

"And you took a lot of pictures," Agnes said. She gestured, and Honor looked—two were framed, hanging over the sideboard. No one captured lost possibilities like John: jagged timbers sticking out of the sand, dark against the moonlit sea. Honor stared at the pictures, tears scalding her eyes.

"We had lots of projects over the years," John said. "That was just the first one."

"You worked together so much," Agnes said. "Mom would set up her easel in the fields where you were building your installations. You inspired each other."

"We did," John said. "At least, she inspired me."

The girls looked at Honor, but she couldn't speak. She stared at John's pictures of the shipwreck. They inspired her even now; she felt alive, energized. These last weeks she had rediscovered the fire in her art, the only thing on earth that allowed her to express the wild emotions inside.

"The point is, your father and I knew each other well," Honor finally said. "We gave ourselves lots of time before we got engaged. And even then, we waited for a year before we got married."

"And you're still together," Regis said, sounding slightly manic. Had she drunk too much wine? "Let's have another toast! Everyone, come on...wow, I wish Peter were here for this..."

"Regis," Honor said warningly.

"Here's to us all being together," Regis said, raising her glass, clinking with everyone.

"Together," her sisters said; John and Honor looked into each other's eyes, but were silent.

"Why won't you say it?" Regis asked, looking directly at Honor.

"Regis, stop," Honor said.

"It's my fault, isn't it?" she asked. "He went to prison because of me, and now you can't let him back in...I ruined everything."

"That's not true," John said quickly. "I went to prison because of my own actions. I've been away for a long time, Regis. Things don't just get back to normal overnight."

"But why not?" Regis asked. "We're a family, aren't we? I want you to come home. Haven't you been punished enough?"

"My punishment had nothing to do with you or your mother or sisters," he said. "Do you hear me? Nothing at all. Figuring things out will take time. Now let's have dinner, Regis. It's a beautiful night, and I'm so glad to be here. Please, let's just eat, okay?"

"I'm not hungry," Regis said, standing up, running out of the room in tears.

Honor struggled to stay calm. She stood up and went after Regis, leaving everyone silent at the table. Walking down the hall, she could hear muffled sobs coming from the girls' room. She knocked and went in. Regis lay facedown on the bed, crying into her pillow.

"You heard your father," she said. "We have to give him time."

"There's already been too much time," Regis cried.

"Honey..."

"You don't want him back," Regis said. "I can tell. You only had him for dinner tonight because of us...because we wanted it so badly."

Honor sat on the edge of the bed, knowing that Regis was partly right. The letter Bernie had given her was the other reason she had agreed to this night. Her body ached with disappointment and grief. This wasn't how she had thought her life would be—welcoming John home from *prison,* trying to console her daughter about things none of them really understood.

Car tires crunched on the gravel outside, and headlights raked the ceiling. Honor craned her neck to see.

"It's Peter," she said.

"Tell him I'll be right out," Regis said.

Honor leaned down, hugged her. Regis's body was tense, her arms wrapped around the pillow.

There was something about having John home that made all his years away seem like forever—they'd never get back what was lost. And Honor had turned so far away from him—she didn't know whether she *could* let him in again. She kissed the back of Regis's head, then left the room and walked down the hall.

Back in the kitchen, with candlelight illuminating the girls' banners and streamers, Honor swallowed hard. She saw Peter approaching the screen door, and walked over to open it for him.

"Hi, Peter," she said.

"I came to see Regis," he said.

"She'll be out in a minute," Honor said, gesturing toward the table. "Come sit with us, and meet her father. John, this is Regis's fiancé, Peter Drake."

"I'm glad to meet you, Peter," John said, shaking the young man's hand.

"You too," he said. His gaze slid down the hall, toward Regis's door. Then he looked at Agnes and Cece, and they both smiled.

"So," John said, regarding Peter with an admirably open gaze. Whatever his private feelings about meeting the betrothed of his twenty-year-old daughter after the last scene, he was revealing nothing.

Peter smiled confidently. He pulled out the chair beside the one where Regis had been sitting, and sat down. Honor passed him a plate, and he helped himself to fish and corn. "Isn't Regis eating?" he asked, looking around.

"I guess not," Agnes said. And no one else did, either—except Peter, who spread butter on his corn and ate it. Probably to be polite, Agnes and Cece took a few small bites. John and Honor sat still, unable to touch anything.

Honor stared at John, and he tried to smile. It didn't work. They were doing this for the girls. Her heart was beating so hard, she was sure everyone could hear. Facing her husband down the table, she saw the questions in his eyes. He wasn't looking for reassurance; she saw him wondering whether he should leave.

Honor wanted to tell him to stay. She mouthed the word. He nodded slightly.

"Aren't you having any?" Peter asked John, indicating the platter of corn.

"Not right now," John said.

"Too bad; it's good," Peter said. "Butter-and-sugar is the best. Connecticut really does corn right."

"I've always thought so," John said.

"Guess you missed it while you were *away*."

Agnes actually gasped, and Cece just frowned. To Honor, it felt like a slap across the face—and she was surprised by the powerful urge she felt to leap to John's defense. But John just seemed to take the statement in, roll it around his mind, and feel no particular need to react. Still, Honor knew him well enough to see that Peter's words had done their work; she saw the dangerous glint in his eyes.

"Peter," John said, "what are your intentions?"

"About what?"

"My daughter Regis."

"Well, to marry her," Peter said confidently.

"You're in college, right?"

"Yes," he said. "I go to Tufts. Well, I have to finish my education— we both do. We're not going to drop out or anything."

"That's good. But what will you do for work?" John asked.

"I work some afternoons at the golf course."

"That's a summer job. Who's going to pay the rent?"

Honor watched Peter's gaze falter, and she felt a delicious rush of vindication. Hearing John confront him so matter-of-factly sent shivers down her spine.

"The rent?" Peter asked. "Our parents." He tried a laugh on for size, but when he caught John's reaction—pure seriousness—he stopped.

"That's how it works?" John asked.

"My parents give me a hard time, but they'll come through," Peter said. "I just assumed you and Mrs. Sullivan would want to help out…"

"Where I come from," John said, "when you ask someone to marry you, you're old enough to plan for your future, and take responsibility. It's just one measure of how much you love each other."

"Hmm," Peter said, as if he had already judged John's way of loving someone, found it wanting. He used his napkin to wipe his mouth, glanced at his watch, and then down the hall toward Regis's closed door.

"Do you have plans for tonight, Peter?" Honor asked.

"Actually, yes. We're going to movies on the beach. We should head out soon—they start at dark…"

"Well, you might be out of luck," Agnes said. "I have the feeling she's in for the night."

"No, I'm sure she'll want to come," Peter said, pushing back his chair, looking at Honor and not at John. "Could you tell her I'm here?"

"She knows," Honor said.

"I'll get her," Cece said, but Agnes was already on the way to their room.

"I'll wait outside," Peter said.

With Peter standing just outside the door, waiting, Honor was alone with John at the table. His eyes were still sparkling with mischief.

"You never would have gotten away with talking to him like that," she said in a near whisper, "if Regis had been there."

"I am completely aware of that," John said. "Is she okay?"

"She's upset."

He got up and moved down the table to sit next to her, in the chair Regis had abandoned. "I know ... is there anything I can do?"

"She's very upset that you and I aren't 'together' the way she wishes we were."

"Do you want me to leave?"

Honor shook her head. She could see how wounded he was, by all of it. "I'm sorry," she said.

"You don't have to be sorry," he said, taking her hand. She let him hold it, afraid to look into his eyes, afraid he'd see something in hers she didn't want him to know.

"John," she said.

"This is driving me crazy," he said. "To be in this house again, with you and the girls—but to know we're not together. I'm their father, and I feel I barely know them anymore. They've grown up while I was gone!"

"I know," she said, aching and empty.

"And to be sitting here with you," he said. "If only you knew how I've dreamed of this, every single night—I thought if I could look you in the eye, sit beside you and hold your hand ... Jesus, Honor, I thought our love would still be there."

Honor just sat there, staring at their two hands. She wanted to grab him, and she wanted to push him away.

"Let's not do this now," she said. "I wanted tonight to be nice for the girls—and for you."

"I swear, I don't know if I can take it," he said. "Waiting for you to make up your mind about me. It's going to happen, though."

"What?" she whispered as he squeezed her hand.

"Regis will get her wish. We're going to be together."

"John," Honor said, trying to pull her hand away. He wouldn't let her, and when she looked up, she saw fire in his eyes.

"I promise you, Honor. We are."

Honor couldn't reply. She didn't know what she hoped for. Her heart felt pulled in so many directions, and she felt both exhausted and exhilarated.

"I'm actually glad he stopped by," John said, lowering his voice.

"Now I know what we're up against. Why didn't you tell me he's an asshole?"

"She's so in love with him..."

"He's a complete..." John began, but just then Regis rushed past, head down, and banged out the screen door, into Peter's arms. She had stopped crying, but cleaved against his body and rocked with him back and forth, Peter saying something into her ear while glaring at John triumphantly through the screen, across the top of her head.

"I don't think I can go tonight," they heard Regis say. "Next time, though..."

"C'mon," Peter said clearly. "You'll feel better if you get out of here."

Honor felt her blood boiling, but watched John stay calm and if not serene, at least not explosive. She saw the heat in his eyes—where it always was. Anger, rage, sorrow, joy, passion—he could never hide any of it if you knew where to look. But when Regis and Peter stepped back inside, all they saw was John smiling.

"So, you met," Regis said, looking from Peter to her father.

"We did indeed," John said.

"It was good to meet you," Peter said.

"Likewise, Peter."

Peter stared at John, still holding Regis's hand. "You know, I would have asked you for her hand in marriage," he said. "If you'd been here."

"Peter!" Regis exclaimed.

"It's never too late," John said.

"Well, I already asked Mrs. Sullivan," Peter said. "And she gave us her blessing."

"Then consider it done," John said.

"Thanks, Dad," Regis said, throwing her arms around his neck. Honor locked gazes with him. She saw the fighting spirit that she had always loved so much, that prison hadn't quenched, and that Peter Drake had just reignited. "Maybe I'll go to movies on the beach with Peter after all."

"Hubbard's Point beach movies," John said, looking at Honor.

"Your father and I used to go," Honor said, remembering.

"You will again," Regis said dangerously.

And she left with her fiancé, leaving John and Honor standing together, watching them go. As Peter's car drove out the driveway Honor stared at John. They didn't move. They were frozen in the moment, and if Honor closed her eyes, for just that second, she could swear John had never been gone, had been there all this time.

Nineteen

Honor was in her studio, painting with white heat. This new phase had started three nights ago, after John left the house, and hadn't let up since. Her studio was a wreck, filled with discarded sketches, palettes covered with mixed colors, canvases leaning against the wall. Having completed the painting of John carrying his daughter, she had started something new.

She pulled out a box of photos long stowed away. John had never been able to take the final photos he usually made of his sculptures; but here were pictures he had taken of the land in Ballincastle, steps he'd taken before starting to build his installation there. She also found her sketchbook from that trip, and leafed through studies she'd made that first day, trying to capture the dangerous atmosphere—the ruined castle with the sculpture balancing on the cliff's edge.

Going through the box, she'd found the newspaper clippings from the West Cork papers. She had had plenty of time to read them, waiting at St. Finan's Hospital for Regis to get better. Regis had been in complete shock— unable to speak or feed herself. By then John had been taken into custody, and Honor had read the news accounts for details of what had actually happened.

The nurses had brought her tea, oozing sympathy for the woman whose husband had done such a thing. The papers said John had delivered a terrible beating; the evidence showed that the fight had moved across the cliff edge, with White losing a large amount of blood in two distinct spots. Honor overheard the nurses whispering, "Her husband beat his brains out."

Honor had felt sick. They didn't know the whole story. Why wouldn't John let his lawyers mount a case? Yes, he had admitted to killing Greg White, but wasn't he justified in defending himself, defending Regis? He refused to say a word about it, entering a guilty plea at Criminal Court in Cork City.

By the time Regis was well enough for Honor to leave the hospital, it was all over. Honor rushed to Cork, found out that John was facing six years in prison. "Think about the girls!" she'd cried, and he had just shaken his head, hardly able to look at her, saying, "That's who I *am* thinking of, Honor. This way Regis won't have to testify."

She had wept at his iron gaze, at his stubborness and passion and anger now turned into something immovable and terrible that would bludgeon their family to death just as it had killed the man who had dared to attack it. She watched the guards lead him back to his cell, knowing that life as they'd known it was over. She would never forgive him for throwing it all away. All those emotions were swirling around her now as she slashed at the canvas, painting the scene of her family's destruction: Ballincastle, Ireland. As Honor painted the ruined castle, she thought of her ruined family, her unbending husband, as hard in his way as the rocks that were his art, and the tears rolled down her cheeks.

Sleeves rolled up, covered with sweat and paint, she felt as if she were purging something deep inside. She had rediscovered painting as her greatest release, and she needed it now more than ever. Drained from the summer heat, she cleaned her brushes, went into the kitchen for a glass of iced tea.

Sipping the cool drink, she sat at the kitchen table. The girls were all off, busy doing their things. Regis was working in the library, Agnes was on cleanup duty in the convent, and Cece was taking a bike ride.

John's flowers stood in a vase in the middle of the table; a few blue petals had fallen, along with a shower of golden pollen. She stared at the circle of gold dust radiating from the glass and couldn't bring herself to wipe it up—it seemed as beautiful as the flowers themselves. Sometimes what lasted in life was no more resonant than the parts that fell away. The thought made her reach into her writing desk drawer for the letter Bernie had brought her.

Bernie had been wise, doing so. She was throwing Honor's own words right back at her; for Honor had written the letter to Bernie years ago, back when her best friend, the sister of the man she loved, was in a place of sorrow every bit as painful as the one in which Honor found herself now. The picture on the envelope, however, had been drawn by Bernie, sometime after receiving the letter. It showed a sea monster, the Kelly family crest. Staring at it, Honor knew that Bernie had drawn it to claim the connection they all had to each other.

In Honor's family, the past wasn't talked about much. Her grandparents and parents had stressed how lucky they all were that their forebears had come to America.

"Don't look back" had been her father's motto. Whatever suffering had led their ancestors to leave Ireland was better left unexamined.

So when Honor had met John, Bernie, and Tom, it had felt like a true awakening—the way they roamed these hills, letting history be part of their lives.

"I'm going to go to Ireland. And I'm taking you with me, Bernie," Tom had said one day about a year after they had found the box, as they all walked along the wall.

"We'll see," Bernie had said, trying to smile. She was powerfully drawn to the convent, and Honor knew how torn she felt about Tom.

"I can't imagine what they went through," Tom said. "Treated like garbage by the English, dying of starvation. The ones who survived, standing on the docks in Cobh, watching their children sail to America—knowing they'd never see them again, families ripped apart forever. Can you imagine how we'd feel, losing our children that way?"

"We don't have any children," Bernie said, her eyes filling with tears at the image of those people on the docks.

"We will someday, Bernadette," Tom said.

Honor had been watching John. She was deeply in love with him, and she knew she'd die if they had kids and anything like that ever happened. She watched the way he traced the wall with his hand, as if he could somehow comfort the people who had gone through so much.

"Fevers, famine," he said. "The ones who made it here had to have been so strong."

"And so good at what they did," Honor said. She was staring at the wall, at a perfectly round stone fit in among the other shapes. How had they done it? John's stonemason ancestors had been artists in their own way. Perhaps John had gotten his love of natural materials—rocks, branches, water, ice—from them.

"Cormac buried the truth of their journey," John said. "But we're going to uncover it."

"What do you mean?" Honor asked.

"You heard Tom—he asked Bernie to go to Ireland with him. We'll go someday, too. Think of the land in West Cork—the cliffs, and seacoast. And just north, the Ring of Kerry, the Dingle Peninsula. The Cliffs of Moher, up by Galway...all on the west coast, Honor. Just across the Atlantic, America was calling them. You can paint, and I'll do something at the edge of the land, right on the cliff, facing America."

"Sullivan on the brink," Tom said. "Typical. You going to capture the feeling of exile and loss?"

"The feeling of losing one life so you can gain another," John said. "It was dangerous, what they did. Why shouldn't it be for me, too?" Then, putting his arms around Honor, "Promise me you'll come with me?"

"I wouldn't miss it for anything," she'd promised, ripples of excitement running through her body.

Now, sitting at the kitchen table, she thought about the moment when she'd changed. Not John—but her. Back then, she had been falling in love with John and his way of seeing adventure in every part of life. She had loved the way he combined his work and emotions, made sense of everything by building sculptures wild enough to contain it all. Because his feelings were so extreme, so was his work.

And Honor had loved it, been thrilled by the risks he was willing to take, until one day. She knew the minute her feelings had changed: the day that Regis came into the world. With their daughter's birth, Honor had wanted John to stop being so daring. She wanted closeness and safety, not wildness and danger. Children transformed everything, she thought, her gaze blurring as she stared at the Kelly crest on Bernie's envelope.

Just then she heard a knock at the kitchen door. The sun had dipped behind the trees and chapel, so the yard was in shadow. Peering out, she saw John standing there—she felt a jolt, as if she had conjured him. Beckoning him in, she pushed Bernie's letter beneath a placemat.

"How are you?" he asked.

"I'm fine," she said uncomfortably. "And you?"

"I'm fine," he said. "Are the girls home?"

"No," she said. "They're out and about."

"We have to talk," he said. His eyes looked bruised, as if he had just gone ten rounds. She stared at him, knowing she'd done very little to make his homecoming happy or easy.

"You've been painting," he said, staring at the streaks of paint on her forearms.

She nodded, but didn't say anything.

"The other night was nice," he said, standing by the kitchen table. "Thank you for having me for dinner."

"You're welcome," she said. Things had seemed easygoing by the end of that night, but now he looked tense and upset again, and her time in the studio had left her feeling fragile and on edge.

"Look," he said. "Seeing you is hard. I won't lie to you, Honor."

"I'm sorry...it is for me, too."

"I know. I don't want to make this any harder for you than it already is, but Jesus—I have to see the kids. Spending time with you all the other night was so great. It's all I've been able to think about since then."

Honor looked away. She couldn't tell him that it had been the same for her. Her stomach churned as she struggled to sit still, trying to listen.

"We have to figure out a way," he said. "For me to see them regularly. No matter what you think, I know it's the best thing for them. I don't think I'm being selfish here—I'm their father, and..."

"I'm not going to fight you on it, John," she said.

"You're not?" he asked, surprised. He stopped short, looking at her. She could see that he hadn't been sleeping. His eyes were sunken, rimmed with shadows. Yet even so, she saw the brightness in them; his heart and his curiosity about life were as alive as ever. And though he was gaunt, he stood as straight and strong as he ever had. She looked at him, holding back the desire to reach for his hand.

"How could I?" she asked. "They love you so much."

"But I thought..." he said, confused. "I thought you'd made up your mind I'm bad for them—and bad for you."

"Those are two different things," she murmured.

"Honor," he said, reaching his hand halfway across the table, as if wishing she'd hold it. She kept her hands clasped in her lap. "I screwed up so badly. When I think back to what I let happen over in Ireland, I'm so sorry."

"It was a long time ago," she said.

"But I'll be paying for it the rest of my life!" he said, his voice rising. "The worst part is, so will the girls. They have to live with it, people knowing their father went to jail for killing a man. Did you see the way Peter acted?"

Honor nodded, every muscle in her body tensing.

"He's just a kid, and he looks down on me that way. Imagine what that makes Regis feel like. I can't stand thinking what it makes *you* feel like!"

"What he thinks doesn't matter!" Honor said, exploding. "Who cares what Peter Drake says or thinks? All I care about is what happened to your family. Our family, John!"

"I broke everything," he said, grabbing her hands. "That day on the cliff. I didn't protect Regis, I let a maniac into our lives, I turned into a monster myself, and Regis saw. She says she doesn't remember anything—because what happened was too terrible for her to take in. I know that's my fault, Honor. That's the reason you don't love me anymore—just tell me."

"It happened before that day," she cried, pulling her hands away.

"What?"

"You and I," she said. "You and I broke years before we went to Ireland..."

"Tell me," he said, looking shocked, as if she'd just thrown ice water on him.

"You don't even know," she wept. "You went to Ireland and grieved for your ancestors, all those families torn apart by the famine and immigration. But we were torn apart, too. Everything that ever mattered to me—art, love, you—I thought we'd have it forever."

"We could have," he said.

"Don't you know what it was like for me?" she asked. "I was a dedicated 'passionate' artist, too! But once we had the girls, I wanted our family to come first. I loved you so much."

"But I loved you," he said, looking bewildered. "Do you think I didn't?"

"When you had to go to Labrador, to photograph the aurora borealis on the shortest day of the year... and then got snowed in through Christmas, because of a blizzard, and I was home alone with the girls, missing their father. And when you had to go to Churchill, to build a snow cave, an ice house, to get pictures of polar bear families... when your own family was worried about you, terrified you'd get torn limb from limb."

"Honor..."

"And the trip to Ireland," she said. "That I'd been looking forward to ever since we found the box, ever since you made me promise to go with you... only I didn't go with you, John. You went ahead. You crawled through the holds of the famine ships with Greg White—someone you just met on the docks. He had that experience with you, not me."

"That terrible day," he said, "I broke everything."

"You're not listening!" she said, her voice rising. "It didn't all hinge on that one day! Ballincastle was just the culmination of what had been going on between us for *years*."

"You're telling me it's over between us?" he asked.

Her heart pounded in her throat. She looked at him, saw the wildness in his eyes. John's fierce love had gotten him into so much trouble, and she saw it pouring from him now. She couldn't answer his question, even after everything, even now. Tearing from the room, she ran into her studio and slammed the door behind her.

She sat at her easel, staring at her painting of Ballincastle; she didn't move until she heard him leave the house, saw him walking up over the hill toward the beach. Her heart was in her throat. She picked up her brush and went at the canvas, as if she could just paint the truth of their lives.

Or as if she could paint it all away.

Twenty

Regis was nearing the end of her shift at Paradise the next night. She was so tired of serving ice cream; her feet hurt, her face ached from smiling at customers. Most of all, she felt really uneasy about her mother. She'd barely come out of her studio for days. Regis had heard her crying behind the closed door. When she had told Peter, he had listened with disgust, said it was all her father's fault and that he should just realize he was poison for the Sullivan family, making Regis (a) wish she hadn't told him and (b) feel like slapping him.

Right now, everything just seemed wrong. Her stomach was in a knot, and she swore that at twenty she was probably the youngest person ever to suffer from ulcers and bunions, but even worse, something was hurting deep inside, behind her rib cage, as if her heart were being pinched. She twisted, trying to adjust the way she was standing, hoping for the pain to go away, but it was as strong as ever. Luckily, it was seven forty-five, and she got off work at eight tonight.

The line moved quickly, with Regis and her coworkers serving families, couples, tourists, beachgoers. A garland of lanterns—brightly colored, illuminating the trees—waved in the breeze. Regis spied Peter and the Hubbard's Point gang leaning against Matt Donovan's father's old Firebird, waiting for her to finish. Kris and Josh were there, Angela and Mick, but no Hayley or Jimmy, and, Regis was *most* happy to note, no Alicia.

She waved, just before going to fill an order of two hot fudge sundaes, with extra whipped cream on one, no nuts on the other, and Peter lifted his hand in response. He had such a cool way about him, the way he barely smiled, but followed her with his eyes. He had a certain *thereness* about him—a way of holding back, aloof but present—that she had always cherished and found devastatingly attractive. So why, tonight, did it bother her?

Seeing him across the parking lot with his friends, she almost wished she had to work till eleven. There was no clear reason for this unwelcome feeling to be swirling around; none whatsoever. She was so ready to finish her shift, each minute as it ticked down felt like a hammer blow to her spine. But once she was done, Peter would expect her to jump into the car beside him, and astoundingly, she wasn't in the mood.

At precisely seven fifty-seven, the sound of a car badly in need of a muffler came into earshot, attracting the attention of everyone. Regis watched Peter's head turn first, and then his friends checked it out. They snickered, making Regis feel sorry for the poor person caught driving faulty machinery. But as the car came into sight, her heart did a somersault, and she felt like shouting for Peter and his friends to think again.

Brendan and his brightly painted ancient Volvo pulled up right in front. Brendan and Cece jumped out first, followed by Agnes— Brendan held Agnes's door, shielding her shaved and fractured skull from bumping the frame. Once Peter saw that it was Agnes, he held the others back—but Regis saw that Matt had been about to call something out to Brendan.

"Are we in time?" Cece asked, leaning on the counter with folded arms.

"There's always time for you," Regis said.

"You don't have to wait on us," Agnes said. "We tried to get here earlier, but we saw these amazing tree swallows flying in figure eights above Joshuatown Cove, and..."

"The main thing is," Brendan said, "we wanted to pick you up and hang out with you tonight."

"That was before we saw Peter," Agnes said, giving Peter a polite smile and wave. "We know we'll lose out to him...."

"Hmm," Regis said, whipping open her pad. Maybe they could combine plans and all hang out together. She'd ask Peter in a minute. "What'll it be?" she asked.

"Regis! It's the witching hour!" called Angela Morelli, one of the Hubbard's Point kids standing with Peter, as the chapel bell at Star of the Sea rang eight o'clock, the clear tones drifting across the marsh.

"Just a minute!" Regis called.

"Boooo!" Mick and Angela called, anxious to get going.

Agnes, Cece, and Brendan all ordered chocolate ice cream cones, and Regis made them extra large and handed them across the counter. She hung her apron on the hook and left through the back door, wishing she didn't smell quite so much like the fryolator. As she hurried around the corner, she caught sight of Brendan with his hand resting tenderly on Agnes's back. It made her feel happy for Agnes and sad for herself in a way that made no sense.

"Well, I'm glad we got to see you here," Cece said. " 'Cause it looks as if you and Peter already have plans."

"We do," Regis said. "Beach movies—why don't you come with us?"

"At Hubbard's Point?" Cece asked, sounding so thrilled she nearly dropped her ice cream.

"Yes," Regis said, smiling, knowing how much her sisters loved going there.

"That would be so fun!" Agnes said.

"Sure," Brendan agreed.

So Regis nodded and loped over to Peter, slung her arm around his neck, and kissed him.

"Hey, babe," he said. "Looks like a family reunion."

"I just asked them to come to the movies with us," she said.

He gave her a raised eyebrow. "All of them?" he asked.

"Of course," she said. "What are you talking about?"

"That guy's weird," Josh said, staring at Brendan. "I see him around."

"What a loser car," Kris said.

"Actually, he's a great guy," Regis said. "He took care of my sister in the hospital that first night after she nearly died, which means I'll love him for life, so don't call him weird and don't say he has a loser car again, okay?"

"Ooooh, bitchy!" came the voice from the nether reaches of Matt's back seat. Regis looked in, saw Alicia all slunk down as if she were sulking.

"I didn't see you there," Regis said.

"I'm sure you're feeling all warm and fuzzy to see me now," Alicia said.

"Well, I would have been if you hadn't called me bitchy."

"So, you're defending a male nurse," Alicia said. "That's what he is, you know. I saw him at the clinic the other day, when I had an evil reaction to my new tattoo…no looking, Peter—it's somewhere married men aren't allowed to peek."

"He's not married yet, ha-ha!" Josh said.

"What's wrong with being a male nurse?" Regis asked, latching on to Alicia's putdown of Brendan as being even viler than the seductive look she'd just flashed at Peter.

"It's incredibly gay."

"What's wrong with gay?" Regis asked, ignoring the obvious fact that Brendan was in love with Agnes, and even more incredible—and Regis realized this just now, at this instant, gazing over at Agnes and Brendan together—that Agnes was in love with him.

"Never mind gay," Alicia said. "He's just totally déclassé. A nurse driving that car—it's just so off my radar screen."

"Your radar screen—" Regis started to say, but Peter took her arm, interrupted her.

"Girls, girls, no fighting," Peter said.

Regis glared at him—why couldn't he defend her against this awful snob? She had to face the fact that something inside her was acting up—it felt—she couldn't believe it—as if her love was melting faster than the polar ice caps.

"Look, whatever you want to say about the kid," Angela said, "who really cares? I just want to get back to the beach for the movie. It's *Pirates of the Caribbean,* and if you make me miss Johnny Depp, I won't be a happy girl. In fact, I'll be massively devastated and inclined toward self-destruction."

"Yeah, let's go," Josh said.

Regis looked up at Peter, feeling the seconds click by; with every heartbeat, he was missing the chance to defend Brendan, speak up for Regis. What was happening between them, and why did it seem to have started after her father had come home? The pinched feeling around her heart seemed worse than ever. Glancing around, Regis counted up—the car was already full. She stepped away from Peter.

"I'll ride with my sisters and Brendan," she said. "Meet you there?"

"Fine, whatever," Peter said.

Regis nodded; that was just how she felt, too.

Agnes knew that something was wrong; Regis didn't even have to say, or roll her eyes, or raise her eyebrows. It was just there—in her being, the slant of her shoulders, the air around her. It felt funny to Agnes, to sit in front with a boy while her two sisters sat in the back seat—usually it was Regis up front, with Peter, or one of the boys who had come before him—with Agnes in back with Cece. But Regis climbed in back without a word, and driving down the Shore Road, the whole thing started to feel okay, pretty natural.

Especially because Brendan was so nice and funny, letting her pick the music, something her sisters almost never let her do. Cece was going a little crazy, telling him to change stations every time they hit a song she didn't like, but Brendan just chuckled and didn't seem to mind at all.

"You sure there's no problem with all of us showing up for the beach movie?" Brendan asked, glancing into the rearview mirror to see Regis's eyes.

"No problem at all," Regis said, in a purring tone that let Agnes knew there was a lot more to it.

They rattled down Route 156; Brendan had mentioned needing to get his muffler replaced, but he never had any money to spare, and as long as the car ran, he'd just keep driving. That was so different from Peter's way of doing things; he'd just ask his parents for a new car. Turning under the train trestle into Hubbard's Point, Regis leaned forward so the security guard would recognize her.

"It's nice in here," Brendan said, looking around as they headed down the shady road. "I've never been here before."

"Let's show him Mom's old cottage," Cece said.

"Sure," Agnes said. "I can never remember exactly how to get there, though. Do you know, Regis?"

"Yep. We'll take the long way. Go right here...there's the cemetery, and that's Foley's Store, where all the kids leave each other notes...and left at the stop sign...and now loop up behind the tennis courts..."

Halfway down the road that led to the Point, Agnes told Brendan to stop the car. They pulled over and leaned forward to look up the hill. There was Agnes's mother's old cottage: still weathered, nestled into the rock ledge, surrounded by pine trees.

"You can't tell from here," Agnes said, "but it has a beautiful view of the water."

"Our mother used to sit on the front porch and watch down the Sound for our father," Regis said. "He'd hike through the woods, or sometimes he'd row in a dinghy...but he'd always get here somehow, and she'd always be watching."

"Remember she told us about those kids next door who used to climb up on the roof?" Cece asked. "The boy who grew up to be an astronaut..."

"Zeb," Agnes said. "And Rumer. She's Sisela's vet."

"Really?" Cece asked.

"Yes," Agnes said. "Mom used to watch them climb up to the peak of their roof and gaze out at the stars. Once she decided to do the same—except instead of looking for stars, she was watching for Dad. And we all know what happened..."

"She fell off and broke her collarbone," Cece said.

"That's why she gets so freaked out about heights," Regis said. "Like when Dad used to go up the Devil's Hole cliffs. She has a fear of falling, or of people she loves falling."

Agnes felt Brendan reach for her hand. Was he thinking of how she'd looked that night in the hospital, having smashed into the rock? Had he seen her mother's reaction, which, although Agnes couldn't quite remember, must have been terrible?

"If that's true," Cece said, "why do you two keep doing crazy things that land you in the hospital?"

"Because it's how we know we're alive," Regis said.

Agnes felt prickles on the back of her neck. It was, quite possibly, the truest thing Regis had ever said. As Agnes turned around, to look at her and acknowledge the wisdom in her words, she saw Regis staring—dangerously, a million miles away—at her engagement ring, sparkling in the light of the rising moon.

"Maybe now that Dad's home, we won't have to do crazy things anymore," Agnes said.

Regis didn't reply; she just stared out the window.

Agnes stared at her; her sister was worried about something. Deeply troubled—why hadn't Agnes noticed the circles under her eyes before? "What's wrong?" she asked.

"Regis had the worst dream ever last night," Cece said.

"I know. Mom came into our room last night to see if you were okay," Agnes said to Regis. "And you didn't even wake up."

"It was a bad one," Regis agreed.

"Do you remember it?"

"Something about Ballincastle," Regis said quietly

"The usual," Cece said. "Right?"

But Regis just kept looking out the window.

"You might be dreaming about it now because of the fact that Mom's painting the scene—did you see?" Agnes asked.

"That scary old castle," Cece said, shivering. "And Dad's sculpture with the cross on the top. And the three of us looking out the cottage window. It's not one of my favorite paintings. It reminds me of being unhappy, while Dad was away...Regis, did your dream have—"

"I don't want to talk about my dream anymore!" Regis cried sharply.

"Regis, I'm sorry!" Cece said, sounding shocked.

"Let it go, Cecilia."

Her tone stung, and when Agnes turned to look into the back seat, she saw that Cece had tears in her eyes. Starting to admonish Regis, Agnes stopped short. Regis's eyes were wild, staring out the window, as if she'd seen something that scared her to death.

They were late for the movies, so Brendan turned the car around at the dead end. As they drove down to the beach, Agnes felt hot inside, almost as if she had swallowed a burning coal. In some ways, Agnes knew that they were all haunted by Regis's dream. She had cried out in her sleep, in words too garbled to understand. But the meaning was clear, nonetheless: she'd been terrified, fighting to save someone she loved.

What had happened, and what did it have to do with their father's coming home? Agnes knew that the two things were related, and so did her sister, sitting silently in the back seat.

"Cece, I'm sorry," Regis said.

"I didn't mean to upset you," Cece wept.

"Oh God. Don't cry."

"It's just..." Cece sniffled uncontrollably. "I was so worried about you last night. That dream sounded so scary, the way you were talking, and I wanted to help you, but I couldn't..."

"Cece, it was just a dream."

"We're happy now, right?" Cece asked, brushing away tears. "Now that Dad's back home? You'll feel better, Regis."

"He and Mom aren't together," Regis said hollowly. "In my dream, it was all my fault."

"But it's not your fault. And besides, they will be. And she's painting that picture of his sculpture," Cece said. "As if she's thinking of him. And he's building that crazy circle of stones on the beach...out of pieces from the rock..."

"Something good will come of it," Agnes said. "They're artists, and they inspire each other. Isn't it obvious?"

Regis wasn't the only person in the house to have spent a sleepless night. Sometime after midnight, Honor had finished her painting. The large canvas depicted Ballincastle, the ruins of both the old castle and John's sculpture. The cross on top was stark against the stormy sky. In the distance, looking out the windows of the small thatched-roof cottage, were the faces of her daughters. She'd stood back, examining the picture, knowing that she had captured the dark spirit of that time. But she and John were nowhere on the canvas. They were everywhere—and nowhere.

When she heard Regis tossing and turning, crying out in her sleep, she wiped the paint from her hands and ran to comfort her. Agnes and Cece were sitting up in their beds. Regis was weeping, unintelligible words coming from her mouth.

"Honey, wake up. It's just a dream..."

Honor held her, wanting her to wake up so they could confront the terror together, break through to its source. But her daughter drifted more deeply into sleep, and Honor finally kissed her and her sisters and walked back into the studio.

Standing in the kitchen now, she looked out the window. The girls were out—Regis had been working, and Cece was with Agnes and Brendan. They'd called to say they were all going to movies on the beach at Hubbard's Point.

Honor stared toward the water, wishing for John. She thought of how hard his homecoming had been, and wondered how he was doing tonight.

She left the kitchen, closing the door behind her, and walked across the meadow, awash in late-day light. Dragonflies hovered over the green-gold grasses, and asters swayed in the breeze. When she got to the vineyard, she smelled the pungent aroma of ripening grapes; soon it would be harvesttime.

Reaching the wall, she paused. She stood above the beach, feeling the sea breeze ruffle her hair. Down below, John had stopped working for the day. All the fragments of broken rock had been arranged on the sand. At first Honor thought it was just one big circle, but as she stared down, she saw that he had created an intricate pattern— with rocks, stones, and pebbles arrayed around and around in concentric circles, doubling back on themselves, creating a labyrinth. In the center, there was an empty space.

She climbed down the hill. When she got to the stone house, she saw John sitting on the sand, arms wrapped around his knees, staring at the sea.

"Hello," she said.

"Hi, Honor," he said, sounding surprised.

"I saw what you made," she said, gesturing at the labyrinth. "It's so interesting. It's beautiful."

"Thank you."

"You did it," she said. "Put the broken rock together. Just in a different form."

"Wishful thinking, I guess. But it feels so good to be able to work again. I started thinking it's all a puzzle. The rock can never be whole again. And us...we're not fitting together, because something's missing. Maybe we lost it in Ireland, or maybe—as you said the other night—it was missing for a long time."

"Missing?"

"Something we can't find...a place we can't get to. That's why I made a labyrinth. I thought, maybe that's the only thing I could build that would make sense of us. Of you and me, Honor. The path is mixed up, confusing, but if you stick with it, you eventually reach the center." He shook his head. "That was my plan, anyway, but tonight it feels like something else."

"Like what?"

"Going in circles, making wrong turns, trying to get somewhere that doesn't even exist."

"It exists," she said quietly. "We exist."

He shrugged, staring back at the sea.

"Listen to me," she said. "We exist."

"We do?" he asked, looking up.

She nodded. "Do you have a beach blanket in that house?"

"Sure," he said, looking confused.

"I want you to take me to the movies," she said.

"What movies?"

"At Hubbard's Point—remember how we used to go? When my family had a cottage there, and you used to come over for beach movies?"

"Are you serious?"

"Completely."

"But we don't have a beach sticker, to get in," John said, starting to smile.

"I know; that is a problem."

His eyes were sparks in the fading light. "You want to go to the movies," he said, "I'll get us in."

He grabbed a blanket from inside and started toward Honor's house, where she kept the car, but she grabbed his hand.

"The beach way," she said.

"Really?" he asked. "It's almost dark."

"If we have to sneak in, we have to do it right," she said, holding tight to his hand. "Are you saying you can't do it?"

"Trust me on this, beach girl. When you were living at Hubbard's Point and I was here with the Kelly contingent, I found shortcuts to get to you that no one else would ever find. Are you up for it?"

"I am," she said, gazing into his eyes. "You're going to show me *all* your shortcuts?" she said, feeling excited. He had kept so much of himself hidden all these years; in some ways, knowing him more fully was all she had ever wanted.

He nodded solemnly, taking a step closer, so they were eye to eye.

"I am," he said. "And you know what else?"

"What?" she whispered. The air was sunset-still and summer-warm, but she felt a shiver run down her spine.

"Right now, I want to show you everything."

"John," she said.

He put one finger to her lips. "Everything, Honor."

Her emotions swirled as they set off through the vineyard, following the sound of the waves and the smell of the sea, toward the place she had once called home.

Twenty-one

John and Honor started off along the beach, where every narrow creek and gully they came to had them grabbing each other's hands, helping each other across. The wind-silvered driftwood log straddling the mouth of the tidal marsh was slightly rickety, so he crouched down for her to climb on his back. To his surprise, she took him up on it. Her touch sent his heart racing, and all he wanted to do was stop and put her down and kiss her. He couldn't believe this was happening.

He kept carrying her, even after he'd jumped down off the log. Her arms were draped around his neck, her legs clamped around his waist, and her cheek resting gently against his. She didn't tell him to put her down, so he didn't.

They made their way down the beach. The water was to their right, and the woods, part of a nature preserve, rose up on the left. Just past a falling-down jetty, he headed up the beach to what looked like thick, impenetrable brush. Only then did he put Honor down, as he held aside a thatch of vines, ushering her into the warren of hidden paths.

Walking through the darkest, spookiest part of the forest, he slipped a protective arm around her waist. He couldn't stay away from her, and the scariness of the woods gave him an excuse to be close. She huddled against him as they skirted the Indian Grave, as they passed the old foundation, the haunted remains of the mansion called Fish Hill.

"This is the way I came every night to get to you," he said.

"Until you had your license," she said.

"Even then, I sometimes walked. There was always something about coming through the woods—out of the darkness, into the light—your light, Honor—that made me want to do this..." He'd been feeling such despair these last few days, thinking it was all over. Ireland had been the last straw—what had she said? The culmination of so much...But here she was, smiling at him, and he saw that brightness, her radiance, again.

"Were these trails always here?"

"I cut my way through the brush—I guess some of these paths date back to when I was a kid. Someone has kept them up, though."

"Regis comes through here sometimes," Honor said. "To see Peter."

"I showed her the way a long time ago," John said. "Because she wanted to see the route I took to you."

"She wants to be in love like we were," Honor said quietly.

"I know," John said. He wanted that for his daughter, too—but he doubted there could be anything like what he felt for Honor. They walked along, and John thought about Regis blazing trails to Peter—instead of the other way around.

"Do you really believe there are ghosts here?" she asked, ducking under a low bough.

"If you do," he said, wanting her to press right against him.

"I'm not sure whether I do or not. What did you believe in Ireland? I remember you wouldn't answer me there, either."

"There," he said, and his heart shut down just slightly. He didn't like to think about it or talk about it, but if Honor was asking, he owed her a reply. As they tromped through the Tomahawk Point woods, she reached for his hand, making him want to tell her anything she wanted to know.

"They were there," he said. "I felt them in Cobh, on the docks. I thought of how you and I would have felt, watching our daughters sail away, knowing we'd never see them again. And I felt the ghosts of our families down through the centuries, Honor."

"I felt them, every time we had to leave you after one of our visits," she said.

"You know," he said, "as much as I hated not seeing you and the girls, I was almost glad when you stopped coming. Because I couldn't stand when you left."

"We couldn't stand leaving," Honor said, and they walked in silence for a while, the only sounds those of the leaves beneath their feet, and seagulls calling from the beach up ahead.

They rounded the corner, and she leaned into him. A tall hill sloped down to the beach, and getting there required either climbing over or sliding under a fallen tree. John stood still, savoring the weight of her body against his. Maybe they could just stand here for the rest of the night.

"Are you ready?" Honor asked, looking down the steep trail.

"Whenever you are," he said, ducking under the tree, waiting for her to follow.

"Lead on," she said, and he did, taking a first step down the jagged path, scored and furrowed by runoff, pebbles sliding underfoot as he blocked her from slipping and sliding. And when they got safely to the bottom, feet sinking into the soft sand, she gave him her hand again.

When they got to the main part of the beach, they saw that many people had already set down their blankets. The movie screen was a white sheet, hung between the upright supports of what looked like a football goalpost. Honor surveyed the scene, pointed out a spot; John was happy to see it was toward the back of the crowd.

"How's this?" he asked.

"Perfect," she said. "But we have to dig a pit."

"Exactly," he said. They both crouched down, dug a hole in the sand, building up a smooth mound for a backrest.

They got into the spirit of it, scooping sand from the hole, packing it on the sloping back edge. Spreading their blanket in the pit, they were preparing to sit down and get ready for the movie when some-one called Honor's name.

"Honor, is that you?"

"Yes," she said, peering through the darkness. Two old friends of hers from the Hubbard's Point days, Suzi Wright and Darby Reid, came running over. John had met them long ago.

"We sneaked in to see the movie," Honor said.

"Well, we'll never tell," Suzi said. "We're just so glad to see some-one from the old guard here. A few others are around...see, there's Bay McCabe, over there, and there's Tara O'Toole up on the board-walk with Maeve Jameson..."

"Oh, Maeve," Honor said, sounding happy. "She and my mother were great friends."

"What's this I hear about your daughter marrying a Hubbard's Pointer?"

"Peter Drake," Honor said. "Yes, they're engaged."

"Oh, his parents are here. See? Just past Maeve and Tara."

"Oh, yes," Honor said. "I see them. Well, John and I are undercover tonight, just sneaking in to see the movie. I think we'll wait to see the Drakes another time."

"Have you met them yet, John?" Darby asked.

"They've heard about me, I'm sure," John said.

"Well, of course they have," Suzi said warmly. "We're so proud to know such a famous artist."

Honor threw her friend such a grateful look for the support, and in that instant John saw her vulnerability—and wondered how often she'd had to defend him to other friends and acquaintances.

Just then the screen brightened; the movie was about to start. Suzi and Darby kissed Honor, smiled their goodbyes at John, and left them to their blanket. As they walked away, John noticed quite a few peo-ple along the boardwalk looking in his direction.

Honor held his hand, pulled him down on the blanket. The pit they'd excavated kept them snug, and their sand backrest hid them from prying eyes.

"Are you okay?" she asked.

"I'm fine," he said. "Are you?"

"I'm fine, too," she said.

They each smiled; they were both lying and knew it. His heart was racing, and when he glanced over the top of the backrest, at the people Suzi had said were Peter's parents, he saw them staring at him, talking with several others. He felt as if he were about to be lynched.

"Honor," he said. "Are you sure you're okay?"

"I'm very okay," she said. "And getting better."

"This is going to be your life," he said. "With me. People like that staring and talking. I don't blame you if you don't want it. I swear, Honor—I wouldn't blame you at all."

"I told you—I don't care what people think. That's never been the problem." She stood up, brushed sand from her legs. "Come on."

"What are you doing?"

She gave him her hand, hauled him up. Her eyes were blazing as she led him across the beach, toward the boardwalk. John looked up, saw the Milky Way, a filmy swath of white stars across the summer sky. Honor walked directly over to a couple standing under the pavilion.

"Hi, Millie," Honor said, smiling politely. "Hello, Ralph. I'd like you to meet my husband, John."

He stood straighter at that, *my husband*. She could have said *Regis's father* . . .

"How do you do?" John asked. They all shook hands.

"We've heard so much about you," Millie said, dimpling with unrestrained glee, leaving what they'd heard hanging in the air.

"Indeed we have," Ralph said, with the friendly smile of the nineteenth hole. A man who lived the good life, his face was red, his eyes squinty.

Dead silence as the Drakes let the moment pass, letting it be known that, to them, he was famous for something other than his art. He felt as if he contained the eye of a hurricane, the calm before the storm. Trouble was brewing in his chest, low pressure forming. That old rage he'd felt in Portlaoise Prison was building, building, as he felt himself judged by the parents of a boy he already didn't like, a boy who thought he had a right to John's daughter.

"So," Ralph said. And in that instant his puffy eyes went from golf-friendly to bull shark. "You were released early."

"I was released on time," John said.

"I understand from friends at the Dublin bar that Tom Kelly prevailed on a barrister to intervene on your behalf."

"Ralph..." Millie said, authoritative.

"Friends at the Dublin bar..." John said.

"I made inquiries," Ralph said. "Your daughter is marrying my son, after all."

"All you would have had to do," Honor said sharply, "was ask me. I've not tried to hide anything."

"Yet you didn't know he was on the way home," Ralph said.

John felt Honor cringe beside him. He sensed her wanting to defend him, but Ralph's words were true. Down on the beach, the picture stuttered, hesitated—technical difficulties. Everyone groaned; bunches of kids took the opportunity to run to the ice cream truck for movie treats.

"I didn't tell her," John said. "That's on me—I know what my family has gone through, and I didn't want to force anything on them."

"Force?" Ralph asked, with a low chuckle. "That seems a specialty of yours." Shadows wobbled behind him, kids congregating out of nowhere. John narrowed his eyes, couldn't make out the faces.

John opened his mouth to reply, but what was the point? He didn't owe this guy anything—he had seen the contempt in Peter's eyes already, and now he knew where it came from.

Peter's father took a step closer. John felt the energy change—he didn't see it coming, had no idea what was about to happen. All he knew was that Ralph Drake was in his face, leaning forward, in an almost menacing way.

"Don't hurt my father!" Regis shrieked. "Leave him alone!" She came charging out of the shadows, out of control, crying and throwing herself between John and Peter's father. Ralph Drake ducked back, to get away. Regis wouldn't let him go; she started flailing, and suddenly Brendan stepped forward, gently guiding her backward.

Regis dissolved in sobs, hands over her eyes. Everyone around them was silent, in shock.

"He was hurting my father," Regis wept. "I had to stop him."

"I know," Brendan said. Regis's sisters crowded around, trying to get to her.

John watched, stunned. Regis just stood there, burying her face in her hands, as if by not looking she could block it all out. Her sobs were deep and wrenching, almost inhuman, as if they weren't even coming from her.

"Are you all right?" John heard Millie Drake ask her husband. "Did she hurt you?"

"She scratched me," Ralph Drake said.

"Regis, what's going on?" Peter asked, sounding shell-shocked.

But Regis just cried, unable to look up or speak or move. John met Brendan's eyes, gesturing for him to go to Agnes, who stood off to the side, eyes wide with helpless shock. John stepped forward, reaching out to hold his daughter

"Daddy," Regis wept. "I had to make him stop..."

"Stop him?" Millie Drake asked. "From asking a few questions? You attacked Peter's father!"

"This is crazy," Peter said to Regis.

"I'm sorry," Regis said, eyes wide now with panic and confusion.

"You're acting just like him. That's what you come from. Why should I be surprised? My parents were just trying to protect you—from him!"

John heard someone behind him saying that the police were on the way. Agnes and Cece pressed closer to Regis. Her knees went weak, and John tightened his grip to keep her from falling

Honor turned on him, all the love and tenderness gone, replaced by a distant, dead look.

"Don't," she said coldly.

"Honor," John said, "I have to talk to her."

"No," Honor said. "She's coming home with me."

"You don't understand," John said, lowering his voice so no one in the crowd could hear. "It's important...I have to talk to her right now."

"It's too much!" she said, her voice rising. "No more, John. It's over."

"Honor, you have to listen—"

She ignored him, supporting Regis as she walked away. She gestured to Brendan, who nodded and ran to the parking lot to start his car. The other girls followed, glancing back at John with confused regret.

Brendan pulled the car up to the end of the boardwalk, and everyone got in. John walked to the car, looked through the windows at his family.

"Drive them home safely, will you?" John asked.

"I will, sir," Brendan said.

And then he left, with everyone John loved in his car, leaving John alone with a crowd of strangers on the beach, everyone watching him, whispering about what had just happened.

And John was the only one who really knew.

When they got home to Star of the Sea, Regis went to her room to lie down. The next thing she knew, it was past midnight. She heard Brendan and Agnes talking softly outside. Cece was asleep. Regis could hear music drifting from her mother's studio.

The world felt very new. She stared at the ring on her finger as if she had never seen it before. Sitting up in bed, she thought of the scene at Hubbard's Point, running it through her mind frame by frame as if it were her own tiny, private movie.

She saw herself standing back with her sisters and Brendan, so happy to see her parents heading along the beach for the movie. And then they had walked up to the boardwalk to meet the Drakes, and Peter's father had made that snide comment.

That's really all it was. Regis had to face the fact. It was rude and insensitive, but not much more than that. Her father could certainly have survived it—maybe even laughed it off eventually.

But Regis had gone...what had Peter said? Crazy. She had become hysterical, attacking his father. Thinking about it now, she could barely understand what she'd been thinking. But back at Hubbard's Point, it had felt like life and death and she had charged to her father's defense.

Peter had looked at her as if he hated her. His parents, too. But she hadn't cared. She had a mission, to get between her father and Peter's, prevent him from being hurt. She'd have done anything to stop it. She ran the little movie over, picturing the way Mr. Drake had leaned forward. Had Regis thought he was going to hit her father? Yes, that must have been it.

What were the words again? They had burst out of her at the beach. She felt them in her chest now, but once she let them out, she could never take back their meaning again. They had come to her last night; they had been teasing her at the edge of her dreams for all these years.

She was shaking. When had that started? She climbed out of bed. Her mother was in the studio; she knew she should go see her, reassure her that she was okay, but she couldn't bring herself to do that. Regis felt as if she were coming out of the haze, waking up from a long coma. Thoughts were flying, and she had to get them straight before she spoke to either of her parents.

She walked into the kitchen. This was where her family had sat for dinner, all of them, for the first time in six years. She had wanted to believe they could be happy again. She had seen her parents right where they were supposed to be—in their seats at either end of the table.

She sat down. *Don't hurt my father...* Why hadn't he told anyone? Why had he kept it such a secret? Their whole family had fallen apart because he had kept the truth locked inside. Her hands trembling, she covered her eyes. She wished she could block out the images swirling in her mind.

Bowing her head, she rested it on the table. She felt so tired—exhausted from six years of blocking out the memories. She saw the corner of a blue envelope sticking out, and pulled at it. Staring, she saw a strange, sort of primitive drawing on the back of the envelope:

a squiggly snakelike sea creature rising from the waves. It reminded Regis of the sea monster on Tom Kelly's family crest ring. She had loved looking at it when she was young.

The envelope was blue.... It was old, for one thing—maybe not ancient, but many years old, older than Regis, enough to have yellowed slightly around the edges. But the handwriting was as familiar as Regis's own.

It was her mother's, and the name on the envelope was Aunt Bernie's. She pulled out a single fragile sheet.

Regis bent over the letter, and began to read.

Twenty-two

The next morning dawned hazy and warm, with scraps of fog woven like filmy scarves through the vineyards, caught on grapevines and stone walls. Goldfinches attacked thistles, tearing at the purple tufts, releasing delicate fluff into the wind, the thorny stems and leaves silver-green in the morning light. The fields were alive with songbirds and crickets.

Sister Bernadette had barely slept the night before. She had had bad dreams and, unable to get back to sleep, had walked the grounds until lauds. Her brother had been up, too—working on the stone circle again. Now, sitting at her desk, she was working on lesson plans when the call came in.

"It's Tom Kelly," Sister Gabrielle said, poking her head into the office. "He needs to see you at the grotto."

"Tell him I'll be there shortly."

"He says it's urgent, Sister..."

Glaring, then sighing, Bernie laid down her pen and pushed back her chair. She walked briskly down the long hallway. As she passed the house chapel, she glanced in—not that she was keeping track, but she did like to know who was where. Two novices, dressed in white, were kneeling by the altar; one other person was seated in the back, all alone. Honor.

The sight startled Bernie. She didn't see Honor in church much these days. She gazed at her sister-in-law, and nearly went in, but Tom had said it was urgent. So Bernie just continued on, out the hall door, and along the path through the fields.

As she neared the hill's crest, she looked down toward the beach. The stones John had laid out were glistening in the morning sun. From up here, she could see that the concentric circles were perfectly formed and with a start, she realized that the circles were not separate, but actually connected. Her eyes followed the inroads and backtracks, marveling at the intricacies, at John's creation of a labyrinth.

Heading downhill, on the western side of the slope and away from the morning sun, she felt the shade's coolness. And as she walked into the hollow, through the stone archway into the Blue Grotto, she felt a gentle chill that was welcome this hot day.

Tom stood with his back to her, staring at the wall. The statue of Mary was to his right; someone had left freshly cut roses at her feet. Bernie took note, thinking she should bring a vase of water later. She stood very still, staring at the back of Tom's head. If she turned now, she could leave and he wouldn't know she'd been there.

"Hello, Bernie," he said without looking.

"How did you know it was me?"

He glanced back, raised an eyebrow. "I always know," he said.

"Sister Gabrielle said it was urgent," she said.

"We had another visitor," he said, gesturing at the stone wall. "Or the same one again…"

Bernie stepped closer to stand beside him. She read the words:

SET ME AS A SEAL ON YOUR HEART, AS A SEAL ON YOUR ARM;
FOR AS STERN AS DEATH IS LOVE.

It had been written on the wall below the first message, chiseled into the stone, though not as deeply. Bernie reached up, touched it with her fingers. She knew very well that the writer had worked hard to etch the letters into the rock.

"What do you make of it, O Theological One?" Tom asked.

"It's from the same source as the first," Bernie said. "Lines of scripture, from the Song of Songs."

"You know them by heart?" Tom asked.

"I know them," Bernie said quietly.

"Old Testament," Tom said. "Fire and brimstone, right? God throwing lightning bolts, sending plagues of locusts to torment the sinners?"

"The Song of Songs is a love poem," Bernie said. She wanted to
leave the discussion right there, and not tell him that she had lived
in its verses all those years ago. It had been the only reading she could
handle at the time, because it was the only thing she'd found that reflected the depth of her love and pain.

"This doesn't sound like a love poem to me," he said. "Sounds like
some kind of a warning."

Bernie stared at the wall, still touching the letters.

"You disagree?"

"I didn't say that," she said. "A love poem can also be a warning,
and the other way around. Think about it."

His silence made her blush. She could only imagine what was running through his mind. She stared at the wall, at the dark words written there.

"And a warning can be a love poem," he said after a long moment.
"For Bernadette Sullivan and Thomas Kelly, anyway. Well, there are
warning bells going off all over. Did you hear what happened last
night?"

"No," she said. "What?"

"I woke up this morning early, got here before sunrise. Found John
working on the beach. Turns out he's building a labyrinth. I told him
his stonemason ancestors would probably take their hats off to him—
but he wasn't in the mood to laugh."

"Why? What's wrong?"

Tom shook his head. "At first he wouldn't say, but once he saw I
wouldn't leave unless he told me, he started talking. Seems he and
Honor went over to watch the beach movie at Hubbard's Point." He
threw her a look to see if she remembered—of course she did. She
kept her expression very calm, her face immobile.

"I'm glad they went," she said.

"The year he and Honor started dating," Tom said, "we all used to go to beach movies. Remember?"

"A long time ago," Bernie said sternly.

"Here comes the nun's voice," he said.

"That's because I'm a nun."

"As if I could ever forget that," he said.

"What happened between John and Honor?" she asked.

"John said Peter's father made some comment, and Regis attacked him."

"Attacked him?" Bernie asked, shocked.

"Yes," Tom said. "John said she was out of control. He's worried about her. Honor wouldn't let him talk to her."

"What did Honor say?"

"Well, I guess she blamed John for last night, and everything else," Tom said. "Worst of all, he blames himself. I didn't like the look in his eyes."

"What are you thinking?" Bernie asked, her gaze falling on the words written in the wall, thinking of Honor sitting alone in the chapel.

"He wants to talk to Regis and finish his project," Tom said. "Beyond that, I'm not sure. I think he's going to take off."

"And go where?" she asked, her heart plummeting to think of her brother leaving again.

"I don't know. He thinks he's brought too much pain back here to Honor and the girls. Wouldn't put it past him to have done this," Tom said, staring at the chiseled stone.

"He didn't," Bernie said.

Tom shrugged. "He says he was too far away to have done the first one. I'm trying to figure out whether it's the same person who did both."

"What do you think?"

"Well, like you said, the source is the same. So it has to be someone who reads, or knows, the Song of Songs. The writing is just scratched in, done in block letters, so it's not easy to distinguish many differences. But here's something." Tom pointed at the more recent writing, glancing at Bernie, getting her to lean closer. "I won't bite," he said.

Bernie closed her eyes for a moment. She could never fear Tom. Ever since giving Honor her letter back, she'd opened a door she couldn't close again. Last night, trying to sleep, she had finally dropped off after midnight. Her dreams had been of this grotto, piles of coins and books and mass cards and desperate notes left behind by hopeful, prayerful people; the statue of Mary; and Bernie trying with all her might to push a huge rock into the grotto's doorway, to seal the secrets in and keep everyone else out.

"Just show me what you mean," she said now.

"Okay," he said. "Here—see how the person really bore down for the first few words, 'set me as a seal on your heart,' and less so as it goes on? Almost as if the person had thought there was plenty of time at the beginning, but rushed through at the end. Or lost heart."

"The last two words, 'is love,' just trail off," Bernie said.

"Almost as if the person realized he or she was about to be interrupted. Did anyone come out here in the middle of the night?"

"I did," Bernie said, raising her eyes to his. "I couldn't sleep, and I took a walk."

"Patrolling the grounds, Sister?" he asked, towering over her, not touching her, but standing so close.

"Why would I do that?"

"I don't know. Looking out for those wayward nieces of yours? Or just keeping an eye out for romantic idiots carving up the grotto?"

"Just taking a walk, Tom," she said. "That's all it was."

"What's a love poem doing in the Bible, anyway?" he asked, as if she hadn't spoken at all.

"It's a parable," she said. "About the writer being led by God into perfect love. Scholars commonly agree that it's meant to symbolize an exalted spiritual union—not romantic love. So there goes your theory."

"It took some sweat," Tom said, looking at the wall. "To scratch all these words. They're not scored deeply into the stone, but it still took effort. Whoever has been doing this is really in the grips of something. And it seems to be getting darker."

"It does," Bernie said, thinking of John and his labyrinth, Honor in church, Regis striking out, Agnes and the wall, and other unsolvable mysteries. So much love, and so much trouble...

"So you're saying this is about something sacred. Not something personal."

Bernie nodded. She didn't want to lie in here, not to Tom. But it wasn't a lie, not really. She believed that the personal was as sacred as anything in church. And she knew it went against Catholic doctrine, but to her, the Song of Songs had always been about human love.

About what was sacred between two people who loved each other.

She stood there, feeling his gaze on her. His hair was in his eyes; Bernie wanted to brush it back, but she didn't. She said, though, "I can't see your eyes."

"Why would you want to see them?"

"So I can see what you're thinking."

"I'm thinking," he said, "about the depths of union possible between two people on this earth."

"Tom..."

"And I'm thinking we should call the police. I'm not sure whether this is a threat or a cry for help, but I don't like it."

"Don't call them," she said. "We'll handle it internally."

He gave her a long, cold look that she could see even through the hair across his eyes. "And if in the meantime something happens? Someone gets hurt, or does something dangerous? Someone broken by love?"

"Who would that be?" she asked.

"Pick a number," he said.

"Tom, you sound so bitter."

"I know I'm just the groundskeeper, but I consider this place my responsibility. I know what I have to do here, Sister, and I'm going to do it."

She didn't reply.

Tom left the grotto, and she didn't turn around. She could almost see him shaking his head—even after all this time she felt his frustration with her, with what he had once wanted for them. Didn't he have any idea that she had wanted that, too?

Only Honor knew most of the story—but not even she knew all of it. Bernie hurried out of the grotto and knew she had to go find Honor. She had to talk to her friend.

She cleared the rise and started running, robe and veil flowing out behind her. By the time she made it back to the chapel—thinking all the way about what Tom had said about people broken by love—Honor was gone. The two young nuns were still there, praying at the altar, but the rest of the chapel was empty.

Honor didn't know where to start. She had a whole list of things she wanted to say to God, but after half an hour of sitting in the chapel, her mind was blank and her heart felt as if it would burst. She had been such a happy child, and an easygoing young woman. She had married the man she loved, and had three children with him. Blessed with artistic talent, they had inspired and challenged each other, and somehow managed to keep the passion in everyday life.

And then the fall. Literally—their long, slow slide from grace, followed by a sudden plummet. Seeing him charged and inspired by life and the world, taking risks with his art and life—while she felt left behind. Her recent painting had unlocked all the joy and pain she'd felt in their marriage: loving John, wondering about him, fearing for his safety, even his life—welcoming him home, time after time, and then, finally, wondering whether she'd ever see him again.

These last days had been wonderful—she'd rediscovered her own artistic fire, and her paintings of Ballincastle were the best she'd done in years. She knew that John's labyrinth, and of course John himself, had much to do with it. His work was suddenly so grounded—literally nestled into the sand of their own beach. While hers was suddenly soaring—back to Ireland, into her own dark hiding places.

Last night, lying alone in bed, listening to seagulls crying from their rookery across the bay, she'd felt the truth click into place. She blamed John for Regis's daring, for the trauma of Ireland, for Regis's engagement, for Agnes. Everything... And then it dawned on her: she blamed him for leaving her alone. Leaving her behind.

Walking through the vineyard on the way to the beach, she stopped to pick some wildflowers growing along the wall. She continued on her way, spotting Agnes and Brendan sitting in the grass under a big oak tree, with paints and paper. She would have stopped to talk to them, but she had something she had to do first.

When she got to the top of the beach, she saw John. He crouched at the center of the labyrinth, arranging small stones. Sisela lay along the top of a driftwood log; the once feral kitten gazed at him with abject love. Honor stood still, letting the breeze blow the hair back from her face. Then she took a deep breath and walked across the sand to her husband.

John looked up, surprised. From a distance, he had appeared peaceful, meditative; but up close she could see that the expression in his eyes was beyond hurting. She held out the wildflowers.

"For you," she said.

"Why?"

"You brought me flowers the other day, and it made me so happy. I wanted... to do the same for you."

"Thank you," he said, rising and taking them, not smiling.

"I'm sorry about last night," she said.

"So am I," he said.

"But you have nothing to apologize for. It wasn't your fault... none of it was. The girls love you so much, John," she continued. "They all try to be like you, in different ways. Agnes and her photography, Cece starting to sculpt with clay... and Regis..."

"I know," John said.

"Ralph Drake was so out of line. But Regis, screaming, 'Don't hurt my father.' For all her wildness, I've never, ever seen her like that. Why did she overreact that way?"

John crouched again, dropped the flowers by his side, and slowly began moving stones around, arranging them in the sand. She saw his hand shaking.

"John? Do you know?"

"She didn't like seeing me humiliated," he said. "Let it go, Honor."

Honor stared down at him. This close up, the labyrinth looked like nothing more than rows and rows of stones, radiating out from a hole in the middle.

"It's hot out," she said. "You shouldn't be working in the sun."

She crouched next to him and very tentatively, she reached for his hand. Last night they had held hands in the dark; he had carried her through the woods. All the bad years had melted away, and she had let herself start to feel love again. She wanted that back so badly. John's hand was shaking, and he pulled away.

"Honor," he said.

"I'm sorry about last night," she said again.

"Don't apologize," he said harshly.

"I was upset," she said, shocked by his tone of voice. "I just wanted to get her away from all those people, take her home. I shouldn't have blamed you—shouldn't have left you there. I was so overwhelmed, I didn't even think about you getting home."

"They were rude," he said roughly. "I could take it, no problem, but thinking of you and the girls, of Regis having to put up with it. That's what killed me, Honor."

"John," she said, "you're the one it was most terrible for."

He shook his head.

His body was tan, from working in the sun. She looked down, saw a badly healed scar beneath his left arm, over his rib cage. She traced its edge with her finger, and he flinched.

"That happened in jail, didn't it?"

He grabbed both her hands, and looked her straight in the eyes

"Jail is over," he said. "I'm free now. Understand that? You didn't put me there; it wasn't your fault. So don't let me see that look in your eyes now. Get rid of it, Honor—stop beating up on yourself."

"I stopped visiting you," she whispered, a wave of grief rising up.

"It doesn't matter. Do you know what kept me going, the whole time I was there?"

She shook her head, eyes stinging.

He put his mouth to her ear; his whisper felt like the gentlest breeze in the world. "You," he said.

"But I wasn't there," she said. "I wasn't there for you at all. I took the girls away, wouldn't let them visit..."

"It doesn't matter, Honor," he said. "You did what was right for them. You were being their mother, just the way I'd want you to. But you were with me anyway. Every minute, I had you there."

"I couldn't protect you," she said, shuddering with a sob.

"Honor," he said, "don't you know yet, even now? You can't protect anyone. All you can do is love them, and have a little faith."

"I lost faith six years ago," she wept.

He didn't reply; she knew that he had lost his faith, too. He didn't even have to say it; she could see it in the hardness in his eyes.

"I'm not staying," he said.

"What are you talking about?" she asked, staring up at him.

"I'm not putting you and the girls through any more. Tom will help me find a place. Somewhere in Canada—I can work there, I know. I'll let you know where it is, so the girls can visit me when they want to."

"That's not what we want," Honor said. Even as she said the words, she felt all the warmth drain from her body. John had made up his mind—she sensed it in his posture, the way he stood back from her, staring out to sea.

The tide had turned, and the first thin waves were stretching over the hard-packed sand where they stood. Tiny rippling advances, clear as cellophane, they spread across the tidal flats and lapped at John's and Honor's feet.

Just then they heard feet pounding the hard sand, and when they looked up, they saw Cece flying down the beach, arms flailing and waving a white paper.

"Mom, Dad!" she yelled. "There's a police car at the Academy. Is it because of Regis? Because she's gone! She's run away!"

Twenty-three

Regis's note said that she needed to be alone and think. But after last night, Honor said that would be the worst thing for her.

Back at the house, John followed Honor into the girls' room. He stood in the door, looking around. There were pictures of him everywhere: on the bureau, on the nightstands, on the walls above his daughters' beds. Photographs he had taken—some originals, some cut out of magazines—hung on a wall by the door. He stood still, stunned by the evidence of his presence in his daughters' lives, knowing he had to leave them again. The words "Don't hurt my father" seared his mind. If he left, perhaps Regis would go no further down that path.

Honor picked up Regis's pillow and held it. Just held it. She stood in the middle of the room. She wasn't going through Regis's drawers or desks, wasn't rifling drawers. He saw that she was taking Regis in, just absorbing her, trying to pick up some sense of where she had gone . . .

Cecilia was frantic. "We have to find her! Call her or get in the car and go looking for her!"

"Cece's right," Honor said. "I can't bear thinking of what she's thinking."

"I wish," Cece said, bursting into tears, "that Regis had known you were speaking! That you went to see Dad on the beach, Mom!"

"What do you mean?"

"She was so upset last night," Cece said. "At the way we just left Dad there at Hubbard's Point without a ride home."

"I walked home by the beaches," John said. "It was fine, Cece."

"But Regis didn't think so," Cece wept. "She was *beside* herself. She was practically pulling out her hair, she was so sorry. She knew it was all her fault, she kept saying so."

"She was just upset about what Peter's father said," Honor said.

"Maybe that's not what she meant," John said.

"What do you mean?"

"When she said it was her fault," John said grimly, "maybe she wasn't referring to last night."

"Then what?" Honor asked, walking over to the table, absently straightening a placemat. Something caught her attention and she pulled out a blue envelope from beneath the fabric's edge.

"Did you see her before she left?" Honor asked Cece before John could reply to her question.

Cece nodded. "We had breakfast together. Or, I did, and Regis sat there. She didn't eat."

"Did she mention this?" Honor asked, looking pale. The envelope was empty.

Cece shrugged. "I don't think so. What is it?"

"Something that I shouldn't have left lying around," Honor said, sliding the envelope into her jeans pocket.

"Honor, what is it?" John pressed.

"It was a letter I wrote to Bernie a long time ago. She gave it back to me recently... to remind me of what I'd once said to her."

"Look out there," Cece said, standing at the window and pointing. Across the lawn, driving from the main part of the campus toward the grotto, were a police car and a dark sedan. "I saw them before, and I wondered if they'd come to find Regis."

John thought back to last night—Regis's wild explosion, the way

she had charged to his defense—and hoped he could get to her before the police found her, before she talked to anyone.

"Let's go talk to them," Honor said.

"They have to find her," Cece said. "Come on, hurry!"

John hung back, trying to figure out where Regis would go so he
could find her himself, and Honor noticed. She gazed at him, her eyes
filled with questions.

She had no idea, and he hoped she never would.

"You were great last night," Agnes said, sitting on the blanket with
Brendan. "I was proud of you. The way you saw that Regis was in
trouble, and went to help her."

"She really loves your father, just wanted to defend him. You guys
are so lucky, even with everything you've been through. I wish I had
your family."

"But what about your parents? Why don't you just talk to them?
Tell them what their drinking is doing to you..."

Brendan gave her a long, kind look; his eyes were so big and wide,
his gaze so steady. He looked at her with the kind of patient tolerance
Agnes used to feel for people who would ask where her father was,
or when the family planned to visit him, or why her sister wanted to
get married so young. Unanswerable questions. But Brendan didn't
even cringe.

"Stupid question, right?" she asked.

"Nothing you ask is ever stupid," he said.

He reached over, pushed her long hair back from the shaved track
on her head. He touched her scar. She felt electricity tingle through
his fingers, and closing her eyes, she felt him healing her. In that moment, she saw the flash of white light she'd captured on her broken
camera, and saw him pulling her sister, so gently, away from Peter's
father.

"Who are you?" she whispered.

"I'm Brendan," he said. "You know that."

"Brendan...Regis calls you 'the archangel.'"

He laughed softly, his hand still cradling her head. "Brendan was just an ordinary saint," he said.

"There's nothing ordinary about a saint," she replied. "Tell me what he did."

"Brendan was a navigator," he said. "He stood on top of Mount Brandon, one of Ireland's tallest mountains, and looked out across the Atlantic Ocean...just about exactly across from where we are now."

"He was looking toward Connecticut?"

"Maybe," Brendan said. "He had a vision of a magical land, across the western seas, called Tir na nog—'the Promised Land of the Saints.' He felt pulled there, and he sailed out of a narrow creek, just like the one in Black Hall, and set off on a quest for the Blessed Isles. A seven-year quest...No matter how fierce the sea, or how wicked the storms, he kept going. He's the patron saint of pilgrims and seekers."

"Our family's been on a six-year quest," Agnes whispered.

"To get your father back," he said, stroking her head.

"I thought when he came home, everything would finally be right," she said. "I thought my mother would be happy, and Regis would stop having nightmares. I thought she'd figure out that Peter is wrong for her."

"Agnes," Brendan said, looking at her with eyes so blue and glowing she imagined he could see straight into her soul. "She will figure that out. I have the feeling she already has. People have to make their own mistakes."

"What was she saying?" Agnes asked.

"You should ask her," Brendan said softly, thinking of what Regis had said to him later, after they'd returned to Star of the Sea.

"It sounded as if she thought Mr. Drake was going to attack Dad—I thought I heard her say 'Don't hurt him.'"

"She did say that," Brendan admitted, not wanting to say more until he'd had the chance to talk to Regis again, help her to tell everyone.

"But why was she so upset?"

"I don't know."

"I couldn't believe she hit Mr. Drake. Regis would never hurt anyone...you should have seen her at Ballincastle, after she saw my father kill Gregory White. She was pure white, just staring into space. She couldn't move, couldn't talk."

"I can imagine," Brendan said. "After what she'd been through."

"The police took our father away, and an ambulance took Regis to the hospital. She was there for days—we were afraid she wouldn't come out of it. My mother couldn't even go to Cork City to help Dad."

"How could she have helped him?" Brendan asked gently. "He was in custody, right?"

"Yes," Agnes said.

"It must have been terrible," Brendan said.

"Yes," Agnes said. "It must have. Regis can't remember what happened, and our father would never really talk about it, to *anyone*. But Regis was bruised, and she had a huge bump on her head. The doctors said it probably accounted for why she couldn't remember anything."

"That and the trauma," Brendan said. "People shut down when they're scared. Emotions can be just as brutal as being physically attacked. That's why I want to be a psychiatrist."

"I wish it were so much easier," she whispered.

"Like in Tir Na Nog," he said.

Holding her hand, he leaned forward to kiss her, and Agnes closed her eyes, tasted his lips. She felt herself melting into him, so lost she barely realized they were no longer alone. Looking up, she saw her parents and Cece standing there. Cece tugged Agnes's hand, looking frantically from her to Brendan.

"Have you seen Regis?" she cried.

John shepherded his family through the vineyard, toward the Academy. Cece talked quietly, filling Agnes and Brendan in on Regis. Honor strode along in silence, her shoulder brushing against John's as they walked. From the top of the rise, John spotted the police cars, one of them unmarked, at the dead end of the lane that led to the Blue Grotto. His stomach flipped, just seeing them.

When they got to the bottom of the hill, they followed the sound of voices into the small stone chamber: the Blue Grotto. Seeing it filled with strangers—two plainclothes detectives and two uniformed officers—felt jarring. They were talking to Bernie and Tom.

Bernie and Tom turned as John and Honor moved forward. Tom stood close by her side, but Bernie was clearly the one in charge; the police were all looking at her, taking notes.

"Excuse me," one of the detectives said, attempting to block the way. "This is a police investigation. You'll have to come back later."

"What happened here?" Honor asked.

"Please step outside," the female detective said.

John realized that the officers assumed that his family was just visiting the grotto—worshipers, or tourists, visiting Star of the Sea. Bernie caught it at the same moment and edged forward.

"This is my brother and sister-in-law," Bernie said. "They live on the grounds here at the Academy. Maybe they've seen something. John, Honor, someone scratched some messages into the wall, and they're causing... consternation."

"They sound a little desperate," Tom said.

"Aunt Bernie," Cece cried, her voice breaking. "Regis is missing! She's very upset, and she's run away. Never mind this... please, you have to help us find her."

"Slow down," the male detective said. "What happened? How old is she?"

"She's twenty," John said.

"And you say she's run away?"

"She said she has to think," Honor said, visibly shaken. She twisted her hands, trying to keep them steady. Her face was pale, her lips dry. Her gaze darted to John, as if making sure he was okay; he nodded, supporting her, taking her arm. "She's been through a lot, and last night had words with her fiancé's father."

"At Hubbard's Point," one of the uniformed officers said sharply, suddenly taking notice. "We got a call about that, but by the time we arrived, she was gone."

"I don't think that was necessary," Honor said. "For you to be called."

"Mr. Drake could have pressed charges," the officer said. "He chose not to."

"For a little shove?" Agnes asked. "She didn't mean it."

"He claims she attacked him, scratched him."

"Barely," Honor said, but she looked scared.

"She's very loyal to her father," Bernie said.

"She was defending him," Honor said.

The cops all turned their eyes on John. "That's you?"

"It is," he said, feeling nervous to have the attention of four members of the police department on him.

"You're John Sullivan," said the younger cop—and John recognized him as Officer Kossoy. He had been here the night of Agnes's accident.

"I am," he said.

"The artist?" the woman detective asked.

"Yes," John said cautiously. Was she familiar with his work, or had she heard about Ireland?

"I'm Detective Cavanagh, and this is my partner, Detective Gaffney," she said.

"You've been in trouble, Mr. Sullivan," said Gaffney. "We know about you."

"What does this have to do with our daughter?" Honor asked. "Please—"

"We ran a check on you," Officer Kossoy said, "after the last incident, when Agnes fell off the wall. Your daughter Regis was with you in Ireland, wasn't she? When you killed that man?"

"We were all there," Honor said, her voice rising. "My husband was protecting Regis from him!"

"It's true," Cece cried as Officer Kossoy reached for John's arm. "Get away from my father!"

"Cece," Agnes said, grabbing her sister in a hug.

"Do you think Regis's running away has anything to do with the message on the wall?" the female detective asked no one in particular.

John remembered seeing the first carvings with Tom just two

weeks ago, and now he read the new words, etched just about even with his eye level:

> SET ME AS A SEAL ON YOUR HEART, AS A SEAL ON YOUR ARM;
> FOR AS STERN AS DEATH IS LOVE.

"Are you saying you think she wrote this?" Honor asked. "She could barely reach it—she's only five-four."

"'Set me as a seal on your heart, as a seal on your arm; for as stern as death is love,'" John read, and the lines sent a chill down his spine. "What is that from?"

"The Bible," Brendan said. "The Old Testament."

Everyone turned to look at him. Red-haired, sparks in his blue eyes, he gazed up at the carving. John saw that he had wiry strength in his thin body; like Regis, he was too short to reach up that far. But John found himself looking around for a step, something that could boost the boy up.

"Do we have a religious scholar in our midst?" Bernie asked, smiling.

He shook his head. "Not really," he said. "But I went to Jesuit school, so..."

"Ah," she said. "The Jesuits. They're the Marines and intellectuals of religious life. Very rigorous. Funny, I wouldn't think of them as giving so much emphasis to the Song of Songs. That scripture is so filled with love; it would take a kinder, softer Jesuit to teach it."

Brendan nodded, as if he knew what she meant.

John found himself wondering about this boy who could talk the Old Testament with Bernie and Tir na nog with Agnes, as he had heard him do a few minutes earlier. Again, he read the message, shivered at the words "for as stern as death is love."

"Do you think love is stern as death?" John asked, looking straight at Brendan.

"Hey," Officer Kossoy said, "this is a police investigation. Why don't we leave the metaphysics till later."

"They go together sometimes," Brendan said, as if the policeman hadn't spoken, looking straight at John. "Not everyone knows that, though."

"You know it?" John asked.

Brendan nodded slowly, and held John's gaze.

"His brother died," Agnes said softly, inching closer.

"Did you do this?" John asked, pointing at the wall.

Not replying, Brendan cleared his throat and looked away.

Just then, the sound of a car squealing into the parking lot echoed off the stone walls, and everyone looked toward the Academy. A Jeep pulled into view, and Honor gasped, "Regis!"

But it wasn't. It was Peter Drake, followed by three friends. They started toward the Sullivans' house, but caught sight of the crowd by the grotto and changed course. Peter's eyes were wild, his shoulders bursting with tension. His tan privileged-beach-boy looks were contorted with panic and rage.

"Where is she?" he shouted, rushing toward Brendan.

"Peter, stop!" Agnes said, getting between them.

Peter stopped short of physically moving her, but glared at and through her and stepped around her. Brendan folded his arms, gazing back with fire in his eyes.

"First you show up out of nowhere, big hero, taking care of Agnes. That would win Regis over if nothing else, and you had to know it. Then that stunt last night—stepping in, taking her away, so close to her, whatever the hell that was. And now, this note from Regis—"

"She left a note?" Brendan asked.

"She left one for us, too," Honor said.

"We'd like to see them," Detective Gaffney said.

Honor willingly gave him the sheet of paper. Peter started to hand his over, but then jammed it into his pocket and flung himself at Brendan. His fist cracked Brendan's nose, sharp as a gunshot, blood bursting everywhere. Brendan, bleeding, fought back, landing some punches of his own as Peter kept pummeling, until the police finally pulled them apart.

"She left me," Peter snapped, wiping his bloodied lip. "Gave me back my ring! And you know why. You know why!"

"Peter, what are you talking about?" Agnes asked.

"Ask him," Peter said, shuddering with sobs as Officer Kossoy and his partner held his shoulders. Brendan bent double, pressing his hands to his face. Bernie crouched down, handed him a handkerchief, her hand on his back.

"Are you all right?" Bernie asked.

"I'm fine," Brendan said.

"You shouldn't care whether he's all right or not!" Peter yelled. "Don't any of you get it? Regis is gone because of him! Ask him!"

"Do you have any knowledge of Regis Sullivan's whereabouts?" Officer Kossoy asked. For the first time, fear had entered Brendan's eyes, sending a cold splinter into John's heart. John had seen fear like that before—primal and untamed—in the eyes of men in prison. He pushed Bernie aside and looked straight into Brendan's eyes.

"Do you?" John asked, his fingers gripping the boy's skinny shoulders.

"Dad, don't hurt him!"

"Back off, Mr. Sullivan," Detective Gaffney said, yanking his arm.

"What do you know about Regis?" Honor asked. "What did Peter mean?"

"I know that she had something to think about," Brendan said quietly.

"I think maybe we'd better talk this over," Detective Gaffney said to Brendan. "Down at the station house."

"That's right," Peter said. "Take him in—that's where he belongs."

"He didn't do anything wrong!" Cece cried out.

"Brendan," John said, turning his back on Peter, "we'll help you if you just tell us the truth."

"Goddamn you," Peter said, wrenching John's arm. "You should have stayed in Ireland, left Regis alone. My parents looked your case up. You beat a man to death. That's what Regis has to live with—what she's running from. Right, Brendan? Can anyone even blame her?"

"You don't know anything," Brendan said.

"Shut up, loser," Peter shouted. "I checked on you—asked around. You're a *bastard*. You don't even *know* who your parents are. Your sister Agnes and this a-hole have been talking behind our backs. She's been cheating on me with this creep—and he's been doing the same to you. Couldn't you see it in their eyes last night, at Hubbard's Point?"

"Don't you dare talk to me about Brendan. He has parents who adopted him, who *love* him," she said, looking at Brendan. "And I saw him trying to help my sister," she whispered, growing pale.

"She looked at him the way she should be looking at me!" Peter exploded.

"Regis needs a lot of help right now," Brendan said quietly. "If you love her, you should know that."

"What do you mean, she needs help?" John asked.

"Tell us," Honor said.

"Don't you understand, even now?" Brendan asked gently, reaching for Agnes, looking into her eyes.

"Understand what?"

"Regis is the reason your father couldn't come home. She's the reason your family couldn't be together." Brendan stared at John, still and unwavering. And John knew that he knew the truth.

"What are you saying?" Agnes shrieked, whirling to look at John and Honor. John felt her and Honor's gazes boring into him, sensed Tom taking a step forward, as if to mitigate the force of their emotions.

"Come on, let's clear this up down at the station," Officer Kossoy said, leveling a look at John, too. "Both of you."

"Dad," Agnes wept, "what does he mean?"

"John, please," Honor said, her voice breaking.

"I can't say anything without Regis," John said.

And at that, Agnes wheeled, burying her head in Honor's shoulder.

Detective Gaffney stepped forward, grabbing John's arm and doing what John knew he would: marching him away with Brendan, toward the two police cars. He looked back over his shoulder.

Of all the things he might have expected to see—his daughters crying, Honor staring after him with despair, Peter smug and triumphant—what he did see shocked him.

Bernie—standing with Tom in the middle of the grotto, her right arm stretched out, reaching, as she watched the group of police marching John and Brendan toward the squad car, right past Brendan's crazily painted Volvo.

Only her gaze wasn't on her brother, John—not at all. Her arm trembled, held straight out, grasping at nothing John could see, her eyes full of light and pain, locked on Brendan McCarthy, the boy with the red hair, as the police led him away.

Twenty-four

The police took John and Brendan away, and Honor stood and watched them go. Agnes and Cece raced after the cars, stopping only when they turned out of sight. Peter and his friends stormed off, as angry as when they'd arrived.

Glancing over at Bernadette and Tom, Honor felt the energy pouring off them and knew they needed to be alone. She started back through the vineyard; not toward home, but along the path that led to the beach. Her skin tingled as she neared the sea. The waves rolled in, and the air felt moist. The long stone wall ran in its relentless way along the crest of the hill to her right. It shimmered in the sun, sparkling with mica.

She climbed the bluff, followed the narrow trail through bayberry and beach roses, looking past the labyrinth, up and down the strand. There was John's stone cottage, darkly silhouetted, and when she saw it, she started to run. Regis would be there—she knew it. Their daughter, their wonderful, mixed-up girl—if she was searching for answers, and Honor knew she was, the only place to find them was right here.

"Regis!" Honor called.

Climbing up the steps, she rattled the door; it was locked, but the latch was old and fragile. She knew she could force it, but she also knew where Tom had always hidden the spare key—on a rusty nail just behind the kitchen shutter. If only John hadn't taken it, changed the hiding place...and he hadn't. Her fingers closed around it; fumbling, she sliced the heel of her right hand on the nail, but she didn't even care—she had the key.

Managing to get it into the lock, she opened the door. "Regis," she said into the cool darkness.

But the room was empty. John was once again with the police, and Regis was once again lost. Honor leaned against the door and closed her eyes. She was thrust back in time. When the police took John away from that windswept cliffside, someone else was also gone—Regis. Lost and numbed, unable to remember or speak about what she had just witnessed.

What had Brendan meant?—*Regis is the reason your father couldn't come home. She's the reason your family couldn't be together.* He had sounded so clear, so certain. There was something otherworldly about him; Honor had heard the girls saying that Regis called him "the archangel." She'd taken it in stride. Living on the grounds of Star of the Sea, the girls often spoke of saints and angels. But there was something about this boy, so caring and true.

She tried not to think about what Bernie and Tom must be imagining. If she could turn the clock back, she would never have left Bernie's letter under the placemat, for Regis to find. There were so many ways to lose a child, none of them possible to recover from. Honor thought of the Christmas crèche—installed outside the chapel each Advent by Bernie and the nuns. Bernie had always been so kind, to let the girls join in. But Bernie herself was always the one to place the Christ child in his crib. Even when Regis had begged and pleaded—and Bernie was notorious for being unable to say no to her goddaughter—this was one duty Bernie considered hers alone. And Honor had never been able to watch her do it without starting to cry. Bernie herself never had dry eyes when she installed the crèche.

So, now Regis knew the truth about her aunt—from her mother's own words. If Regis had ever guessed at the story of Bernie and Tom, she had never said—and Honor, no matter how honest she tried to be with her daughters, had never discussed it. Not even with Regis, her most straightforward and demanding-of-the-truth-the-whole-truth-and-nothing-but-the-truth daughter.

Still leaning on the door of the beach house, Honor opened her eyes. Why was it so dark in here? John kept the shutters closed—which seemed so unlike him. He lived for light, the brighter and more scalding the better. His photographs were a study in light, and like the Tonalists and early American Impressionists, he celebrated Black Hall for its river- and ocean-washed light.

But the room was pitch-dark. The photo-processing smell made her think he'd been working here—which made her even sadder, considering he had a perfectly good darkroom in the studio attached to their house.

Honor felt her way to the bed. She sat down, and as her eyes became accustomed to the darkness, she saw that John kept his camera on his pillow. His old, predigital Leica. She smiled, because that was so like him. He lived to get the right shot, the picture that would define the moment, the day, his feelings. She also saw that he kept the box—*the* box—on his makeshift night table, a driftwood stump set beside the bed. Tom must have given it back to John.

Lifting the lid, she peered inside. There was Cormac Sullivan's death certificate, old and crumbling. It pierced her heart—with love for John's great-grandfather, the man who had been brave enough to come to America. In all his hunger and longing for home, Cormac had built the beautiful walls that defined this land. He had started a family, putting down Sullivan roots for John and Honor and their children. The ring was there, too: the gold ring with the red stone.

Her attention was suddenly drawn to a paper and pen beside the bed. Lifting it, squinting in the dim light slanting through the cracks of the shutters, she saw that John had been making notes. Lifting the notepad, she read: "train—Montrealer—bus to Quebec—8 a.m./12 noon/3 p.m.??—or Tom drive?—Hotel St. Jacques—inquire weekly rates."

He was planning to leave.

This morning when she'd come to him, to apologize for last night, he'd told her that he wasn't staying—and now she saw that he meant it. She had known it then. She sat still, feeling her heart pound in her chest.

She couldn't lose him again.

Standing up, feeling shaky, she went to the window and pushed the shutters open. The salt breeze blew back her hair, and she blinked into the sunlight. When she turned around, she gasped in shock.

Daylight revealed what had previously been hidden: pictures hanging on strings bisecting the room; it was a wonder Honor hadn't walked straight into them. He must have decided to process what he had in his camera before he left, and when she saw what he'd been photographing, her eyes blurred with tears.

The pictures were all of her.

Honor at her easel, in the garden, walking through the vineyard; Honor sitting on a driftwood log beside Sisela, holding Agnes's hand, laughing with Cece; Honor standing in the darkness, looking up at the sky as if she were wishing on a star; Honor with her arm draped over Regis's shoulder—and the last one . . . Honor walking along the tide line, gathering moonstones.

She remembered that moment—it was the day John's letter had arrived, letting them all know that he was coming home. So he hadn't been in Canada still, as Tom had said. He had been here all along. He *had* chiseled the verses into the grotto wall. . . .

Her heart had ached for years, but this was something different. Surrounded by the pictures her husband had taken of her, holding his notes for departure in her hand, feeling the loss of Regis, Honor knew her heart was breaking.

She did the only thing she could think to do: sat down hard on John's bed, reached into the box they had pulled from the wall all those years ago. Removing the gold ring with the red stone, she slipped it on her finger.

The room had been dark, and now it was filled with light. The ring had once been forbidden pirate gold, and now it was family treasure. John had been gone, and now he was home. Bernie had hidden from her own truth for too long, and she knew it—Honor had felt it in the grotto. Things could change: they could.

But first they had to find Regis.

"It's him," Tom said. The grotto was shot through with shadow and light.

Bernie looked anywhere but at him. "It can't be. How would he have gotten all the way from Dublin?" she said.

"I don't know, Bernie. His age, though—he'd be the right age. And that bright red hair—exactly like yours. Your hair is just as red now, isn't it? Under the veil?"

"A lot of people have red hair."

"You heard Agnes say he was adopted!"

"Tom—listen to yourself! He's not the only adopted boy in the state of Connecticut! And Connecticut is a long, long way from Ireland!"

"Why are you doing this?" Tom asked her, grabbing her by the shoulders. "Why won't you at least listen to me, consider the possibility?"

"Because I can't, and you can't either. For one thing, you're dreaming, and for another, he has a life. And we can't get in the way of it!" Bernie was shaking, as if from the cold, but it was eighty degrees, even in the shade of the grotto. She didn't want to tell Tom about her dreams, or about the voice she'd heard calling lately: a young boy, riding on the back of a sea monster, straight out of the Kelly family crest, laughing as he traversed the waves.

It was a pagan dream, unbefitting a nun. Sisters of Notre Dame didn't believe in sea monsters, not even the legendary one said to have watched over the fallen body of Tadhg Mor O'Kelly, after the battle of Clontarf.

"He has your hair color," Tom said now. "And he has my eyes."

"You're flattering both of us," she said.

"Have you looked in the mirror lately?" he asked. "Do you even *have* mirrors in the convent?"

"None of your business," she said.

"Jesus Christ, Bernie—don't you know a miracle when you see it? You think it's him, too. I know you."

Bernie walked away. She prayed he wouldn't follow her, but of course he did. She heard his footsteps behind her, on the stone path from the Blue Grotto toward the parking lot. Her route to the convent would take her right past the boy's car—his lovely, mysteriously painted old Volvo. Bernie had noticed it on his visits to Agnes. One night she had come out after vespers, just to read the messages in his images.

The white cat, gazing at the moon: that was her favorite. Brendan had somehow captured the very essence of Sisela—her yearning mystery and nameless desire. Bernie wondered whether Brendan knew the story of the white kitten, homeless and motherless, adopted by the Sullivans.

"Here's his car," Tom said, over her shoulder.

"Well, he'll come back and pick it up soon," Bernie said, feeling a jolt of guilt—knowing she should have spoken up for Brendan to the police, saying he couldn't possibly have carved those words into the wall, or have had anything to do with Regis's disappearance.

"That's not my point," Tom said. "Have you looked at what's painted here?"

"Yes," she said, tensing.

"You've seen this?" he asked, gesturing with his right hand.

Bernie stared at the images: a young red-haired boy riding on the back of a sea monster, slipping across the waves, cliffs rising on two sides of the same ocean. Ireland and Connecticut, she had thought when she'd first seen it.

"What about it?" she asked.

"For the love of God, Bernie," he said. "It's the Kelly family crest!"

"And what?" she asked. "Brendan is supposed to know that? He's somehow figured out that he's a Kelly? He somehow sailed across the Atlantic—how, by the way? On the back of a *real* sea monster? One that he's immortalizing along with cats and foxes and white whales?"

"Why else do you think he's hanging around here?" Tom asked.

"He must have gone to Catholic Charities and petitioned to see his file. The hospital in Dublin never promised the baby would stay in Ireland—Catholic adoptions can happen anywhere, as long as the parents promise to raise the child in the Church. Jesus, Bernie—he's looking for his birth parents!"

"I think you're wrong," she said. "I think it's simple. He's in love with Agnes. He met her after her accident, and he's fallen in love with her."

"How do you explain this picture of the cat?" Tom asked, pricking Bernie with one of the doubts she kept trying to chase away. How would Brendan have known about the tiny white kitten, saved from the wilds by the Sullivans, unless he'd been hanging around for a while, doing research into the families of Star of the Sea?

"The cat's an archetype," Bernie said. "She represents his longing."

"That's bull. It's Sisela. He's been here looking for his family."

"He *has* a family," Bernie said. "He was adopted, and they are his parents now."

Tom shook his head. He narrowed his blue eyes, and Bernie felt his disappointment in her. She kept up her stern expression, honed to perfection after ten years as Superior here at the convent—she could issue disapproval to any novice with just the slightest glance. But Tom saw through it, and she knew that she had about twenty seconds before she fell apart.

"Archetypes, huh?" he asked.

"Yes." She babbled on, anything to keep from talking about the red-haired boy with the calm blue eyes. "Artists have been known to use them as inspiration. Like John, the way he's building a labyrinth. And the installation at Ballincastle, echoes of the ruins. Another of his sandcastles, like his most famous shot, the one at Devil's Hole—"

"Sandcastles?"

"Yes," Bernie said. "Symbolic of how fleeting life is, how things fall away. The need to appreciate beauty—love, connection—while it is there, but then to let it go. Something you should consider right now."

"Bernie," Tom said. "Are you serious? Ever notice the irony in John calling them sandcastles? He builds them of stone, and tree trunks, and fallen branches. Big stuff, Bernie. Anything but sand. Has that ever occurred to you?"

Bernie didn't reply, didn't let on that she had often thought the same thing.

"Things that *last,* Bernie."

"Stop, Tom," Bernie said.

"The joke is, John can't stand to build anything of sand," Tom said. "Because he wants to hold on. Anything he's ever tried to let go of has his claw marks all over it. He does it eventually, but only if he has to. Even that goddamn rock he smashed. He couldn't just let it go; he had to haul the pieces out of the sea, swirl them around the beach in that goddamn maze."

"We've said enough."

"Brendan is using our families for his inspiration. That's because he knows..."

Bernie shook her head. She couldn't stand to listen. She grabbed Tom's left hand, raised it so he could look straight at his crest ring, the one that had belonged to Francis X. Kelly, the one with the Kelly family insignia on it.

"That's a sea monster," she said. "*That's* your family crest. Does it bear any—*any* resemblance to this picture on this car?"

She watched him gaze from his ring to the left rear fender. The two images had so little in common. But as Bernie stared herself, the sea monster might very well have just disappeared, swum into the deepest valleys of the sea beneath. Because all she could see—and she knew that all Tom was looking at—was the smiling image of the little boy on the creature's back.

The red-haired, blue-eyed little boy, looking just the way a child, if there was such a child, of Thomas Kelly and Bernadette Sullivan might look.

"You're thinking the same thing I am, Sister Bernadette," Tom said. "I know you are."

"You don't know at all," Bernie said. "Now, excuse me. I have to get inside."

"Got praying to do?"

"I have a convent to run."

"You know? We're just like *Casablanca*. Ingrid Bergman and Humphrey Bogart had nothing on us...."

"I'm not in the mood, Tom," she said.

"Well, neither am I," he said. "But don't worry. We'll always have Dublin."

Her heart scathed by the thought of what Dublin had meant to them, she walked quickly away.

Twenty-five

T he Black Hall police station was located in a small brick
building on Shore Road, just before the turnoff for
Hubbard's Point. It had a well-tended front lawn, and there was a
Black Hall town flag, depicting marsh grass, a lighthouse, and a blue
heron, flying from the flagpole on the peaked roof. John and Brendan
were led into a small room and told to wait.

They weren't restrained; they weren't separated, or told not to
speak to each other. The officers were polite and respectful, if not exactly friendly. Officer Kossoy handed Brendan an icepack for his nose.

Moments after John and Brendan first sat down, an alarm rang,
and all but two officers on duty scrambled—there was a brawl down
at Deacon's Reef, the seaside bar where bikers gathered on hot summer days.

John glanced over at Brendan to see how the boy was holding up.
He sat still, erect, as if he were on high alert. John had seen young
men his age imprisoned at Portlaoise for violent crimes, some politi-
cally motivated, kids who were hardened by oppression and hopelessness, and by their time in jail.

Brendan was the opposite; to John, he looked like just about the
least hardened person he'd seen in a long time. Even his own wife
and children seemed so wounded by life, by what he had put them

through. Brendan, in comparison, looked to be at ease and at peace; even holding the ice to his bloody nose, he had bright eyes and a mouth ready to smile.

"Everything's going to be okay," John said to him.

"I know," Brendan said.

Even that reply shook John: what kid in police custody knew, without seeming to doubt, that everything would be okay?

"They're going to ask you if you carved up the grotto," John said.

"I figured that."

John paused, waiting to hear what the kid would say next. But when Brendan just lowered the ice, checked to see if the bleeding had stopped—yes, it had—he remained silent. John refrained from asking again whether Brendan had done it or not. The question hung in the air, left over from before. So John went on.

"And they're going to ask you what you meant about Regis." Just saying the words made John's pulse start to race. Brendan might as well have seen his heart beating right under his skin, because he turned his head and looked into John's eyes.

"You want to know, too," Brendan said. "Right?"

"Of course I do," John said. "I want to know anything that might help her. Did she talk to you?"

Brendan nodded. For the first time since being brought into the station, he looked nervous. He seemed paler, and he licked his lips as if he was thirsty. A bubbler sat in the corner of the room; John glanced around. It didn't come naturally, to move freely in a police station, but for Brendan's sake he steeled himself, walked over, and filled a paper cup.

"Did she talk to you?" John asked again, handing him the water.

Brendan nodded, downing the water in one gulp. "Last night," he said. "After we left the beach movies at Hubbard's Point, and we all went back to the Academy, Regis was ... well, pretty unsettled. Upset, because she thought Mrs. Sullivan was mad at you."

"She was just tired of it all," John said. "Rightly so."

"Regis didn't think it was fair. She did what she did on her own."

"Our family has a long history," John said, "of being divided into two categories: the cautious and the daredevils. Regis seems to have followed me into the daredevil group."

Brendan smiled. "You can't always choose who you take after."

"Well," John said. "You might be right about that." He looked at Brendan, saw sorrow behind his smile, remembered Cece saying that his brother had died, and that he was adopted. He wanted to ask Brendan about his family, but first he had to find out about Regis.

"What else did she say?"

"It was after Cece and Mrs. Sullivan went to bed, and Agnes was getting tired. I said good night, and started out to my car. Regis came after me. First, she asked me for a ride back to Hubbard's Point. . . . I asked her if she was going to see Peter, and she said no—she wanted to find you."

"She was worried about me," John said.

Brendan nodded. "I told her you had probably walked back along the beaches by then."

"You were right," John said, wondering how he knew.

"Well, then she told me she wanted me to look after Agnes again—both of them actually, Cece too, not just Agnes. She sounded funny, as if she had something planned. I asked her what was going on. . . ."

"What did she say?"

Brendan took a deep breath. "She said she'd been having really bad dreams. Ever since you came home. She's been dreaming that the wrong person went to jail; that it should have been her instead of you."

John's stomach was in a knot. He felt sweat running down his back, between his shoulder blades. "Dreams are just dreams," he said. "They're not reality."

"But you know what she was talking about, don't you?" Brendan asked quietly.

"No," John said. "I don't."

"She said she dreams . . . that she killed someone."

John shook his head. "She didn't. I did."

"In her dreams, she saw him him going after you—and then she killed him."

"It wasn't like that," John said, his heart pounding.

Brendan's blue eyes glinted in the dim light coming through the blinds covering the station house windows. John saw something familiar there—a flash of knowledge, cutting through to the core—that reminded him of Tom Kelly.

"You know what, Mr. Sullivan? I can tell you're a good father—I see the way your girls feel about you, and right now I can hear how much you want to protect Regis."

John's shoulders tensed up, and just as in so many of Tom's preambles, he knew that there was a "but" coming. "She's my daughter," he said. "Of course I want to protect her."

"Then tell her the truth."

"Hey," John started.

"Kids always figure out when their parents are lying to them," Brendan said.

John glared at him—how dare this kid he barely knew say such a thing? But even as his anger rose, it washed away. There was something in Brendan's eyes—a compassion that seemed too deep and old for his years—that made John listen.

"For me, it started when they said Paddy had the flu. I knew it was more than that, because he didn't come home from the hospital. Then he did come home, and they had to tell me that he had leukemia. . . ."

"I'm sorry," John said.

Brendan nodded, hurrying on, letting John know that that wasn't the point. "They told me his chemo would work. I kept waiting for that to happen. But Paddy kept getting sicker. He couldn't play anymore. They said he was just tired from the treatment. He got these terrible mouth sores—he'd cry, and the salt from his tears made it worse. They told him to think of the fishing trip we were all going to take when he got better."

"Did he like fishing?"

Brendan nodded. "It was his favorite thing. We had a rowboat in the creek, over behind Paradise Ice Cream. We used to go out when the snapper blues were running and catch so many we thought we'd sink the boat."

"Maybe your parents were just trying to ease his pain," John said. "Give Paddy something happy to think about, and look forward to."

"I know," Brendan said. "But they lied to me, too. They kept telling me we'd get to fish together again. When I knew we'd never make it back to the creek, back to the Sound."

"Did you—"

Brendan shook his head. "Nope. Never fished with him ever again. He just kept getting sicker. My parents just kept saying it was the chemo. The strong drugs, making Paddy sick. They said he'd turn the corner. . . . I got mad at the doctor, because Paddy never got to that corner."

"Don't blame your parents, Brendan," John said quietly, thinking of how he might act if one of his girls were that ill. "They were doing the best they could."

"I know," Brendan said. "They were crazed, they really were. They loved Paddy so much. We all did. I found out about a kid at school whose brother was saved by a bone marrow transplant. I told my parents I wanted to do that for Paddy, and they told me I was too young."

"Were you?"

Brendan shrugged. "I don't know. It was beside the point. The real reason I couldn't donate my marrow was because I was adopted."

"And you didn't know?"

Brendan shook his head. "Nope. I had no idea. They never even gave me a straight answer—I had to ask my aunt. She's the one who told me. It was after Paddy died, and by then my parents weren't in the mood to answer any questions. She told me they couldn't conceive, so they adopted me. But then, a few years later, my mother got pregnant. And Paddy was born. . . . My parents won't talk about it."

"Brendan, parents love adopted kids as much as if they were their birth children," John said. "So much so, they might not think the truth, the details, matter."

"But the truth and details *do* matter," Brendan said softly. "Just the way they matter to Regis."

John was seized with memories and images. The silver-green hills of West Cork, turning black under storm clouds. The sharp cliffs of Ballincastle, waves smashing the rocks down below. Rain coming down sideways, his sculpture teetering on the brink, the ruined tower looming over everything. Greg White insane, attacking his work, screaming that John owed him money.

"If only she hadn't come onto the bluff," he heard himself say now.

"You owe her the truth," Brendan said.

"I've never lied to her," John said, his throat closing up. Even as he spoke, he realized that he was lying right now.

"You took the blame," Brendan said. "You rewrote history, just so Regis wouldn't have to face the truth—and she lost her father for six years."

John couldn't speak. He looked over at the young man—he couldn't be any older than twenty-four, but he had such sorrow and wisdom in his eyes.

"She's haunted," Brendan said, "in her dreams."

"Where is she? Where did she go?"

"That I don't know," Brendan said.

Just then the two detectives walked into the room. Detective Gaffney beckoned Brendan to go with him, and Detective Cavanagh held the door for John to precede her into a small anteroom.

He looked around, finding it hard not to relive the initial questioning at the garda station in Ireland. Brendan's words were ringing in his ears; he thought of what he had said about lies, about a person deserving the truth, and as he spun back six years, to his state of mind and what he wanted, needed, for Regis, he wondered whether he'd made the worst mistake of his life.

"Mr. Sullivan," Detective Cavanagh said, motioning for him to take a seat. He did, and she sat opposite him, at a small desk. She was in her early forties, dressed in dark pants and a crisp white shirt, with sun-streaked light brown hair. Behind a genuinely kind smile, she had a stern steadiness that reminded him of the officers he'd encountered at Ballincastle.

"I need to find my daughter," he said.

She nodded, gazing at him with silent appraisal.

"She's . . . going through a lot," he said, stumbling over the words. If only he could appeal to the detective's kindness—which he had seen at the grotto, and felt now—he could convince her to get out there, look for Regis, and let him do the same.

"What do you mean, 'a lot'?"

John paused. This was the instant he should ask for a lawyer; that's where he'd made his big mistake in Ireland. Trying to protect Regis, he had given a statement, and they'd used it against him. A barrister might have been able to mitigate the impact in court without involving her.

He should clamp down, shut up, refuse to answer anything without calling a lawyer now. He could call Tom—the Kellys had more lawyers in their family in Hartford than there were stones in the Academy walls. These were heavy hitters—lawyers who represented the archdiocese and insurance companies. The chief prosecutor was a second cousin; half the assistant DAs in the state had Kelly blood. The public defender was named for Francis X. himself.

The pro bono league, lawyers known for taking on long shots and last chances, were all found at Kelly family reunions each summer. John knew all he had to do was exercise his constitutional right to counsel, and a Kelly would be at his side within the hour.

But he was innocent right now, and he was notoriously pigheaded, and he believed that this detective was a human being who would understand that he loved his daughter and had to get out of here to help her.

"She's twenty," he said. "She's engaged, but I think she's rethinking that. She was in Ireland with me when—when . . ."

"When you were arrested for manslaughter," Detective Cavanagh finished for him, looking through a sheaf of papers that made John's heart skip; why would they have his arrest file from Ireland?

"Yes," he said. "And I've just come home. Our family has always been close; we've just come back together. It will take some adjustment."

"What do you know about the vandalism at the Academy?"

The transition shook John; had he misjudged Cavanagh? He thought she looked as if she cared, but here she was worried about words scratched into stone instead of Regis.

"Look," he said, "I know that's why my sister called you initially, but I think there's something much more important to deal with—my daughter. She's not someone who just runs away, disappears—she's never taken off before. Her mother and I are worried...."

"I can appreciate that, Mr. Sullivan," the detective said. "We're trying to sort it all out, figure out whether your daughter's decision to go away has anything to do with what happened in the grotto."

"What happened in the *grotto*?" he asked, leaping up, nearly exploding. "That's just someone trying, I don't know, to get their message across. A vandal, or a religious fanatic, or who knows what? Never mind that—I thought you cared about finding Regis!"

"Sit down," she ordered.

John buried his face in his hands, unable to believe this was happening—time passing while Regis was out there, needing him more than ever now. He kept thinking of Brendan, of what he'd said about her dreams. Was Brendan talking to Detective Gaffney, telling him what Regis had talked about to him?

"Last night," Detective Cavanagh said, reading, "Regis behaved very erratically at Hubbard's Point, physically assaulting a man. She was screaming, 'Don't hurt my father.' "

"She didn't assault him. She was a little out of control, yes."

"One person said she was defending you from a verbal attack."

John knew then. That's how she'd found out about his record; last night, when the police had been called at Hubbard's Point, someone had told them about him. He shook his head now.

"Look, Detective. It's between her and me. Can you just believe that, and let me go find her?"

"It would really help if you'd tell me what happened."

"With a name like Cavanagh, you know how the Irish are. My

daughter has the soul of a poet." He struggled, knowing he had to sound convincing so she'd let him go. "She feels things very deeply. That was her future father-in-law last night. She thought he was being too hard on me, that's all. It hurt her feelings."

"That's interesting," Detective Cavanagh said, reading from the original sheaf—the papers that even from across the desk John could see bore the stamp of the Irish court. "Were her feelings hurt in Ireland, too?"

"No," John said, his heart falling, knowing what was coming next.

"Because the initial report filed by the gardai at Ballincastle, where you were arrested for killing Gregory White, says that when they arrived on the scene Regis was crying uncontrollably, repeating one phrase over and over: 'Don't hurt my father.' And then she went silent, and didn't speak to the police again. Ever."

John's heart thudded. They did have the investigation report from Ireland. Peter's parents must have given it to them.

"You don't understand," he said. "She's sensitive. Wouldn't you be, if you saw a man die? It was terrible for her."

"I'll bet it was," the detective said, pushing something out on the table in front of him. It was Regis's letter, the one that Honor had handed the police back at the Blue Grotto. John glanced down, didn't even have to read it....

Dear everyone,

Dad tried to take the blame, but I can't let him do that anymore.

I thought being grown up meant getting married, and that's what I wanted to do. I was missing the most important part.

It means taking responsibility for myself.

You've all taught me so much.

Unfortunately, one of the things our family does best is keep secrets. The letter Aunt Bernie had from Mom proves that beyond any doubt.

I have to think. I want to do the right thing.

*Please don't try to stop me; you couldn't if you tried, anyway.
I love you all—*

Regis

John sat back in his chair. He stared out the window. Traffic sped by on Shore Road; through the glass and over the hum of the air-conditioning, he could hear the muffled sound of cars passing, taking people to and from the beach, their boats, their families. He thought of how worried Honor must be about their daughter, and gripped the arms of his chair to keep himself from shouting at the detective.

"What does she mean," the detective asked, "when she says she wants to take responsibility for herself?"

John just kept staring out the window.

"And here," the detective pointed at the last paragraph, "when she says she wants to do the right thing?"

"I would like a lawyer," he said quietly, knowing it was more for Regis than himself.

Twenty-six

As Bernadette walked through the convent, she stopped and looked out the window—there was Tom, still standing by Brendan's car, no doubt staring at the picture of the sea monster. Even from here she could see Tom's eyes burning bright, as if all their secrets were fueling him.

Knowing what lay ahead of her just now, she straightened her veil, brushed the dirt off the front of her skirt, from where she'd knelt in the grotto, and headed toward the cloister. Clasping her hands, she tried to stop them from shaking. It was nearly *none*, the two o'clock office, and the sisters had gathered in the cloister chapel.

Bernie walked in. She bypassed her usual spot in the last choir stall in the first row, stood right in front of the altar. The sisters remained silent, in private prayer. Several kneeled; most sat.

"In the name of the Father," Bernie began, blessing herself; all the other sisters followed. She caught some of their expressions—surprise that she was standing up here. Normally she just took her seat, a sister among sisters. She ran the place, but that was just administration. When it came to prayer life, they were all equal.

"I'd like to ask you all to pray for a special intention," she said. "For my niece, Regis Sullivan. Please…" She stood tall and steady, but her voice trembled. "Please pray that she finds her way."

The sisters bowed their heads, and Bernie led them in the rosary.

She heard beads clicking. Bernie held the crystal beads her grand-mother had given her when she made her First Communion. She thought of the connection, strong women all related to each other. Regis was a woman after Bernie's grandmother's heart, brave and lov-ing and adventurous.

After all the Hail Marys, Our Fathers, and Glory bes, she finished with the Memorare. It had been Tom's grandmother's favorite prayer, imported straight from Ireland. Bernie remembered the first time she heard it. It had seemed almost incantatory, calling for the power of Mary. When Bernie had gone through her darkest time, months after returning from Dublin with Tom, the Memorare was the prayer that had led her into the convent:

Remember, O most gracious Virgin Mary, that never was it known that anyone who fled to thy protection, implored thy help, or sought thy intercession, was left unaided. Inspired with this confidence, I fly unto thee, O Virgin of virgins, my Mother! To thee I come; before thee I stand, sinful and sorrowful. O Mother of the Word Incarnate, despise not my petitions, but in thy mercy hear and answer me. Amen.

The sisters bowed their heads; Bernie looked out over them. She loved her community of nuns so much, just as she loved Regis, the girl for whom they prayed.

Bernie's heart ached, and she prayed her niece wouldn't do any-thing crazy, anything to harm herself.

Agnes and Cece walked the grounds, looking in all of Regis's secret places. The tunnels, of course, and the pine barrens; the formal gar-dens behind the convent, originally planted in the 1920s, for the wed-ding of Francis X. Kelly's daughter; the Blue Grotto, which now bore the chilly reality of a crime scene, the chalky words with their dark meaning scratched into the granite; the marsh and the creek; and all along the winding stone wall.

Agnes wondered whether the stones had actual magical or spiritual power—like the dolmens or standing stones her family had seen near Ballincastle. They must have, she thought now, walking along, looking for Regis, feeling electricity bouncing off the wall. Every single stone, each rock, had been lifted and placed by one of her ancestors.

"Regis!" Cece yelled now. "Come out! We're looking for you!"

"She won't come out," Agnes said, feeling the truth in her bones.

"What do you mean?"

"She doesn't want us to find her."

"But why? She can't want us to worry about her."

"She's not thinking of that," Agnes said. "There's something she has to do before we find her...."

"How do you know?"

"I know Regis," Agnes said.

And it was true. Although they were three sisters, and had lived much of their lives as a unit of three, Agnes and Regis had been a twosome for five years before Cece was born, and were forever bonded. Agnes remembered looking out from her crib as an infant, seeing Regis's face smiling in; she remembered Regis giving her a bottle.

Agnes thought of the nights Regis had cried in her sleep. She had mumbled words, and now Agnes swore they were the same ones Regis had called out that night at Hubbard's Point. *Don't hurt my father.* How could she not have known what Regis was saying? What good were sisters if they couldn't help translate the language of each other's dreams?

"Sisela," Cece said.

Agnes saw her then, the old white cat—older than both Agnes and Cece. She lay curled on the wall up ahead, gazing at them with emerald green eyes.

"Maybe she'll lead us to Regis," Cece said.

"I think that only happens in the movies," Agnes said.

"But look," Cece said as the cat stretched, white fur seeming to glow—beyond the sunlight streaming down.

"What's she doing?" Agnes asked as Sisela looked back over her shoulder, as if to make sure the girls were following.

"She's taking us to Regis," Cece whispered.

"No," Agnes said.

But that's just what Sisela seemed to be doing. She strode along the top of the wall . . . not east, toward the Sound, but west, toward the convent, and then Black Hall, and then who knew where. In that moment, with the sun as bright as Agnes's camera flash had been the night of her accident, she knew that the picture she had taken was not of an angel at all—at least, not one with wings.

It had been an angel with fur. Sisela must have been sitting on the wall, just waiting to jump into the void, fly toward the beach where their father had come to stay. The cat had led Agnes and the family to him, so why shouldn't she lead them to Regis now?

Agnes and Cece began to follow the old cat, walking toward the Academy. And even though it wasn't a Tuesday, Agnes felt speechless. There wasn't anything left to say, not until they found her big sister.

It took exactly fifty-seven minutes from the time John placed his call to Chrysogonus Kelly—better known as Tom's cousin Chris—for the star of Connecticut's Superior Court and legal forums everywhere to drive down Route 9 from his house—a sprawling Georgian mansion on seven acres in Farmington—to Black Hall's police station.

John heard the engine before he saw the man; he didn't know what Chris was driving, but it sounded expensive. The low thrum was exciting and dangerous, and a testosterone ripple ran through the whole building as Chris parked the car in the small parking lot just outside.

"What's that, a Lamborghini?" Officer Kossoy asked as Chris came through the front door.

"It's a Pagani Zonda," Chris said.

"Yeah? Never seen one. Got to be pretty much the only one in America," Kossoy said, glancing out at the rare car.

"Only one in Connecticut, anyway," Chris said. He grinned with obvious delight.

"Far out," Kossoy said.

"So," Detective Cavanagh began. "Enough with the car talk. To what do we owe the pleasure of Chrysogonus Kelly's company?"

"I'm here to see my client," Chris said, giving her his most flirtatious smile.

"We have two gentlemen here on suspicion of vandalism, and one of them calls you?" Officer Kossoy asked.

"Yeah, aren't you supposed to be in Washington, arguing some low-life killer's death penalty case before the Supreme Court?" Detective Gaffney asked.

"I'll be arguing prosecutorial misconduct next week," Chris said. "But today's business is just as important. The Sixth Amendment knows no hierarchy."

"That's really a Pagani Zonda?" Officer Kossoy asked.

"Yep. I'll give you a ride after Detective Cavanagh," Chris said.

"You're dreaming," she said. "Ever since you grilled me on the Duncaster case, I wouldn't go anywhere with you. You twisted my words from here to eternity...."

"*From Here to Eternity*. My favorite movie," Chris said. "Especially that scene in the surf..."

Detective Cavanagh narrowed her eyes at him. "Defense lawyers are arrogant by definition, but you're in a class all by yourself. I went to Star of the Sea Academy. I know all about you Kellys. You might be *named* for a saint..."

"Yep," Chris said, smiling. "I love being part of the lineup. Linus, Cletus, Clemens, Sixtus, Cyprian, Cornelius, Chrysogonus..."

"Don't flatter yourself," Detective Cavanagh said. "You can talk to your client in there." She gestured at the same room where she'd interrogated John, and John led Chris in, shaking his head.

"You can't help yourself, can you?" John asked.

"What can I say?" Chris asked. "She and I have a long history in court. She can give as good as she gets, believe me. I need to be on my toes when I'm around Doreen Cavanagh. She's one tough cop. Tell me what's going on."

"First of all, thanks for getting here so fast."

"You're family, John. Tom and Bernie, and you and Honor—we're practically blood. Francis would have it no other way than that I pull out all the stops for you. I'm sorry about what you went through in Ireland, by the way. Tom and I talked about it. I wish to hell I'd been a member of the bar over there. I'd have gotten you out within the week."

"My barrister wasn't the problem," John said.

"No," Chris admitted. "I've heard. You had your own ideas about what you wanted to do, left your barrister pretty much helpless at sentencing. If the court had been in Dublin instead of Cork, my cousin Sixtus would have gotten you off."

John shrugged. His shoulders were so tense, he thought they'd crack. Every minute he sat in this police station was a minute Regis was out there, needing help. He couldn't talk about it, but he had to.

"You said Cavanagh is a tough cop," he said.

"She is. She nearly put a client of mine away for life, an ugly case, I won't go into it; she would have won, too, if I hadn't come through on appeal. A little problem with discovery. Nothing against her, though. It was all on the state's attorney. Not one of my cousins, thank God. Why?"

"She's onto something about my daughter."

"Which daughter? They can't possibly be old enough to have the likes of DeeDee Cavanagh onto them."

"Regis. She's twenty." And she'd been fourteen when the real trouble began...and ended.

"What did she do?"

John glared at Chris. He'd known him since he was born—Tom's cousin, younger by six years. They used to tease him unmercifully, calling him "Chrysanthemum." Even now, staring at the confident attorney in his expensive summer sports clothes, John could see traces of the young boy they used to make cry by nicknaming him after a flower.

"It happened at Ballincastle," John began, then stopped.

"Go on," Chris urged.

"You're my lawyer now, right?" John said.

"Yes."

"Attorney-client privilege applies?"

"Of course."

"None of what I tell you leaves this room."

"Understood, John."

So John took a deep breath, and then he told his lawyer what happened one stormy day on a windswept cliff across the ocean, a lifetime ago.

Bernie couldn't rest. It was nearly vespers, Tom was out in the garden pruning the same rosebushes he'd clipped yesterday, Honor was keeping vigil on the beach, and Agnes and Cece stood outside now, Sisela between them, staring at the building. There was such a sense of terrible anticipation. But for what?

Bernie wondered about Brendan. Was he with John? Was her brother looking after him at the police station? She knew his last name, thought maybe she could look it up in the phone book, call his parents to let him know where he was. But something kept her from doing that.

She had work to do, and she was worried about Regis. She knew the sisters would pray at vespers, and at compline, and on through the night; but all the rosaries in the world couldn't keep her head-strong niece from doing what she was going to do. Because the Academy library was where Bernie felt closest to Regis, she headed there now. When she glanced out the window, she saw her other nieces and Sisela still hovering outside.

Bernie went straight toward the rare-book room. She had a safe inside, where she kept the Academy funds; it was also where she kept important documents and her personal diaries. She had come here so often in her early days as a nun, when all she wanted to do was pray and forget.

"Hi, Aunt Bernie."

Shocked, she nearly jumped, looking up.

"Regis..." she gasped.

Her niece stood on a stepladder, kerchief tied around her head, dusting the books on the top shelf, as if it were a normal workday. Hanging back slightly, Bernie watched as the girl took each volume down, holding it in her hands, rubbing it slowly with the flannel square before replacing it in the bookcase.

"You were scheduled to work today," Bernie said, "but I didn't expect you."

"I'm taking my responsibilities very seriously these days," Regis said.

"Your family is looking for you."

"Families look for each other all the time," Regis said.

Bernie's heart skipped a beat; what did the girl mean by that? "Regis, why don't you come down? There's really no rush to dust all these shelves today."

"That's the wrong attitude to have," Regis said, gently dusting a green book cover.

"Excuse me?"

"You said 'shelves,'" Regis said, "when I'm thinking in terms of *books*. Do you know the last time some of these were read?" She opened the jacket and looked at the library stamp. "This one was last taken out in 1973. This might be the very first time it's been touched by human hands since then. Poor old book."

"What's the title?"

Regis peered at the spine. "*Vita Sanctus Aloysius Gonzaga.*"

"'The Life of Saint Aloysius Gonzaga,' in Latin," Bernadette said. "It's about an Italian nobleman who grew up in a castle. His father was a compulsive gambler. His mother was wretched."

"A lot of saints have wretched families, I guess," Regis said. "A lot of people, as a matter of fact—not just saints."

"What's gotten into you, Regis Maria?" Bernadette asked. "First I hear about you creating a spectacle last night, and then you run off and make your family worry, and now you're saying something like that? Come down now, and tell me what's wrong."

They stared at each other, Regis's eyes sparkling with tears. Fighting to hold them back, she started down the ladder.

"Hand me that book on Gonzaga, will you?" Bernie said. As Regis passed it over, Bernie gave her a hand, and they clasped fingers. She saw Regis's shoulders trembling. Walking slowly, she led her niece through the library. Long and narrow, it was built on the same plan as the Long Room at Trinity College in Dublin, with a barrel-vaulted ceiling and gallery bookcases, a mezzanine encircled by an oak balustrade, and two levels of bookshelves. Tom's great-grandfather had spared no expense. Bernie and Tom had visited the library when they were in Dublin; she remembered that every time she walked through here.

When they got to the office, Bernadette placed the book on top of the ones about Saint Francis of Assisi: another saint who had defied his wealthy landowning father. A portrait of Tom's great-grandfather gazed sternly down from the wall, as if he had some inkling of what her interest was in these particular books, how they reminded her of Tom Kelly. Turning her back on the painting, she faced Regis.

"Tell me what's going on," Bernadette said.

"I'd rather ask *you* that."

"Your parents are really worried, Regis. Peter is, too. He was here, looking for you."

"We're not engaged anymore," Regis said. "I gave him back the ring late last night."

"I know," Bernie said.

"The priest will be happy. He was always trying to talk us out of getting married. Did you put him up to it?"

"As much influence as I have over the Holy See and the archdiocese, it pretty much stops dead at the doors of Father Joe's rectory. What did he say?"

"That we should put everything on hold, and be absolutely sure of what we want, and the usual stuff. Pretty much what you, Mom, and the Drakes were saying."

"And now you see the wisdom in it?"

"Wisdom," Regis said, "is remarkably overrated."

"Really."

"Yep."

"What's better than wisdom?"

"Love," Regis said. "And passion. And don't tell me you don't understand."

"I'm a nun," Bernadette said.

"Yes," Regis said, narrowing her eyes. "But you weren't always."

Bernie's heart skipped a beat.

"I realized Peter and I would be making a mistake. I was marrying him for the wrong reasons; it wouldn't have been fair to him. I was just hiding out..."

"From what?"

Regis shook her head. "Does it matter?" she asked. "Hiding out is just another way of keeping secrets. You should know."

"What are you trying to tell me?"

Regis stared at her, steel in her lovely young eyes. Bernadette saw herself there, and she felt herself blush.

"I know about you and Tom," Regis said.

Bernadette's pulse was racing, but she didn't react. She just stared at the stack of books on her desk. Saint Francis of Assisi had been such a generous soul, such a dreamer. He had loved all creatures, loved the poorest of the poor, left his family's riches behind. And Tom Kelly, scion of one of the great families of the East Coast of America, was the groundskeeper at Star of the Sea Academy on the Connecticut shore, intimately familiar with, so tender about, everything within its gray stone walls.

"Regis," Bernadette said, approaching her. "I know you think you know something, but you don't."

"He loved you, and wanted to marry you, but you wouldn't, right? It all came together for me, all about what my father and Tom found in the wall, and why our family went to Ireland. About you and Tom going there first."

"Regis, it had to do with tracing our roots. Tom's people were from Dublin, so we went there. You know that."

"But I didn't know the secret...."

Bernadette didn't speak; she took a deep breath and stared.

"You have a secret that started on your trip to Ireland," Regis said, staring right back. "And I have one that started on mine."

"Stop," Bernie said.

"Your secret is that a life began, and mine is that a life ended."

"Regis," Bernie said, reaching for her, but Regis pulled away.

"Maybe I'll regret breaking up with Peter. Don't you ever wish you had married Tom?" Regis asked, challenging her, eyes on fire.

"Regis, you don't understand. Our stories are not the same," Bernadette said. "It's so important to me that you know that."

"But they are the same," Regis said, her voice rising. "All love stories are the same!"

"They're not," Bernadette pleaded. "You only think you understand. You don't. It was so much more complicated than you think."

"But you loved Tom, didn't you? You were in love with each other?"

"I loved him, yes," Bernadette whispered.

"And something happened in Dublin," Regis said, a sob breaking out. "You created a life."

"Regis, please," Bernadette said, grabbing her hand. "You can't understand, you don't have all the information."

Regis reached into the back pocket of her jeans, pulled out the letter Honor had written twenty-three years ago, placed it ever so gently on the desk. Bernadette's eyes filled with tears when she saw it.

She saw Honor's writing—her friend's youth and excitement, her unconditional love and support, were manifest in the all the exclamation points she had used in the letter. Bernie had kept the letter all this time—and had drawn on the envelope one afternoon, reading and rereading Honor's words, trying to decide what to do—the sea monster from Tom's Kelly family crest. She felt her face grow scalding hot.

"I kept that letter hidden all these years," Bernie said. "I just gave it back to your mother."

"I know. She must have read and reread it; I found it under a placemat in the kitchen. Funny, her saying these things to you—about being honest with yourself, knowing what was important in life, telling the truth."

"Oh, Regis..." Bernadette said, struggling for control of her voice. "You have no idea."

She remembered that Honor had quoted from the diary of Bobby Sands, the young Irishman who had gone to prison and died in a hunger strike against British rule. His words came to Bernadette now, filling her heart: *I am standing on the threshold of another trembling world.*

Oh, the trembling world. Bernie knew it so well.

"You called my mother from Ireland, to tell her you were having a baby," Regis said.

"She was my best friend," Bernie whispered. "The only person I could tell, besides Tom."

"She wrote to you, trying to convince you to come home and have the baby. She'd have helped you tell your family. She told you it wasn't wrong, that you loved Tom and shouldn't be ashamed. That you had to tell the truth, or you'd regret it your whole life. She said she'd help you through the hardest part," Regis said.

Bernie closed her eyes, as if she could block out the hardest part: hearing their baby cry, holding him, feeling his heart beat against hers, handing him to the nuns in the hospital...

"When Tom and I decided to give the baby up for adoption," Bernie said. "That was the hardest part."

"Why did you do it," Regis asked, "if you loved each other?"

"Things were so different back then. We weren't married; we're both from such strict Catholic families. We didn't want to bring shame on them, or on the baby. And since you've read your mother's letter, you know that something happened, that I had a vision." Bernie watched Regis for her reaction.

"*Everyone* knows you did," Regis said. "We don't know what it was, but Agnes, especially, talks about it. But Mom says in her letter that even you might have misinterpreted what the vision meant."

Bernie stared out the window toward the Blue Grotto; she didn't want to admit to her niece that she had had many dark nights of the soul, wondering that very thing.

"Last night," Regis said, "after everything happened at Hubbard's Point, and my sisters and mother went to bed, I went outside to talk to Brendan."

Bernie shivered, just to hear his name.

"What did Brendan say?" she asked.

"He was able to get birth records," she said. "By going to Catholic Charities, and matching the information he got there with what he found, working at the hospital. It's why he's been hanging around here."

"Around here?"

"Around the Academy," Regis said. "He believes that Tom is his father."

"I know that," Bernie said. "Tom figured it out."

"Which would make you his mother."

Bernie couldn't answer. Her throat caught, remembering the shock of red hair on her son's head, the sleepy softness of his blue eyes. She had had him at Gethsemani Hospital, staffed by Sisters of Notre Dame des Victoires, the order of nuns that she would soon join.

"I never knew why you used to cry at Christmas," Regis said. "When we'd set up the crèche, and place the infant in his crib. Now I do."

"Now you do," Bernie whispered.

"People make mistakes," Regis said. "And entire lives can change forever."

Bernadette held her breath as Regis looked over at her.

"Aunt Bernie, help me," Regis said, starting to sob.

"I'll do anything," Bernie said, reaching for her. "Tell me, my dearest girl..."

"I did something terrible," Regis cried. "And, oh, Aunt Bernie, my father took the blame for it."

Twenty-seven

Three men in a Pagani Zonda was a very tight fit, but Chris Kelly managed to drive himself and his two clients—for he had also agreed to represent Brendan McCarthy during questioning—the mile and a half from the Black Hall police station to Star of the Sea Academy.

John sat in the front seat, and Brendan was squeezed next to him, trying to avoid the gearshift. Chris's driving was fast and painless. He was used to getting quickly from one courthouse to the next, and then back to his office, to maximize his potential. Today he had a late-afternoon golf game up in Avon, and he wanted to make his tee time.

"So," Chris said, Persol sunglasses giving him more the look of a movie star in the South of France than a defense lawyer driving two clients along the sleepy Shore Road. "They're not going to file charges."

"That's good," John said. "Considering we didn't do anything worth charging us for."

Brendan's silence made him wonder whether that was true; had the boy vandalized the Blue Grotto?

"The police aren't taking your daughter's disappearance seriously," Chris said. "They say she's 'of age,' and she left a note that seems very sound and well thought out. Does that worry you?"

"It's better this way," John said. "Her mother and I will find her ourselves."

"Well, the way they were talking at first," Chris said, "I was afraid the cops were going to give you grief about her disappearance. But the important thing is that you get her straightened out. You go the shrink route here, and I'll make discreet inquiries across the way."

"No, Chris," John said.

"Shut up, Sullivan. I'm not 'Chrysanthemum' anymore, and you're an idiot who knows shit about the law. If you'd called me when you should have, we wouldn't be doing this now. I'm your lawyer, got it?"

John stared out the window, feeling so tense he might kick out the windshield. Only the presence of Brendan McCarthy, looking painfully uncomfortable to hear the lawyer talking this way, kept John in line.

"Cops love to throw their weight around," Chris said. "I remember it from childhood, don't you, Johnny? When Uncle Frank would show us his nightstick and blackjack, tell us how many skulls he'd cracked?"

"The Black Hall police were hardly rough on us," John said.

"No," Chris said. "But they wanted to draw a line in the sand. They have your court papers from Dublin, thanks to Ralph Drake. I've known him since law school, and he's a jerk. Anyway, the cops know you went to prison for manslaughter, and they're letting you know they know. That's what this was all about, you realize."

"And Brendan?" John asked, worried about the idea of another young person dragged into a police inquiry.

"Brendan has nothing to worry about," Chris said confidently. "They call you again, Brendan, you tell them to call your lawyer."

"I can't really afford a lawyer," Brendan said. "But thank you for what you did today. I'll pay you when I can...."

"Hah," Chris said, turning off onto Old Shore Road. "No need. You're practically family."

"Family? We've never even met," Brendan said, his eyes shining.

Chris glanced over. "True, but when John called me, he said you're a friend of Agnes's. That makes you family in my book."

"I thought maybe...well, that you meant that you think we could be related," Brendan said.

John could feel nervousness pouring off the young man—he was surprised Chris hadn't sensed it. Brendan was practically shaking.

"Well," Chris said, "it's true that you have a lot of Kelly to you—those killer blue eyes, and a fighting spirit. And it's also true that if you're an Irish Catholic Democrat in this state, the chances are good we're related."

"That's all?" Brendan asked, letting the question hang.

Chris chuckled. "That's all, kid. Of course, anything's possible."

He downshifted, and the car's roar turned into a throaty purr. Turning in through the stone gates of Star of the Sea, John felt a jolt. He was coming home, to go away. His experience at the police station had convinced him, more than ever, that he had to leave.

The police had drawn a line in the sand, but that was nothing compared to the one John had drawn for himself. He no longer knew what the borders of his life should be. He loved Honor and the girls with the force of his soul, but every move he made seemed to hurt them. He had taught his daughters long ago that the way to escape the boundaries of life was to go as far out on the edge as you could. And Regis, his firstborn, of all the girls had made that philosophy her own.

He just hoped she wasn't so far out that she couldn't be found and brought back. He'd find her. He'd go to Devil's Hole, climb the cliff, and see if she was hiding out there. He'd go anywhere it took to find her. And then, once she was safely back at home, he'd leave. He never wanted to see pain in Honor's face again—not like he'd seen last night. He had caused enough of that to last a lifetime.

"Well, well," Chris said, driving through the vineyard. "This sure brings back memories. Remember when we were kids down here, John?"

"I could never forget," John said quietly, gazing out the car window at every inch of this land that he held so dear.

"Brendan, John's great-grandfather built all these walls that you see. He was a stonemason, straight off the boat from Ireland, an incredibly strong and gifted man," Chris said.

"And Chris's great-grandfather owned the house and the land," John said. "He was a true philanthropist; generous to everyone he came into contact with."

"My great-great grandfather," Brendan said quietly.

John heard him, but Chris wasn't sure.

"What did you say?" Chris asked, laughing.

"Here we are," Brendan said as the car purred to a stop in front of the main Academy building, the stone mansion that had once belonged to Francis X. Kelly, right in front of Sister Bernadette Ignatius—standing on the sidewalk, arm around her eldest niece. Agnes and Cece were pressed close, and Sisela was sitting at their feet.

"Regis!" John said, jumping out of the car.

"Dad!" she cried out, leaving Bernie's side.

"Sweetheart!" he managed to get out, folding her in his arms. "Are you all right?"

"Dad, I am," she said. "For the first time in a long time…"

"Where were you?" he asked, holding her out at arm's length. "Why did you run away?"

"She didn't run too far, as it turns out," Bernie said. "She was waiting for me in the library."

"Is that true?" John asked.

Regis nodded. "I couldn't go too far," she said. "Because I had to talk to you. Mom, too, but you first."

"Should I stick around?" Chris asked John. "I'll cancel my golf game," the lawyer said.

John shot him a grateful look and nodded.

"Hello, Chris," Bernie said. "Make yourself at home. You know your way around."

"I do indeed, Sister."

"Let's talk," John said to Regis. Brendan had gone to hug Agnes, whisper a few words to her. Agnes listened, kissed his cheek, and grabbed Cece's hand. They gave their sister a quick hug and went off toward the beach.

Then John saw Brendan turn his gaze toward Bernie. As John walked away with his daughter, he left them standing together. His heart went out to them both, but for now, all his attention was on Regis. She needed him more than ever. And whatever she had to tell him, he had a few things to say to her, too.

Regis's heart soared, and her stomach sank. Talking with her father, really talking—this was what she had dreamed of and dreaded all these last nights. They walked across the grounds, through the vineyard, already spicy with the fragrance of late-summer grapes.

Someday soon she would take him to Devil's Hole, the scariest place she'd ever been before Ballincastle. She'd show him how brave she was, how close she could stand to the edge—how she had learned from him how to trust her instincts and strengths. But right now there was somewhere closer that seemed an even better place to have this talk, and they both knew what it was.

They started up the hill, toward the long stone wall. From here it looked almost like a backbone, the spine of the Academy property, strong and structural, as if the land couldn't exist without it. Regis ran her hand along the top stones of the wall as they walked beside it; she remembered doing that when she was very small, maybe five years old. The stones felt warm from the sun's heat.

When they reached the spot where he had found the box, they both stopped at the same time.

"Dad, I have something to tell you."

"I know," he said. "So have I."

"It's about Ballincastle, Dad."

"Regis…"

"You have to listen to me."

"There's nothing left to say."

The look on his face was so profoundly troubled, for a minute she wanted to back down, let the whole thing rest. But she had done that for too long, and she *knew* she had to tell him what she *knew*.

"I remember, Dad," she said.

"What do you think you remember now," he asked carefully, "that could possibly be new? It's over, Regis."

"That's the thing," she said. "I thought memories were solid—that once you had them, they lasted forever. But ever since that day on the cliff, I haven't trusted my memories." Blinking into the late-day sun, she looked up at him.

He just stared down at her with the saddest eyes, as if he wished he could prevent her from going through this. But she had started, and she knew she had to continue.

"At first there was nothing." She paused, staring across the fields to the calm and sparkling water. "Just blackness. That's all I could see, just as if it were a curtain. Thick and dark. For such a long time, that was all I remembered from that day."

"Let it be, Regis," John said, begging her.

She shook her head. "Dad, listen. After a while, I remembered hearing him yelling for you to pay him more money, and to tell him where the gold was buried—pirate gold. You and he were fighting, and you told him you'd already paid him what you owed him, you'd warned him about this....I heard myself screaming, and I tried to pull him off you. He cracked me with his elbow—it hurt so much, and I went flying. Dad, you went crazy when you saw that. You were punching him so hard—I could hear your fists pounding his head. And then he was down on the ground, bleeding, and you were hugging me, telling me everything would be okay."

"That's what happened," her father said, resolute.

"But not all," Regis said.

"Sweetheart, let it stay there."

"No, Dad. Listen. I remember more now..." She closed her eyes tight. What was a memory, what was a fear, what was a scrap of nightmare? Voices, feelings, a shove, stepping away...

"None of it changes what happened," her father said. "I crossed paths with the wrong person. I did that too often back then...I never should have hired him. I paid him once, and then I couldn't get rid of him. Then I made the mistake of threatening him in a crowded bar."

"I know."

"People say things they don't mean," John said. "I was just so angry at what he'd already done to my sculpture. I should have let it go, called the police. But I didn't, and I paid for it."

Regis closed her eyes tight again—tighter. A flash of conversation between her parents, just before her father had left the house in the storm. Her father talking about the strange man who had helped him with his sculpture for a few days, but that he'd fired him. The man had sounded scary, and Regis had wanted to go after her father, to help him.

She pictured Gregory White that day in the rain, when he'd attacked her—tall, thin, with curly, shaggy brown hair and piercing green eyes. And then, after her father had fought him, the man lying on the wet ground, blood pouring from his head.

Memories were like rocks at low tide: they were there, visible, obvious. But the first wave came in, sliding over them, making the rockweed swish in the rising water, undulating and advancing and receding, and then the second wave, a little higher, and then the third: until you weren't sure there were rocks underneath the water at all.

Her father was staring at her now, his eyes full of fear for what she would say next.

"I killed him, Dad," she said.

"Regis, no…"

Her father sat on the wall, shaking his head, as if he could make the past go away, send her memories back into the blackness. She welled up, hating what had happened, feeling the dread all over again.

"It was after you hit him," she said. "And he was down on the ground."

"Honey," her father said, pleading now. "All this time. You've kept it buried, and for a good reason. Please, Regis…"

"Your sculpture was in pieces. You thought you'd knocked him out, and after you saw I was okay, you turned to look at what he'd done. Rocks, driftwood, everything had been dislodged, just lying there on the ground."

"God, Regis," John said. "Why did I even care about that right then? I should have just gotten you out of there."

"You were stunned at what he'd done. All your work, torn down. You were standing right at the edge of the cliff, gathering up the stuff he'd kicked over there. I guess he'd planned to pitch it off."

"I should have taken you right home," John said.

"But Greg White wasn't knocked out—you had your back turned, he stood up, and picked up a rock—one of the big ones he had pulled down from your sculpture. He was going to hit you with it," Regis said, feeling as frantic as if it were happening all over. "And I couldn't let him. He was too big for me to fight, or to pull back from you— and you were right at the edge of the cliff, and I thought he was going to hit you and push you off."

She stared down at the stone wall, could nearly see the rock in Greg White's hands. He'd lifted it high over his head, ready to smash it down on her father's skull.

"And I started screaming, 'Don't hurt my father!' The rain was just pouring, and the wind howling—I felt as if the words were caught in my throat. I was trying to warn you, and stop him, but he just kept going..."

"Sweetheart, no."

"So I picked up a piece of driftwood..."

She felt as if she was in a trance. Her father held her hand, and she knew she was safe now, and didn't pull away. She wondered if this was what it was like to be hypnotized. The breeze blew softly, the opposite of the wind howling at Ballincastle; she felt it in her hair. She felt so alive now, so alert to everything around them. Her father's breath sounded steady and tense, and tears ran down his cheeks.

"I saw him start to turn around," she said. "He was between me and you. I looked down, and the cliff just dropped away."

"Regis," her father said, and his eyes looked scared. Regis's heart opened up; if only he knew how she needed this.

"You still didn't hear. That screaming wind... It was louder than my voice. I couldn't stop him any other way, Dad."

Regis took a breath, then looked her father straight in the eye.

"He had this look on his face," Regis said. "He glanced at me, then back at you. He didn't think I'd do it. He raised the rock, to smash it down on your—"

Her father listened, right there with her.

"And I raised the driftwood branch. I screamed, 'Don't hurt my father,'" Regis said, the memory flooding back. "I hit him as hard as I could. Dad, the way it felt in my hand when it smashed...his *skull*."

"Regis," he said, reaching for her, but she wouldn't let him hold her yet.

"We all went over," she said. "I'd charged him so hard. If there hadn't been that little ledge beneath the cliff, we'd all have died. Instead...Oh, Dad. When I looked at his face, and he was still alive. Blood just pouring out of his head; running into his eyes, and he looked at me, so shocked. And then he died!"

Her mind was suddenly so clear, and she started to cry. She remembered how scared she had been—not for herself, but because she had thought someone was about to kill her father.

"Sweetheart," her father broke down, holding her. "You saved my life."

"Why couldn't you have told the gardai?" Regis asked, weeping. "Why did you have to take the blame for something I did?"

"Because I had threatened to kill him," John said. "People heard me. White and I had history with each other."

"But if you said I was just trying to protect you!"

"Regis, you're my daughter. All I could think of was keeping you out of it. I had gotten us into the situation. When the gardai first arrived, I told them I was trying to protect you—my little daughter. Do you think they would have believed me if I'd said it was the other way around?"

"But you must have thought," Regis cried, gulping air, "that I let you go to jail!"

"I didn't think that at all," her father said.

"Then why didn't you let me testify?" she asked.

"Regis, you didn't remember. Your mother told me, and I was so grateful. I didn't want you to have these memories...."

"I have them now," she said softly. "The worst part is remembering how close he came to killing you."

"I know."

"Last night," she whispered, "when I saw Peter's father getting right in your face, it all came back. I didn't even think—I just acted. My heart was beating so fast, I just felt it happening all over again. I shoved him, just the way I did Greg White. 'Don't hurt my father...' I've been dreaming that for six years. Last night I yelled it at Mr. Drake, and something clicked inside. It felt like the missing piece."

"You're safe now, Regis," he said. "And so am I."

Golden light from the setting sun spread all over the river and Sound, over the fields and vineyard, over the slate roof of the Academy building, and the long stone walls meandering from west to east, all the way to Ireland.

Long shadows had begun to spring up—from trees, rocks, the steeple, the walls, the hill itself. They hid things that would be obvious in midday: a rabbit eating grass by the wall, a slash of red foliage in the maples near the pond, the glimmer of purple grapes on the vines, Aunt Bernie and Brendan sitting on a bench by the Blue Grotto. And Regis's mother...

Hidden in the wall's shadow, Regis looked down the hill, saw her mother sitting right in the middle of her father's labyrinth—the very center of all the stones he had gathered, silvery and magical in the soft, summery light. The tide was coming in, waves lapping up toward the biggest rocks on the labyrinth's outer edge.

It was a strange place for her mother to be waiting. On an August evening, she might be home painting or getting dinner ready. She might be walking with Cece or talking to Agnes. But Aunt Bernie had called her after she'd found Regis in the library, so maybe she was sitting in the labyrinth, gathering herself for the talk they'd have later.

"There's your mother," her father said.

"I noticed," Regis said.

"She can't see us sitting in the shadows here," he said. "Let's go down and show her you're okay."

"Aunt Bernie told her."

"It's not the same as letting her see you with her own eyes," he said. "It would make her happy."

"I thought maybe you might want to talk to her alone," Regis said.

Her father looked surprised, as if he hadn't thought she could tell. His lined cheeks turned ruddy, blushing.

"She wants to see you," he said.

"Dad," Regis said, squeezing his hand, "she wants to see *you*, too. Besides, you have to tell her about Chris Kelly."

"What do you mean?" he asked.

"I heard you tell him he should stick around," Regis said. "You knew what I was going to say, didn't you?"

"I feared," he said, touching her cheek. "I didn't know for sure."

"Am I going to be in a lot of trouble?" she asked.

He shook his head—but of course he would. That was her father, always trying to protect her from the worst. No matter what, she was just so glad to have told what she remembered. So they could all face the truth.

And be together again.

Twenty-eight

Sister Bernadette sat beside Brendan McCarthy, staring down at the ground, looking at his shoes. Funny, she had stared into his beautiful blue eyes, and taken note of his slender fingers, and listened to the deep intelligence and sensitivity of his spirit pouring forth as he spoke. But nothing, none of it, made her throat catch quite in the way that looking at his shoes did.

"So, you see," he continued, laying out his "case," his most persuasive arguments, "once I checked with Catholic Charities, and found out my mother had come from Star of the Sea...and once I realized my father's last name was Kelly, then it all just seemed so clear."

"I can imagine how it would," Bernie said, unable to take her eyes off those shoes. They were brown, laced up, quite scuffed. They looked to be size 9 or 10; Brendan was a medium-sized boy, with medium-sized feet.

"I didn't even start looking until a couple of years ago," Brendan said.

"No?" she asked. She thought of her boy; how he had looked as a baby. She had held him the day of his birth, fed him, gazed into his eyes. She had marvelled at his feet—perfect tiny feet, with ten perfect toes. She had kissed them.

Over the years, she had imagined him learning to walk. Now, looking down at Brendan's feet, she imagined him taking his first steps, learning to tie his shoes.

"No," he said. "I thought it would be disloyal to my parents. The ones who raised me."

"And what changed your mind?" Bernie asked.

"Well," he said, thinking. "Something inside me. It won't go away. I keep thinking, I want to know the people who gave me my life. It doesn't mean I love my adoptive parents any less." He paused. "They drink. A lot. They held it together for a long time, but when I went to college and started working…it got really bad. They're just lost."

"The grief of losing your brother must have been terrible," Bernie said. "For you all."

"It has been," Brendan said. "I don't want to blame them for what they feel. They loved him so much."

"That doesn't mean they don't love you, too."

"I know," he said. "I wouldn't want to hurt them. But they've been— not there. I mean, they're sitting in the room with me, we're all together, but they're just—gone. Not present. It made me think they might not even notice if I tried to find my birth parents."

"And that's what led you here," Bernie said.

"Yes," Brendan said.

And as Bernie raised her eyes—from his tired, scuffed old shoes, to his bright, sharp, intelligent blue eyes—she saw Tom standing just behind him. Perhaps he'd been standing in the background this whole time, listening. But now that Bernie had seen him, he came forward.

"Hi," Tom said, staring at Brendan as if he was taking in every detail—the shape of his face, the profusion of freckles, his slightly crooked bottom teeth.

"Hi," Brendan said. Suddenly he seemed shy. He had been so friendly, and open, and exuberant. But at the sight of Tom, whose entire being was gleaming, shimmering, as if he really were in the presence of his only child, the boy turned slightly inward. Tom wanted it all, he wanted his family to be here right now, sitting on this bench by the Blue Grotto, he wanted Brendan to be their son. Bernie moved over a few inches, and so did Brendan; Tom sat down on the other end, with the boy in the middle.

"Tom," Bernie said. "Brendan was just telling me that he started searching…"

"I heard," Tom said. "I know that he is looking for his birth parents. And that his search has led him here. To us."

Brendan nodded. "Well, to you…there was a Star of the Sea reference, and the last name being Kelly…"

Bernie closed her eyes. Brendan couldn't know about her and Tom. He had no idea she was thinking she might be his mother. She was missing vespers, and she could hear the voices of the sisters, high and clear. They were singing the psalms, and their prayers rose and mixed with the summer air and filled her heart. How often, after her baby was born, had she sat in that chapel, singing line after line, page after page, believing there weren't enough prayers or psalms in the world to treat the pain she was feeling?

"It all makes such sense," Tom said, his voice low and thrilling.

"Do your adoption papers say where you were born?" Bernie asked quietly.

"Yes," Brendan said, fumbling in his pocket. The fact that he pulled them out—that he carried them with him—pierced her heart more than almost anything. More than his shoes, more than Tom's expression. "It's right here—'Place of Birth: New London, Connecticut. Shoreline General Hospital.'"

Bernie swore she could hear Tom's breaking heart echoing off the stones of the Blue Grotto behind them. She could feel the cold despair pouring out of him, and she was shocked to feel it even in herself.

"New London?" Tom asked. "You're sure?"

Brendan nodded—digging back in his pocket. This time he pulled out a small plastic bracelet—a hospital bracelet just the right size for an infant's wrist. It was blue, and beneath the words "Shoreline General" was printed "Baby Boy Brendan."

"See?" he asked. "They didn't have a last name for me yet, but apparently my birth mother wanted to make sure I was called Brendan."

Bernie looked across his head at Tom, but Tom couldn't meet her eyes. She could see disappointment welling in his as he gazed down at the document, the bracelet, and the young man he had willed to be their son.

"Did you want to name me that?" Brendan asked Tom. "Was there a reason?"

Bernie opened her mouth to reply, to take the burden off Tom. But he beat her to it. His voice was soft and low, filled with compassion and love, and he gazed straight into Brendan's blue eyes.

"Our son was born in Dublin," Tom said.

"No," Brendan said, looking confused. "I was born in New London..."

"Dublin, Ireland," Tom said. "We had gone there to research some family history, the year before Bernie..."

He didn't finish the sentence: *the year before Bernie joined the convent.*

She listened to the sisters' chanting, felt her insides trembling as if the earth were shaking. Tom had tried to talk her out of a religious life ever since she'd felt the calling—right here on the grounds of Star of the Sea. Her family was so proud of her. And so were the Kellys. She was the first member of her generation—of both families—to have a nun's vocation.

Night after night she had walked the grounds, praying for answers. She loved Tom; she always had. She longed to be with him, to marry him and have his children. But at the same time, she felt another possibility tugging her in a different direction—she loved God with all her heart, and she kept dreaming that there was so much to be done— ways of helping the world that she could do only if she gave herself over to him fully: if she was a nun.

She resisted the dreams; she prayed to have them stop. If she didn't dream of being a nun, she could ignore the thoughts that were starting to enter her daytime hours. She could resist the desire she'd been feeling to enter the order right here at Star of the Sea—the place where she and Tom had met, where they had spent so many happy hours.

But the dreams didn't stop. She kept hearing a voice, telling her that she was needed—that she had to pray, to begin a life of prayer and contemplation, of devotion to the Lord, and to Mary. She felt herself being ripped apart, her heart pulled in two wildly different directions—between a life spent loving Tom and the life of being part of the order.

And then one day, Bernie had come here, to the Blue Grotto. She had come to pray, to tell God that she had chosen Tom. Her dreams had changed. Instead of nights filled with images of the convent and cloister, she'd started having dreams of a family—her, Tom, and a little boy. And that day, on her knees, Bernie had had a vision, right here at the Blue Grotto.

The Virgin Mary had appeared to her. Bernie had been kneeling on the stone inside, praying at the altar, asking for guidance. She remembered how hot the day had been; there wasn't any air moving anywhere on the property, not even near the beach. But suddenly a strong breeze filled the grotto, bringing with it the scent of roses. Bernie had felt almost dizzy with their sweetness, and suddenly she'd felt a cool hand on her forehead.

It was Mary, wiping her brow with a white linen cloth. Her mouth had moved, but Bernie had heard no words. The breeze was too strong—almost like a hurricane or a sirocco. Bernie had reached for her hand, but Mary disappeared.

Kneeling there, Bernie had wept. She had cried out loud, begging for Mary to come back. She had so many questions. She loved Tom so much—how could she be called away from him?

Devout young woman that she was, Bernie couldn't ignore the vision. She couldn't just put it aside, pretend it hadn't happened. She took it as a sign that she was meant to dedicate her life to Mary, to God. But when she'd told Tom the next day, he grabbed her hands, frantic, wild.

"Maybe it was a sign about love," he said. "Come to Ireland with me, Bernie. We'll do what we always dreamed—see where our families came from, where *we* come from. Maybe you'll get another sign over there. Give me this time with you, with who we are."

The sisters themselves had told Bernie it was better not to rush, that she should be sure of her vocation before she took her vows. When she gazed around the convent and Academy grounds, knowing that so much of this place would always remind her of Ireland— the land of the Kellys and Sullivans—she knew that if she didn't travel there with Tom, she would be haunted forever.

She'd agreed to go. And they'd flown to Shannon.

Never had she seen such brilliant green, spreading everywhere, grass, hillsides, fields, hedges. Bright, vivid, emerald green, traced and divided by silvery stone walls. She saw her family's heritage everywhere—even from the plane—and from the instant her feet touched the ground, she felt she was home.

She loved the way people talked—their soft, melodic voices, the way they had of telling stories, the music in the pubs, romantic ruins everywhere, Celtic crosses in the graveyards. She was overwhelmed with love. Seeing this country with Tom, knowing how it all echoed back to their home in Connecticut, at Star of the Sea, where their families had come together again to build something timeless, filled her with passion and emotion.

She and Tom drove to Dublin and conceived their baby the first week they were there.

"Tom is right," Bernie said softly now, to the young man sitting between them. "We did have a child. But he was born in Ireland, not America."

"The two of you? Together?" Brendan asked, shocked.

Bernie nodded. She couldn't quite look at Tom. She remembered finding out she was pregnant, how rocked they'd been, how worried for her Tom was. But underneath his concern, she'd seen his joy. Even as he'd helped her make arrangements to stay in Ireland until she had the baby—because she'd said no one could know, she'd die of shame if anyone found out—he'd never stopped hoping she'd change her mind about giving the baby up for adoption.

"But what if I was really born there, and sent over here, right away, to the hospital in New London..."

"What is your birthday?" Bernie asked.

"September 17, 1984," he said.

"Our boy was born on January 4, 1983," Tom said. Bernie heard hopelessness in his voice. She remembered that winter day in Phibsboro, Dublin 7, a flat in a row of brick houses. The slate gray sky, stray flurries falling as they walked outside, Tom's arms around her. They'd walked in silence, except for Bernie's crying. Tom had at last stopped begging her to change her mind. That in itself had made her weep.

For Brendan's sake, she turned her thoughts back to the present. "You said that your birth mother attended Star of the Sea?"

"Yes," he said, sounding bereft, almost hollow. "She did."

"Until twenty years ago," Bernie said, "there was a wing of the school devoted to unwed mothers. Now we're a little more progressive, and we don't keep them separate. But perhaps your mother came here during her pregnancy; she would have been very welcome."

"What about the name Kelly?" Brendan asked. He turned to Tom. "Were any of your relatives...?"

"Not that I know of," he said. "But you know the name Kelly is a little like Smith. It's not uncommon. We can certainly check, though. And we will check. We'll help you, Brendan, won't we, Bernie?"

"We will," she said. "We'll help you look into it, any way we can."

"I saw the painting you did of the sea monster, on your car," Tom said, putting his arm around Brendan's shoulders. "That's how I knew there was a Kelly connection." He showed Brendan his crest ring; the boy stared at it for a long time.

"I got it all wrong," Brendan said quietly.

"No," Bernie said, tapping his heart. "You've got it all right. You're searching...that's what matters. You've brought such light to our family this summer. Agnes has come out of herself because of you."

"I guess that's one good thing about not being related to you," Brendan said, glancing up. "It means I'm not related to Agnes either...I hadn't even thought of that, because I only knew about being a Kelly."

"I wanted this to turn out different, for my own sake," Tom said. "And Bernie's. You're a great young man; we'd be proud if you were ours."

"And I'd be proud if you were mine," Brendan said, standing up. He went to shake Tom's hand, but Tom pulled him close, hugging him.

Looking up at them, Bernie imagined him hugging their son, and she had to close her eyes. Brendan leaned down, kissed her cheek. She smiled, stood up.

"Thank you," she said. "You have opened my world, Brendan. In a way I never really expected..."

"Well, I hope you find your son someday," Brendan said. "He'd be a lucky guy."

He started to walk away—and Bernie noticed that it wasn't toward the parking lot, where his car had been all this time, but toward the right, the path that led to Agnes's house. "Just a minute," Tom called out.

"What is it?" Brendan asked.

"Tell us one thing," Tom said, lowering his voice so no one else could hear.

"Sure," Brendan said. "Anything."

"Did you carve those words into the grotto walls?" Tom asked.

Brendan hesitated, his eyes sparkling. "I almost wish I could take credit for them," he said. "They're beautiful. I love their mystery, and what they say, and even more, what they don't say. Kind of what I'm trying to get at with the pictures on my car, and kind of what I want to become a psychiatrist for. But no. No, I didn't do them... You'll have to keep looking."

He turned and kept walking, and then he started running—straight over the rise to Agnes. Bernie's heart cracked to see him go. She hadn't realized how much she yearned to know her son, the boy she'd had known for such a short time that cold January twenty-three years ago.

"Bernie," Tom said, standing beside her.

"I know," she said.

"You don't know," he said. "You have no idea."

She jerked her head, to look into his eyes. Expecting to see resignation, maybe sadness, she saw fire and anger instead.

"Sister Bernadette," he said. "Mother Superior of Star of the Sea."

"Yes," she said. "That's who I am."

"So much so that you've blocked everything else."

"What do you mean?"

"That boy. He could have been our son."

"Tom, I know..."

"Bernie, don't you ever think of it? Think about him? Think about us? Think about how we were? What might have been?"

"I think about it," she whispered. "Of course I do..."

"I'm haunted, Bernie. I'm like a ghost, do you know that? I'm here every day, working in your garden just so I can be near you."

"I don't want you to feel haunted," she said.

"The only way for me to stop that," he said, "is to go back to Ireland."

"Don't say that!" she burst out, turning away.

Tom grabbed her shoulders, shaking her, accidentally dislodging her veil. She reached up, tucked her hair back inside. He barely noticed, just staring her down.

He had never left Star of the Sea, never worked anywhere else. He had never taken any other job—even though he had had plenty of offers. Many board members, benefactors, parents of students had tried to lure him away. And although Bernie could never admit it, she knew she would be lost if he were to go.

"Think about it," he said. "Brendan has shown us what's possible. People can be reunited."

"What do you mean?"

"We can go to Dublin. You and I."

"My place is here," she whispered. "You know that!"

"Yes, I know it. Do you think I could ever forget? But I saw your eyes, that first moment when Brendan said he was adopted—I saw what it did to you. The same thing it did to me, Bernie. Made me think of..."

"Our baby," she finished.

"Yes," Tom said. "Our baby. *Ours*, Bernie. It might have just lasted for a minute—before you pushed it away and got back to business, being Sister Bernadette..."

"It didn't last just a minute," she said.

"No?"

She shook her head. Her heart was in her throat, her blood felt like galloping horses. She turned away, leaving Tom in the sunshine as she walked into the grotto. The summer day was hot, just as it had been twenty-four years ago, when she'd prayed for guidance—hoping to be told she should marry Tom, but seeing Mary instead.

What if Honor, in her letter, had been right, and Bernie had interpreted everything the wrong way? She had felt Mary calling her, pulling her into her life. And Bernie had been so honored, so incredibly moved, that Mary had appeared to her, calling her to follow her early dreams and become a nun.

But Mary had had another aspect, as well. She had been a wife and mother. No woman had ever loved her family more.... What if Bernie had given all that up, just because of her own Catholic upbringing, the pride of two families pushing her into the convent, crossed signals of a miraculous vision?

"I saw Mary here," she said now, her voice so hoarse she could barely speak.

"I know," Tom said. "You told me back then. When you turned down my proposal once and for all. How could I compete with the Virgin Mary?"

Bernie stared at the cross. Another mother's son had died; Bernie had always related to the Blessed Mother, imagining that she knew how it felt to lose a son. But her son wasn't lost—he hadn't died. He was living out a life, perhaps in Ireland. The nuns in Dublin would know. There would be records.

Tom walked closer to the wall, where the two messages had been carved. Bernie felt a shiver go down her back as she watched him trace the words with his finger.

"Song of Songs," Tom said. "Like you said that first day, when I called you down here to see the first message: a love song."

"A love story," she corrected.

"The kid didn't do this, or so he says," Tom said, still facing the wall.

"He didn't," Bernie said.

"How do you know for sure?" he asked.

Ever the stonemason, Tom picked up one of the fallen stones—the one that had tumbled two nights ago, when Bernie had tried to deepen the carving.

"Because I did it," she said.

Tom turned slowly, holding the rock. His eyes were wide open, and Bernie felt shock waves pouring off him.

"My great-grandfather built this place," she said. "I still have his stonecutting tools, in the shed behind…"

"The cloister," Tom said. "I know."

"I used to watch my grandfather, when I was a child. I saw how he did it, and I used to admire the way he left his mark on the rock, on the land. It sometimes seemed to me like prayer made visible."

"Prayer—"

Bernie nodded. "It takes such devotion, to work with stones and rocks," she said. "It takes a very deep faith to believe that you can make any difference, any at all, when it comes to the immovable, the impenetrable."

"But why did you do this, Bernie? Why here?"

"I have visited this grotto every single day since I was a very young woman. The Virgin Mary came to me here; I wanted her to come again. I wanted to know. I wanted her to tell me what to do."

"So you had to write her a love story?"

"She knows my love story," Bernie said.

"What did she tell you to do?" Tom asked.

Bernie closed her eyes. She felt the dark, closed space growing hotter, stiller. She swooned, and had to reach out her hand, to touch the walls with her fingertips, just to steady herself. Tom was right there, standing beside her. He didn't touch her. He didn't have to.

"Bernie?" he asked, standing so close she could feel his breath on her forehead.

She opened her eyes. Finally, as if for the first time, she opened her eyes and saw. Tom looked just as he had the first time she saw him: exactly. He was so tall. His eyes were so blue. He looked as he had all his life here in Black Hall, and over in Dublin.

"What did she tell you to do?" Tom asked.

And Bernie told him.

Twenty-nine

Honor's nerves were raw, waiting. Low tide was extreme; tonight there would be a full moon. She gathered moonstones, trying to calm herself. When the tide began to rise, she retreated to the stone circle. John had used the largest pieces of rock for the outside ring—protecting the inner circles from waves and wind. Yet the labyrinth was still vulnerable; the slightest breezes covered the smaller stones with drifts of sand.

Starting at the outer edge, she began to walk. Around the circle once, then left into the next ring, doubling back on herself. It felt good to be out in the sun and the salt air, and she felt John's presence as she moved through the labyrinth, deeper into its center.

Once she reached the very core, she sat down. Her heart was beating hard. She sat very still, looking straight out. The Sound was calm tonight; there hadn't been any storms at sea to stir up the waves. There was barely a whisper of wind; the surface registered hardly a ripple.

"What are you doing in there?"

She heard his voice before she saw him coming up behind her, and she swiveled slightly, to see him standing on the bank—dressed in the same jeans and T-shirt and old sneakers he'd worn to the police station.

"Waiting for you," she said.

"The tide's coming in."

"Yes, it is," she said, her mouth dry. "Oh God, John. What happened? What did they say to you?"

"I have to tell you something," he said.

"What is it?"

"Can I come in there with you, and tell you?" he asked.

Honor nodded, making room at the labyrinth's center. She watched him kick off his sneakers, jump down from the seawall, and walk over to the outer circle. Instead of following the circuitous path, he stepped over each line of stones to get straight to her. He brushed her shoulder as he sat down beside her, and she saw him holding himself back, knew that he was figuring out how to tell her this.

She knew him so well; his touch was so familiar. Yet this was brand-new. The look in his eyes, so tender and bruised, nearly as worried as she'd seen him in Ireland, when the police were taking him away. Had something happened at the police station? Were they going to take him into custody?

"What is it, John?" she asked. "Tell me, I can't stand it."

"I just saw Regis," he said.

"Bernie told me she was in the library," Honor said. "I wanted to give her the chance to be alone for a while. Breaking up with Peter is such a big deal. I can't let her see how happy I am about it, so I'm staying away. I'm worried that she'll see the relief in my eyes."

"That's not why she disappeared," John said.

"What do you mean?" Honor asked.

He paused, trying to find the words.

"Was it because I got angry at you last night, at the beach movie? I know it upset her terribly...and I'm so sorry. I really overreacted. I just thought—"

"That's not it either," John said. "It has to do with Ballincastle. What happened there..."

"What are you talking about?" she asked, frozen, scared by his tone.

"Something that Regis just remembered," John said. "Honor, you'll tell me that I should have told you. Maybe I should have. But I didn't want Regis to suffer more than she already had, and I didn't want you to, either."

"What is it, John?"

"That day," John said. "When Greg White showed up..."

"He attacked you and Regis," Honor said.

"You know what I told the police," he said, watching her.

"You told them it was self-defense," she said. "It was, right?"

"It was Regis," he said, his voice so low, she could barely hear.

"What?" she asked, feeling a shiver down her spine.

"She threw herself against him, Honor. To keep him from killing me. Grabbed a piece of driftwood and hit him with it. And that's when he went over. When we all did."

"She— Regis hit him?" she asked with disbelief. "*Killed* him?"

"Yes."

"Oh God, Regis," Honor said, her heart pounding, thinking of Regis at fourteen. How terrified she must have been. How brave... She made a small fist, fingers closing around the ring she had put on earlier that day. "Why didn't she ever tell me?"

"Because she didn't remember," John said. "It all happened so fast. It was a blur, and she was so young—she couldn't process it, and really, neither could I."

"Why didn't you tell me, then?"

"Oh, Honor. My instincts kicked in. I didn't want her involved. I was worried enough about her. I thought if I told you, told anyone, the story would get muddled. We'd have to decide what to do. So I just decided myself."

"God, John," Honor said.

"I couldn't bring Regis in. I couldn't stand to think of her getting caught up with the investigation. It was just my word, and hers. I could already see what they thought my word was worth."

"So you protected her."

"As much as I could," John said. "After the fact."

"It wasn't after the fact," she said, lowering her head to her knees, taking the information in. "It was very much during the fact—while

the gardai were charging you, and the courts were sentencing you...
you kept Regis out of all of that..."

"Honor, I promise you—I'm not going to hurt you anymore. Any
of you. It's too much right now. I love you, and I'm going to get out
of here. Not forever, but until everything calms down. Until we figure out what to do for Regis—we have to help her...."

"You're not going anywhere," Honor said in a low voice.

"You know that's the best thing for..."

"It's the worst thing," she said. "For all of us."

She touched his lips with her finger. Her thoughts were racing,
and she knew they had to get to Regis. The tide was really coming in
now, small waves lapping at the outer edge of rocks, trickling in over
the rows of pebbles to soak their bare feet and the bottoms of their
jeans.

Honor thought of what Regis had said, about John's bringing the
color back into their lives. He was so passionate, quick to anger, and
drawn to dangerous places; and as much as that scared her, it also
made him the man she had always loved—always ready to embrace
life fully, to love completely, without reservation or limits. She
thought of her new paintings and knew that his work, his being, had
deeply inspired her own.

"We're going to need you now," she said as the Sound came up another inch. "More than ever."

"Even though..."

"Even though everything," she said.

"Chris Kelly came down from Hartford," John said. "He's waiting
up at the convent. I think we should talk to him, see what he advises."

"Advises about what?"

"Honor, she needed to get this off her chest to me. Do you think
it's going to stop there? Regis is determined to set things straight."

"But you've already paid—"

John grabbed her, looked her straight on. She felt the fear well up,
suddenly knowing that Regis would never stop until she cleared his
name. She jumped up, frantic to see her daughter, talk her out of
whatever she might be planning to do. John caught her, steadied her.

"You mean confess, or set the record straight—in Ireland?"

"I don't know," John said. "You haven't seen the look in her eyes. But you know Regis."

"We can't let her," Honor said.

"Honor," he asked gently, looking into her eyes. "I love you, and I love her so much. I would do anything I could to keep her from this."

"I know," she said. "You already have."

"And look what's happened. She's torn up with guilt. All those bad dreams you say she keeps having. Let's just listen to her. Not try to tell her what she should do, or how she should feel. We can handle this together."

"You mean, you'll stay?" she asked.

"As long as you want me," he said. "You just said we need each other. I *know* how much I need you."

Honor nodded, holding her husband in her arms, and he kissed her, filling her with strength and letting her know she wasn't alone anymore, that maybe she'd never really been alone at all.

"Chris is waiting," he said. "Let's go talk to him. He'll give us good advice about how to handle it."

Honor nodded; John was right. Her bare feet were planted in the sand, and for a moment, she couldn't quite bear to move. A cool breeze blew off the Sound, from the east. It made her shiver, staring down at John's labyrinth.

As they walked away, she reached into the pocket of her jeans, pulled out her hand and poured the moonstones she had gathered into his open palm.

John's gaze traveled up the hill, took in the stone walls reaching across the Academy land. They were dark in the twilight, but sparkling with quartz and mica, as if stars had fallen to earth, become trapped in the walls themselves. Honor thought of Cormac Sullivan, of all that he had brought with him from Ballincastle, of all that he had given to her family.

The big orange moon rose out of the Sound. It crested over the smooth surface, glimmering on the small waves. Heading home to see Regis, and Agnes, and Cecilia, Honor stared at her husband with fierce love, here on the beach where they had first met.

Ten yards from the labyrinth, John suddenly stopped walking. As she watched, he opened his hand, looked down at the moonstones she had given him. Was he remembering the ones he had found for her, the night he proposed? Without speaking, he turned and led her back, hand-in-hand.

Bending over, John let the moonstones she had chosen trickle from his fingers, into the labyrinth's exact center, where he and Honor had just been sitting. They formed a swirl, like the whorl inside a shell, something eternal without beginning or end. As she followed it with her eyes, from the inside out, she saw that the circle's outer edge led her gaze straight up the vineyard's gentle slope.

To the stone wall. Did he plan it that way? She didn't know, and she knew it didn't really matter. It all connected. It always had, and it always would. The stone wall had endured all this time, holding back secrets of love and sorrow. She knew that the sea would wash the labyrinth away, just like their sandcastles of long ago.

But Honor also knew what the people of John's family had known all along: that rocks and stones were made to last. The Sullivans used material forged by fire and ice; you might knock it down, but they could always rebuild. When the moonstones drifted out with the tide, her family would find them again. John took her outstretched hand. The labyrinth he had built was proof of how far they would travel, how hard they would work to find the core of what mattered.

The air smelled of salt and grapes, the end of summer. Honor shivered in the light breeze, and John put his arm around her as they walked back down the beach. Across the marsh grass, she could see the lights of their house, just coming on, cozy and warm. The girls were there, waiting for them. Regis needed her parents, and they were on their way.

The moon rose higher. If Honor turned around, she would see its path on the water, stretching all the way across the sea, all the way to Ireland. But for now, she had eyes only for home.

Epilogue

Dublin's Four Courts stood on the bank of the River Liffey. The copper-covered shallow lantern dome and six-columned Corinthian portico, and a sculpture of Moses flanked by Justice and Mercy, were reflected in the pewter gray river, coursing out to sea beneath one somber bridge after another.

Early that morning rain had poured down, blowing off the Irish Sea sideways, in slanting sheets. Although the rain had stopped for the moment, the sky remained overcast with low clouds. To Agnes, staring at it through the huge windows, it echoed the weather on that fateful day six years earlier. She could almost feel the wind roaring up the cliff.

Now she and Cece sat on a bench in the main waiting area, under the enormous dome, waiting to find out what punishment, if any, Regis would face for what had happened to Gregory White.

"What's going to happen?" Cece asked nervously.

"I don't know," Agnes said.

"But you must have some idea, right?" Cece asked. "Can't you try to have a vision, and find out?"

Not long ago, she would have taken the weather, so similar to what it had been the day that Gregory White had died, as a sign from above, meaning that things would go badly. She would have seen the dark, blowing clouds as angry angels on the move. It had been exhausting, trying to be a mystic. Taking a deep breath, she looked down at her sister.

"Have faith, Cece," she said, "that everything is going to work out right."

"But how do you know it will?" Cece pressed, staring at the door that led to the criminal courts, knowing that Regis and their parents were inside.

The family had flown over, all together, to support Regis. She had wanted to go alone or with her mother, to spare her father having to return to Criminal Court. But neither he nor their mother would hear of it; neither would Agnes nor Cecelia.

Even though the girls would be missing the first few days of fall term, they had insisted on coming. Chris Kelly had spoken with their father's barrister, arranged for Regis to have her own legal counsel—a Kelly relative who lived in the family's original stately Georgian house on Merrion Square.

His name was Sixtus Kelly, and he had joked about his name coming from the same lineup of saints as Chrysogonus, that the family had law, justice, and the Almighty on their side. He had explained that since the act had occurred when Regis was fourteen, her statement would be given in Children's Court here in Dublin, instead of Cork City.

They were all inside now, behind the closed door. Agnes trembled, forcing herself to breathe steadily. She wished she could rely on her old ways—using silence and visions as a hedge against what scared her most, begging for a miracle in return for her own clarity.

Brendan had taught her so much. He was helping her to not be so afraid. Having a friend who had faced loss and fear, who knew something about Agnes's own life, meant so much to her. He was somehow helping her bridge the gap between her truly deep faith and the wishful thinking her religion had become.

"Agnes?" Cece asked again. "What's going to happen?"

"Regis is going to tell the truth," Agnes said, holding her sister's hand. "All of it, that she can remember."

"Will they arrest her? Lock her up?" Cece asked.

"No, they won't," Agnes said, her stomach jumping at the thought.

"Why did she have to do this?" Cece asked. "No one had to know. She didn't mean to hurt him, so why tell?"

"Because the truth matters," Agnes said.

"Hiding from it gave her nightmares," Cece said. "And made her want to marry Peter."

Agnes held back a smile. Cece was a little young to understand; Agnes knew that Regis had truly fallen in love, but she'd also latched on to Peter as a sort of savior. With her father locked up, gone during such an important time of her life, she had needed something, someone to grab onto. And Peter had been there.

"He was wrong for her," Agnes said, thinking of how totally Peter had cut Regis off once she'd told him the whole story.

"Love is weird," Cece said. "At least in our family."

"No," Agnes said, shaking her head. "Love is wonderful. *Especially* in our family." That was one belief that had never been shaken. Even during the time when her mother was so angry at her father, she had known that her parents' love was real and true. They had passed it on to their daughters, and it was going to carry them through now.

She thought of Brendan, back home in Connecticut. He was working part-time at the Academy, supplementing his hospital income to earn enough money for medical school. He was working for Tom on the grounds crew, and once Regis returned to college, Aunt Bernie was giving him her library job.

If Regis returned to college, Agnes thought. She checked her watch. They'd been inside for over an hour now. Surely there had to be some resolution soon. For the first time all day, her faith really faltered. What if everything went wrong? What if they charged Regis, threw her in jail? And what if they were so angry at her father for withholding information that they arrested him again?

Just then the door opened, and Regis came walking out. Agnes and Cece started toward her, and she threw herself into their arms. She was sobbing so hard, they couldn't hear a word she was saying.

Looking over Regis's head, Agnes saw her parents standing in the doorway, shaking hands with Sixtus Kelly. He nodded and walked away. But it was Agnes's mother's smile that told the whole story.

It told everything Agnes needed to know. Her mother's face was so open, her eyes so bright, and her smile so sweet, a sight more welcome than any vision. Agnes's eyes filled with tears, and she was finally able to make out what Regis was saying.

"It's over," Regis cried. "It's all over."

When they got to the airport, they learned that their flight would be delayed. The plane from the States hadn't arrived yet, due to inclement weather off the eastern seaboard. While the girls walked through the duty-free shops, Honor and John stayed near the gate.

They sat in the last row of seats, against the wall. Holding hands, they could see everything. People walking through the airport, hurrying to reach their flights, mothers with small children, couples sitting together. Through the glass window, they could see people arriving, on their way to customs. Watching a family arrive—parents and three young children—Honor felt a shiver go down her spine.

"There we are," she said to John, pointing. "Six years ago..."

"They look so excited to be here," he said, following her gaze.

"There's a lot to be excited about," she said. "Traveling together. Seeing everything—so brand-new, such an adventure."

"I wonder whether they're Americans, searching out their roots," John said. "Looking for explanations of how they got to be who they are."

"Is that why we came?" Honor asked. "Was that the big question we stumbled upon in the stone wall?"

"One of them," he said, sliding his arm around her. "I've forgotten the rest."

She laughed, leaning against him. The girls passed by, to check on their flight status, then went running off to see what else they could find in duty-free. Regis would be twenty-one in a month, returning to college for her senior year, but she looked younger than ever.

"We're really free," Honor said. "All of us."

"We are," John said.

"I was so worried," Honor said. She pictured the judge, tall and dour, sitting at the bench, listening to Regis tell her story. Being led through the recitation by Sixtus, straightforward and knowledgeable, asking her questions that set forth all the details of what she had come to remember about the death of Gregory White, and the part she had played.

"She did a great job," John said. "I was so proud of her."

"So was I," Honor said. "And of you, too."

"Me, why?"

Honor held his hand. "For letting her do this. Deep down, I was scared they might charge you with obstruction of justice."

"Letting her do it?" John asked. "I couldn't have stopped her if I tried. She was determined to clear my name."

"And she did," Honor said.

The judge had apologized to John, while also chastising him for not telling the truth. He had said that Regis's version of the events proved that they had both acted in self-defense, that Gregory White had been trying to kill John, and maybe Regis too, and that John would not have been sentenced to prison.

"We wasted all that time," Honor said.

"Then we have to make up for it," he said, putting his arm around her shoulder.

"As soon as we get home," she said. "We'll have a party. We'll invite Bernie, Tom, Chris..."

"And the Drakes," John said. "They can be the guests of honor."

Honor laughed, imagining the disappointment they'd feel when their barrister friend in Dublin informed them of today's proceedings. Just then the loudspeaker announced that the aircraft had just arrived from Boston, and that as soon as it was cleaned and refueled, they would be ready for boarding.

"Okay," John said, looking around. "Where are the girls?"

"Let's go find them," Honor said, standing up.

They didn't have to go far. Their daughters were in a woolen shop just past the boarding area. They had picked out a sweater for Brendan, a tweed cap for Tom, and a white linen scarf for Bernie. Regis paid for the purchases, and then they all headed down the hall, returning to their gate.

On the way, they passed the large glass window overlooking the arrivals area. People from the Boston flight were streaming down the wide corridor, carrying bags and hauling suitcases behind them. Honor paused to gaze down at all the families. So many of them, coming to Ireland for their own reasons. She thought back, again, to how she had felt arriving six years ago. Even without the terrible events at Ballincastle, she had been so close to leaving John.

What if she had? If she had given up on them, on their marriage, on all the dangers and challenges that came from being in love. She looked up at him, waiting for her now. His hair was so short, mostly gray. When he smiled, as he did now, she saw starbursts of lines around his eyes and mouth. She also saw the boy she had loved forever, whom she had first met on their beach at Star of the Sea.

"Honor," he said now. And she thought he was going to tell her to hurry, that they had to get to the gate.

But he was looking past her shoulder, staring through the glass at the walkway below. The crowd was thick, people filing off the 747. John was pointing, directing her gaze downward. She tried to see what he was looking at, scanned the faces for someone familiar. Her eyes settled on a nun, her long black veil and habit reminiscent of a Sister of Notre Dame des Victoires.

"Bernie," she gasped.

"And Tom," John said, pointing at the man walking alongside the nun.

"Oh God," Honor said. "We should have called them! They must have come over to support Regis." She looked around frantically. "Can we get to them and let them know what happened? So they can fly home with us?"

"I don't think they want to fly home with us," John said.

And immediately, Honor knew that he was right. She waved,

through the window, praying that Bernie would look up. The throng was pushing her along, and there was absolutely no reason for Bernie to glance anywhere but straight ahead.

But miracles, small and large, do happen. And just before the crowd would have jostled Bernie out of sight, she stopped still. Catching Tom's arm, she raised her eyes up toward the observation window, and she looked straight into Honor's eyes.

"She sees us," John said, waving. He gave a thumbs-up, letting his sister and Tom know that all was well, that they were on their way home.

Honor was gazing into Bernie's eyes. She put her hand over her heart—to give her sister-in-law her love and support. Not just friend to friend, but mother to mother. Bernie did the same; touched her heart, and stood gazing up at Honor.

"I hope you find him," Honor mouthed through the glass.

Bernie just nodded, and a radiant smile spread across her face.

"Should we skip our flight?" John asked. "Stay and help them with their search?"

"I think they have to do it alone, just the two of them," Honor said.

And John agreed. They stood together, smiling and waving at their best friends in the world. Honor slipped her hand into her jacket pocket, the pirate ring catching slightly on the fabric. She pulled out the blue envelope that she carried all the time now. She had written the letter to Bernie twenty-three years ago, the year she was pregnant, in Dublin with Tom. She held it up to the glass.

Honor knew that Bernie remembered it all. Honor's own words had bounced back to her this summer, giving her strength to deal with John and their past, hope to move forward into their future. She wanted them to do the same for Bernie, just starting this new part of her own long journey.

You don't have to feel afraid, Honor had written. *No matter what happens, you're not alone. One thing the stone wall has taught us, we come from wonderful, brave people, who would travel across the sea to make things right for the ones they love. We're with you, Bernie—John and I. We love you and Tom, and we'll love your baby. No matter what you decide to do, know that we are right there with you. We're a family, Bernie. Don't ever forget that.*

"We're with you," Honor whispered through the window.

And then Tom put his arm around Bernie's shoulders. They both waved up at the glass, one last time, and disappeared into customs. Honor pressed her head against the window, watching them until the last possible moment. She turned to John, saw him doing the same thing.

The girls had run ahead, but now they came back, wondering what was taking their parents so long. They came over to stand by the window, looking down at the crowds still arriving in Ireland.

"Don't you want to go home?" Cece asked, looking up at John and Honor.

Regis and Agnes didn't even ask. They didn't have to.

"More than anything," John said.

And he put his hand in Honor's, and together they all began the journey home.

PHOTO © GASPER TRINGALE

Luanne Rice is the author of twenty-eight novels, most recently *The Deep Blue Sea for Beginners, The Geometry of Sisters, Last Kiss, Light of the Moon, What Matters Most, The Edge of Winter, Sandcastles, Summer of Roses, Summer's Child,* and *Beach Girls,* among many *New York Times* bestsellers. She lives in New York City and Old Lyme, Connecticut.

www.luannerice.com

PRAISE FOR LUANNE RICE AND *SANDCASTLES*

"With deft style, Rice delicately handles heartbreak and redemption, once again pleasing her fans with her latest story about the inhabitants of her beloved shore town." —*Booklist*

"This potent brew of love and longing has echoes of Colleen McCullough's 1977 Australian saga *The Thorn Birds*....One of those books you'll be longing to carve out time to read." —*USA Today*

"Readers looking for...enduring love and family drama won't be disappointed." —*Kirkus Reviews*

"Rice seamlessly weaves family dramas and the many varieties of love into this heartfelt book." —Barnes & Noble

"Family and conflict, love and heartbreak, redemption and forgiveness...*Sandcastles* is certainly brimming over with emotion....A deeply satisfying and emotional read." —Romance Reviews Today

"Author Luanne Rice once again shows her readers how complex life can be." —*The Decatur Daily*

"Set in Connecticut and Ireland, this story will appeal to fans of family-relationship novels." —*Library Journal*

"*Sandcastles* is about family—how strong the ties that bind families are, as well as how fragile those ties can become if honest communication does not take place...and the healing of painful memories and the importance of forgiveness." —Bookreporter.com

"Ms. Rice has seamlessly woven the tale of two separate tragedies into one gripping family tale." —A Romance Review

"Luanne Rice explores that issue [the balance between artistic freedom and a stable home life] in her rich new novel *Sandcastles*....The author manages the mean feat of never underestimating the turbulence of the [characters'] lives while still coming up with a satisfying resolution that doesn't tie everything up in an unrealistic manner.... *Sandcastles* shows us that there are still huge challenges for women who are determined to explore their art and have a life partner and family." —*Connecticut Post*

"Few…authors are able to portray the complex and contradictory emotions that bind family members as effortlessly as Rice."
—*Publishers Weekly*

"Full of all the things families are made of: love, secrets, traditions, and memories." —*The Providence Journal*

"Luanne Rice handles with marvelous insight and sensitivity the complex chemistry of a family that might be the one next door."
—Eileen Goudge

"Rice, a terrific storyteller and a poetic stylist, takes on a difficult and brutal subject and transforms it into a source of light and hope."
—*Booklist*

"Irresistible…fast-paced…moving…vivid storytelling. Readers can almost smell the sea air. Rice has a gift for creating realistic characters, and the pages fly by as those characters explore the bonds of family." —*Orlando Sentinel*

"What the author does best: heartfelt family drama, gracefully written and poignant." —*Kirkus Reviews*

"Rice is a master of…emotional intensity." —CinCHouse.com

"Rice, always skilled at drafting complex stories…reveals her special strength in character development." —*The Star-Ledger*

"Rice's ability to evoke the lyricism of the seaside lifestyle without oversentimentalizing contemporary issues…is just one of…many gifts that make…a perfect summer read."
—*Publishers Weekly* (starred review)

"Rice, as always, provides her readers with a delightful love story filled with the subtle nuances of the human heart." —*Booklist*

"Luanne Rice touches the deepest, most tender corners of the heart."
—Tami Hoag

"Pure gold." —*Library Journal*